CH00649853

The Beautiful Decay

Tombtown, Volume 2

Veo Corva

Published by Witch Key Fiction, 2023.

First published in 2023 by Witch Key Fiction
Copyright © 2023 Veo Corva
All rights reserved.
This book or any portion thereof may not be reproduced or used in any manner whatsoever without the express written permission of the author except for the use of brief quotations in a book review.
All characters and events in this publication are fictitious and any resemblance to any real persons, living or dead, is purely coincidental.
EPUB ISBN: 978-1-7394742-0-1
Print ISBN: 978-1-7394742-1-8
Veo Corva
Website: https://veocorva.xyz
Witch Key Fiction
Website: https://witchkeyfiction.xyz
Cover art by Dona Vajgand
Website: https://dona.neocities.org/
Proofread by Nicole Evans | Thoughts Stained With Ink
Website: https://thoughtsstainedwithink.com/
Many thanks to the supporters of the
The Beautiful Decay Kickstarter campaign.

Table of Contents

For Joh, who always helps.

CONTENT WARNINGS

Contains undead, mild-moderate fantasy violence, fungal horror, abusive sex, and fantasy threat.

CHAPTER ONE

Usther

Deep beneath the Dead Mountains, in a secret and sprawling necropolis that smelled of dust and carried the chill of death, a woman with colourless eyes and a long trailing gown of black lace snorted and jerked upright, knocking over the complicated array of bobbins and partially-knit lace on the table in front of her.

'Shit,' she said with quiet fervour, scooping up the now tangled mess.

An undead creature swayed in the doorway, breath rattling in and out in long, rasping gasps. Dark purple flesh peeked from the rag strips encasing it, obscuring all but the dark hole of its mouth and a trailing plait of dark hair. It raised its hand again, preparing to scratch at the open door.

'Yes, yes, *I'm awake*, Misery darling,' said the woman. Her name was Usther of the Ashes. She was in her mid-twenties, tall and with slate-coloured skin that was once a warm brown-black. Now, necromancy had tinged it a grey-black. Her hair was pulled into neat box-braids, their smooth shape making the sharpness of her cheekbones all the more dramatic. Around her waist was a ropey belt of treated intestine. But most shocking were her colourless eyes, with only the faintest line ringing her irises.

She set about trying to untangle her lace bobbins and set them back the way they'd been before. After a moment, she sighed and shunted them across the table. 'Morrin's teeth.' She rubbed her eyes. 'Ugh. It'll take me an *age* to fix that.'

Usther stood up, wincing at the soreness in her back and legs. She stretched, shoulders cracking. 'I suppose she snuck in like a little cockroach?' she said to Misery. The minion sighed, which could mean anything. She went to her housemate's door and rapped on it irritably. 'Get up! The suneye's been up for hours and—' The door swung open. Stale air greeted her. Usther gazed at that empty, book-strewn room solemnly, then closed the door without another word.

She washed in icy mountain water stored in a cistern above her tub and emerged shivering in robes of dark purple fabric with lace cuffs. She pulled her box-braids into a long tail and turned to a shard of mirror in one of the sconces of the main room. There, her own tired, un-made up face stared back at her.

She bared her teeth at herself before she ran kohl carefully around her eyes and painted her lips black. She bared her teeth again. 'Good. Less like a wounded animal, more like the animal that did the wounding,' she said.

There was a small chirp and bump at her legs. She looked down and her expression softened. A stocky, short-haired cat with black patches gazed up at her, kneading on the stone floor with stumbling paws. The cat's scarred little face was split half-and-half between white and black. She had a collar around her neck so saturated with runes and wards that it glowed.

Usther knelt and scooped up the cat. The warmth of a living creature had once been startling to her, but now it was as reassuring as the cat's gravelly rumble. 'That's right, Dichotomy. We ought to leave or we won't be on time for the town meeting—or, gods forbid, *late.*' As she squished her cat's ear, the cat purred and dribbled happily, then bit her hand, drawing blood.

Usther didn't flinch. 'Well, that's enough petting then, if you're going to be rotten about it.' She put Dichotomy down and swept toward the door. The cat followed, still purring and dashing around her legs.

'Misery, darling! It's time to go.' She put her hand on the door, then stopped when there was no response. She glanced over her shoulder. 'Misery?'

Misery sighed. She stood in the corner of the kitchen, staring at the wall with her back to the world.

'Come on, darling. You know I can't leave you here.'

Misery shifted, leaning her head against the wall.

As she did every day, Usther considered leaving her minion home. After all, Misery *was* a house-minion; she had no liking for the outside world. But even as she thought it, she remembered flames and a drenched blanket and the horrible, choking taste of smoke and ash.

'Come on,' she clapped her hands. She didn't put any necromancy into it. It was rare that she used magic to command this particular minion.

Reluctantly, Misery shuffled away from the wall and followed Usther out the door, her head hung low and her arms hanging limp. 'Good,' said Usther. 'And I see you've been listening to me about your posture as well. Much better!'

She locked up her home, waiting for the comforting feel of her wards locking into place, before setting off for the Town Hall. Dichotomy wove about her legs and darted ahead only to come trotting back again. She seemed as reluctant to let Usther out of her sight. And no wonder. When Usther had found her, she'd been a stray cat lost in the crypt, dodging undead and giant spiders and subsisting on tomb rats.

'Misery, keep up!' Usther called over her shoulder. She looked back at her minion lagging behind with tiny, shuffling steps and held in a growl of frustration. 'Misery darling, we'll be late at that rate.' She walked back and tucked her minion's rag-wrapped arm firmly around her own. It was icy cold and might have burned an upworlder, but Usther was deep enough into the Craft that the chill barely registered.

'They *have* to declare a new council member now, surely!' she said. Her voice quavered and then held; she banished the image of Ree's empty room from her mind. 'I know those pompous bastards love to hang on to their power but with only three of them, how are they supposed to make *any* decisions?'

Misery sighed in what Usther thought was a supportive way.

'I'm going to call for the empty council seats to be filled,' Usther continued. 'There were seven once and there should be seven again. Morrin herself blessed it. We can't continue letting everything *decay*—no offence, darling.' She glanced at Misery, who rolled her eyes. She couldn't tell whether that was out of sarcasm or whether she'd just lost control of them.

Usther inclined her head to other denizens as she passed. Some were outside their tombhomes enjoying the morning must and mist. A few others seemed to be making their way to the Town Hall early, as she was. She kept her back straight and her expression imperious, as if it was perfectly normal to take one's house-minion for a stroll to the town meeting. She repressed the twingeing thought that she wouldn't feel so uncomfortable if Ree had been here, as they'd planned. Ree never seemed to be around anymore.

As they hit the end of the street, Usther enjoyed the familiar sight of the central mausoleum, or Tombtown proper. Though she often resented that her tombhome was so far from the centre where the council members and other important denizens resided, she secretly loved the view from this high-up street before she descended the stairs, with all of the town laid out in stone, shadow, and fractured sunlight.

Once an enormous collection of individual tombs beneath a great domed ceiling, now those tombs had been converted into grim stone houses and businesses still engraved with the names of the dead once interred there.

Usther glanced up at the domed ceiling. Cracks in it let through trickles of water or glimmers of distant light that flashed in her darksight. A comforting reminder that this place was home and hidden from those upworlders that would destroy her kind; but not without an ache at the memory of warm sunlight on her face, the scent of fresh air, the feel of grass beneath her feet. Even as distant and faded as those memories were, they could still bite.

They passed down spidery stairs and into the square, taking them slowly so that Misery wouldn't trip. The market was as bustling as ever, perhaps less a few stalls than usual today. It was always busy at the market on town meeting days, as much for gossip as for shopping.

'Bone flutes for sale! Bone flutes!' Mazerin the Bold shouted raspily from his usual bone stall. He was a weedy necromancer with a slight hunch, wispy hair, and visible fangs. He'd been a fixture of the market for as long as Usther had lived here. 'Good for occupying kids and banishing ghouls! Or the other way around!'

Usther would have glided past, but Dichotomy trotted over to Mazerin and started twining about his legs.

'Oh! There's a good cat. No, I won't pet you—I know you'll only savage me. Here, I've got some nice smoked cavefish just for you ...' Dichotomy continued to twine about his legs until the fish was dropped, at which point she growled and sprinted away with fish in mouth to hide behind some crates.

Mazerin watched her go with a bemused expression, then caught Usther's stare. 'Oh. Uh. It's all perfectly safe, I swear. Deboned and all. She always comes a-begging for my lunch and cats are good luck.'

Usther was torn a moment, between her desire to be first to the town meeting and this nagging sense of debt. She stopped at Mazerin's stall. 'Do you have a *zyk* scry knuckle?' she asked, as casually as she could. 'Mine is getting worn out and won't roll properly.'

'Ahh…that's the danger bone. Must have a lot of excitement in your future, eh?'

Usther didn't deign to answer. Mazerin handed her the knucklebone and she dropped three large gold coins onto the stall top. Mazerin raised his eyebrows—though gold was plentiful among the denizens, three coins was still a vast overpayment for a replacement knucklebone.

She avoided his questioning gaze and went to wait until her cat emerged from behind the crate, licking her chops with a much-satisfied expression. 'All done?'

Dichotomy flicked her tail, staring at Usther.

'Well, come on then.'

As they walked, she considered her cat. A cat minion would be much prized in Tombtown, particularly as cats were so hard to come by in a crypt. She'd spelled all kinds of wards and curses into Dichotomy's collar to protect her from other practitioners who might prefer her undead to alive and she rarely let the cat out unsupervised. It had never occurred to her that any of her neighbours might be *kind* to her. And indeed, Mazerin had seemed quite familiar with her…

'I suppose I know where you disappear to when you run out of the house,' Usther said. 'All those times I was imagining you caught in a giant spider's web.'

Dichotomy sniffed a door rather than responding.

They came at last to the towering black iron doors that gated the Old King's Tomb, now used as the town hall. They'd been opened enough to let through a few denizens at a time, but nobody was walking in currently.

'Look at that,' Usther said. 'We're still early, in spite of our little detour.'

She laid a hand on the cold metal surface of the door, thinking of Ree. Ree had seen this place not as an ancient ruin but an active throne room; had knelt before the now nameless king and learnt him to be a cruel tyrant. It was still wild to Usther that it could be true: that her friend had been cast into the past by an ancient lich, and been brought back only by Usther's magic.

Did Ree still think about that when she passed through these doors, or did her experience of the present outweigh the heft of memories past? If she was here, Usther might ask.

But she was never here.

Usther took her hands from the door, drew a long breath, and straightened. 'Misery, darling, keep an eye on Dichotomy for me. And don't leave the town hall. I'm going to sit up front so the council can see me glaring.'

She took one last look around, thinking perhaps her friend might come running up, looking tired and travel-worn, then squared her shoulders and went inside.

The town hall was empty. The dais holding the Old King's sarcophagus was devoid of council members, as were the marble stairs leading up to it. The rows of rickety chairs, some of which were now well on their way to being firewood, were largely uninhabited as well—except for old Uzma Plaguebringer, who dozed in the back with her rat minions curled up on her shoulders and lap. She'd likely arrived hours ago to light the torch sconces that lined the walls.

The once-grand hall was now worn and dilapidated, though with patches of shiny new-ness that was a constant reminder of the terrible ritual that had almost been completed here, exchanging the modern town and denizens for the necromantic kingdom of old. The torchlight cast long and angry shadows across the hall, glinting off the neatly organised treasure at the back—treasure which belonged to the town, and could be claimed by any denizen with the council's blessing.

Usther took a seat at the front, carefully sweeping her skirts so that they'd fan out as she sat. She crossed her arms and frowned up at the dais.

A swirling storm of screaming spirits and icy winds. The eerie glow of a growing portal. It had been eight years since Chandrian Smythe had been exiled from Tombtown, and she still couldn't look at those stairs without seeing it. Without remembering the feeling of air being sucked from her lungs; remembering dragging herself up those steps to stop the man she'd come to think of as a friend from killing her.

She hadn't made it, of course. Nobody had made it. Not the council. Not the high priestess of Morrin. Not even the Lich, the most powerful necromancer of the crypt and several centuries old. Their only saving grace had been that Smythe had excluded Ree from his spell, and thus she had been able to climb the steps and stop him—along with Wandering Larry, the crypt's oldest and most gormless minion.

She rubbed her chest and looked away, letting her pulse settle back down. Smythe was gone, and good riddance to him. Just another in a long line of people who had betrayed her.

The town hall filled in trickles and spurts, necromancers filing in either in small groups or edging for lonely seats at the back. She kept an ear out for rumours and subtly took a pinch of gravemould from a pouch at her hip, summoning an invisible spectre to be her eyes and ears at the back. It had taken her years to get her spectres to be fully invisible—for a long time, she'd been able to hide everything but the glow of their ghostly eyes—but now it was so complete that it was rare that she got caught spying.

She listened, with her own ears first, to the rows nearest her.

'Have you seen old Ursula?' asked Etherea Eversworn. 'She swore bloody vengeance on me when I bumped into her the other week but my mushroom garden is completely untouched. It's not like her.'

'Heard she'd gone fishin',' replied another denizen—she wasn't sure who. A man, most likely. *Fishing* referred to searching the crypt for corpses to raise as minions or feral undead to master.

'Well...I'll keep an eye out. She's a hateful old ghoul but I worry about her.'

Usther shifted her senses to her spectre, now hovering far enough above the back rows that the practitioners wouldn't sense its cold and know themselves to be watched. She rubbed her eyes at the cold itch as her vision transferred to her spectre, hoping that, as far forward as she was, nobody would notice a ghostly glow in her own colourless eyes.

'*...didn't see them when I scried...*' said a teen practitioner with their hair shaved on the sides and plaited on top.

'*They prob'ly don't want you spying on them,*' said another teen. '*You know how El is about scrying. Emergency only...*'

'*...saw a strange little shroom while out with Dead Percy,*' said an older practitioner, fondly patting his undead dog. The dog panted silently, its fleshless skull devoid of tongue. '*I wanted to pick it and bring it home for my son's collection, but something spooked Perce and he went haring off.*'

'*Yeah, I heard there might be ghouls in those parts...*'

Nothing particularly interesting. A feud between two practitioners had led to the first bannings at *The Bone & Brew* in a long time. Someone had stolen some treated organs from one of their neighbours...nothing big enough to sink her teeth into. She sifted through the conversations, bored and a little irritated by the wind-like whooshing that accompanied sitting inside her spectre's head.

Something groaned piteously. A familiar groan, followed by the faintest yowl. Usther sighed and massaged her temples, ejecting from her spectre's senses. 'Go help Misery with the cat, would you?' she murmured, and sensed her spectre go to do her bidding.

She looked around, blinking a few times to refocus her eyes and clear any residual glow. The town hall was nearly full now, and the council had begun their procession up the aisle to the dais. Kylath Bane at the front, her robes dusty and dreary but a cut of vibrant red paint across her lips. Igneus the Undying behind her, looking like someone had drained all the colour from his skin and dipped his long hair in ink. Tarantur behind him, naked and hairless from the waist up but for the tattoos crowding his skin.

All of them moved with a kind of ritual pace that made Usther roll her eyes. She supposed they thought it gave them gravitas, but honestly it just made her feel impatient. Nobody was really paying them attention, anyway.

When they got to the dais, they all stood behind the sarcophagus as if it were a particularly long lectern, and Igneus stomped his staff with a boom, amplifying the council's voices across the hall.

'Under Morrin's blessing, we survive another week in this bounteous crypt,' he said. He launched into his usual self-important blather, which Usther listened to with narrowed eyes.

'Front row again, Usther? Ever the dutiful denizen.'

Usther startled at the familiar voice and eerie tone. She hadn't noticed the High Priestess of Morrin slip into the seat beside her. Apparently she'd once been a huntress—perhaps that was where Ree had inherited her creepy stillness and silent movement.

Arthura raised her eyebrows while she watched her husband address the town hall. 'Wait for me after the meeting,' she said quietly. 'We have much to discuss.'

Usther inclined her head, trying to hold in her nervous apprehension. Something about Arthura's manner made her feel that it was more than an invitation to dinner with the family.

The meeting went on. Kylath took over from Igneus, taking complaints and solving disputes between denizens—practitioners fighting over fishing rights in certain tombs, neighbourly disputes about minions tearing up each other's mushroom gardens, that sort of thing. Once, Usther would have been hanging on every word, scheming for the day when *she* would be the one the denizens came to for advice. Those dreams had crumbled with maturity. The council was nepotistic and near-immortal, and she no longer desired power over others. She wanted purpose. And that was something altogether different and entirely more difficult to find.

So when Tarantur interrupted proceedings to call for volunteers to be part of some 'Grand Expedition', Usther only raised her eyebrows.

Tarantur sidled to the front of the dais, steepling his bony fingers. 'Prestige awaits,' he said. 'As well as necromantic discoveries such as we have never seen before. I vow that all who accompany me will receive my special thanks.' He nearly hissed the last word, a sound that tickled Usther's ear unpleasantly.

People started shouting back their questions and responses, some complaining about the vagueness of the offer, others asking when it would start and what form the thanks might take. Usther tuned out of it, focusing instead on the other council members' reactions. Igneus looked disapproving, Kylath harried. Interesting.

When the meeting ended, the town hall gradually emptied except for a few denizens here and there and a clump of eager practitioners around Tarantur, who basked in the attention.

'Not drawn by the prestige?' Arthura murmured beside her.

Usther glanced at the priestess. As ever, she wore a cassock of plain brown sack-cloth but wore it so regally it might have been silk. Her bare feet poked from the bottom, pale and neat. Her mane of ash-coloured hair and been wrestled into a loose tail that even now it fought to free itself from.

'Not particularly,' Usther said. 'It takes more than vague promises of a pat on the head to pique my interest.'

She didn't say that sometimes it felt like nothing piqued her interest, these days. That she clung to her house-minion and her cat because it seemed like there was nothing else for her. That some days, she looked forward to visiting the Altar of Many Gods to make an offering to Morrin simply because it was nice to think that anyone was listening.

Those kinds of thoughts were unworthy of a practitioner of her stature. Nonetheless, when she met Arthura's ice-chip eyes, she could not help but feel pierced by them. Like she was made of glass and her thoughts floated around inside her for Arthura to examine as she pleased.

'...of course,' said Arthura, her tone entirely too mild. She stood and smoothed her cassock. 'Come join me at the Altar,' she said. 'Though Morrin sees all, some things are best discussed right in front of her.'

'Sorry, what is this about?'

Arthura's expression was very grave. 'It is about you, Usther of the Ashes. It is about your fate.'

CHAPTER TWO

Usther

Usther made excuses to stop at home first; Dichotomy needed feeding, Misery needed a few moments to stare at the wall. Arthura took this all with the serene calm Usther both admired and hated.

Now, Usther sat down in her armchair, fussing at the lace that was still too tangled to tat. She tried not to look at the door.

Arthura walked along the walls, gently touching the various bones, candles, books, and other knick-knacks they'd accumulated there. Whether she was performing some silent benediction or it was merely for the tactile pleasure of it, Usther couldn't say. Usther couldn't remember the last time she'd been here. Though she was Ree's mother, most of their visits had taken place outside the house.

Like everything Ree did.

Time passed. Dichotomy attacked Arthura's skirts as she walked, pouncing with claws extended and then rolling around on the floor, getting tangled in them. When she got properly stuck, Arthura knelt and picked up the squirming cat, heedless of the deep scratches the cat left in her hands.

'You are more fearsome a warrior than you look,' she said. 'You'd do better to seek smaller prey, however.' She gave the tiniest smile, shocking in its sincerity, and placed Dichotomy back on the ground.

Arthura turned and caught Usther's eyes, her gaze sharp and clear as shattered glass. 'She's not coming.'

Usther stiffened. 'I'm sure I don't know what you're talking about.'

Arthura said nothing, only holding Usther's gaze.

At length, they left again, Dichotomy leading the way with tail raised, Misery shuffling behind. Usther watched the priestess surreptitiously as she walked, trying to make sense of how she moved so swiftly but with such a sedate, unhurried air. There was something otherworldly about Arthura that Usther had hoped she might have discovered for herself by now. But somehow she still felt like an awkward teenager in her presence—just a lot older, and a lot more tired.

It didn't seem fair. She had been in this town for more than ten years now, gathering secrets and training her power. She'd clawed her way out of being known as an acolyte, only to receive a title from her greatest hurt. 'Usther of the Ashes' sounded like an insult, not an honour.

What 'fate' could there be for someone like her? Her dreams of power and influence were ashes, just like her title. Truthfully, it was a relief to lay them to rest.

Perhaps Arthura needed someone to take over sweeping the Altar of Many Gods.

A bump against her leg. 'Prrt?' Dichotomy chirped questioningly. Usther realised she'd fallen out of step with the priestess.

She picked up her cat and cuddled her against her chest. 'Thank you,' she said. She squished Dichotomy's ears and strode to catch up with Arthura, who acknowledged her with the faintest nod.

There were worse fates than a quiet life at home caring for her cat and minion. And if Arthura needed someone to labour at the Altar, well, she'd happily accept. Time spent in service to Morrin was purpose enough for anyone.

Arthura didn't speak as they made their way to the Altar of Many Gods. Usther's feet knew the way, but she felt like she was seeing the town with new eyes in the priestess' company.

Even as quiet as the town was today, the mood was different with Arthura. Passing denizens inclined their heads respectfully, or even sketched slight bows. Arthura met each of them with a steady gaze and the barest nod of acknowledgement, which somehow angered nobody, even though necromancers hated it when someone acted superior to them.

The thing was, Arthura existed outside of necromancer power struggles. As the avatar of Morrin, she naturally garnered respect, but that respect didn't threaten anyone else's power. Indeed, Usther wondered whether the denizens were really bowing to Arthura, or whether they were bowing instead to the goddess she represented.

She felt...strange...about it. A kind of longing that wasn't based in jealousy. What must it be like for Arthura to give and gain respect without it being part of a complicated web of anger and hurt? What was it like to surrender all of that to Morrin?

She stewed on that as they walked, but Arthura didn't remark on her uncharacteristic silence. She was probably used to it, given her daughter's taciturn demeanour. Gradually, tombhomes gave way to bare stone as the domed ceiling of the central mausoleum sloped down to meet the floor. Here, on the outskirts of town, was the Altar of Many Gods.

Unlike the rest of the town, it wasn't a repurposed tomb. Instead, it had been constructed from salvaged stonework from all around the crypt—pieces that had survived collapse and been recovered from rubble. Some of it was large hunks and bricks of simple stone. Other parts were formed of stone carvings or even statues. The result was a mosaic structure formed of all different stones from across the crypt. Beautiful and strange, a series of makeshift columns holding up a decorative roof.

And at the base of most of the columns were small shrines of lit candles and offerings: purple flowers brought in from the frosty mountain top; herbs filched from Andomerys' garden; little paper prayers sealed with wax or twine or, in some instances, gut;carved bones and trinkets here and there, depending on the god.

Arthura swept past all these, sometimes pausing to straighten a stray offering or relight a candle that had gone out. None of these shrines were to Morrin, though Arthura had built this altar herself—with the aid of local minions, of course.

They came, at last, to Morrin's shrine. No larger or grander than any of the other gods', though more offerings had been left at it. It was a simple framed painting of a woman with all-white eyes and a hole through her head, nestled on a recess in a column of carved stone. On the shelf beside it was a small sack pouch with teeth spilling out of it and a small bone knife.

On approach, Usther immediately ducked her head and bowed to the portrait. Then she let her fingers hover just above the pouch of teeth.

Maybe she imagined it, but it always felt like a tiny spark of static leapt between the pouch and her fingertips. It was comforting nonetheless.

Arthura watched, saying nothing. Though the tight-lipped nature of their family sometimes irked her, Usther was glad of the chance to greet the goddess unhurried. She closed her eyes a moment, took a deep breath, and turned away. Dichotomy twined around her legs, a mouse wriggling in her mouth.

'That's not kind,' Usther said, and with a brush of her will against the mouse's, sent the mouse into a peaceful, painless death.

Dichotomy meeped around the mouse and slitted her eyes in a smile.

Arthura smiled at the cat, an expression so human and unguarded that Usther had no idea what to make of it.

Usther cleared her throat. 'So why did you want me here? I'm assuming it's not for the pleasure of my company.' She sniffed.

Arthura's head canted slightly to one side. 'I don't know why you would assume that,' she said, proving once again how easily she could slit Usther open.

Usther wondered if there would ever come a time she didn't crave the approval of a mother figure. If so, she hoped it would come soon.

'I wanted to see what you would do,' she said. 'And see how Morrin responds.' She caught Usther's gaze and held it, ice-chip eyes locked with colourless ones. 'I think there may be a connection between you.'

The words hit Usther like a punch to the stomach. One hand went to her chest as she considered the words. 'Between the goddess...and me?' She wanted to laugh it off, but she couldn't seem to draw the air, her lungs suddenly thin.

'You sound surprised,' said Arthura.

Surprised wasn't quite the right word. Usther cleared her throat, which suddenly felt full and tight. 'Not at all,' she said, as smoothly as she could, wildly hoping Arthura didn't notice how affected she was.

Arthura still hadn't looked away. 'I need your help.'

Usther blinked, struck unawares yet again. 'I beg your pardon?' she spluttered, before she could think better of it.

Arthura at last looked away, her expression becoming once again the distant priestess. 'There is something the goddess needs dealing with, and

I cannot do it alone. When I cast the teeth, I could make little sense of it...only that it is a danger of three parts. The empty tomb, the monster at the door, the sun and moon in love and at war...'

Usther bit her lip, holding back a scathing remark. She had little patience for riddles, but this was the High Priestess. She deserved Usther's respect. 'Sorry...what?' she asked, her voice only half as cutting as she felt.

Dichotomy scampered off, chasing something Usther couldn't see through the candlelit columns of the altar.

Arthura focused back on her again. 'I believe there is something wrong with the crypt,' she said. 'A danger that cannot be defeated by force. I am called elsewhere, but the danger must still be dealt with. I believe *you* are the one who should deal with it.'

Usther digested this. 'Why me?'

Arthura's mouth firmed, and she said, 'I believe Morrin has chosen you. I believe the danger is coming from the Lich's Wing,' she said. 'And I think we both know it would be a mistake to send my daughter there.'

Usther frowned, then inhaled sharply. 'Oh. *Oh.*'

It was well-known that a certain practitioner had taken up residence in the Lich's Wing.

Usther had taught him everything he knew about necromancy.

And he had tried to kill her with it.

CHAPTER THREE

Ree

A crow soared through the central mausoleum, beady eyes sweeping the town below with a singular purpose. Birds were unheard of this deep into the crypt, but the denizens below didn't so much as glance up as the winged shadow flitted over them, rasping a loud, hearty caw as it went.

The crow rolled on the wing, dodging a translucent spectre as it glided off on its master's orders, then circled twice around the spire of *The Bone & Brew*, wings fluttering as it perched on a narrow lip of stone. Then the bird...unravelled, like rags dragged from mummified flesh, blue light edged in shadow unspooling from inside. When the light cleared, the crow was gone and only a woman remained, black haired, silver-skinned, and with a tiredness about her eyes and mouth that even the immortality of magic could not erase. Her name was Ree. She perched just as easily as the crow had, one arm wrapped around the spire, her soft-soled boots flat against the incline. Her eyes searched the town below just as intently as had the crow's, dark eyes beneath a stripe of dark blue face paint. She hummed under her breath and then her eyes glowed strangely, briefly taking on the beady yellow appearance of a hawk.

After a moment, she sighed and swung herself down from the roof—a little clumsier than she had in her youth, and landing a lot heavier, the years having given her a plump padding. She dusted off her robes, tucked the wispy strands of her neck-length hair behind her ears, and headed for the market square.

There was a small bustle in the square today, with minions stumbling in all directions carrying bags and boxes for their masters and denizens at stalls haggling imperiously over bones, organs, and basic goods like food and herbs.

Ree made for the single blaze of colour in the shifting sea of black and grey. It was a woman in orange robes picked with red and blue flowers, her brown skin warm with health, her curly black hair pulled into a loose topknot. She had one full arm; the other ended cleanly at the elbow. The woman glared at a handful of garlic she grasped by the stem, then awkwardly thrust it into the basket hooked onto her belt and picked out some more produce from the sparse market stall. The denizen running the stall—Terra Blackthumb, necromantic farmer—kept offering the woman things which she rejected with a wave of her hand.

'These'll do,' she said, taking a handful of purple carrots that had disturbingly face-like profiles. 'Will three be enough?' She withdrew three vials of glowing blue liquid, which Blackthumb accepted eagerly.

'Andomerys,' Ree greeted her as she turned away from the stall. The woman stiffened then turned to her, her expression tight with emotion. Suddenly, it was hard to face what she must say, so Ree asked, 'What were those potions?'

'Moisturiser,' said Andomerys. She was a great healer, and an excellent potion-crafter besides. 'I do good trade with them. Most folk suffer from dry skin down here.' She gave Ree a considering look. 'You could probably do with some. I'll get you a batch.'

Ree made a face. 'I'll manage,' she said.

Andomerys turned them away, striding further into the market. 'Have you seen him?' she asked in a low voice.

Worry kicked Ree in the guts. No avoiding it now. 'No. I take it he's not back yet.'

A family of denizens crossed their path, two men with a small girl toddling between them, hugging a little rat minion with an exposed skull and glowing eye sockets. It nuzzled her chin and she shrieked with laughter.

Andomerys shook her head. 'It's...it's worse than that.'

Worse. The word coiled in Ree's chest sickeningly.

She had known. When Andomerys had asked her to keep an eye out for Emberlon on her outing, she had known that it was more than an idle request.

'Come to mine,' Ree said. 'We can talk while I pack.'

Usther would be furious that she'd not even taken the day at home, but some things were more important than that. If she was lucky, she'd catch Usther at home and explain.

The wards on her tombhome deactivated easily at her touch in a burst of familiar necromantic energy, a chill breeze with the feel of Usther. She ushered Andomerys inside and closed the door behind her, the wards thrumming back into place as the door sealed.

Andomerys took a seat in one of the threadbare armchairs, resting her chin on her hand. She looked tired, Ree realised; bags under her eyes, a heaviness to her mouth. She wasn't used to seeing that from her old friend. Andomerys was ageless, the only bright and lively appearance in the town.

Ree hesitated a moment, half-hoping that Usther was home, half-dreading it, but she didn't hear a sigh from the kitchen and a black-and-white blur didn't attack her boots, so Usther must be out. Ree settled into her friend's usual seat at the small table, noting the mess of lace and bobbins in a tangled heap there. She looked to Andomerys, waiting.

The healer sighed and rubbed her face. 'Emberlon is missing. He should have returned from his last trip a week ago. I hoped he was just delayed, which was why I asked you to keep an eye out for him.'

Ree frowned, anxiety kicking her again. It was never good when denizens went missing. Adventurers were an infrequent but deadly threat. And Emberlon was not a particularly powerful necromancer.

'I'll find him,' she said. She'd thought to spend the next week at home—catch up with her parents, help out Usther and Misery around the house. Rest. It had been weeks since she'd taken more than a day at home and it was beginning to wear on her.

She could rest when Emberlon was home safe. She pressed her lips into a thin line, considering the logistics. 'What does it look like when you scry him? Is it brick or rough stone? Are there columns? Wooden beams?'

Andomerys went very still.

'You can scry him now if you can't remember,' said Ree.

Andomerys licked her lips. 'I can't scry him.'

Ree waited uncertainly for her to explain. She'd known for years that Emberlon and Andomerys were exclusions to each other's anti-scry charms specifically for situations like this.

'I've tried. Many times. But each time I do, all I see is...white.'

That couldn't be right. When scrying worked, you saw the subject and their surroundings. With the right spell, you could even communicate. When it didn't work, your scrying surface—usually a bowl with water—was inert. Just water.

Ree went into the kitchen at the back of the tombhome. She pulled a wide, deep bowl from the shelf and filled it with cold mountain water from the cistern.

'Show me?' she asked. When Andomerys nodded, Ree took a small, curved knife from her belt and pricked her finger with it, letting the blood fall into the water. Though it was only a single drop, it swirled and spread like a red cloud.

Andomerys gripped the sides of the bowl tightly. A golden glow suffused her, seeming to seep from her skin. A warmth like sunlight emanated from her. '*Illathitar serath,*' the healer intoned, the silken language of *iyad-anar* a startling contrast to the guttural necromantic language, Old Antherian.

The blood in the water flashed gold, becoming a shining thread. Then the surface of the water did the same. The surface became disturbed, shifting. Ree waited for it to reform and still into the image of her friend and former mentor. Instead it became a blank, brilliant white so stark she had to shade her eyes.

Andomerys let the spell fade and the water again became still, the blood only blood.

She didn't know what this meant. If a scry subject was protected or dead, the spell would simply fail. This obfuscation was something new entirely.

She knew, however, that it couldn't mean anything good.

'I'll track him, then,' she said. 'There'll be records of where he went and why. That's as good a place as any to start.'

Maybe he was somewhere full of white light? Maybe the scry hadn't failed but simply been impossible to see?

Where could he even *be* where that would be the case?

She put those thoughts aside. 'I just need a few hours to get ready,' she said, standing up. She hadn't even unpacked from her last trip. She needed to wash all the grave dust from her skin and hair, needed to replace all her clothes with fresh ones, and needed to collect new rations. It was a market day, so the last part shouldn't be awkward, at least. She rubbed her eyes tiredly. So much for sleeping on her nice comfy stone shelf...

Andomerys rose as well. 'I'll need the same. I'll meet you here.'

Before Ree could even express her surprise, Andomerys pressed on, 'I can't stay home knowing he's lost, and I'll never have a better guide than you.'

Ree thought about all the reasons that Andomerys shouldn't come. Ree could cover more ground in her crowskin than she could on foot. She could focus better alone than she ever could in company.

But Andomerys and Emerblon were friends. Would Ree be content to stay home, knowing Usther was in danger?

She nodded. 'The crypt's been unsettled recently. I'd be glad of your magic.'

Andomerys' expression softened. She nodded and left the tombhome, the wards sealing behind her.

It didn't take Ree long to get ready; a few hours had been a much-inflated estimate. She rushed through her wash in icy mountain water, picked up her supplies, and re-packed her bag with frantic speed. It was only her note she hesitated over. What did you say to your friend who'd been waiting for you for weeks? She wanted to apologise; she wanted to say that even though being at home was hard for her, she still loved Usther and had been planning to see her. That this wasn't her idea.

But putting that into words seemed like it would only make things worse. In the end, she kept it brief.

Travelling with Andomerys. Scry if I'm not back in a week.

~ Ree

CHAPTER FOUR

Ree

Andomerys arrived not long after that. Her clothes were more practical than Ree had ever seen them, replacing her long silks and sashes with thick cotton robes, but no more muted. She'd stick out in the crypt like a flower patch in a swamp, but Ree wasn't entirely sure undead could even see colours, so she tried not to worry about it.

'We'll need to stop by the archives so I can check where he was headed when he disappeared,' Ree told her, joining her outside. The flare of the wards sealing behind her felt like a condemnation.

She led the other woman to the archives, a small room with a heavy iron door that it took both of them to budge. Ree watched as sunlight flared around Andomerys' body, no doubt giving herself a strength boost with her healing magic. It was a gentle pulse of warmth, like the sun coming out from behind thick clouds, and then gone again.

It didn't take much searching. They'd left notes for each other in a journal open at the small, cramped desk. Ree ran her hands over Emberlon's familiar, cramped script. *Taking a bag of returns to the eastern tunnels, sixth and eighth libraries,* it read. *One week, maybe two.* He'd dated it three weeks ago.

Andomerys wandered in behind her, awkwardly skirting the various stacks of books she and Emberlon had left waiting to be returned when a trip presented itself.

'We need a bigger archive room,' Emberlon had said once, when floor space was direly lacking and they'd knocked over their neatly stacked books more than once.

'We need a central library,' Ree had replied. 'Why don't we move them to a new space, like we did with the treasures?' She'd referenced the enormous sorting and cataloguing task they'd worked on at the beginning of her apprenticeship.

Emberlon had considered carefully, never dismissive of his much younger assistant. 'It seems wrong, doesn't it? To steal from a library, even to build your own? These libraries have stood for hundreds of years. The way they're sorted, the books they hold...it's all pieces of a history that would quickly vanish if we plundered it.'

'You're a necromancer,' Ree had said blankly. 'Isn't plundering old things part of the job?'

'I'm an archivist,' Emberlon had said firmly. 'I believe in borrowing.'

She'd realised, later, that she'd rarely seen Emberlon with any minion but Wandering Larry, who was nobody's minion at all. And now, with years more experience as a necromancer archivist, she had to agree with him. They didn't need a bigger library. They needed more archivists.

Maybe then they wouldn't have to venture out alone.

'Ree?' Andomerys asked warily.

'Mm?'

'I said, do you know where he's gone?'

'Oh.' Ree closed the journal, smoothing the craggy leather cover. She cleared her throat and blinked at the sudden heat around her eyes. 'He went to the eastern tunnels. It's...you know, it's probably easier if I show you.' She strode into the middle of the room, raised one hand, as if calculating, then confidently went to a case of scrolls. She unrolled a map and showed it to Andomerys.

'Eastern tunnels,' said Andomerys. 'Isn't that the old Lich's Wing?'

Ree shook her head. 'Much further east. He's gone to libraries six and eight.' She pointed them out. 'It's a week if you go the safe way, a few days if we go the dangerous way.'

Andomerys raised her eyebrows.

'The dangerous way it is,' Ree said. 'By the way: how do you feel about heights?'

ANDOMERYS DID NOT CARE for heights.

It made for slow going, coaxing her up ladders carved into stone walls, or across rope bridges over vast chasms below. The crypt was a world of cramped tunnels and enormous underground expanses, something that Ree was just now realising might make for a journey of unpleasant extremes. She did her best to keep Andomerys appraised of what they would come upon next, pausing frequently to show her the map.

Ree had spent her whole life travelling the crypt alone, and didn't care much for company. The times when she'd appreciated having a mage companion to turn aside the undead had long passed. She was a beastmage now, and frequently, her fingers twitched toward her crowskin pouch, wishing she could shed her human shape and let her wings carry her the rest of the way.

But Andomerys was capable enough, and muscled through her fears with a determination Ree couldn't help but respect. Moreover, she was not prone to chatter, and Ree enjoyed their companionable silence more than she liked to admit.

But mentally complaining about their travel was only a distraction from the thoughts Ree didn't want to face, and on that first night when they sat together around a campfire in a room with a ceiling that vanished into the distance, the worries came bubbling to the surface once more.

Andomerys stared into the flames, poking the wood with a long spoon. They'd assembled the wood from damaged crates and furniture. As old as it was, it still burned, and Andomerys had set a pot bubbling over it. Her expression now was tight-lipped, her eyes hard.

Ree licked her lips. 'How do you and Emberlon know each other?' she asked into the quiet.

Andomerys glanced up at her and then away. She shrugged. 'We never met until he moved here,' she said.

Ree frowned. She knew there was more to it than that. More to their strange friendship.

Andomerys tossed aside the spoon and leaned back on her hands. 'Gods,' she said. 'That was over thirty years ago now.' She shook her head and looked up into the long dark above them. 'I hate this place, and it's been thirty years.'

Ree held in a flinch at her words. Andomerys had the right to hate whatever she wanted.

'The place,' said Andomerys. 'Not the people in it.'

She was watching Ree, must have caught what Ree had been trying to hide.

But she still didn't understand.

You couldn't hate the crypt without hating part of Ree.

But Ree didn't know what to say about that, so she said nothing. Andomerys served them a mushroom stew with some stale but serviceable bread, and then they curled up on opposite sides of the fire and went to sleep. Andomerys basked in the warmth, while Ree backed to the very edge of their small room.

REE WOKE IMMEDIATELY to the sound of frantic, shuffling footsteps. Ever since she'd acquired her ratskin, her hearing and sense of smell had become a little sharper, even when she wasn't wearing it. She rolled to her feet, muscles protesting at the movement so soon after sleep, and moved quickly to Andomerys' side. She woke her with a gentle shake on the shoulder, still alert to the footsteps. They were drawing nearer.

Andomerys groaned. 'Ughh. What?'

'Minion,' Ree said.

Andomerys' face scrunched up. 'I'll blast it if it comes in.' She waved a dismissive hand.

Ree didn't doubt that she could, but a minion approaching might not just be a feral undead. There was every chance there was a necromancer attached, and not every necromancer in the crypt was friendly.

She tried Andomerys again, but Andomerys only mumbled a threat and rolled over, leaving Ree alone.

Ree reached into her herb pouch, where she carried burial herbs that could soothe or stun a feral lesser dead, and crept to the doorway.

Closer...closer...she pinched the herbs between her fingers, dry and leafy.

Rattling breath, just the other side of the door...

Ree spun out the doorway and flung the herbs into the minion's face. The minion howled and started to pat its own face in a panic, a wailing, staggering figure with withered green skin pulled tight over a skeletal build.

Ree froze, watching the minion flail and complain. Ridiculous. Familiar.

'Larry?' She took two quick steps forward. 'Larry, is that you?'

She reached for the minion's hands, dragging them away from his face. He blinked at her, still speckled with burial herbs—herbs which not only didn't hurt undead, but which had never had any effect on this minion at all.

Tears stung at Ree's eyes. She flung her arms around the minion. 'Gods! It's really you, isn't it?'

Wandering Larry returned the hug with the fumbling awkwardness of an undead. After a moment, he started to chew on Ree's hair.

She gently smacked him, making him grumble, and she pulled away. She had no idea what he was doing here, but Morrin's teeth was she delighted to see him. 'Come on,' she said, gesturing for him to follow. Part of her wondered whether he would, but when he dutifully shuffled after her, her heart lifted.

'Andomerys!' Ree said loudly. 'We have a visitor!'

When Andomerys finally deigned to wake, they gathered around the embers of the fire. Ree handed Larry the hard heel of the bread to gnaw on, which he excitedly started to mash against his blunt black teeth. Minions like Larry didn't need food the way humans did. They were sustained by necromancy, or sometimes by the wild death energies that formed in places where many bodies had been buried. Minions nonetheless were rather...bitey...as a species, and none more so than Larry.

'What is he doing out here?' Andomerys said. 'I've seen him a handful of times in as many years. It was my understanding that his...new master...was keeping him busy.'

His 'new master'. Ree looked down, twisting her hands in the skirts of her robes, and tried to keep her breathing steady. 'I see him around sometimes,' she said, which made it sound a much more regular occurrence than it was. Like it didn't make her heart ache for a different time to have him sitting nearby and gargling excitedly. Like she had known what to do with herself for eight years of travelling utterly alone. Larry had been her shadow since she was old enough to walk. Everyone in town knew him, and all the children who grew up there were fond of him. But he'd been her minion in a way he'd been no one else's, her lack of necromancy be damned.

More than the Lich who'd raised him.

More than his new master.

WHEN THEY SET OUT AGAIN that day, it was difficult not to feel light in a way she hadn't in weeks. Difficult not to smile a little when she glanced back and saw him determinedly plodding after them. Difficult not to snort a laugh when he tested his teeth on a stone column, then howled unhappily when it was too hard.

Though their path took them skirting precarious ledges and climbing collapsed stairs, Larry would always eventually catch up, determination making up for what he lacked in co-ordination—or perhaps magic making up for the lack, once he was away from their sight. Larry, Ree had discovered, had hidden depths.

Often, Andomerys caught her smiling at him, her own expression troubled. Each time, Ree quickly looked away.

That night, sleeping cold in a dark room with only travel rations to fill their bellies, Andomerys asked, 'Don't you wonder why he's here?'

'No.' Ree said, and turned her back to her.

The next few days continued much the same, until at last Ree stopped in the middle of the corridor and held out her hand. 'Library six is just up that staircase.' She gestured to a narrow opening in the wall that just revealed a steep spiral that was more ripple than carved stairs. She started up it, squeezing through the gap. Her feet slipped a little on the over-smoothed stone, but she braced her arms against the walls and made it up okay. When she got to the top, she waited to pull Andomerys up the last few steps.

At the bottom, Larry yelled and scrambled, his awkward minion gait not suited to this challenge. 'We'll be back soon,' Ree told him, as she'd done many times before. This time, her heart was in her throat. She had no guarantee that Larry would be there when she returned.

Then she took a key from her pack and unlocked the carved wooden door, in which, in Old Antherian script, the word KNOWLEDGE was boldly scribed, surrounded by the points of a many-petaled flower.

Inside, it was a long, narrow room, lined on both sides with shelves. A large desk took up the far end, surrounded by a framework of metal vines that climbed the wall. There were more scrolls than books here—an older library, and even the books had a strange sort of concertina binding, opening out in odd ways.

'Cozy,' said Andomerys.

Ree nodded, scanning the shelves for anything obviously out of place. 'We get a surprising amount of use out of it,' she said. 'A lot of these are unique texts. Wear gloves if you touch any of them.'

'My hands aren't dirty.'

Ree glanced at her. 'All hands are dirty, but it's not about that. The oils in human skin degrade old parchment.'

'Ah.'

Ree shrugged. 'Make sure you lock the door behind you. Larry has destroyed more books than I can count and he'll find a way up those stairs eventually.'

She looked for signs of Emberlon. A stack of books. A note left tucked under a paperweight on the desk. But she found nothing. No sign of him. For a moment, she just stood there and breathed.

'He wasn't here, was he?' Andomerys' voice was soft.

Ree made for the door. 'We'll try library eight.'

Library eight was a burial collection accessed through a trapdoor in a queen's tomb. Ree steeled herself before she entered.Until she'd learned therianthropy, she'd never been able to access this tomb alone. Dead monarchs made for nasty undead, which some claimed was due to inherent power but Ree thought was more likely due to inherent assholery. Sometimes particularly malignant deaths or acts could leave behind unstable death energy, and she'd rarely heard of a monarch who *hadn't* done terrible things. She'd always been glad that Tombtown didn't have them.

Sure, the town had problems, but the cruelty of monarchy wasn't one of them.

The antechamber was made of successive archways centering an ornate sarcophagus with gold filigree carvings. As they walked in, the temperature in the room dropped to the point that Ree could see her breath mist the air in front of her. She headed straight for the trapdoor, maybe twenty feet left of the sarcophagus. 'We'll have to be quick,' she said. She'd normally run in as a rat, which wouldn't wake the sleeping queen. But with Andomerys, she had little recourse.

Andomerys hurried after her, hovering as Ree pried at the trapdoor.

'Festering rats,' Ree muttered. 'It's stuck!' She took a small knife from her belt and dragged it around the edges of the door, trying to find the obstruction.

The sound of stone grating on stone interrupted her. Ree glanced up, wreathed in her own breath, as the lid of the sarcophagus slid aside and long grey fingers gripped the edge of the stone box.

Ree dropped the knife and wrenched at the handle.

A crowned head with cobweb hair appeared, hollow eyes burning with two points of eerie green light.

'Andomerys, I can't lift it—'

Its jaw opened in a lipless snarl with a sound like sucking wind.

'Andomerys—'

The healer raised shaking hands, but when she spoke, her voice was firm. 'Enough.'

Golden light bloomed from her hands, seeping from her skin, glowing brighter and brighter until Ree had to shield her eyes. The greater undead hissed and there was a sound of grinding stone.

Andomerys let her magic fade, and when Ree looked up, the undead queen had sealed herself back inside her sarcophagus.

'Well,' Ree said. 'That's one way to deal with it.'

Together, they descended into the queen's library.

Ree leapt from the ladder and took in the room, heart-pounding. Her gaze swept the shelves; it was all scrolls here, each slotted into a curved holder. Each in their place.

Larry landed on his back after her, howling.

'He wasn't here,' said Ree. Static grew in her head, loud and crackling. She took another step, hands clenching and unclenching at her sides. 'Andomerys, he wasn't—'

'Hey.' Andomerys seized her shoulder and spun her to face her. Ree was too stricken even to flinch. 'Panic won't help. This is one more thing we know than I did when I came to you.'

Ree nodded vaguely, the static growing louder. Emberlon, lost. Panic was a clenched fist under her ribs.

'Look at me.'

Ree started to lift her eyes, but froze. There was a slash of violent red beyond Andomerys' shoulder.

No. Her stomach lurched at the sight. It couldn't be.

'Wait,' she said, and Andomerys released her.

Ree crouched at the other end of the library. In the corner, beside the ladder, there was a large crack in the wall that hadn't been there before. And blooming at the base of it was not the blood she'd feared, but a trail of crimson fungi.

VEO CORVA

CHAPTER FIVE

Usther

Usther knew she was being manipulated. She kept the knowledge like a barb in her chest, and she had to be careful not to hope too much or it would spike her expanding heart. But she tried to set that knowledge aside and focus instead on her goal.

Arthura was one of the most respected denizens in town. She was beloved by the goddess. And for whatever reason, she had chosen Usther to help protect the town. Usther could use that. She'd needed purpose, something to draw her away from her lonely tombhome, and here, it was provided. Arthura might be manipulating her by offering her prestige, but she had unknowingly answered the prayers Usther had been laying at Morrin's altar for months.

She wanted to tell Ree as much, to let her know that she had an important mission, and would be away for a while. Perhaps to filch some of her many maps. After years of watching Ree come and go on various archivist errands, it would have been sweet to be the one leaving on important business. Would have been sweet merely to see her friend again, however briefly.

But of course when she got in, it was to find a slip of paper sitting on the table beside her lacework.

Travelling with Andomerys. Scry if I'm not back in a week.

No indication where, or why. As considerate as always.

So Usther packed her things and left her own ambiguous note. She hoped her housemate found it galling. Then she gathered Misery and Dichotomy and set out, one of Ree's maps rolled up and tucked into her pack.

The journey, of course, was uneventful, but edged with constant tension. With the Lich dead and gone, there was little in the crypt a skilled practitioner had to fear—and Usther had honed her skills to a fine edge. With Ree's map, she could avoid the tombs of the greater dead and largely escape her biggest threat: getting lost. All else she could turn aside with a word and brush of her will—or at worst, a blast of necromancy reminding them who was master.

The tension was because of her entourage. Misery was an able (if reluctant) houseminion, but Usther doubted her ability to defend herself. Even now, she lagged behind Usther whenever she thought she could get away with it. And Dichotomy...

Dichotomy had been a small, scarred stray when Usther had found her a handful of years ago. Now, she was plump and healthy, and wore a collar so rife with warnings and curses that even Ree, who was specifically excluded from them, was wary to touch her. She was generally good about following Usther, a devoted little thing, but she was still a cat. Prone to wandering off, or, when threatened, fleeing to goddess-only-knew where. Usther had no idea how she might react to a longer journey, or what danger she might unwittingly putting her cat into.

But she couldn't leave her at home. Couldn't leave anyone at home.

They trailed her easily enough. Dichotomy running ahead and then running back, or leaping out from behind crates or from drainage tunnels. Misery sighing and dragging her feet but never quite dropping out of sight. The tunnels were long and cold, labyrinthine in places, but the company made them a little warmer. At night, they camped in small rooms where Usther could easily see the door. Misery stood on watch while Dichotomy crawled into Usther's lap and purred. Usther massaged the little cat's ruff, wondering exactly what she was bringing them into.

WHEN AT LAST THEY CAME to the Lich's Wing, Usther lifted her chin. 'Stay close,' she ordered Misery, necromancy lacing the words. 'And keep watch on Dichotomy.' She hoped the quaver in her voice didn't frighten her minion. If anything, she hoped it made her cautious. It was rare that she used magic to command Misery, but some things were too important to leave to chance.

She had never been to the Lich's Wing, and Ree's maps of it were still vague and incomplete. She'd only begun mapping them since the Lich's demise, and Usther suspected she only did so out of her obsessive sense of duty. If she'd ever run into Smythe on her map-making missions over the years, she hadn't told Usther about it.

There was one path, however, that was clearly marked. Bold against the faintly sketched tunnels and halls that surrounded it. It was a path that led to the Lich's library, and it was that which Usther followed now. If Smythe was anywhere, it would be in a library. He was like Ree, that way. One of his few character traits that wasn't an obvious flaw.

She didn't like it here, and she couldn't quite convince herself it was just because of Smythe. The rooms were empty, the tombs hollow. There was no distant shuffle of restless feet, no clatter of bones or rasp of gentle breaths. When she extended her senses around her, reached out with necromancy, it was to find nothing at all. An entire wing of the crypt, devoid of death and undeath. A suffocating silence compared to the noise and activity of the crypt she knew.

Ree had once called it over-fished, suggesting that after centuries of occupying this wing, the Lich had used up all its 'natural resources'. But walking through these halls in-person, it felt like more than that. A lingering malevolence in a void.

She read the map as carefully as she could, stopping often and discussing her path with Misery and Dichotomy, though the former only sighed and the latter only smiled, equally uncomprehending. The loneliness of her journey pressed on her in this place in a way it hadn't in the rest of the crypt. And if she were to step off the path here, she would have very little chance of getting back. The map was unfinished, and the crypt felt...unmade.

When at last she found her way to the library, she hesitated at the door. Her chest was tight, suddenly too small for her lungs. The last time she had seen this man, she'd been barely more than a girl. She'd stayed up all night helping him research a way to save his life. And then she'd been dying on the stairs as he sucked the energy out of her and the whole town to fuel his ritual.

Necromancers rarely felt cold the way non-practitioners did, but the ice riming the stairs, her robes, her hair, would always stay with her. The terrible howl of spirits on the wind, leeching the warmth from her as they went, would stay with her. The savage satisfaction on his face as he opened a portal atop the dais would stay with her.

For a moment, she could feel that chill again. She shivered.

A touch at her ankle. Dichotomy twined around her legs, chirping a question. A bump at her shoulder, and Misery turned away, pretending she didn't care.

Usther took a shuddering breath. 'We can do this,' she said. She scooped up Dichotomy, holding the little cat against her chest, and walked inside.

It wasn't what she'd expected. Grander than most of the libraries Ree dragged her to, but chaotic and disarrayed. They stood on an upper landing with stairs curving down either side. There was a door at the other end—perhaps leading to more of the library, perhaps to something else. The bookcases here were tall, and a wheeled ladder rested against one, likely necessary to reach the top. Books were stacked or scattered across the floor, many seeming to pin piles of notes in place. Discarded quills and ink pots littered the tables and floor.

There was no sign of Smythe, beyond the horrendous mess. She couldn't quite bring herself to believe the Lich had left it so.

Dichotomy started to squirm, so she let her go. The little cat leapt easily from her arms to trot down the stairs, exploring with interest. Usther followed, but Misery made a small groan of discomfort.

'I feel quite the same,' Usther said. 'You can stay up there, if you like.'

Misery didn't reply, but she didn't follow either.

Usther walked the library, skirting the mess. The trail of her dress caught an ink pot and sent it tinkling across the floor. She winced, but no angry spirit came rushing down on her. Smythe didn't burst through the door, demanding to know why she'd come.

Dichotomy chased the pot, batting it further. The constant skittering and scratching did nothing to ease Usther's discomfort.

'So this is where you've been hiding all this time,' Usther muttered. She spun on the spot, taking it all in. 'She'd hate it, you know. She believes a library ought to be ordered.'

Usther approached the door at the other end. No wards, seals, or curses were etched into the wood there, or reacted when she sent a wave of necromancy rolling over it. She tried the handle.

The room it led to was meticulously clean in comparison to the library. Stone walls that looked regularly washed. A small pallet bed with a straw mattress and feather pillow, the blanket neatly folded on top. A journal closed beside it.

The journal was equally un-cursed, so Usther picked it up and flicked to the most recent page.

I saw it again today. It was growing in one of the storage rooms not far from the library, as lurid as fresh blood. It resisted my necromancy, just like the others did. I poured some acid on it, and that seemed to take care of it.

I'm tempted to take a sample and find out more about it, but I fear that may lead me down a path best untaken. I can't help but think of others better suited to the task, anyway. Not that I would ask.

'Usther? Is that you?'

Usther startled, the journal falling from her hands as she formed a spell-casting shape. A man stood in the doorway of the library, eyes wide behind his spectacles. His dark hair, with its waves and ringlet curls, had been pulled back into a messy ponytail. His sepia skin was shadowed around the eyes and faintly tinged with grey, marking him as a necromancer. He was dressed differently than she remembered; instead of his khaki adventuring clothes, he wore a long blue coat with brass buttons and a tall collar.

He raised his hands palm-out. 'I'm terribly sorry, I didn't mean to—I—what are you doing here?'

Red bled at the edges of Usther's vision. Power whipped around her, comfortingly cold.

She could attack him, right now. He was more powerful than anyone had guessed, maybe more than she knew now, but he had summoned no magic to himself. He'd set up no wards or traps. He'd left himself completely helpless.

He looked frightened. No, not frightened...something else. Worried.

'I say,' he said, his voice almost a whisper. 'Are you all right?'

The red faded. She let her magic dissipate into the air, leaving her numb. She dropped her hands.

She wasn't a teenager any more. She could feel the years past now like a yawning chasm, and it left her tired.

'We need to talk, that's all,' she said.

She thought he might smile and bluster, as he used to, but he only nodded. 'I'll put on some tea,' he said. 'Uh...here, take a seat.' He took her into the library and hastily removed a stack of parchment from a chair of burnished wood. 'I'll be right back.'

And, having lost the terror that urged her to fight, she sat.

THE BEAUTIFUL DECAY

CHAPTER SIX

Ree

'What do you think it is?' Ree asked.

They crouched before a vast crack in the library wall. Ree had no idea what might have caused it. Though the crypt did shift and crumble over the years, this was too vast and sudden to be believed. It had been cracked and split like an egg over a bowl, revealing a jagged tunnel like nothing she recognised.

And a fungus like nothing she recognised. The sight of little red caps, each a different shape and shade, each a little too vibrant and shiny as if slick, turned her stomach.

Andomerys shrugged. 'Nothing medicinal. I don't know much about fungi beyond that. Probably toxic, judging by its colour. We should leave it.'

A mushroom twitched.

'Ahh!' Andomerys flinched back. 'What in all the realms was that?'

Ree shook out her sleeve and covered her mouth with it, leaning closer. 'They shouldn't do that,' she said. 'Mother taught me about fungi when I was little. They're a bit like plants; they can only move by growing, and they can spread via seeds—spores, even.'

As she drew nearer, the mushroom's cap lit up from beneath like a lamp; a violent pink, clashing horribly against the crimson cap and stalk. When she drew back, the light faded.

'Odd,' she said. She felt a finger of chill run down her spine. There was something to this. Emberlon missing, the library cracked open, and now...this. In the place Emberlon had been headed.

'Leave it.' Andomerys' voice was sharp. With fear or frustration, Ree couldn't tell.

Ree stood, peering down the crack in the wall. 'This shouldn't be here either.'

'He's not here.'

'He might have been,' Ree said. She peered into the narrow space. Wide enough for a person, even one as wide as Ree, if they weren't too claustrophobic. Certainly someone as narrow as Emberlon could have squeezed through.

Below her, the mushroom lit up again. And then, as if by relay, a dozen other points of light appeared down the tunnel. On the walls, on the floor. On the ceiling. Pinks, purples, and reds.

Intrigue and concern warred within her.

She stepped carefully over the fungi and started to squeeze into the gap. The rough-hewn stone scratched against her skin, snagging on her robes, but she didn't complain.

'Ree!' Andomerys hissed.

Ree glanced back. The healer's hands were clenched at her sides. Her jaw was tight. She looked hunted.

'You don't have to come,' Ree said. 'You can wait here, and I'll come get you on the way back.' Andomerys looked poised to argue, so Ree added, 'He came this way. This is why I'm here. He came this way, and I'm going to find him.'

'Fine!' Andomerys huffed. 'Get trapped in some lonely crack in the crypt.'

Ree took this for assent, and continued her squeeze. She considered her ratskin, magically folded into a pouch on her belt, but after a minute she heard swearing and glanced back to see Andomerys squeezing in after her.

She did her best to avoid the fungi. It wasn't easy; they were sparse, but there was very little wiggle room. She had to duck beneath ones at head height on the walls, and half-climb over those higher than her knees, bracing herself in the small gap. Ahead, she could see the walls begin to widen. The red speckles fell away. 'I think it opens out ahead,' she said to Andomerys. 'Not much further—'

Her words were consumed by a desperate wail. Ree glanced back, dreading what she would see. Sure enough, Larry shoved himself into the crack. 'Larry, stop!' Ree cried. She had no idea what the fungi might make of undead flesh, but she didn't want to find out. Some very nasty things could grow in a crypt of this size. 'Andomerys! Can you stop him?'

'I am barely squeezing through here,' she replied, somewhat muffled. 'Larry. Go back. Go back!'

Larry howled and tried to jam himself in further, smashing right into the fungi, which released clouds of glittering spores that settled on his face and shoulders. He continued to push in with desperate force.

'Larry, calm down!' Andomerys said sharply, but Larry's struggle grew no less frantic. He might barrel into her in this state and do her real harm. Minions like Larry had a feral strength to them when riled up.

Ree hesitated only a moment. She slipped her hand into the second pouch at her waist, her fingers brushing short, smooth fur. She sang the spell, a trilling, winding tune in a long-dead language. Blue-and-black light surrounded her, breaking her apart into smoke and pouring her into the skin, filling it up. And then Ree hit the ground on all fours and scampered back along the crack.

Her ratskin was from a dead cave rat being sold in the town market for meat. She'd requested to take the whole thing rather than have the butcher cut it up, which wasn't an unusual request in Tombtown. Then she and her mother had ritually tanned and treated it until it was ready for therianthropy. It wasn't a particularly large rat, but it was small and nimble, ideal for a space like this. She skittered up a wall, over a cluster of fungi, and then skidded back down to slip past Andomerys' legs. Her small hands could find purchase on the slick stone, which was intangible to her as a human, and her whiskers twitched and helped her navigate the tight space with speed and confidence,

As she got to Larry, whose body was now coated in red spores, she stopped, straightened, and dropped her skin. It was a strange sensation; a sort of unspooling, like she was both thread and liquid at the same time. As a human, she was pressed flat against the wall—the sudden tightness uncomfortable and unsettling—but she clamped down on that feeling, focusing instead on Larry.

Larry goggled at her, the howl dying in his throat. Her sudden appearance had stunned him, and she took full advantage of that before he could work himself up again. 'Larry,' she said, firmly but not unkindly.

'You are doing this all wrong. You need to stand side-on, look...' She began the tedious process of coaching Larry through the space, as she had done many times before, whether that be climbing up a crumbling staircase or balancing along the precarious edge of a cliff. Minions were rarely clever and never co-ordinated (and Larry less so than most). But Ree had found that if she was patient and helped him position his hands and feet, he could eventually be gotten through most spaces.

Getting him around the fungi in so tight a space seemed almost impossible. However, as covered in spores as he already was, she didn't know that another coating could do much worse.

Eventually, she and Larry emerged. 'We made it,' Ree panted. She glanced at Larry. 'I missed you, but I did not miss *that*.'

Andomerys paid them no mind. She faced the other way, taking in the environs. The crack led to an odd, cave-like passage that looked bored straight into the rock. More fungi sprung up here and there in clusters, some of them pulsing or twitching ominously.

'Wait...' Ree took a few steps after her friend. The passage went only one way—further east, by Ree's estimation. 'I don't remember this place.'

Andomerys turned to face her now. 'It's a big crypt. Larry, come here, I'll get those spores off you.' Her hands started to glow and Larry howled and stumbled away from her, shielding his face with his hands. 'Larry! I won't get *you*...'

Ree ignored these antics, staring frozen at the cave around her. 'You don't understand...I don't *remember* this place.' She unslung her pack and cast about for her travel map. She found it in a protective fold of rat leather and unwrapped it, flipping open the worn parchment with a crisp crackling sound.

Her eyes immediately found the eastern tunnels. She followed a winding path with her fingertip until she found a small mark for Library Eight. But the cracked wall in the library should have brought them out into a large Hall of the Dead, with almost a hundred bodies lining the walls in shelves. Not...whatever unbuilt place this was.

Had something bored it through the Hall and destroyed what should have been there? She stared at the map, uncomprehending. But there would be signs. There would be debris. There would be restless dead, screeching their rage at being disturbed.

Here there was...nothing.

Only stone.

Only the cave.

Only crimson fungi spattering the walls and ceiling like droplets of blood.

Ree felt, in a horrible lurch as if the earth were moving beneath her feet, that something was *wrong* with the crypt.

Then Larry screamed.

VEO CORVA

CHAPTER SEVEN

Usther

Usther sipped at an oddly sweet cup of tea and watched the man who had almost killed her play with her cat. Finding her purpose was going very differently than she'd thought it would.

'Ow!' Smythe jerked his hand back from where he'd been spidering it across the ground and stuck his bleeding finger in his mouth. 'Rascal,' he said, waggling a finger at her white-and-black cat. 'You're rather quicker than I expected!'

Dichotomy licked her paw in what Usther thought was a distinctly pleased manner.

She watched him for any sign he would take vengeance for her actions, but he only smiled and shook out his hand.

Then again, if you'd asked Usther several years ago whether Smythe was a threat before he'd nearly destroyed the town, she would have laughed. She wouldn't underestimate him again.

'So who's this?' he asked, nodding to Misery. The minion hovered behind Usther's seat, back half-turned and head drooping. 'Forgive me, but she doesn't look like much of a bodyguard.'

Usther stiffened. 'This is Misery,' she said. 'She's my personal assistant and is quite capable, thank you.'

That wasn't true, of course. If there was any danger, Usther's first command to Misery would be to run. She was fragile in both build and temperament, and Usther couldn't bear the thought of losing her first and oldest minion. Nearly everything else she raised was temporary, but Misery was for life.

Smythe stood up and approached Misery with hand outstretched. 'A pleasure to make your acquaintance—uh. Oh. Jolly good.' He let his hand fall as Misery turned away with a sigh.

For a moment, Usther could only see his back. His shoulders slumped and he stared at the ground. Then he straightened and turned back to sit across from Usther with a strained smile.

'Not that I'm not glad of the company,' Smythe said. 'I am—I *really* am—but I don't understand why you're here. Why anyone would come here after—why anyone would come here now.'

Usther shrugged and crossed her legs, hoping the movement would school her features to smoothness. She didn't have Ree's gift for hiding her emotions. Though, to be fair, sometimes she wondered if Ree had any emotions to hide. 'Checking in, I suppose,' she said, her tone bored. 'It doesn't do to ignore a threat forever.'

Smythe wrung his hands in his lap and nodded. 'Of course,' he murmured.

'Have you seen any red fungi about?' she said. He'd absolutely caught her reading his journal, but the pretence gave her an element of advantage, and she needed all she could get.

But while Smythe had been noticeably, vulnerably open thus far, now it seemed like shutters went down behind his eyes. He crossed his arms and shifted on his seat. 'I have,' he said.

Usther raised her eyebrows. 'And what do you know about them?'

'Very little. But they're dangerous, whatever they are, and best left alone.'

They considered each other; Usther with lip curled, Smythe with a sullen glare.

The red fungi might have nothing to do with the threat Arthura had foreseen but Usther still wanted to learn more. Wanted to press Smythe simply because he didn't want her to. Instead, she looked away, as if she'd lost interest.

She stood up and strode over to a bookshelf, pretending to examine the many titles there. 'Have you had many visitors, in your time here?' she asked. She cast him a sidelong look. 'I mean, I know very well someone who *hasn't* visited you, but you never know, perhaps there is someone who can still pretend to tolerate you.'

Smythe looked down and Usther felt a curl of satisfaction. 'No,' he said. 'It's just been me. Quite lonely, if I'm completely honest. Larry, I can lure back on occasion, but he doesn't like me like he used to since I...' he trailed off, no doubt remembering the moment he'd absorbed the Lich's powers. A feat that thankfully most of the town hadn't witnessed, as it was likely to cause all sorts of problems.

Indeed, Smythe and Ree had created many problems for the town, not the least of which was Smythe himself.

'And what have you been working on?' she asked. 'I suppose there's little for you to do but work, given your status as a pariah among pariahs.'

She'd meant it to be a sting, something to draw him out in revealing his work. It was laughably easy to play most practitioners into monologuing about their grand plans. Wound his ego and he'd be unable to help himself from blustering and spilling all his secrets. And after all, even before learning necromancy, Smythe had had a necromancer's ego. But instead Smythe only looked abashed, and shook his head. 'Nothing very important,' he said. 'I've mostly been working on uncovering the history of this place but...I don't suppose that would interest you.'

'It wouldn't,' Usther said, struggling to contain her annoyance. What did he think he was playing at, with this kicked puppy act?

He took a sip of his tea, frowned, and set it carefully atop a saucer with a tiny clink. 'So. Uh...how are things in Tombtown? All rather exciting, I expect?' His attempt to rally seemed uncharacteristically feeble.

Usther had had quite enough of him. 'Not really,' she said. 'In fact, though Morrin has warned us of a great danger, the town has been positively boring. You wouldn't know anything about that, would you?'

Smythe flinched and leaned back.

Usther shoved aside her teacup. 'You know, don't you? Of course you know. Eight years you've been hiding away in the Lich's Wing—even though nobody wants you—filling up on old books and strange magic, like a hideous fat spider, waiting for us to fall into your trap—'

'I didn't—'

'Go on!' Usther said. As she got angry, her magic sparked at her fingers and filled her lungs like a breath of icy air. Her eyes started to fill with ink; she could see the shadows at the corners of her vision that marked it. 'Pretend you're just some harmless little bookworm. I won't fall for the same trick twice.'

She expected him to draw magic around him as well, but he only lifted his glasses and rubbed his eyes tiredly. 'I'm not harmless,' he said. 'Though sometimes I rather wish I was. I think maybe I never have been. Even before the magic. I think maybe that's why...it doesn't matter. I haven't done anything to the town, or any denizens in it. I haven't uncovered any dark and mysterious secrets in the Lich's library. Truthfully, I've had very little heart for necromancy of late, apart from questioning the odd spirit when I can't find what I need in a book. And I'm also afraid,' now he met her gaze levelly, 'that whatever you try, you won't be able to hurt me. I'm quite beyond that now.'

'Like fuck I can't—' before she could so much as crook her fingers for a spell, his eyes changed. Not noticeably in colour or shape, and yet she couldn't look away from them. She felt the pressure of it like her brain was being locked in a vice; like any wrong move might crush her entirely. Then he blinked and looked away. He looked, if possible, even more miserable than he had before.

Usther panted at the sudden release of pressure. She stared at her hands. They were shaking so hard she'd have been pressed to even lift a teacup.

She clenched her fists. Weak. Always too weak.

'What are the red fungi?' she asked quietly. She'd have liked to have sneered it, liked to have made him feel small, that she knew his secret. But she felt terribly tired.

Smythe shook his head. 'No. Tell me why you're here.'

She threaded her hands in her lap, as much to affect calm as to hide her trembling. 'I already told you. The town is in danger. Arthura believes the source is near here.'

Very near, though Usther didn't say that.

Smythe rubbed his eyes. 'And you assumed it was me. I can hardly complain.'

Usther looked around at this library, which Ree fumed about giving up to him even to this day. All the collected knowledge of the most powerful Lich she had ever heard of.

Ah.

'And what of the Lich's notes? It's grimoire? Surely you'd be able to make quite a lot of trouble with that?'

Smythe sighed. 'I'm sure I would, if I still had it. I destroyed it.'

Usther blinked. 'You...you what?'

Smythe took off his glasses and cleaned them. He looked almost sheepish. 'I was upset. I blamed the Lich for—it doesn't matter. It's gone.'

Gone? She scrutinised him, looking for any sign of insincerity, any hint of a lie, but he only looked tired and sad.

The knowledge of a necromantic mind so brilliant, he had learned to manipulate *time*. Destroyed.

She needed to focus. 'The fungi, then. You're hiding something about it!'

Smythe sighed and stood up. 'Well, I could use another pair of eyes, truth be told. I'll show you.'

He gathered his things. He took a lot longer than Ree would have. Though he had a pack ready to go, there seemed to be all manner of small knick-knacks and other nonsense he refused to leave without. There was much, 'Oh, I couldn't possibly travel without Hirsten's *A Brief Burial Biography* to keep my company,' and 'I don't suppose you've seen my ink? No, not that ink—my *good* ink, the one with the wax seal?' and 'How long do you think we'll be gone? Do you think two gender balance potions will be enough?' He seemed so posh and fluttery that Usther could see shades in him of the historian she'd trained so many years ago.

But when they left the Lich's library, he was again quiet and contained. No bluster, no chatter. And he looked, if anything, nervous.

Usther wished she could take solace in that but he had already proven how very little he had to fear from her.

CHAPTER EIGHT

Ree

Ree had chased Larry many times in her life. She'd chased him when he'd stolen her books and then tried to flee so he could gnaw on them in peace. She'd chased him when he'd gotten his head stuck in a sack of flour and had panicked when walking backwards didn't get it off. But she'd never had to chase him like this: while he was screaming, actually screaming, and tearing at his own flesh with his fingernails.

She chased him now. 'Larry!' she tried to yell over his desperate cries. 'Larry, hold still!'

She caught him when he ran into a wall and wrapped her arms around his middle to stop him fleeing. He squirmed in her grip, his hands scrabbling not at her, but at his own skin. Up close, Ree could see the tiny red filaments growing from his skin, seeking outward like tiny maggots.

'Festering rats,' Ree whispered, her eyes going wide. She fought back the impulse to jerk away from Larry, away from the hideous, fast-growing fungi embedded in his undead flesh. If she let him go, he would run, and who knew what might happen to him then?

'We need to kill it,' Ree said. 'We need to get him to Usther, or Pa, or—or—'

Larry's head wrenched back, thumping into Ree's. For a moment, she saw white, and Larry burst free of her suddenly slack grip. 'Andomerys—!'

'Hold him still,' the healer replied tiredly. 'Let's get a look at him.'

Ree grappled her undead friend again, pinning his arms. She knew he was capable of incredible strength, but that seemed dormant in him now as he continued to wriggle and struggle in panic.

Andomerys leaned close.

'The fungus is spreading.' She put a finger near one of the sprouting filaments, which poked at her and then retracted. 'It appears to prefer undead flesh.'

Small relief that it wouldn't eat her, when it was already eating her friend. 'Necromancy will kill it,' Ree said. She'd watched Usther sterilise things with magic more times than she could count. Nobody had to be more careful about disease than a necromancer. Human remains were dangerous until they were properly treated and preserved by magic.

'We don't have a necromancer,' Andomerys said. She withdrew, and her hands started to glow.

Ree immediately spun to put her back between Andomerys and Larry. 'You can't cleanse him with healing magic. You'll kill him!' Her heart thumped a terrible beat. Some minions could even be killed by direct sunlight. The idea that any minion, even Larry, could survive a brush with healing as powerful as Andomerys' was unthinkable.

Andomerys made a sound halfway between a growl and a sigh. A wave of sunlight blasted past Ree, surrounding her in its light. She hugged Larry close, her scream mingling with his.

'Ree. Ree...' A touch on her shoulder. Larry was still whole in her arms. She backed away, looking him up and down. Larry looked down at himself, where the red filaments were crumbling into ash. He patted his own body, as if testing it, and looked up at Ree with mouth agape.

She realised she was mirroring his expression and closed her mouth.

Andomerys dusted off her hands and put them on her hips. 'You don't get to be a healer if you can't precisely direct your magic. And healing is just as capable of killing as necromancy.'

Ree stared at her. 'You only targeted the fungi? But you couldn't even *see* all of it.'

Andomerys shrugged. 'With the right parameters in your spell, you can be very precise.'

Larry hugged his now fungi-free body and then hurled himself down to sprawl on the ground in relief.

Ree allowed herself a moment to enjoy the sight of her friend, safe, before Andomerys' words really sank in.

Parameters. It wasn't something she'd heard mentioned before. Necromancers talked about limitations, which sounded similar but was usually said with more cursing. In therianthropy, she'd paid a lot of attention to what the witch Wylandriah called 'the pitch and cadence' of the song. It controlled for things like intensity in spells that didn't use therianskin. But she'd never really had much to do with healing magic; her mother had only a passing interest in it, and she'd done her best not to look too eager, lest someone try to force her into learning it.

Ree pushed down the burning desire to ask more. She could pester Andomerys for details once Emberlon was safe at home.

Now, Andomerys paused and crouched beside a cluster of crimson fungi. Ree came to stand at her shoulder. 'They don't look related,' Ree said. 'They aren't even all the same colour of red.'

Indeed, many of them were hues of garish pink or had caps or stalks that verged on purple. They were a riot of reddish colour, but each had some part that was the exact same shade of bright crimson, glistening as if doused in fresh blood.

A mushroom with a serrated purple cap and luminous filaments twitched as she spoke.

Andomerys reached into her pack, withdrawing an empty vial and a pair of forceps. As her hand neared the cluster, the mushrooms seemed to lean toward her, but she moved quickly, plucking an edge from one of the caps and transferring it to the vial. There was the faintest plink against the glass as the fungus tested its new restraints, before falling silent.

'Why take it with you?' Ree asked as Andomerys returned the vial to her pack. Ree couldn't imagine willingly keeping the bizarre fungus so close to her person.

'I'm a healer,' Andomerys said. 'It's a requirement of the job to keep track of dangerous and toxic plants in case they have a beneficial use or can be cured. But apart from that,' she dusted her hands and straightened her robe, 'I was able to cleanse it with a sterilising spell, but it wasn't easy. It...resisted my magic. I find that concerning.'

Ree did, too. Her eyes flicked to the cluster Andomerys had taken a sample from. Spidery filaments were already growing over the spot where the previous sample had been, regenerating and reforming. She repressed a shudder. There was definitely something sinister about the crimson fungi. She only hoped that their connection to Emberlon's disappearance was coincidental.

Somehow though, she doubted he'd just gotten locked into a tomb somewhere.

Once Larry had calmed down, the three of them set off down the tunnel marked on none of Ree's maps.

CHAPTER NINE

Usther

'So...' Smythe thrust his hands into his pockets, looking at Usther side-long. 'How have you been?'

'Adequate.'

'Any exciting magical developments?'

'Some.'

'Did things work out with that girl you liked? Uh...Symphona, was it?'

'She tried to kill my cat.'

Smythe nodded. 'Romance is like that sometimes,' he said, and grimaced.

They were travelling to a part of the Lich's Wing Usther didn't recognise, though it seemed to be heading back toward town. The halls were wide and the ceilings high. The walls were decorated with carvings and mosaics, the colours faded with time. Lesser dead frequently shuffled by or hissed at them from the doorways lining the halls. Smythe paid them no mind at all. Usther occasionally turned them with a gentle exertion of will when they seemed especially aggressive.

'Ree said this part of the crypt was over-fished,' she observed, making a mental note to fold the corners in her favourite books in punishment. Even in a crypt of this size, finding a healthy population of minions largely untouched by other practitioners was rare. It irked her to think this trove of lesser dead, clearly saturated with death energy, had just been sitting here untapped all this time.

'Oh it was,' Smythe said. 'It was so quiet in here that it was positively airless. But I don't use many corpses for my work. Over the years, the undead have gradually been drawn here from other parts of the crypt. Residual death energy, I suppose, from when the Lich was here.'

Or from the current occupant. She had already felt his power and it was every bit as frightening as the Lich's had been. Perhaps more, since the Lich hadn't nearly destroyed the town, as Smythe had when he was only a teenager. She said none of this aloud.

Dichotomy prrted and trotted ahead, tail held high. The bell on her collar danced silently, but where she walked, the dead made way. Usther smiled to see it. It hadn't been especially powerful magic, but it had been clever, and she prided herself on clever things.

'How does that work?' Smythe asked, following the cat with his eyes. 'I assume it's something to do with the sound...?'

Usther raised her chin. 'Well deduced,' she said. 'I got the idea from all Ree's ugly magic singing...that perhaps you could trap a spell within a sound. So when the bell rings, it turns undead away. They are lightly but actively repulsed by the sound of it.'

'But it isn't making a sound...so you worked it to only affect undead. How?'

Usther waved a hand. 'It required quite a long incantation, etched onto the bell, and a crystal to contain the resonance...nothing too draining, of course, but I couldn't build much on existing work.'

'That's brilliant,' said Smythe.

'Of course. That's *me,*' Usther replied, though privately she was pleased by his response.

It felt almost like she was his mentor again. Her mood curdled. Perish the thought.

Dichotomy paused to sniff something against a wall. She hissed, tail fuzzing, and ran back to Usther, who immediately scooped her up.

There was a spray of crimson against the wall. Or mostly crimson. When she had imagined the fungi, she had pictured something closer to the amanita that grew in her childhood village, or the bloodcups that formed in the amphitheatre outside Tombtown. Something red and recognisable. But this was like a colony of dozens of fungi of all shades and shapes. Luminous purples and shocking pinks shot through with red of all shades. But predominantly that vibrant, unsettling crimson.

On spotting it, Smythe jogged ahead. 'I didn't know it had grown this deep into the Wing,' he said. He crouched beside it and gestured to Usther. 'Watch this.' He held out his hand above the cluster; a narrow purple mushroom twitched. Below it, red filaments extended from the base of the cluster, seeking his hand. When he pulled away, the filaments retracted.

Usther did not consider herself squeamish. After all, she regularly played with internal organs, working elbow-deep in the kind of gore that haunted the nightmares of others. But something about those thin filaments questing outward like curious little worms turned her stomach.

'How many of them are there?' she said. 'Why are they so varied? How long have they been here?' In spite of her questions, she drew no closer. Dichotomy squirmed, asking to be put down, but Usther hugged her closer. She would not let anyone she cared about within sneezing distance of those things.

'I don't know.'

'Which question are you answering?'

'All of them. I'm terribly sorry, Usther. I just don't know. I noticed them maybe a few years back? Thought little of them. It's not until you get close enough for them to reach for you that you realise there's something strange about them. I thought they were endemic to crypts like this.' He hesitated. 'And watch this.' His eyes filled with inky darkness as he turned to the fungi. He pointed at it. *'Erz vorhett zarak!'*

An arrow of red light shot at the mushroom to burst across its surface. It glowed at the touch, filaments flashing and crackling with energy, before fading. Usther held her breath, transfixed by the sight. Waiting for it to wither and crumble into dust, as any living thing must when struck with a killing curse so powerful it sucked the air around it as it travelled and rimed the stone around its target with frost.

But the mushroom remained.

'That...can't be right. Only the dead are unharmed by a killing curse.' Behind her, Misery shuffled closer, leaning over her shoulder to look. Usther adjusted Dichotomy and put an arm out to hold her minion back.

Smythe shrugged. 'I don't know what to say. I've attempted to kill it many times, to no effect.'

'So it's what...an undead fungus?' The idea was bizarre. There were stories of undead trees, of course, though Usther thought they were little more than stories. No respectable necromancer would fart around trying to raise a tree from the dead.

Well, maybe Veritas would try it. He wouldn't be *successful*, though.

'It's not undead,' Smythe said. His eyes were troubled behind his glasses. 'I've tried every variation of turning and laying to rest I know. It's not reanimated. It's *immune* to necromancy.'

'That isn't possible.' Usther couldn't keep the irritated snap out of her voice. Dichotomy squirmed at her tone. She shifted the cat so she was resting against her shoulder.

Smythe spread his hands helplessly.

Something moved beyond him, a flash of white. Usther's gaze snapped up just in time to see a fluttering skirt disappear down another passage. She stiffened and seized Smythe's shoulder. 'Who was that?'

Smythe blinked at her. 'Sorry but...who was who?'

She tightened her grip, making him bluster a bit in protest, and towed him after her.

The figure had disappeared not through a normal passage nor a doorway off the hall, but a wide, jagged crack leading into a tunnel that looked as if it had been bored into place by a giant worm. Crimson fungi spiralled down it, coating the walls, the floor, the ceiling. All but a narrow path down the centre.

In the distance, a man in a white dress paused. He was shockingly beautiful, his features drawn in delicate lines, his short red hair stark against his ochre brown skin. He was barefoot among the fungi, which burst into light and colour at his feet.

Even at this distance, his smile was a perfect white slash.

And then he ran on, vanishing into the distance, leaving a trail of fading light in his wake.

'I say, is that a friend of yours?' Smythe asked. His voice shook the barest bit.

Perhaps he, too, was revulsed by the thought of bare feet among the greedy, bloody fungi.

'Not at all,' she replied. Her desire to hunt down the outsider and question them warred with her fear of the fungi. Arthura had sent her here to discover the danger in the Lich's Wing, but neither of them had imagined the threat might look like this.

Smythe put a hand to the crack in the wall. 'Look at this. It's–well, it's quite phenomenal. There's no crumbling; the lines are jagged like teeth, but would fit together perfectly. This...this wasn't here, the last time I was in these parts. I wonder who created the entrance to this tunnel. How did they know it was here? This was all wall before!'

Usther wiped her hand across her forehead and backed away from the tunnel. 'I need a moment.'

'Are you all right?'

'Just shut up, would you?' Usther glared at him, and he did, clasping his hands and looking contrite.

Usther pinched the bridge of her nose between her fingertips and turned away. Dichotomy twined around her feet. Misery sighed. The sound was calming.

It was increasingly clear that Arthura had seen truly. There really was a danger here, which meant Morrin really had sent her here.

The question was: what was *she* supposed to do about it? Even Smythe, with his unseemly amount of power, was unable to affect the crimson fungi.

'Ughhh. If only Ree wasn't such a miserable hermit...' she muttered. Her friend was an expert at dealing with situations she was woefully unequipped for, and Usther could really use her expertise right now.

A sharp intake of breath. Usther turned and Smythe watched her with worried eyes.

'Is—' he cleared his throat. 'Is she well?'

Usther shrugged and turned away again. 'You don't get to ask that.'

'No,' Smythe said quietly. 'I suppose that's fair.'

VEO CORVA

CHAPTER TEN

Ree

The tunnel had many passageways, criss-crossing seemingly at random. All as oddly formed as the original. It unnerved Ree how difficult Emberlon was to track in this place, where he might have gone in any direction and they had no way to know. The shorter passages, she did investigate. Most seemed to open out into the crypt proper, as had the one they'd found in the library, through cracks and crevices that looked almost as if something had ripped open the wall between its claws.

Worse were the longer tunnels, where Ree had to decide whether they were worth pursuing. They wouldn't be able to search all of them with any kind of haste, but it pained Ree to think that they might be going the wrong way.

Mostly, they picked the passages that had the most fungi. Ree didn't think it was a coincidence that they had appeared at the same time as these bizarre tunnels and Emberlon's disappearance.

They were picking their way down one such tunnel which Ree thought was heading north (and sinking lower) when she heard a shout. She froze in her tracks; Larry bumped into her and grumbled.

Andomerys raised her eyebrows. 'What?'

'Did you hear that?' she asked.

Andomerys said nothing, watching her.

Ree strained to listen. Surely that hadn't been the cry of an undead.

She thought she heard a distant, echoing laugh, but could see no recognition on Andomerys' face. The hairs on her arms lifted. 'It's this way,' she said, motioning to her friend. 'Move quietly.'

Ever since she'd started practising therianthropy, she'd noticed certain heightened senses and instincts. It wasn't reliable; it varied from day to day, from spell to spell. Some days she could barely stand to be in the same room as other humans because she could smell them so strongly. Sometimes the sight of Usther's cat made her want to flee.

She hadn't seen anything about it in her main source of therianthropic knowledge, the journal of Wylandriah Witchfeather, who was the first therianthrope to make a written record of the magic. But then that was a very limited resource even by the author's own admission. And it wasn't exactly an *enormous* change from normal. It was just...noticeable.

Now, she was glad of it. It was always better to get a look at other people in the crypt before they got a look at you. If it was a town necromancer, they had nothing to fear. Well...*little* to fear, anyway. If it was a newcomer necromancer, they might have a fight on their hands, but it was unlikely. Most necromancers were eager to learn about the town, enough so that they would overcome their desire to terrorise and impress.

The problem was upworlders. Non-necromancers who lived in the world beyond the crypt. As Ree had found out the hard way, even the nice ones weren't to be trusted.

Now, she moved swiftly and stealthily down the passage she'd heard the voices coming from. Andomerys followed her at a casual pace, occasionally shushing Larry, though his gargles and sniffles didn't sound amiss in a crypt where undead were plentiful. It wasn't long before the tunnel closed on a narrow crack. This one was blissfully shallow, and it was barely a squeeze to get through. She hunkered low on the other side.

It was a wide chamber lined with shelves of the dead sleeping peacefully with their arms crossed over their chests. It was old; early Third Era, by her guess. The dead had been preserved with ointments and lotions that had dried their skin and turned it shades of blue and green. She couldn't see any of the crimson fungus out here, which was a small relief. Her skin had been crawling the entire time they'd been in the passages. Though the fungus seemed much more interested in Larry's undead flesh than her living one, she still felt...violated, somehow, in nearness to it.

They were on the second floor of the hall, with two exits below on opposite sides of the room. One was filled with flickering orange torchlight.

Her stomach clenched. Adventurers.

Larry made to squeeze through after her and Andomerys, but Ree shushed him and waved for him to stay back. To Andomerys, she whispered, 'Stay out of sight.'

'Gladly,' the healer replied. She eyed the growing light with lips pressed tightly. While nobody would mistake her for a necromancer, she had been the one to heal Ree's near-fatal gut-wound from adventurers when Ree was just a teenager. Ree suspected it hadn't been the first time she'd had to do it.

At the thought, Ree's hand went to her abdomen. Even with Andomerys' intervention, the attack had left an ugly scar on her that still pained her from time to time. They had killed Larry in front of her (or so she'd thought), and they had treated her as less than human, dragging her after them like so much old meat, hoping they might get some treasure out of her before she died. She had been certain she would die. If Emberlon hadn't scried on her to check in, she would be.

She only wished it had been her harshest lesson in the dangers of upworlders.

Now, Ree crept to the edge of the upper floor, ducking behind a crumbling column and looking down. Upworlders couldn't see in the dark, so she felt plenty hidden. Sure enough, when they appeared, their torchlight made a glowing orb around them—so bright that, for a moment, Ree had to cover her eyes to let them adjust. She couldn't help but internally *tsk* at the foolishness of entering a crypt of this size without approaching a necromancer for a darksight ritual.

But then she was looking at them, really *looking* at them, and her scorn quickly withered into fear.

Two strong, sturdy people strode into the room. One had a tumble of green curls that faded brown at the roots, and a flash of green paint on their eyelids. They had a broad, sturdy build and wore mail armour with a green surcoat embroidered with golden leaves and vines. Two gleaming, hooked blades hung at their belt—sickles, Ree thought they were called, though she only remembered seeing them used by upworlder farmers at the village she sometimes accompanied her father to for trade.

Somehow, she didn't think these were for farming.

Their companion was extremely large in build. A woman with silver hair falling in a long plait down one shoulder. Her armour was made of overlapping plates. It was a deep ocean blue and etched in silver on the front was a design of an owl with wings spread and water flowing from the wings. Ree recognised it immediately as a holy symbol, but couldn't remember which. It wasn't any god that appeared in the Altar of Many Gods in Tombtown. A spear hung from a strap slung over her shoulder, and a shield hung on her back.

Their voices bounced around the chamber, still muffled and hard to make out amongst the clatter of their armour and heavy, echoing bootsteps. They didn't look up at the higher level; it was outside their bubble of torchlight and, to them, must be impenetrably dark.

Ree put her hands into a pouch on each side of her belt. In the first, she touched the soft fur of her ratskin. In the second, she felt around until she found a smooth bone carved into the shape of an ear. Some of Mazerin the Bold's best bone work.

She hummed a gentle tune under her breath. Her ears went cold and then all at once, she could hear *everything*. The ultrasonic squeaking of other rodents, the skittering of many-legged things over mossy stone, the ringing melody of the armour and chain. She took a moment to adjust and then filtered out the noise, focusing instead on the voices of the two intruders.

'...exactly what you signed up for,' said the green-haired person. Their voice was animated, and seemed halfway between exasperation and laughter. 'You shouldn't have let that necro escape. She might be the one we were sent here for!'

'She was terrified,' their companion replied. Her voice was deep and musical. Both she and the green-haired person had an accent Ree couldn't place. It wasn't quite the accent of the village in Zenk, though it had a similar rolling quality. Perhaps it was nearby? 'Do you truly believe a being of great evil would squeak and flee at the sight of us?'

The green-haired person shrugged. 'We'd *like* to believe it.'

We?

A touch on Ree's shoulder, feather-light; Andomerys crouched beside her as the pair passed into another room. 'This is growing more complicated,' she said grimly. 'We're tracking Emberlon and we find necromantic fungi and witchkillers.'

A shiver went down Ree's spine. She thought of the holy symbol marked on the silver-haired woman's chest. 'Witchkillers?'

'Those are paladins, Ree. Gods only know how they found this place.' She glared at the place where their torchlight was slowly disappearing.

Paladins. The word seized Ree's chest. Holy warriors trained specifically to kill necromancers at some evil island academy. They used to be as common as any kind of warrior but had fallen out of grace decades ago. Unfortunately, there were still some around.

'Festering rats,' Ree whispered. 'What do we do?'

Andomerys leaned past her, scanning the room. 'How do you get down from here?'

Ree scratched the back of her head. 'I don't know where we are. I'd just climb down.'

'Climb?' Andomerys made a face. She walked to the edge of the floor, light gathering in her hand. 'Stay here.'

Alarm bells rang in Ree's mind. 'I don't think you should–!'

Andomerys stepped off the edge. She landed lightly on the floor below, golden light suffusing her body.

Ree swore under her breath. Healers must be able to augment their bodies with magic, similarly to how Ree did with therianthropy.

Andomerys glanced back at her, glaring, and strode after the paladins, her magic fading like the sky at dusk,

Ree swore again and fumbled with the pouch at her belt. She hurriedly sang herself into the skin, becoming a column of shadow and light that poured itself into the skin, filling it. Then, she skittered down a column to the ground floor on four paws, scaly tail whipping behind her.

It didn't take her long to catch up to Andomerys. She darted in front of her and stood up on her hind legs to chitter her annoyance in the sharp, lisping vocabulary of a rat. Ahead of them, the light of the paladins was still visible. If anything, it looked like they had stopped.

Andomerys glared down at her. 'Keep out of sight. They aren't going to hurt me. I'm not what they're here for.'

Ree still remembered the awful feeling of a knife in her gut. She hadn't been the target of *those* adventurers, but it hadn't stopped them. She squeaked even louder, her tail thumping the ground behind her.

Andomerys sighed. 'They cannot possibly kill me. Stay out of the way.'

She strode on, sidestepping Ree's tiny cave rat form. Ree fumed, furiously smoothing her whiskers, before scurrying after her. *She* wasn't at risk here. As far as those witchkillers were concerned, she was just another cave rat. Not even a particularly large one,. Emberlon was already missing and she refused to let Andomerys walk into danger alone.

She kept a few steps behind and stuck to the edges of the passage, where the shadows were thickest and the torchlight was unlikely to reach. Her ears twitched as the echoes of the witchkillers' voices reached them.

'Another festering crossroads,' came the voice of the green-haired paladin. 'How exactly do the gods expect us to find our way around this place without a map?'

'Take a deep breath,' their companion replied. Her voice was more soft, and didn't carry as well. 'We'll look around until a lead presents itself.'

'Your patience is giving us hives.'

It looked like the paladins were standing in a hall not terribly different to the one they'd just left. Their torchlight barely licked the exit of the passage they'd just walked through, but it still burned Ree's retinas with its brightness. As a rat, they seemed mountainous, two enormous automatons of metal and blades.

One of the automatons blew air derisively.

'Hail!' Andomerys called from in the passage. Ree startled, surprised by both the formal tone and the volume.

As one the paladins drew their weapons, the torch falling to the floor and shrinking the circle of light. 'Who hails?' The silver-haired paladin asked, her voice cold.

Andomerys sighed. 'There's no need for any of that.' She called golden light to her hand, so that they couldn't mistake that she was a healer. They relaxed as she emerged from the passage, though they didn't sheathe their weapons.

'I didn't realise there were people here,' said the green-haired paladin. Their companion raised her eyebrows, and they quickly added, 'Non-necromancers, I mean. Obviously, Sef.'

Ree's fur stood on end at the blunt de-humanisation. She crept closer, keeping to the shadows.

Andomerys put her hand on her hip. 'I'm Andomerys. I know this area well. And you are?'

'Tabris Root-and-Sickle of Paladur-Ez,' said the green-haired person. They tilted their sickles toward the light, and hung them again at their belt.

'Persephone Owl-and-Spear of Paladur-Ez,' said the silver-haired woman. She slung her spear back over her shoulder.

Neither of them looked any less intimidating without their weapons in hand. Indeed, the silver-haired woman alone looked like she could punch through a crypt door with a single blow of her gauntleted hand. They were both so gods-awful *large*.

'What are you *doing* here?' Tabris asked. 'You can't go five steps in this place without tripping over an undead.'

'Or having one grab your ankle,' Persephone added in an undertone that perhaps only Ree caught.

'Are you a priest?' Tabris continued. 'This place isn't safe. I can't imagine why you would come here.'

Ree stiffened, concerned that Andomerys would reveal that she lived here. Something that raised too many questions, and which she had cursed herself many times for once revealing to a lost historian. But Andomerys only sighed and tapped her foot. 'I'm not a priest,' she said, and as always, she made the word sound like a curse. The paladins both tensed at her tone. 'Do you have a moment to sit and talk?'

The paladins exchanged a look. Persephone nodded.

'A moment, sure,' said Tabris. The pair both took their weapons and set them aside, presumably in a show of faith. Both had more weapons on them than Ree had first realised, drawing knives from their boots, from their belts, and from their gauntlets.

'Feel free to sit,' Tabris said, gesturing to Andomerys. 'We would but, uh...'

'We might not be able to get back up again,' their companion explained with a fleeting smile.

They looked able enough to Ree, but then she realised they meant the armour. She supposed carrying around what looked like a coffin-load of metal would severely limit your flexibility.

She made a tiny ratty snort. Foolish of them to wear it. You didn't need armour to get around undead, you just needed a pouch full of burial herbs and a no-nonsense manner.

Though they looked more comfortable in it than their words suggested.

Andomerys sat, folding herself down with the kind of deliberate precision Ree had come to expect from her in all things. If she was worried these two witchkillers might attempt to lop her head off, she was masterful at hiding it.

Ree decided to worry enough for both of them. She crept a little closer, all her rat senses on high alert.

'This place is no danger to anyone who doesn't enter it,' Andomerys said. 'I am intimately familiar with it. A bunch of old tombs—enough that the dead wake themselves, as often as not. They can't leave, because there's not enough tree cover for them to face the sunlight. And there are no settlements for days in any direction even if the odd mi—uh, undead did manage to find its way out safely.' She caught herself on the word 'minion'. Ree wondered if it was an uncommon term for undead among upworlders.

'I harvest various mushrooms and lichens here that are good for healing potions,' she continued, and that was true even if the ones she harvested she grew herself. 'But in general, there's not much here. The odd necromancer, a pack of adventurers every now and then come to plunder the place. I've not encountered anything that would warrant a paladin, let alone *two*.'

'You know it that well?' Persephone tapped a foot on the ground.

'As I said, I come here often.' Andomerys' voice was hard, and Ree winced. Aggression was unlikely to put them off their guard, but then Andomerys had never been a soft person.

Persephone frowned. She was quite beautiful, Ree realised as she crept closer still. Both paladins were. Perhaps that was a requirement of paladins. Perhaps upworlder gods were vain as well as cruel.

'It seems a long way to travel,' Persephone said softly. She seemed to weigh Andomerys with her eyes.

'Not at all,' Andomerys replied.

'Don't be rude, Sef,' Tabris said, and shrugged comfortably. 'Andomerys, we're here on divine business. Truthfully, we didn't even know this crypt existed until the gods gave us a little knock-on-the-head and directions. There's meant to be a great evil growing here. You wouldn't know anything about that?'

'I wouldn't, no,' Andomerys said. 'Like I said, there's nothing worse than the odd necromancer here.'

'Necromancers can be plenty terrible. Well, I don't suppose you know where we are, then? In this particular part of the crypt, I mean. This place is larger than—'

Persephone's head turned toward Ree. 'No,' she said and reached out a hand. Silver light as dazzling as Andomerys' suffused her hand, and wrapped around Ree as well. Ree squeaked as she was lifted into the air, struggling against the force that held her.

It burned.

'Father's piss, Sef, how the hell did you pick up a rat?' Tabris glanced over with interest.

Andomerys went very still. 'Put her down.' Her voice brooked no argument.

Persephone frowned. 'It's not a rat,' she said. 'I think...it's some kind of necromancy.' Her hand flexed; Ree squealed as her skin started to pull and tug in opposite directions, the burning sensation increasing.

Tabris got to their feet, grabbing a sickle. 'Necromancy?'

Morrin's *teeth,* it hurt. It was taking all her concentration to hold herself together. It felt like at any moment her skin would rip into shreds.

She released her hold on the spell. In a flurry of blue-edged shadow, she poured out of the skin to land hard on the floor, the silver light no longer able to keep its grip on her. At once, her hand went to the pouch that held her ratskin. It was still there, folded and whole. She breathed a sigh of relief.

Tabris took two steps toward her jabbing forward with the sickle. Ree scrambled back out of the way.

'What in all nature was *that?*'

71

Andomerys stood up and dusted off her robes. 'That,' she said, 'Is my friend Ree.'

Ree continued to back up, hauling herself to her feet as quickly as she could. She gave a tiny nod at her name.

Persephone's eyebrows drew together.

'Now,' said Andomerys. 'Put your damn weapons away, or we are going to have a problem.'

But as neither paladin made any move, Ree thought they already had one.

CHAPTER ELEVEN

Usther

In the end, Usther refused to go further until Smythe went back for spare clothes to bundle Misery in, including an over-sized pair of boots. The minion went utterly limp when Usther tried to dress her, sagging to the floor and moaning piteously.

'Oh don't be ridiculous, Misery!' Usther scolded, attempting to shove the minion's arm through a long sleeve but struggling with her loose wrist. 'You don't fuss when I change your rags!'

But it seemed rags and clothes were completely different, as far as Misery was concerned.

'Starting to make sense that you never see minions in proper clothes,' Smythe said conversationally, helping Usther pull on the trousers of a minion that was more accurately imitating a corpse than she ever had before. 'I suppose they rip off as much as they can as soon as they're raised, assuming they're wearing clothes when it happens.'

'She's not some feral undead woken by a random spark of death energy!' Usther growled. 'She's a civilised house-minion. You're civilised, you dratted ungrateful meatbag!'

Misery rolled over onto her stomach, twisting up the trousers as she went.

Several necromancy-enforced orders later, they set off with Misery shuffling miserably in her boots and Dichotomy purring happily in a sling against Usther's chest.

They'd been walking for a few hours when Smythe said, 'I didn't know you were the religious type.'

'Mm?' Usther shifted Dichotomy. The cat's contented drool was starting to soak through her robes.

'I didn't know you were the religious type. Working for the high priestess.'

'Oh, that.' Usther shrugged. 'I found Morrin not long after finding the town. Sometimes it feels like fate that I did. Like she brought me here.' Her eyes scanned the fungi spiralling ahead of them. Those nearest lit up as they passed, their clear acknowledgement of their presence worrying her. 'It's not as if Eldunar or the Rootfather would welcome a necromancer.'

Indeed, the village priestess of Eldunar had done quite the opposite. She still remembered the window shattering as a stone smashed against it. The angry cries of the villagers. The baker who'd always given her a jam bun on her birthday, now holding a torch. The hedgewitch who'd taught her to sew, mixed among the crowd, her expression cold. The children she'd played with, clinging to their parents. Some frightened. Some...excited.

And her, twelve years old, with her parents' hands on her shoulders dragging her to the back of the house. A rabbit skeleton rattling at her feet, accidentally raised in play when she'd been left alone with her grandfather's hunting trophies.

A natural talent, the denizens would call it, when she was discovered two years later in the crypt and the wild minions had shambled up and moved to shield her. To raise the dead with only will and no conscious spell was a gift from Morrin, even if she could rarely do it intentionally. And, she would learn, her story was not so uncommon among practitioners of the Craft. A whole town of lonely children grown into bitter adults.

Smythe was quiet for a moment, taking her words in. It still disconcerted her, this thoughtfulness. She wondered whether age and experience had led to it or whether he'd always had these depths but had hidden them at the time.

'...No,' he said at length. 'I suppose not. But their loss is Morrin's gain.'

Usther's throat tightened and she looked away, furious with herself for being touched. What did it matter what Smythe thought of her? Was she really so starved for praise that she was overwhelmed by it even from a man she hated?

'Why are you still here?' she demanded, not meeting his eyes.

'You wanted my help with the crimson fungi—'

'Not *here*. Here in the crypt. Nobody wanted you when you first arrived, and they damn well didn't want you after your festering ritual in the town hall.' Just talking about it made her tense and angry all over again. Good. She wanted to be angry.

But when she turned her glare on Smythe, it was to find him looking...small. Lost. 'I didn't have anywhere else to go,' he said.

'Phaw. You never shut up about your ghastly university. "Youngest graverobber ever to graduate" or whatever nonsense.' She waited for him to correct her, waited for that flash of the young man he'd been so that she could take out her anger on it, but he only shook his head.

'It's possible they would take me back,' Smythe said. 'Truthfully, I haven't tried. The University...didn't care for me. I ruffled a lot of feathers. I was young and arrogant and made no attempt to make friends, so it's no wonder. If I went back, I'd have to stop using the Craft. It's completely prohibited by Iyadi law. And my family...well. I love them, but I don't know how they'd react to the news I learned how to raise the dead.'

'But you *could* go back, then,' Usther pressed. 'You'd just have to stop using necromancy, and—and—'

'Would you?' Smythe turned a questioning gaze on her. 'Would you give up the Craft? Pretend you didn't know anything of spectres and minions?'

She frowned. 'I didn't have a choice.' A twelve year-old on the run used whatever protection she could muster.

'Well, I did have a choice. I could have gone back. It was always in the back of my mind that I should. But at first, I thought I would stay just long enough to explain myself. That you or Ree would come find me and I would...I don't know, convince you of my good intentions. As pitiful as they were. Deluded, even.'

Usther rolled her eyes. 'Yes, please do wallow in self-pity. It's all the entertainment I'm going to get in this awful tunnel.'

Smythe ducked his head. 'I—no, you're right. I'm sorry.' He fell silent.

They came to a patch of fungi that was particularly thick. It looked like they'd have to jump across, and Usther had no belief that Misery would manage. And the idea of crushing the things and releasing their spores was more than a little daunting.

'Perhaps a few spectres could lift her across?' Smythe suggested. 'You're rather good at spectres, aren't you?'

They were her specialty, in fact. Near formless minions summoned with gravemould, they made excellent spies due to their ability to pass through walls. They were poor defenders but they could move with the force of a powerful wind. It could well be enough to lift a single, skinny minion across a short gap. 'I'll need four to be sure of lifting her properly,' she said. Four was a stretch to summon at once. Spectres, like skeletons, required more magic to run than fleshier minions due to the increased demands of a form without muscles to move it.

'We'll summon two each then,' Smythe said. 'If you'll permit me to borrow some gravemould? I'm afraid I rarely raise anything heftier than a spirit.' He smiled apologetically.

Wordlessly, she held out her pouch of gravemould. In a whoosh of air and ghostly rags, four gasping spectres carried a struggling Misery high across the crimson fungi and deposited her safely on the other side, before vanishing in a puff of dust.

Usther sighed and scooped up what she could of the remaining gravemould. Most of it was lost when the spectres dispersed, but she'd hate to waste any of it.

Misery groaned and collapsed onto the floor.

'Oh don't be melodramatic,' Usther said. 'You were perfectly safe.'

Smythe knelt beside Misery and pat her shoulder. 'I know just how you feel, old chap. I don't fancy flying, either.' He paused. 'You don't think one could *actually* fly via spectre...?'

Usther straightened her braids, which had knotted atop her head. 'Not with spectres. Not safely, or for any real distance. With a greywraith, perhaps, but I don't need to tell you the ethical implications of *that*...'

His expression turned grim. 'No, indeed.'

As they walked on, the odd, naturally-bored cave passages gave way to smooth white marble hallways. Usther put a hand against it. Fuschia-coloured eyes and a jagged white smile flashed in her mind. She yanked her hand back. 'It's warm,' she said, while she tried to steady her breathing. She stared at her fingertips, not quite believing what she'd just felt. 'Why is it warm?'

Smythe frowned and looked ahead at the rest of the hallway. At the way it seamlessly merged into the cave wall, with no cracks or edges in sight. 'I rather think we might be in over our heads here,' he said.

CHAPTER TWELVE

Ree

'I mean you no harm!' Ree said. She raised her hands in a placating gesture, still backing away. 'I'm just here for Andomerys.'

The paladin in front of her, Tabris, stopped with their sickle still raised threateningly. 'You just...materialised. Popped out of thin air when Sef killed that undead rat.'

The other paladin hadn't moved, but she watched Ree with cold eyes. 'You look like a necromancer.'

In spite of her terror, she couldn't keep the bitterness out of her voice. 'Everyone sees a black robe and *immediately* leaps to necromancer.'

Tabris scoffed. 'You're sneaking around in a gods-damned *crypt!*'

'So are you.'

Andomerys cleared her throat. 'You're pointing a weapon at my friend, who has done neither you nor anyone else any harm. Is this really how paladins behave these days?'

Tabris hesitated. 'No. Of course not.' They lowered their sickle, then took a few steps back, standing beside their armoured friend with their arms crossed.

Ree eyed them warily and kept her hands raised.

'Please explain the rat, if you don't mind,' Persephone said calmly, as if her companion hadn't just leapt forward to gut her only moments ago.

Andomerys glared at her. 'You don't owe these people anything, Ree. They have no right to treat you like a criminal on trial.'

Ree nodded, her heart pounding as she looked between the paladins. The *witchkillers*. And she might not be a necromancer, but she was *undoubtedly* a witch.

But if she could put these people at their ease, maybe they knew something about Emberlon. Or the red mushrooms. Or if nothing else, perhaps she could convince them to *leave.*

Her eyes went to the awful, naked hooks still hanging from Tabris' belt. To the jagged spear still visible above Persephone's shoulder.

One hand went to her belly without thinking. Both paladins tensed, which caused her to flinch.

After a moment, Persephone's shoulders dropped. 'We're scaring her. Back up.' She took her spear and placed it on the ground, then took two long steps back. She motioned for her companion to do the same.

'But I'm not gonna—fine! Fine.' Tabris removed the sickles, flipped them in-hand, then placed them neatly on the ground.

Andomerys came to stand in front of Ree, blocking them from view. She seemed utterly unconcerned that she'd turned her back on two trained killers. 'Ree.' She put her hands on Ree's shoulders, squeezing firmly. Ree startled at the touch, focusing on her friend's face. Nobody ever touched her.

'We can go,' Andomerys said. 'We have nothing more to say to each other.'

Being touched was normally unpleasant and Ree avoided it. But right now, Andomerys' grip on her shoulder was grounding her. It felt like maybe the only thing tying her to her body...

She licked her lips, tongue rasping against the dry skin. She was here and now. And it was important that she was.

'I'm okay,' she said. She twitched her shoulder and Andomerys let her go, swinging aside to flank her. A powerful ally in confidence alone.

The paladins waited. Tabris fidgeted, thumbs in the rings of their belt, but Persephone only watched her. Steady and unreadable.

'I'm not a necromancer,' she said. 'But it would be wrong to attack me, even if I was.'

Tabris frowned, but at a look from Persephone, said nothing.

Emboldened, Ree continued, 'I appeared because I *was* the rat.'

Silver eyebrows raised.

Tabris tapped their boot on the ground. 'You did *what?*'

'I'm a therianthrope,' she said. They both stared at her, non-plussed. 'It's probably easier if I show you. It's magic. Just...don't stab me or anything.'

Reluctantly, both nodded, and Ree put her hand slowly to the pouch at her belt and started to sing. Tabris crossed their arms while Persephone frowned, listening intently. Light and shadow wrapped around Ree, a cold liquid embrace. And then she blinked and she was treading air as a crow. She cawed at the paladins, then flew to land on Andomerys' outstretched arm.

'As you can see,' Andomerys said. 'Not a necromancer.'

Ree, emboldened by the crowskin, turned and flipped her tail, cawing again.

'Beast magic.' Tabris reached out a shaking hand toward Ree, as if to stroke her, before letting it fall to their side. They knelt in front of her. 'Truly, you must be blessed by the Rootfather. I was told all beast magic was lost when the Queen Illis of Iyad purged the wilds.'

Ree cocked her head to one side. This was an unexpected development.

Persephone said, 'It *felt* like necromancy. Why would healing break the spell if it wasn't?' But she looked shaken too, one hand pressed to her chestplate.

Before Ree could even begin to unpick the significance of any of that, a howl echoed around the hall where they stood. Larry loped awkwardly in, reaching for Andomerys.

Persephone rolled back and grabbed her spear; Tabris kicked up their sickles and caught them. And Ree burst back into her human shape in a swirl of robes and shadows, throwing up her hands and blocking Larry from their sight. 'Stop! Please! He's a friend! He's a *friend*.'

Heart-pounding, she and the paladins faced off. Andomerys watched with arms crossed, the air around her rippling with waves of heat.

Larry peered around Ree, gargling curiously. She pushed him back.

The paladins didn't lower their weapons this time.

CHAPTER THIRTEEN

Usther

They made camp in a chamber of that alien marble, a room so bright that Usther felt she was sitting in a room of light. There were no cracks in the ceiling to allow for a campfire, but it was hardly needed; the floor pulsed with warmth. It beat in time with her heart and it terrified her.

She could feel Smythe's eyes on her as she laid out her bedroll, shifting it here and there. They'd chosen a room where the crimson fungi was pushed to the corners, to avoid touching it in their sleep, but nowhere felt far enough. It seemed to her it would creep across the distance in the night and she would wake with mushrooms sprouting from her cheeks and growing over her body, as if she were a mound of soil.

'We could go back,' Smythe offered quietly. He'd placed his own bedroll without fuss, though he had no more defence against the fungi than she did.

She almost snapped at him, but swallowed her words on seeing him. His sepia skin had a sweaty sheen and his eyes, shadowed by necromancy, sagged with tiredness. The day's travel had taken its toll on him and he looked on the verge of passing out. He wasn't asking for himself.

She started to tell him that she couldn't go back, then stopped. She tried to say that she finally, finally had purpose, but stopped again. Finally, she asked, 'Why did you do it?'

It wasn't what she had meant to say, and her face heated. She looked away.

Smythe didn't ask what she meant. He was quiet a long time. When she mastered her embarrassment enough to look at him, she found him staring at his hands, twisting his fingers.

'I thought I was going to die,' he said at length. His voice was hoarse, quiet. 'I thought *she* was going to die. I knew I had to try it, or we would—die, that is. I knew she would try to stop me. Trusted that she would, really.'

Usther leaned forward. 'You could have excluded me.' She touched her forehead, where Smythe had painted an exclusion sigil on himself and Ree. 'I thought we were friends.'

The apple of his throat bobbed as he swallowed. 'I had to mean it, the ritual. The intention was everything...you must have heard that curse expert. If I had painted an exclusion on everyone in town, it would be meaningless. If I had stepped aside when she asked me to, it would have achieved nothing.'

'You enjoyed it,' Usther accused.

'I don't...enjoy is too strong a word. But a part of me wanted it to happen. Quite a large part of me, actually.' He met her gaze then, his eyes bleak behind his glasses. 'I'm not a very good person. I'd always thought I was, before. But when I was doing the ritual, and I had all that power, and there was so much knowledge to be gained if it succeeded...' he shook his head. 'And I can't even regret it.'

'Can't?' Usther asked sharply.

'Because we're alive,' he said. 'All of us are still alive.'

'You're a coward,' Usther said.

'Yes,' Smythe replied sadly. And he laid down with his back to her and went to sleep.

It took Usther longer. Dichotomy curled up inside her bedroll, and Misery huddled at her feet, keeping watch on the door. But now there was more than fungi on her mind.

She hated him, she realised. Hated him so much it brought tears to her eyes and set fire to her throat. And she had no idea what to do about it.

IN HER DREAMS, SMYTHE leaned over her while she slept. Fungi climbed his clothes, tendrils wrapping around his throat and seeking through his curls. He reached for her, tendrils extending from his hand.

A woman with a hole through her head and white eyes grabbed his wrist. *'Not yet,'* she said. Her face split into a toothless grin.

Usther stirred and sat up. The man in the white dress crouched beside her, close enough to share breath. He smiled, baring brilliant white fangs.

Usther yelled and lurched away from him, throwing up her hands.

'Ahh!' Smythe woke with a shout, looking around in panic. His hair was a mess, his glasses gone. 'I say, are you all right?'

Usther swallowed hard, her heartbeat frantic. The man was gone. 'A nightmare,' she said, though it had felt viscerally real. She started to get up.

'Wait!'

Usther stopped, pushing back her annoyance. Smythe looked frantic, his glasses jammed awkwardly onto his face. He pointed at the floor near Usther, where a trail of crimson as vibrant as fresh blood led from the corner fungi right up to her bedroll.

'Festering *fucking* rats!' she yelled, yanking her bedroll back.

'Steady on,' said Smythe, earning him a glare. 'Right. Sorry. Force of habit, you know. My tutor would scold me terribly for crude language.'

'Of course you had a tutor,' Usther muttered. Smythe came over and the two of them studied the thin trail of fungi.

'It's like it went directly for you,' Smythe said. 'Fascinating.' But his eyes behind his glasses were worried as he looked at her. 'Can these things be intelligent?'

A translucent red cap that was full of red liquid twitched.

'Ahh!' They both yelped and scrambled back.

'Smythe.' Usther paused and tried to bring moisture into her dry mouth. 'The nightmare...I woke up. And when I woke up, I saw that...that man we saw. The man in white. Crouching right in front of me.' She swallowed. 'Right there.'

And she pointed to where the fungi stopped.

He frowned. 'That...that's a rather worrying coincidence.'

'Yes.'

He ran a hand through his tangled curls. 'But you don't think it's a coincidence?'

'Of *course* not!' she snapped. 'I wouldn't be telling you if I did!'

'Not coincidence, but fate,' said a gentle voice.

Usther seized Misery and the bedroll Dichotomy was still curled up in and yanked them toward her as a figure stepped out from the corner of the room, the fungi lighting up in all shades of red at the movement.

It was the man in the white dress. His feet were bare, the ragged skirt of his dress splitting at his movement to bare dark legs that were utterly smooth. He was beautiful; sharp cheekbones and fuschia eyes, blood red hair in a short, tight curl with unfamiliar symbols shaved into the sides.

'Oh,' said Smythe. His voice sounded oddly dry, as if perhaps the man's appearance had stolen the moisture from Smythe's mouth as surely as it had Usther's. 'I'm...terribly sorry. I didn't realise we had company. I'm Chandrian Smythe, historian, and my companion is Usther—uhh—'

'Usther of the Ashes.' Usther lifted her chin and clenched her hands to hide their tremble.

The man smiled, his teeth perfectly white and even. It made him look warm, softening the harshness of his carved features.

Beside her, Smythe audibly swallowed hard. But the man's beauty was lost on Usther, whose pace quickened not from attraction but fear.

'Why were you spying on us?' she asked, forcing imperiousness into her tone. It couldn't quite mask the tremor.

'I might ask you the same thing,' said the man. He spoke slowly, with laziness or deliberation, she couldn't tell. 'You are in *my* home, after all. But let's not concern ourselves with accusations and harsh words. After all, we have only just met, Usther and Chandrian.' He bowed, the movement perfectly smooth, one hand over his heart. 'I am Mykol. You seek to know more of the Many-That-Hungers. I can show you all that you seek.'

The Many-That-Hungers? Before she could even piece that together, Mykol gestured to the crimson fungi all around them.

Not a reassuring name.

'That's a very...generous...offer,' Smythe said haltingly.

'How do we know we can trust you?' Usther asked.

Mykol put a hand on his hip and shrugged. 'What is trust? I have knowledge. So do you. We have need of each other.'

Usther stared. The way he spoke' had unnerved her. It had sounded almost like a genuine question.

She glanced at Smythe. He looked...if not eager, at least deeply curious. The young man she had known would have leapt at this offer. But Smythe looked to her instead. 'What do you think?' he asked. 'This is your expedition, after all.'

She thought of Arthura, tasking her with something too important to be left undone. She thought of how this was her chance to prove herself to the town, to Morrin, to everyone. She thought of the heavy debt she owed to the Goddess of Undying, who had given her a home and a purpose.

Mykol waited expectantly, his smile perfectly bland and utterly terrifying.

'We would be interested in learning more,' Usther said. She wished it didn't feel like she was signing their souls away.

'I am pleased to hear that,' he said, syrup-slow. 'I believe you will come to love the Many-That-Hungers. It already loves you.'

With that, he turned and strode from the room, and there was nothing Usther and Smythe could do but gather their things, hold their minions close, and follow.

CHAPTER FOURTEEN

Ree

Ree's eyes fixed on the tip of the spear pointed at her. Her every instinct screamed at her to run, to hide. Reminded her of the feel of a knife sliding into her gut. But her oldest friend was behind her, patting her shoulder and gargling his confusion.

'So you *are* a necromancer!' said Persephone. She looked larger than ever now, with spear raised and poised to strike, her gently falling silver plait the only soft thing about her.

'No,' Ree said, hating herself for the denial. 'I'm not—this isn't—'

Tabris sheathed one sickle and nudged their companion. 'She's a beastmage, Sef! And she's not hurting anyone. What are you going to do, stab her?'

The spear-point wavered. 'Of course not. But the undead...'

'He won't hurt anyone!' Ree's voice was hoarse. 'He's harmless, truly.' A bigger lie than she wished; there was no minion more powerful nor more mysterious than Wandering Larry. But none kinder, either

'Winds guide us,' Persephone said. A prayer said like a curse. But she lowered her spear and looked to Tabris. 'Why are the gods testing us?'

Tabris shrugged. 'Why do the gods do anything?' As Persephone slung her spear back over her shoulder, Tabris said, 'We won't attack if it won't attack.'

Ree nodded and seized Larry's wrist. It was all too easy to imagine him curiously nibbling at the new, exciting humans. 'If he bites me or Andomerys, please don't defend us. He's harmless, truly.'

Persephone's eyebrows raised, but she nodded.

'Now that we're all certain we aren't going to kill each other,' Andomerys said. 'Have you seen a man with greying hair and a miserable disposition?'

'And a bag full of books,' Ree added.

Andomerys nodded. 'He's been missing for some time. We're concerned about him.'

'His name is Emberlon,' said Ree. 'Emberlon the—just Emberlon.' Larry tried to pull free of her but she held fast. He sighed, sounding for all the world like Misery.

Persephone and Tabris looked at each other.

'We haven't seen him,' said Persephone. 'But we'll help him, if we can.'

Tabris' mouth shifted to one side. 'Though if he's lost this deep in the crypt, he's more than likely corpse food.'

'He's a necromancer,' said Andomerys. 'So I doubt it.'

'Not a very good one, but still,' Ree added under her breath. Emberlon had always been only vaguely interested in the actual practice of the Craft. He was much more interested in necromancers themselves—and in the knowledge and history of the crypt.

'Another necromancer...' Persephone said. 'We've already encountered one, and then there's...whatever you two are. How many people are there here in this crypt, I wonder?'

Neither Ree nor Andomerys replied.

Tabris rubbed the back of their head. 'Look, if we're all done here, could you give us some directions? We honestly have no idea where we are.'

Ree tilted her head to one side. 'Where are you trying to go?'

'It's less about where we're trying to go and more about having no idea where we are. It would be nice to know where the exit is.'

If they were fellow denizens, Ree wouldn't hesitate to get out her maps and help them retrace their steps. But considering how close they had come to skewering her and Larry, she felt no desire to hand over the secrets of her crypt.

Truthfully, Ree didn't actually *know* where they were right now. The tunnel of crimson fungi had spat them out in these enormous burial chambers, but she didn't recognise them out of context. There were many similar chambers across the crypt.

But then...it would be prudent for her to work out where they were, at least. And maybe keeping a close eye on the paladins was a good idea. There were too many coincidences here, too many terrible things colliding all at once.

Larry tried to nibble at her shoulder. She swatted at him with her free hand and led him over to Andomerys. 'Watch him, would you? I'm going to try to get my bearings.'

'Ree, I don't really—'

She transferred a struggling Larry to the healer, over her protests. Andomerys would be plenty able to handle him, even if she rarely had anything to do with minions.

Ree turned her attention to the room around them, her eyes sweeping the many shelves where the dead lay neatly stacked, some shrouded, some with arms crossed peacefully on their chests. 'A mass burial chamber,' Ree said. 'Not nobles...possibly honoured servants.' She approached one of the walls. 'No possessions, preserved with...oils maybe, but not with rags. Probably not late Third Era, but possibly early Third...'

She studied a body free of a shroud. 'They're all facing the same way...probably south?' She fished her compass out of her pack and checked it. 'North. Okay, so they aren't Antherian.'

'How do you know all this?' Tabris demanded.

Ree ignored them, continuing to study the room. She put her back to the corpses and went to study one of the columns. 'These are quite plain, unmarked, but they flare in the middle. Could be Iyadi, I suppose.' Her mind spun as she tried to picture her maps.

An early Third Iyadi burial chamber of this size, connected to another roughly the same? That rang a bell. But was it near the subterranean waterfall? Or was it nearer the surface and further east?

She swore under her breath. She knew her way around better than anyone but Emberlon, but it was still an enormous crypt and the maps served much better than her memory, especially so far from town.

A presence at her side. She startled as Persephone rested a hand on the column she'd been studying, taking it in herself. 'You're a historian?' she asked quietly.

Ree shrugged. 'Of a sort,' she replied, because that was safer than explaining that anyone who grew up in the crypt would become one by necessity. Her mother had once put it in very neat terms.

'When I was a girl, I grew up in the woods of the Serpent's Spine,' she'd said. *'There it was wild and the footing treacherous, but by the time I came of age, I could follow paths none but the animals could see, and could feel my way around in the dark with nothing more than my hands and my memory.'*

It was the same for Ree, albeit her 'woods' were rather light on trees and heavy on corpses.

It struck her then that she *did* know where they were, but before she could say anything Persephone drew her spear, looking at something past Ree's shoulder. Before she could lunge, Ree grabbed her arm. 'Wait!'

A lesser undead stirred on the shelf beside them, its stretch languid, its moan half a yawn, as if waking from deep sleep. Persephone tensed but didn't struggle. Gently, Ree released her and reached into the herb pouch on her belt. 'Morrin bless you and bear you to peaceful rest,' she said. She dodged the undead's lazily grasping hands and threw a pinch of burial herbs in its face. Its arm dropped. After a moment, it crossed its arms again and went still.

The whole room went quiet, apart from the gentle sound of Larry trying to wrench free of Andomerys.

'How did you do that?' Persephone asked. 'I didn't sense any necromancy.'

'Because it wasn't necromancy,' she said. 'It was just kindness. Lesser undead wake up confused. It doesn't take much to remind them they are dead, and they go back to sleep.'

'Who raised it?' Tabris had drawn their sickles, and scanned the upper floor of the chamber.

'Nobody,' said Ree. She was getting tired of these two, of their violence and paranoia. Of the constant need to explain.

'Undead occur naturally in places where many have died or been buried,' Andomerys said. She studied Tabris with an unusually blank expression. 'Surely you know that?'

The paladins said nothing. Persephone looked thoughtful, Tabris angry. Tabris shoved their sickles back through their belt.

Ree got parchment, pen and ink from her satchel and got to work sketching their vague location. 'I think we're here,' she said, sketching the chambers. 'Which means the nearest exit is...a few floors above us now, and a day's travel east.' She got another sheaf of parchment so that she could sketch out the path across the different floors. 'It's probably not very accurate, but it'll do.'

'Not very accurate?' said Persephone. She accepted Ree's hastily drawn map, studying it with eyebrows raised. 'This is better than some of the maps the Priest Masters issue us with.'

Tabris ran a hand through their hair and came to look over Persephone's shoulder. They glanced at Ree, then back down. Their mouth shifted to one side. 'You didn't draw anything but the way out.'

'No.' Ree left it at that.

Tabris made an aggravated sound and stomped away, armour jangling, but Persephone only folded the map and tucked it into her breastplate. 'We're not here to hurt anyone,' she said. 'We were sent to stop a great evil. You don't strike me as a great evil.' Her eyes flicked to Larry as he let out a plaintive groan and sagged in defeat.

Ree took him back from Andomerys, keeping him behind her. 'I think we might disagree on what evil means, and what punishment it deserves,' she replied coolly.

The paladin paused. 'Perhaps.' She touched her breastplate, where the map rested. 'If we encounter your friend, the necromancer with greying hair, we'll tell him you're looking, and where we met.'

'Thank you,' said Andomerys, sounding genuine for the first time since the conversation began.

'And if we find a great evil, we'll be sure to point it in your direction,' Ree said.

Persephone nodded, but Tabris grinned widely. 'I can live with that,' they said. 'I hope we meet again, beastmage. I'd like to know more about you.'

They collected their packs and stomped away, further into the crypt.

Ree stared at their retreating backs until they were gone, taking their torchlight with them. 'Can't say I feel the same,' she muttered.

CHAPTER FIFTEEN

Usther

Where in the realms of the living and dead this creep was leading them, Usther couldn't say. This looked nothing like the rest of the crypt. The walls were too white, too new, too clean, and too warm. The fungi here—or perhaps the Many-That-Hungers—were numerous and active, lighting up as Mykol passed, reaching their feelers out to touch his feet, his legs, the trail of his ragged skirt.

She didn't like how comfortable he looked here, either. How easily he fit in, with his red hair and stark white dress, somehow spared the dust and grime that coated the rest of the crypt.

He didn't talk, either. Not to them, at least. Occasionally, when a clump of fungi would stretch its tendrils eagerly toward Misery, he would kneel beside it and whisper something she couldn't hear, and it would reluctantly retract them. The sight never grew less chilling. For the humans, Mykol seemed to have exhausted his desire to speak.

Smythe didn't talk much either, apart from to offer to carry Dichotomy for a while, which Usther gratefully accepted. Or, to occasionally direct Misery when she was at risk of stumbling into a fungi patch. He bracketed the minion with Usther, body blocking her from the fungi as best as he could. She wondered if he was as scared as she was, or if his silence was merely due to him building some terrible scheme he would never regret.

At length, the passage began to take on some character. Doors lined the walls, white doors as smooth and stark as the walls they opened. Some of them were open; necromancers watched them pass solemnly, bowing at the waist.

She recognised many of them: Erfur of the Bones, who flinched at the sight of them; Hestia the Harrowed, who hugged herself with tears streaming down her cheeks; Melancholia, flanked by fungi-wreathed minions, shoulders hunched; other practitioners her own age. Each wearing a slash of red at their wrists in the form of lurid red ribbons.

There were others. Neighbours. Rivals. Ursula the Underqueen hobbled down the corridor and bowed so low you could hear her bones creak. The ancient woman had lost the arrogance and spite that Usther had once admired. Now she only looked fragile. Vellum nodded their approval, as if they'd expected them. Etherea Eversworn curtsied, then waved one ribbon-wrapped hand.

'Cheerful,' Usther murmured under her breath. She had no idea what to make of any of this. Of the appearance of so many denizens so far from town. Of their wildly varying dispositions.

'Our beloved servants,' Mykol said. 'Each one was once an honoured guest. Like you.'

Usther tried to ignore the chill that trickled down her spine.

There were other minions too. All covered in crimson fungi like a bulbous rash. Their eyes were white and blank, and they moved wrong. Too smoothly, Usther realised. Too close to the gait of a living human. Misery whimpered and bumped into Usther's shoulder each time they encountered them, and Usther patted her and tried not to imagine what the fungi might do to her. She almost asked what had happened to them, and why, but held her tongue at the last moment.

Smythe gently elbowed her and nodded toward a set of double doors. Outside two necromancers stood, looking bored. Usther thought she recognised one of them as someone who lived on her street, but she couldn't remember their names. Both wore the red ribbons.

As their group passed, they straightened up. Smythe caught her eye. 'Guards,' he mouthed.

She was inclined to agree. But what in the crypt required guarding? All the treasure found so far had been moved to the Town Hall, and was for use by all. And nobody would ask another practitioner to guard the secrets of their own Craft.

'We're here,' said Mykol, and gestured for them to precede him.

They stepped forward into a vast hall. The ceiling was almost too high to see but for the constellation-like scattering of glowing mushrooms that glared down like angry stars. Enormous pillars of white marble held up the ceiling, reaching so far that they almost seemed to bend into the distance, flexing rhythmically at the edge of her vision, as if alive.

The hall itself was bustling with activity. Denizens directed minions to place bookcases or sent spectres to hang tapestries on the walls. Six fungi-ridden minions carried a long feast table on their shoulders with a chilling synchronicity, while several others rolled out a long, intricately woven rug. At one end, a necromancer painted on a vast canvas with rapt attention while a woman with terracotta-coloured skin and a curtain of red hair posed with perfect stillness.

It was busier here than on market day in Tombtown, but with so many of the same faces. Each of them paused to bow to Mykol as they passed. People came in and out from the various entry passages, each doorway framed by fungus.

'I don't understand,' Usther said. 'What is the purpose of this?'

Mykol smiled. 'All humans require a home, do they not? We are making one big enough that all can share in it.' He spread his arms and called out, 'Beloved servants! Please welcome Usther of the Ashes and Chandrian Smythe, our honoured guests! Assist them in any way they require. Celia, would you join me?'

'Later, brother,' replied the woman posing for the portrait. Usther realised with a shock that she did bear a shocking resemblance to Mykol, though they appeared to have completely different heritages. There was something similarly sharp about her features, and her long, straight hair was the exact same shade of red as Mykol's short, tight curl. If Usther looked into her eyes, would they also be that unnatural shade of fuschia pink? Usther shuddered at the thought. Celia, too, wore a perfectly white dress and stood barefoot on the white marble. The strangest uniform Usther had ever seen.

It was hard not to notice the perfect curve of her thigh as the skirt split across her arched leg, or the elegantly long fingers that cupped her chin. As she stared, Celia turned to look at her. Her smile widened, and she bit her lip.

Usther startled and looked away, heat rushing through her. No, definitely not someone she ought to be staring at.

Smythe was staring elsewhere, a frown nestled on his brow. 'Where are you getting all these books from?' he asked.

Mykol gestured at the denizens walking in with armfuls of books stacked up against their chests. 'This land has a bounty of knowledge. Our beloved servants collect it for us.'

Smythe only looked more worried. And it suddenly struck her what it meant that they were collecting all these books. They were stealing them from the crypt. From all of the town, who could browse and borrow whatever they liked.

They were stealing them from Ree.

Dichotomy meowed from the sling on Smythe's chest. 'Pass her here,' Usther said, and accepted the sling and the now squirming cat. 'Hush, darling,' Usther said, holding her close. 'I'll put you down soon, I promise.'

Mykol's smile morphed to an expression of earnest concern. 'Your companion will not be harmed,' he said. 'She is also an honoured guest.'

Usther desperately wished he would stop saying that. 'Thank you, but I'd prefer to keep her close. Listen, I'm eager to learn more about the Many-That-Hungers and the wonderful redecorating you're doing in the crypt, but is there perhaps somewhere private my companions and I could rest for a moment? I need to tend to them.'

'Of course. You have had a long journey which must have been tiring.' Mykol's sympathy felt slick and greasy on Usther's skin. 'There will be plenty of time to get to know each other better.' He gestured across the room at a denizen, who hurried over. It was Ellenil, who had grown up in the town. They were only eighteen, and had been practising for only a few years, as per town law. Usther had babysat them when they were child, making a rat skeleton dance for them. *They're an insufferable brat,* Usther had told their mother, unable to suppress a smile. *I'd be happy to watch them again.*

It seemed to her that ten years hadn't aged them much. The same button nose, face still round with youth, the cheeks barely hollowed by the Craft. They were almost as tall as Usther but they were gangly and awkward, grown too quickly for grace to catch up. Anxiety pecked at her to see them here, in this of all places.

Ellenil bowed to Mykol. 'Yes, my lord?'

She didn't remember them being this polite, either.

'Ellenil. Please show our honoured guests to a free chamber.'

They bowed again, their hood flopping forward over their mass of curly hair and the two horns they'd formed out of it.

When they looked at their charges, their eyes widened in recognition. But then they smoothed their expression to stillness.

'Follow me,' they said smoothly. They turned, their robes swirling behind them. They wore an intricate lace cloak over plain robes. Usther was a little jealous of the style.

They left the chamber through another archway, walking down a corridor identical to the one they'd come from. If Ellenil found it hard to navigate, they didn't show it. Their steps were sure and swift.

They didn't say anything, leading them in silence.

Smythe cleared his throat. 'Pardon me, I don't believe we've met. I'm Chandrian Smythe. Pleased to meet you.' He sped up so he could offer Ellenil his hand.

Ellenil looked startled, and shook it. 'Smythe?' they asked. 'Not the same Smythe who—?'

'Ellenil, what are you *doing* here?' Usther's voice was half-whisper, half-shout.

Ellenil glared at her. 'I might ask you the same thing!'

'I'm twenty-eight years old, Ellenil. If I'm going to do something foolish I can at least be smart about it—'

'Does that make *complete* sense? Because—' Smythe began.

'You should go back to town. Do your parents know you're here?'

'They think I've gone fishing with my cabal,' Ellenil said. Their defiance faded a little. 'I can't go anywhere, Usther.' They raised their right arm, where a red ribbon was tied around their wrist, just below the end of their sleeve. 'I belong here.'

'Ellenil—!'

They stopped. 'This is your room.' They gestured to an open door. The door was carved with a series of symbols Usther didn't recognise. Was it a name? A number?

Usther grabbed their sleeve as they turned away. 'Ellenil, what is going on here?'

Passing fungal minions immediately reached for Usther, but Ellenil waved them off and pulled their sleeve free. They gave Usther a look she couldn't read. 'What is it people say? Civilisations rise and fall.' They straightened their sleeve, the ribbon an almost gory slash of colour. 'You should decide where you want to be when that happens.' They strode away, the fungal minions forming a wall behind them.

Smythe took Usther by the elbow. 'I think we'd better settle down for a moment, don't you?' he said. His voice sounded forcibly light. He dragged her into the room and shut the door.

CHAPTER SIXTEEN

Ree

Another two days of searching and they were no closer to finding Emberlon. Ree sat down on a sarcophagus and put her head in her hands. Natural light filled the chamber; this tomb was close to the surface, and light trickled in through cracks in the ceiling. 'What are we doing?' she said. 'We've completely lost his trail, if we ever had it.'

Andomerys sat on the shallow steps leading up to the sarcophagus, tucking her robes around her legs. 'He has to be out here,' she said. 'If we've lost his trail, we keep looking until we pick it up again.'

Larry wandered the edge of the tomb. He gargled curiously at an inanimate skeleton holding a spear. It had been tied to a post to prop it up, but as Larry leaned close, red lights appeared in its eye sockets. It clacked its teeth in Larry's face; Larry toppled over backwards, yelling. The skeleton cackled once with the silent, teeth-chattering laugh of a bone minion, before going still again.

Ree shook her head. Her hands moved to the back of her head. 'He could be anywhere. He moves just as fast as I do.'

'Stop it,' Andomerys said tiredly.

'And I have *no idea* how to track him when the crypt is...wrong. When there are tunnels where they shouldn't be, and freaky moving mushrooms and—and paladins!'

'Please stop.'

'Morrin's teeth, what are *paladins* doing in *our* crypt?'

'Ree!' Andomerys stood up, fists clenched, and wheeled away from her. 'This is not helping, all right? It's *not helping!*'

Ree stopped. The tomb suddenly felt incredibly quiet. Even Larry stopped flailing on the floor.

Ree was struggling to remember the last time Andomerys had raised her voice.

The healer's back was to her now, the shoulders high and bunched with tension. After a moment, she unclenched her fists. Her shoulders lowered. And when she turned back, her expression was very calm but for a burning light in eyes that pinched with suppressed pain. 'He's all I have,' she said. 'We swore...when he came here, we *swore* we would be there for each other.'

Ree searched for the right words. 'I didn't know it was like that between you two,' she said.

Andomerys snorted, and Ree couldn't parse the emotions that crossed her face. 'It's not. Not the way you think. I am only interested in women that way. Emberlon...he's never been romantically interested in anyone at all. But there are many kinds of love.'

Many kinds of love. And Ree had little experience of any of them. Only once had she thought...but that had been disastrous. These were all thoughts for another time.

But Andomerys was right. Berating herself over losing Emberlon's trail wasn't going to get them any closer to finding him. She loved the old archivist too; he'd been her mentor for many years, and a friend for almost as long. The thought of the quiet, thoughtful man trapped somewhere in the crypt made her chest hurt, but dwelling on her own emotions was self-indulgent, not productive.

She hopped off the sarcophagus and started to pace the low stone dais, the soft soles of her boots slapping gently. 'None of this is coincidence, is it?' she said.

Andomerys raised her eyebrows. 'Ree?'

Ree waved away her question, continuing to pace. 'Emberlon was definitely in library eight, where we found the tunnel and the red fungi. The paladins are here to stop a great evil. Well, if that was anything to do with the town, they're half a century too late. I don't think their gods give a single rat about us. They said they didn't see Emberlon, and little as I trust them, I believe them.'

'They did wear their emotions on their sleeves,' said Andomerys.

'More like on their spear points.' Ree flexed her hands, and turned on her heel, picking up speed. 'What's changed? The Lich isn't here anymore. We haven't had an Incident with any of the denizens since the last time Veritas tried to conquer the town, and not only did that fail, he's been doing that for years. The only change is whatever made those tunnels. Maybe the same thing spreading the crimson fungi.'

'Which means the paladins are on the trail of the fungi...'

'Which means we need to get on the trail of the paladins,' Ree finished. 'If their gods are really guiding them, they'll have a better time of it than we're having.'

Larry wandered over, gargling hopefully. She dodged his attempt to bite her shoulder, instead patting him on the arm and nudging him toward Andomerys. 'We could really use a practitioner right now,' she said. 'Usther can make quite a few spectres at once and send them to scout. They can even pass through walls. But I suppose we'll have to make do with what we have.'

She pulled her crowskin from her pouch, smoothing the feathers beneath her fingertips. It looked almost like a pool of ink in her hands, but felt silken rather than oily.

'Stay here,' Ree said. 'I'll find them, and come back.'

Larry tried to bite Andomerys. She smacked him in the chest, startling him. 'That's a terrible idea,' she said. 'If we separate, I'll have no way to know if you're safe, or coming back at all.'

Ree shook her head. 'You can scry for me. You've been an exception on my amulet since you and Emberlon saved me when I was a teenager.' She touched her chest, where beneath her robes, her father's amulet of protection pulsed with a reassuring chill. It protected her from scrying, as well as giving her additional wards against curses and mind-snares. As her mentor, Emberlon had already been spelled in as an exception. When he'd brought Andomerys with him to save Ree, her father had agreed to make the healer part of that exception.

It was a small group. Her father and mother, Usther, Emberlon, and Andomerys. All people she trusted not just with her life, but with her privacy. Somehow, it felt a much greater show of trust.

Andomerys must have felt the same, because she looked shocked to hear it. Then she nodded with a small, sad smile. 'I'll scry every few hours,' she said. She fished in her pocket and held out a suneye, a necromantic tool for tracking the sun. The marble-like eye rolled in her hand until the iris pointed directly up. It must be noon in the upworld.

Ree took a deep breath, letting magic flow in and out of her lungs like chill winter air. When she sang the spell, her voice cracked but confident, she gave one last look to her friends before shadow-edged light and feathers enveloped her and the world spun and re-shaped into the world of a crow.

She tread air with her wings, feeling the air run along each finger-like feather, adjusting to the shape in only a few heartbeats. She felt light, but also powerful, the joy and wickedness of the crow rushing through her. It was easier every time. After so many years, the crowskin had become as real to her as her own body. Realer now, certainly, when her body was so much shadow stuffing the crow.

'Be careful,' Andomerys called, and Ree cawed a laugh at the thought, taking off out of the tomb and into the wider crypt.

She travelled fast as a crow. There were no heights to climb or depths to painstakingly descend. There was only the open air, as good high as it was low. Lesser undead sometimes snatched at her but she was gone too fast to pay them much mind. She could take secret ways in this form. Where once she'd had to hoist herself up to reach windows or vent passages, now she could swoop up and through them with utter ease. It was tiring, flying, but no more so than walking for a human.

She tried to focus herself on her task, because the crowskin always made her a little reckless, a little too prone to fun.

Ree backtracked on the path she and Andomerys had taken, cutting across a vast chasm and through a high-up door instead, before spiralling down through a wide crack in the ceiling of the mass tomb in which they'd met the paladins. The dust on the floor here was heavily disturbed from the many feet that had crossed it.

Taking the exit the paladins had, she pumped her wings for greater speed, her excellent vision picking up the dust trails in the air and the scuffs on the floor, allowing her to make a choice at each crossroad.

She stopped and roosted several times, pausing to rest her wings and preen her feathers back into order. The breaks, while they helped the soreness in her wings, did nothing to lift the strain of holding onto her spell. But she was a practised therianthrope; she knew her limits, and thought she could push on for longer yet.

When she caught the distant orange dance of torchlight, she knew she had them. The paladins marched along a narrow ridge. Below, a subterranean river rushed, the echoes of its roar loud but distant enough not to be deafening. Water fell in gentle trickles from a high-up ceiling, dampening the entire passage. Ree perched atop a crumbling column to watch them.

'I hate this,' Persephone said. She was too wide and too nervous to walk easily along the ridge, so instead she scooted along with her back to the wall, gritting her teeth at the enormous drop before her.

Tabris looked over their shoulder at her. 'It's not that bad. We don't really mind, except for Nara.' They were not much narrower than their companion, but they walked with confidence anyway, keeping one hand on the wall while the other held up the torch.

Again, that 'we'. Who was Nara? An aspect of their god?

'What isn't that bad about being inches away from a long fall to a painful death?'

Tabris laughed. 'What, are you afraid of heights now?'

Persephone punched their shoulder lightly, then gasped when her own weight shifted.

'Oh, Sef.'

As Persephone glanced around, as if hoping for a railing to hold on to, her gaze alighted on Ree where she perched.

Ree cocked her head to one side. Could the paladin possibly see her at this distance, with nothing but the torchlight to see by?

But Persephone's mouth pressed into a grim line, and she gave Ree a small nod before continuing to inch her way along the ridge.

Ree considered. She'd meant to return to Andomerys with news of their whereabouts first of all. It seemed rash to face these people alone, when they'd squeezed her out of her ratskin and pointed spears at her.

But then again, they hadn't hurt her, or even seemed likely to, once they'd calmed down. And it was a long way back. It would be a lot easier to follow them if the paladins would obligingly wait for them to catch up.

She cawed loudly, the sound cutting through the atmospheric drone of the river. Tabris startled with a shout, but Persephone only watched her. Ree flew over, keeping out of reach and treading air above the chasm.

'Sef, is that the beastmage?'

'It would seem so.'

She flew ahead and, careful of the gap, let her crowskin fall away, spilling in a flurry of cloak and shadows onto the ridge. 'There's actually a parallel passage you can take,' she called. She felt along the wall until she found the right spot and shouldered it hard. The disguised door gave way in a cloud of dust. She gestured inside. 'I thought you might prefer it.'

'Oh, thank the Owl,' Persephone said.

The paladins met her inside. Persephone leaned on Tabris' shoulder, panting. Tabris patted her sympathetically. 'Give us a minute?' they asked.

Ree nodded and leaned against the wall, arms crossed. She was ready to flee if the moment arrived, but neither paladin seemed eager to reach for their weapons.

'That...was the worst place...I've ever been...' Persephone said between gasps. She slung off her pack and pulled out a waterskin, taking a long draught. Ree watched her curiously. Her pack and waterskin looked practical but inexpensive, though even the cap of the waterskin was engraved with the holy symbol of her god: the owl with river wings.

'It absolutely wasn't,' Tabris said, flashing a grin at Ree. 'Remember the stink swamp? With the necro hippos?'

She shook her head. 'This was worse.'

Ree held in her question about 'necro hippos', though everything about the words intrigued her. Weren't hippos the fat horses that lived in Vendala? She remembered her mother saying something about them having swords for teeth. She could think of any number of her neighbours who would kill to get their hands on a corpse that had sword teeth.

'So, what brings you back into our path?' Tabris put their hand on their hip. 'I didn't get the impression you wanted us around.'

'Not so strange,' Persephone said. She seemed to be calming down. 'Nobody likes paladins.'

'Maybe nobody likes *you*,' Tabris said. They gave Ree a smile that oozed charm.

Ree had never had much use for charm. She said, 'I was hoping you'd let us travel with you. My friend and I know the crypt, and no necromancer will attack you if we're there.' That latter part was *almost* certainly true. 'And...truthfully, we could use your help.'

Tabris raised their eyebrows. 'I thought you didn't want us to kill anyone.'

'I don't,' Ree said. 'I want you to *save* someone.'

The paladins considered her. She steeled herself to their gazes, which felt heavy on her skin.

'Sure,' said Tabris. 'I'd be honoured to travel with the only living beastmage. Sef?' They elbowed their companion, armour clinking at the contact.

Persephone's mouth shifted to one side. Her dark eyes were weighing. Ree remembered her assertion that therianthropy 'felt like necromancy'. The way she'd squeezed Ree out of her ratskin like one might squeeze juice from a berry.

'Will you interfere with our work?' said Persephone. 'If we attack a necromancer, will you try to stop us?'

Ree gritted her teeth at the question. Could she really travel with people so casually violent? She considered lying, telling them no, of course she wouldn't dare. But Ree had never been much of a liar, and Persephone's question had gotten too far under her skin for her to try it now.

She locked eyes with the silver-haired paladin. 'Without question,' she said.

Tabris looked ready to argue, but Persephone held up a hand and they fell silent. 'Good,' she said. She extended her gauntleted hand. It took Ree a few seconds to realise she expected her to shake it.

Gingerly, Ree took the paladin's hand. She expected a crushing grip, like necromancers trying to intimidate one another, but the paladin's hold was gentle in spite of the armour.

'Wait here and I'll bring my friends,' she said, taking her hand back and flexing it curiously.

Persephone bowed slightly, fist over heart. 'Of course.'

As she winged her way back to the tomb where Andomerys waited, she wondered if she'd made the right decision.

CHAPTER SEVENTEEN

Usther

'Did you see that?' Usther jabbed a finger angrily at the door, pacing so quickly that her skirts whirled around her legs. 'Ellenil is still a *child*. What are they doing, mixed up in all this?'

'Usther—' Dichotomy wriggled in Smythe's arms.

'Half the festering town is here! Did you know I saw the Underqueen? Not only is she a hundred and fifty years old, she didn't even start practising until she was seventy! She literally *creaks when she walks* and she's, what, joined a cult now?'

'Usther, please. Keep your voice *down,*' Smythe said in a low voice. 'We don't know who might be listening.'

Usther froze. Her hands came up and she crossed them, which didn't quite satisfy the urge to hug herself. 'Half the town is here!' she whispered. 'And I don't know about you, but I am not comforted by the thought of meeting the "Many-That-Hungers", which sounds rather like something looking for a necromancer-sized snack!'

Dichotomy sprang free of Smythe and started to explore the room. Usther took a shuddering breath and watched her. The room was large. There were four beds in it, though it looked uninhabited.

Just the sight of the beds gave her pause. It had been years since she'd seen one; most denizens lived in tombhomes and placed padded mats on converted stone shelves where the dead had once rested. These beds were plush. Red covers over white pillows. She couldn't help but walk over and run her hand over the covers, softer than any she could remember. She picked up the pillow and squeezed it. Feather-soft, not straw or fur coarse.

'Where are they getting all this?' she asked, turning to Smythe. 'How did they turn the crypt into white marble? Why have so many denizens joined them?'

'Perhaps they like the luxury,' Smythe said. 'Perhaps it makes them feel important. Or perhaps they had no choice.'

'Like there's anything stopping them from just walking away and returning to town,' Usther scoffed, but Smythe looked thoughtful.

'Well...there are more things than physical barriers that pen people in,' he said quietly. 'I know that very well.' He paused. 'As, I suspect, do you.'

Usther made a sound of wordless disgust and flapped a hand at him. She didn't like this new, thoughtful Smythe.

Misery made a worried sound and bumped into her shoulder, her head hanging low. Usther patted her rag-wrapped cheek. 'I'm sorry, darling,' she said. 'I know this has been hard on you. You didn't get any of those nasty mushrooms on you, did you?'

Misery shook her head pendulously.

'Good. You can do whatever you like now. Just don't leave the room without me, and don't take off your clothes.'

Misery shuffled to the corner and stood facing it, sighing her relief. Usther stared at her a moment, feeling a peculiar mixture of fondness and envy. She could do with mindlessly staring at a wall herself...

Smythe sat down on one of the beds. He immediately sighed and flopped down. 'Gods, I've missed this ...'

'Stop that!' Usther said. 'You're getting into the bed of the enemy!'

'You know, I don't think that's how that phrase usually goes.'

'Hilarious. I'm splitting my sides right now,' she said coldly.

Dichotomy leapt up onto his belly and started circling.

'Di, no.' She scooped up her cat and put her back on the ground.

Smythe lifted his glasses to rub his eyes. 'You're spiralling.'

'I'm doing no such thing!' Usther said, a little too loud. She flinched. 'Fine.' She steeled herself and took the bed across from him. The bed bounced gently under her weight. Morrin's teeth, it felt good to sit down.

Smythe reluctantly sat up and faced her, hands clasped between his knees. He looked at her; she looked at Dichotomy instead, who danced at her feet begging for scritches. 'Morrin chose you, right?'

Usther pursed her lips, still refusing to meet his eyes. 'Sort of,' she said. Really, Arthura had chosen her. And judging by where they'd ended up, it hadn't been a kindness.

Was she a fool for thinking she was ready for something more than hiding away at home and spying on her neighbours? These people she had never met had turned up in the crypt and gained the loyalty of more denizens than even respected the council. They commanded strange organisms that were immune to necromancy. And she? She had only a little cat, a house-minion, and a handful of gravemould to face them with. Not minions that could be flung into battle, but vulnerable, fragile beings that needed her protection and attention.

She wanted to go home. She wanted a cup of mushroom tea and to curl up in bed while her spectres whispered reports in her ears. She wanted to play Scrolls and Skulls with Ree, and laugh when she crushed her. She wanted the comfort of cold stone and cluttered shelves.

But she couldn't have any of that.

Smythe was watching her. His gaze wasn't appraising. It was expectant. Like he was waiting for her to tell him what to do.

Dichotomy brushed her leg again, and Misery sighed tiredly in the corner. Festering rats, when had *she* become a leader?

'We need to find out why everyone is here,' Usther said. 'Like you said, they can't *all* be here willingly. Not all of them looked happy. And I don't know a single necromancer who chooses to be called a servant.'

Smythe nodded. 'But how do we ask them, if Mykol is always watching us?'

Usther shrugged helplessly. 'We'll have to look for opportunities. But Mykol seems keen to tell us more about the Many-That-Hungers. Perhaps if we show interest, he'll let his guard down.'

'I won't have to feign it,' Smythe said. 'The whole thing seems...unreal. Did you notice how oddly those fungal minions moved?'

She nodded, remembering their smooth gaits and dextrous fingers. 'Almost like the living,' she said. 'Uncanny.'

'And they didn't seem to be directly under anyone's control,' Smythe said. 'I didn't sense any necromancy in the room. Did you?'

Usther frowned. 'I had other things on my mind.' One of those things had been Celia, but she'd be damned before she said it.

'Nobody was casting. No commands. When I focused, there was just ... *nothing* linking the necromancers and the minions. Or the minions and Mykol or Celia. Maybe someone has developed a more subtle form of raising, I don't know. Or the necromancer commanding them could have been absent, but...' He trailed off.

'You think they're, what, feral dead? They've just civilised themselves into helping out with the redecorating?' Her scorn covered the chill she felt at the thought. She remembered the way the fungus seemed to reach for her. And the way it reached for Misery. What would happen if her minion had stepped on the mushrooms? What kind of soil did a minion make for necromantic fungi?

'Maybe.' Smythe shrugged. 'I don't know. I'm just a Soul Summoner.'

Usther's eyebrows lifted. 'Still?' Most practitioners moved on to more practical schools of the Craft once they'd mastered the basics of soul summoning. There wasn't much you could do with something that was intangible and constantly screaming...

Smythe shrugged, non-committal. She narrowed her eyes. He'd clearly deepened his practice of the Craft; he'd remained in the crypt, afterall, and looked shades greyer than she remembered him.

'What are you hiding?' she said suddenly. 'Smythe, I *refuse* to be blind-sided by some scheme of yours while I'm dealing with all this, so if you'd just *tell* me—'

'I'm not hiding anything.'

'—ridiculous to think I'll let you pull the same trick twice—'

'No tricks. No schemes. No secrets...well, beyond the usual embarrassing childhood stories and such.' He shook his head. 'I'm just here to help.'

He looked honest. Earnest. And tired. He rubbed his hands together, perhaps in a nervous tick, perhaps merely out of awkwardness.

'I don't believe you,' she said.

'Well, that's fair, isn't it?' he replied, and they both lapsed into silence.

At length, Smythe said, 'What about them?' He gestured to Misery, still in the corner, and Dichotomy, who leapt up onto the bed and was attempting to climb into Usther's lap.

Usther pulled at the scruff of her cat's shoulders, her expression turning stormy. 'What about them?'

Smythe rubbed the pack of his neck. 'They'll be vulnerable out there,' he said. 'Dichotomy isn't going to tolerate being in a sling all day. And Misery might step on a mushroom when we aren't looking.' He gestured around the room. 'There's no one here, though. No fungus, either.'

'No. Absolutely not!' Dichotomy fled at the sharpness of her voice, darting under the bed.

'I'm not trying to tell you what to do,' Smythe said. 'I just thought it was worth considering.'

'*It isn't,*' Usther said, then cringed at the death echo in her voice. She closed her eyes and breathed in deep through her nose, releasing the magic she'd unconsciously reached for. Illusory flames danced in her mind's eye. A haunting memory. She put them out.

She stood up, crossing her arms. 'Your plan to question people alone is a good one. I don't want to stay here any longer than I have to, so let's go.' She crouched by the bed and pulled out Dichotomy, who clawed at her hands.

'That's enough, darling,' she said, ignoring the swipes. She put the squirming cat into her sling, refusing to look at Smythe while she did so. 'Misery, if you wouldn't mind?'

Her minion sighed and shuffled over to follow her.

She cracked open the door, peering outside. Pressure on it from the other side forced her back and out of the way.

A woman in a sleek black dress that fell away from her shoulders stood framed by the doorway, flanked by two fungal minions. Usther swallowed hard, her hand immediately going to her throat.

The woman's curly hair was cherry blossom pink, longer than Usther remembered it. It still set just as beautifully against the other woman's slate dark skin. She put a hand beneath her chin and smiled, exactly as cold and cruel as Usther remembered it.

'Right on time,' said Symphona. 'If you'll follow me, the Lord and Lady are waiting.' She turned and strode away, hips swaying, but all Usther could see was fire.

CHAPTER EIGHTEEN

Ree

'Well, this isn't right,' said Tabris.

They'd been travelling for hours in uncomfortable silence, the paladins leading, the denizens following. Ree, who normally revelled in silence, had felt oddly stifled by it. She could see the comradery between the paladins fraying in her presence as much as she could sense Andomerys' restless disapproval of the paladins.

But at least there had been the crypt. Cold, crumbling stone and the comforting mist of death energy. Carved walls and plentiful tombs. Home.

The paladins hadn't even managed to destroy any of the undead in these parts. They'd encountered precious few, and each Andomerys had scared away with a flare of sunlight before the warriors could so much as loosen their weapons.

Ree had begun to feel hopeful.

Until this.

Ree went to the wall, where the ancient stone of this part of the crypt gave way to smooth white marble. She laid her hand against it, then snatched it back. 'Warm,' she said, rubbing her fingers together as if she could rub away the warmth like grains of sand.

She took a few quick steps back, not wanting to stand on the alien floor. Her heart pounded in her chest, her every instinct screaming at the wrongness of it all. She dragged her gaze to the paladins. Tabris was making a face, while Persephone was unreadable as ever.

'*I* know this is wrong,' she said. 'But how do *you* know?'

'Well, it just feels wrong, doesn't it?' said Tabris. 'Do you ever get that?' Ree frowned and they continued, 'We're trained for it in Paldur-Ez. To listen to your gut. It's the whispered warning of the gods all creatures carry. And that,' they pointed at the stark white tunnel streaked with trails of red fungi. 'That is giving me a hell of a warning.'

'Also, you looked like a cat about to hairball when you saw it,' Persephone said. 'And you don't often seem surprised by this place.'

A cat about to hairball...if she didn't feel so sick, she might have smiled at the aptness.

More mysterious was the way the paladins had seemed *drawn* here. She might know the best and safest paths around, but she had no direction. With no destination, it was hard to chart their path. But the paladins hardly seemed to need it. For all their complaint on their first meeting of being lost, they seemed to get lost *with purpose.* And judging by where they had entered the crypt, they had been drawn to this bizarre white passage like a twinned lodestone.

She tucked her questions about that away for another time. 'Well, you're right,' she said. 'This isn't supposed to be here.' She hesitated. 'I...I don't think.'

Andomerys glared, but Ree didn't think it was for her. Her worry tended to manifest more like anger. 'What *is* supposed to be here?'

She'd have to get out her map to be sure, but she wasn't doing that in front of the paladins. Her trust only went so far. 'More tomb,' she said. 'Much like what we're in already.' She gestured around at the hall in which they stood. The walls were lined with upright corpses, their arms crossed.

She'd urged the paladins to stick to the middle of the crypt to avoid disturbing them. Dead that were laid to rest in guardian poses like these were especially susceptible to ambient death energy. It was entirely possible all of them would wake up if disturbed. Indeed, there were a few standing empty already, the two bracketing the white passage and another on the left.

To her relief and surprise, the paladins had agreed without complaint.

Larry followed her point and immediately started toward one of the standing corpses, hands outstretched curiously. She caught him by the wrist with speed borne of long practice and pulled him back to heel. 'You know better,' she told him sternly. He hung his head and gargled piteously, but stopped trying to pull away. Satisfied, she let him go.

Tabris strode forward to examine the passage, but Persephone's eyes were on Ree. Ree stiffened under the inspection, raising her chin.

Persephone was not intimidated. 'It's almost like it understands you.'

Larry gargled a question. She patted his shoulder. 'You can't play with them. You can go chew on Andomerys if you like.'

Larry wandered away, and seconds later she heard Andomerys say, 'Don't even think about—stop that!'

Persephone followed him with her eyes, her expression bemused.

'He does understand,' Ree said. 'Most minions do, the longer they're about. And Larry's been about a long time.' She almost added, 'We grew up together,' but stopped herself. It raised too many questions. And it wasn't completely true, either. Larry, it turned out, had been raised hundreds of years before Ree was born. That he'd been her playmate when she was little just made it feel like they'd always been a pair.

'Minions?' Persephone's eyebrows twitched.

'Undead are unthinking,' Tabris called. They crouched down, studying a patch of fungi. 'They just follow their master's orders. Less going on than in a mushroom.'

Ree frowned at them while they poked at the fungi. She hoped they got spores in their gauntlet. 'Minion is a word for undead. Especially undead that have masters.'

Persephone nodded thoughtfully. 'It's what we're taught, you know,' she said. 'That the soul departs on death, and doesn't return when raised by a necromancer. Even necromancers don't believe it, as far as I can tell.'

Ree shrugged. She had known Larry for too long to believe he was an empty husk. He certainly wasn't carrying a human soul—the man who had inhabited his body while it was alive was nothing at all like Larry—and anyway necromancers could summon souls back to bodies temporarily, making the difference clear.

She wondered, sometimes, whether undead grew new souls over time. And most necromancers didn't have the same minions for as long as Larry or even Misery, who was herself very much a person. Her father had made it very clear that on the surface, necromancers had to use every tool at their disposal just to survive, and minions were often sacrificed for that cause. But in the crypt, where the dead raised themselves and necromancer fights rarely had casualties, perhaps a new sort of minion had had time to grow into being.

Though she said nothing, Persephone still studied her as if she could read meaning in her silence. Her eyes went to Larry again. 'He seems almost friendly.'

'He *is* friendly,' Ree said, stung. Then she noted the change of pronoun, and her outrage melted away. She followed her gaze. Larry was trying to gnaw on a tired Andomerys, who held up a hand that glittered with faint sunlight to ward off his attempts.

'He's not really trying to hurt her,' she explained quietly. 'He just...likes to bite things. More than most minions, I think. He's a terror when he gets into my books—'

'I can imagine,' Persephone murmured.

'—but his teeth are quite blunt and he's not managed to damage anything beyond repair.' She watched him, something warm and anxious all at once stirring in her chest. 'He saved my life.'

More than once. Had saved the whole town too, though that hurt to think about. 'How many minions have you killed?' she asked quietly. 'How many necromancers? Because him? He's never hurt anyone. He's afraid of a housecat. Maybe think about that.'

Persephone shifted where she stood. 'We should move on,' she said. 'If this marble is out of place, then we are on the right path.' She strode away, armour clanking. Ree frowned at her back.

Andomerys came to stand beside her. 'You okay?'

Larry bumped her shoulder. She shifted her pack as he started to tug at it. 'Did you know any paladins? You know, before you came here?'

Andomerys nodded. 'You couldn't escape them at the King's court.'

Ree blinked. 'You didn't tell me you were a noble.'

'That's because I wasn't. I'm a healer, Ree. I've always been a healer. Just not always to necromancers.'

Ree frowned at her. 'Healer to the King? The one that went missing?'

'Does it matter? Paladins were more numerous in those days. They were a mixed bunch, like any warriors. I never liked them. Too concerned with the gods, too little concerned with the people. The Queen Regent was right to kick them out of Iyad, as far as I'm concerned.'

'Yeah, Andomerys. Everyone knows you hate the gods.' Ree smiled as they followed the paladins.

'I don't hate the gods. Hate the way everyone always assumes they know what they want.' She shook her head. 'That's something I like about Emberlon,' she says. 'Sensible boy.'

Ree nodded, not twitching at her calling a man who'd been old when she was a child 'a boy'. She knew by now that Andomerys was far, far older than she looked, and that she wouldn't be drawn on the matter of her age.

She did wonder about her opinion of paladins, though. Were paladins today still too little concerned with people? Persephone and Tabris had both seemed worryingly close to violence on first meeting, but thus far they hadn't hurt any denizens and seemed to see reason as far as not killing any minions that weren't attacking them.

But then, neither she nor Andomerys were necromancers. Perhaps if they were, it would be a different story.

'Are you coming?' Tabris called.

Ree hesitated. She didn't want to, to be honest. The strange bored tunnels had been weird enough, but this white marble was terrifying. She was once again overwhelmed by the sense that there was something wrong with the crypt—*her* crypt—and that she was being forced to work with its enemies to protect it. She liked nothing of what was happening, and couldn't shake a sense of foreboding that the worst was still to come.

Larry seemed to have no such concerns. He ambled into the tunnel and at once, the mushrooms came alive. Little caps of red that looked like blood and fuschia brackets leaned toward him, producing little red tendrils that reached greedily for his passing legs.

'Festering rats!' Ree lunged forward and pulled the minion back before the fungi could get a hold of him. As he left the white marble, the fungi retracted their filaments, settling back into a semblance of innocence. Just every day luminous red mushrooms.

Larry hugged her, gargling in horror. 'Yeah, I know, buddy.' She patted him. 'It's okay.'

Tabris stomped back to study the mushrooms again. 'What was that?'

Andomerys put her hand on her hip. 'This fungus is not native to the crypt. It seems particularly interested in undead. It was all I could do to get the spores off him when he stepped on one.'

'It was eating him,' Ree said, her stomach dropping at the thought. 'He acted like he was on fire...'

'You *healed* an undead?' Tabris' tone was disbelieving.

Andomerys sniffed. 'My sterilisation spell excepted him. It only killed the spores.'

Tabris shook their head.

Persephone leaned her shoulder against a bare patch of marble. 'Leave him behind, then. Surely the crypt holds no danger for him.'

'It doesn't...' Ree said doubtfully. Larry had no master and wandered where he chose. She'd hardly seen him over the last few years, though she didn't know what had held him up. But he was also very hard to leave behind. Just because he understood her didn't mean he'd listen. She wasn't his master; she couldn't actually *command* him. 'Shoo,' she said, waving at him. 'Go find someone else. We're going somewhere dangerous.'

Larry's head tilted to one side. He gargled in confusion.

Ree narrowed her eyes. 'I know you understood that.'

Larry shunted past her toward the tunnel again, and she was forced to tackle him and drag him back. 'Just go *home*, curse you!'

Larry flailed and tried to shove her aside but she held fast, gritting her teeth.

'Do they always do this?' Tabris asked Andomerys.

'More often than you would think,' the healer replied, stony-faced.

'Fine!' Ree released him and straightened her hair, which had fallen in her face during one of Larry's wild blows. Larry didn't rush straight into the tunnel now. He waited, howling his triumph at the ceiling.

But if he was going into the tunnel, he would need protection. More than she did, that was certain.

She rubbed her eyes. 'I can't believe I'm going to suggest this,' she said. 'Larry, come here.' She knelt down and started rummaging in her pack. She pulled out her spare robe. She wasn't very tall, but then neither was Larry. And as an ancient undead, he was very thin indeed. His jaw hung open as he stared at her, uncomprehending.

'Oh, isn't this pretty?' she said, standing up and bouncing it up and down. Larry leaned closer, chomping his teeth. 'It's so interesting, I love to play with it...'

'What in all of divinity is happening right now?' asked Tabris.

Andomerys snorted.

'I bet it would be very fun to bite and ruin forever,' said Ree, swishing it in front of Larry. Larry took a few steps closer, and grabbed for it. 'Aha!' Ree whipped it out of reach and then pounced on him, pulling it over his head. He screeched and tried to fight her off but she started to wrestle one of his arms in. 'Andomerys, get his other arm!'

'What? No!'

He started to shove her off but then someone took his other arm. 'Easy now,' said Persephone. Ree stared at her in surprise, but in spite of the terrifying thickness of her armour, she handled Larry gently. Together, they eased Larry into the robe, and Ree even got Persephone to hold him while she forced him into a pair of her trousers.

'Okay,' she said. 'One last thing.' She started to pull off her boots.

'Uhh...'

'Your *boots?*' said Tabris, sounding disgusted.

'He's more at risk than I am!' she said. 'I can't let him go in defenseless.'

She'd wandered the crypt barefoot as a child. Her mother had encouraged it; said it was important to make that connection to the land, and the crypt was *her* land. She could do it again. As much as the thought of walking near the fungi with bare feet made her skin crawl, it had clearly rejected living flesh. She would be fine.

She tried to get a boot onto Larry's kicking feet. He burst out of Persephone's grip and started sprinting toward the tunnel, howling wildly. 'Larry! Stop!' Festering rats! She'd had no idea he could move this fast.

She charged after him. He tripped and she tackled him, pinning him to the ground. 'The boots!' she yelled.

Much howling thrashing later, and a very cowed Larry stood beside a barefoot Ree. 'There!' Ree said brightly. 'We're all good to go.'

Tabris had their face in their hands.

'All good to go,' Andomerys agreed wryly.

Ree looked at Larry and cringed. Odd enough to see a minion in clothes. Seeing a minion in *her* clothes? That was just unflattering.

They set off. Larry walked beside Ree, lifting his feet extra high, as if he could step out of the boots with each step.

'Thanks for your help,' she said to Persephone, who watched Larry with an unreadable expression. 'He's really clumsy. I couldn't let him walk through here without some kind of protection.'

'My...pleasure?' She sounded as if she didn't quite believe her own words. 'He is very different than most of the undead I've met.'

'He's been around a long time,' Ree said with a shrug. 'That's how it works. And he's not feral; he was raised. That helps as well.'

'Ambient death energy,' Persephone said, recalling her earlier term.

'Why did you help?' Ree asked. She'd been turning it over in her mind, and she couldn't see what the paladin got out of it. She clearly had a great distaste for Larry, and a hatred of necromancy in general. Why go out of her way to help Ree keep one alive?

Persephone looked thoughtful. 'Well, helping is what we do,' she said. 'That's the job. They train us so that we can help in ways the average person cannot, but ultimately, if we're passing through a village and they need someone strong to do some lifting, or want an extra pair of hands to bring in the harvest that day, that's what we do.'

Ree had nothing to say to that. The 'job' was killing witches. Necromancers and anyone who didn't fit the right profile for a 'good' mage. She'd heard many horror stories of paladins firsthand from the people who'd lived through them. If Andomerys was right, and paladins were fewer now than they were in the past, they were doing more than their fair share of terrorising.

'Are your feet cold?' Persephone asked, breaking Ree from her quickly darkening thoughts.

She looked down at her feet. Cold and pale and a little grey, the toenails short and often cracked from when she'd kicked a brick too hard or stumbled while climbing. 'Not really. I don't get cold very easily. And this marble floor is creepily warm.'

'I noticed that as well,' Persephone said, and she seemed troubled. 'Are there...I don't know, underground vents here? Lava, that sort of thing? I hadn't heard that the Dead Mountains were volcanic, but...'

'No,' Ree said. 'Nothing like that.' She'd delved deep enough to know. The lowest levels of the crypt *were* warmer, for the most part, but they were not what an upworlder would call warm. Her mother and Andomerys, the only non-necromancers in town who had grown up in the upworld, had often complained of the cold. Well. Andomerys complained, her mother would say something cryptic about Morrin's life-giving frost and then would wrap up tighter.

'How did you become a paladin?' she asked.

'Tabris,' Persephone called ahead. 'She wants to know how we became paladins.'

Tabris fell back to join them, laughing. 'Bruises and bad dreams, mostly,' they said. 'That's the way they run things at Paladur-Ez.'

Paladur-Ez. An island off the now defunct country of Paladur. It bordered the Dead Mountains where the crypt lay, so it was a neighbour, of sorts. She'd never been; the few times she'd left the crypt with her father in search of trade, they'd gone to the villages in the Dead Marshes, where people asked no questions as long as they didn't wear black, and welcomed the gold they brought with them. Mortana, the publican of the only inn in town, was from Paladur. She'd spoken of it once, calling it only 'a sad, crumbling heap of rubble where the only currency is superstition.' It had not made it sound inviting.

'So you went there to be trained?'

'We were sent there, more like,' said Tabris.

'When a child wakes screaming in the night calling out the names of the gods and making strange prophecies, people are pretty quick to send them to Paladur-Ez,' Persephone explained. 'We frightened them.'

'Oh. I didn't realise. I thought paladins were well-liked.'

Persephone shrugged. 'When we're helping them clear out monsters, they like us well enough. But as children, we were uncanny.'

'What sort of prophecies?' Andomerys asked. They came upon a particularly thick carpet of fungi and took it in turns to file down the narrow path through it.

'Oh, I don't know. It was all gibberish. The priests made sense of it,' said Tabris.

'Imagery. Scripture, that sort of thing,' said Persephone. 'The priests would study what we said. It identified which god had called us.'

'I think I remember mine involved...iron stakes and poisoned soil?' said Tabris. 'Couldn't tell you what that has to do with the Rootfather, but there you are.'

'A tsunami,' said Persephone. 'And rivers that ran red and gold.'

'I like yours better,' said Tabris.

'Is that blasphemy?'

'I don't know, maybe.' They laughed.

Ree wasn't sure what to make of this. Her mother was sometimes given visions from Morrin, but she was the sole priestess of a powerful goddess. 'Do your priests get those dreams as well?'

Persephone shook her head. 'It's not unheard of, but not usually. They say back in the pre-Silver era, kids who had paladin prophecies were considered witches.'

'A less enlightened time,' Tabris said without irony.

Persephone frowned. 'Perhaps,' she said.

It was uncomfortable to think that they might actually have been called by the gods to their profession. Not least because it was a profession concerned with the extermination of her family and friends.

'Prophecy or not, you're human,' Andomerys said, as if reading Ree's thoughts. 'Fallible.'

Persephone inclined her head and Tabris laughed.

Ree didn't ask them any more questions. She had more than enough to think about already.

THE BEAUTIFUL DECAY

CHAPTER NINETEEN

Usther

U sther couldn't take in the room, the denizens, the lord and lady sat on dual thrones at one end, regal in their rags. The world was tilted around her, set at an impossible angle, skewed by the presence of the sleek woman standing beside her so casually.

Symphona didn't look at her and that was a blessing, because Usther didn't know whether to run or to fight when she did. Usther put a hand on Misery's shoulder; Dichotomy was cuddled safely against her chest. She wondered if they recognised the woman who had tried to kill them when she herself had been barely more than a teenager.

She'd been exiled. Cast out from the town, from necromancer society. Usther could have demanded her life for what she'd done, for breaking the implicit peace of Tombtown. She'd always taken it as a point of pride that she hadn't. Instead, she'd held the knowledge close. She was better than Symphona. She wouldn't use her power to kill if it could be avoided.

Now she wondered if she'd made the right choice.

'Thank you, Symphona,' said Mykol.

'You are especially beloved in our eyes,' said Celia.

Symphona smiled and curtsied, as elegant as an iyadi noble. 'It is my pleasure to serve my Lord and Lady.'

Usther didn't know what to make of that. It had been a long time since she had last seen Symphona, but the woman *she'd* known would never have been described as subservient. But here she was, bowing and scraping, someone else's symbol making a perfectly shaped bow around her wrist.

Mykol and Celia felt like mirror images of each other, Mykol leaning on the left of his throne, Celia lounging against the right. The hall, which

127

had bustled with activity before, was now utterly still. The denizens who had worked here before now knelt with heads lowered. The minions, with their fungal wreaths, stood perfectly at attention, frozen and silent. Usther shuddered. It was like they weren't people; they were ornaments.

'Shall I introduce our honoured guests to the Many-That-Hungers, brother?' Celia asked. She gave Usther a wicked smile.

Symphona dipped a curtsy. 'If it pleases you, my Lady, I was hoping to continue your instruction today.'

Celia considered. 'Oh? It has been useful, I suppose. I leave them to you, brother.'

As one, the siblings rose. Celia strode past Symphona, brushing her shoulder. Now Symphona did look at Usther, the barest smirk curving her lips. Then she turned and followed Celia from the room.

Mykol gestured to Usther and Smythe. 'Follow me, if you would.'

He waved his hand as they exited the hall, and Usther startled as the hall burst back into activity, the sudden noise and bustle shocking after so much silence.

Once again, she was struck by how much power these siblings held over the denizens. People who would never normally allow anyone to tell them what to do. What were they offering in exchange for this devotion and servitude? Or, more frighteningly: what were they threatening?

Mykol didn't lead them far down a white corridor before pausing at a large cluster of crimson fungi. He gestured to them. 'Usther. Chandrian. Observe with me.' He knelt. Usther glanced at Smythe, who shrugged. They knelt beside him, Usther's skin crawling at her nearness both to him and to the hated fungus.

With long, delicate fingers, Mykol gently stroked the cap of a mushroom; it wiggled, as if in delight at his touch, and many of the fungi around it lit up like lanterns, casting a red glow across the white marble. 'These, you already know,' he said. 'The least part of the Many. Tiny cells of a larger whole, spreading out as scouts.'

'The Many-That-Hungers is a fungus?' asked Smythe. 'An intelligent fungus?'

Mykol's expression flickered, so quickly that Usther couldn't quite catch what it had shifted to. He smiled. 'You say that as if any fungus is not. Your understanding is limited. I will teach you better.'

A tendril reached out from the patch to wrap around his finger, caressing. He withdrew his hand and it released him with all tenderness.

He didn't look at them. His entire attention was focused on the fungi. 'Touch it,' he ordered. His tone lost all the gentleness it had held before. Now it was iron-hard and commanding. Usther clenched her fists and gritted her teeth against the urge to talk back. She despised it.

She glanced at Smythe, who looked troubled but shrugged. He must be thinking the same thing she was; that it could not serve their purpose to anger Mykol.

Tentatively, she stretched out a finger. As it drew near, the little pink cap she reached for twitched. She hesitated, but she could feel Mykol's regard, oppressively heavy. And she could not shake the feeling that if she didn't make contact, he would know.

She brushed it with her fingertip. It was as warm and pliant as human flesh, and she quickly drew back. Smythe did the same.

'It knows you,' said Mykol. 'It all knows you. Usther of the Ashes, Chandrian Smythe, and one other.'

One other? A chill ran down Usther's spine.

'But there is more, of course,' he said, rising. 'Come.'

He led them further, to a set of double doors that alone in all this place was black. Like a void at the heart of a star. Fungal minions stood in front of it, but as Mykol approached, they swung aside without a single command or gesture, one pushing the door open.

It revealed a room drenched in red. Fungi mounded on the floor, carpeted the walls, dangled from the ceiling. It was packed with fungi, fungi on fungi, and all of it lit up as Mykol stepped inside, bare feet stepping in among it and crushing caps that burst into glittering clouds of pink and red. Smythe covered his mouth; Usther shoved Misery back and away.

In the centre of the mound, something stirred. Slowly, a figure sat upright. An undead in a tarnished crown, button mushrooms spilling from its ribcage, crimson brackets clinging to the sides of its head. It was little more than bone with a thin paste of skin now, held together not with necromancy but with tightly-wrapped red filaments.

Usther breathed hard through her mouth, assaulted by the stench of it. Necromancy, death energy, and clever burial rites had staved off the worst decay of the crypt. Everything here was ancient and preserved. But there was nothing preservational about the fungi. It was eating the corpse even as it puppeted it. Instinctively, she reached out with her senses for the death energy that permeated the crypt, but in this room, there was nothing. The undead stopped moving, except for the occasional twitch of the fungi growing on it.

'The Many feed on death,' said Mykol. 'It learns as it feeds. This was a queen of your people. Now she is food for the Many. One day soon, she will be part of the Many entire.'

There was a long pause. Usther tried to repress her shudder, crossing her arms to stop her traitor limbs from giving her away.

At length, Smythe said brightly. 'Fascinating. From where do the Many-That-Hungers gain this information? Bodies do not contain souls, and dare I say, I doubt there was much brain left in a corpse of that age.'

'Flesh and blood contain memory,' said Mykol. 'The impression of what came before. The Many-That-Hungers consumes and catalogues all that it touches.'

It sounded nothing at all like necromancy. Necromancy was the cold kiss of Crafted magic. It was ancient words uttered with clarity of intent. This sounded almost biological, though an alien biology she didn't understand. But the word 'blood' still stood out to her. Blood was used primarily in curses and the most experimental of necromancy. It was used in the Black Oath, a curse so binding that it would tether the soul to the realm of the living as an eternal servant. Smythe still bore the marks of that curse on his own skin, where it had been sealed into his blood.

She wanted to ask about its significance, but she was very aware of how narrow the ledge they walked was. Mykol had dozens, maybe more, of denizens at his command. He had the crimson fungi at his command, an entity she could not begin to understand. And he and his sister themselves had an uncanniness about them that made her skin crawl with warning. She hadn't forgotten his sudden appearance at her bedside, having woken neither Dichotomy nor Misery. She had no idea what he might be capable of, when stirred to anger.

Smythe, though, had none of her reservations. 'I had thought it uninterested in living flesh,' he said. 'The Many-That-Hungers seemed to reject my flesh, though it seemed very interested in Misery.'

Mykol smiled. 'Living flesh. But blood is blood, and rare to find among the dead.'

Blood is blood. And where were they finding their blood, so rare among the dead? Her thoughts went to the red ribbons worn at every denizen's wrist. Broad red ribbons like bloody slashes, she'd thought. Wide enough to conceal what they resembled, certainly. The thought did not please her.

'Your beloved servants,' Usther said. 'Did you show them all this, too? Give them a tour?'

Mykol stood and smoothed down his dress. It rippled oddly, as if caught in a breeze, and settled again unwrinkled.

Uncanny, Usther thought again. That was not how clothes worked, any more than the fungal minions behaved the way minions ought.

'Our beloved servants were given what they required to serve us,' said Mykol. 'You are being given what you require as well. Or at least, what I think you require. Only blood will tell for sure.'

Usther wished she could cross her arms again, so uncomfortable did that thought make her.

'Well,' said Smythe. 'I must say, this is rather fascinating, old chap. How did you come upon the Many-That-Hungers? You seem to have rather a strong connection to it.'

Mykol's fushica eyes seemed, for a moment, to flare with inner light. His expression smoothed into something hard and unreadable. 'That is a big secret. To get it, you would need to offer an equal secret. Blood would suffice.' He paused. 'But you are not eager to make that trade now. I understand.'

'Would you mind if we take a look around ourselves?' Usther said. 'Speak to your servants, see what you have created?'

'By all means,' said Mykol. 'The Many-That-Hungers will not allow you to go anywhere you should not. The rest of its kingdom is free to you.'

'Kingdom?' Usther asked before she could stop herself.

Mykol smiled. 'Of course. The first thing that the Many-That-Hungers learned was how to rule.'

He gestured, and Smythe and Usther stepped back. The fungal minions closed the door on the room of the undead queen buried in fungi. Usther caught one last glimpse of the fungi-ridden monarch toppling back into the pile before the black doors clicked shut.

CHAPTER TWENTY

Ree

The deeper into the tunnels they got, the more fungi there was, and the stranger it behaved. There were sections where it was almost a carpet and Ree would puzzle over how to get the others over it, only for it to part in the middle and leave a clear path, shrivelling back only to grow again behind them as they passed.

There were rooms upon rooms, all of them doorless and furnitureless; nothing more than barren cubes of white marble. They slept in the ones that didn't have fungi in them. Ree wondered whether that really mattered, given the speed at which the fungi could spread. For the first time in her life, she slept as part of a series of watches, making sure that someone was always on lookout for danger. The paladins said they did it as a matter of course, though it seemed weird and unnatural to Ree. But even though their only threat was the fungi, she was glad to think it wouldn't sneak up on them in the night, as it did in her dreams.

The paladins, for their part, were more than up to the adventure. They became more comfortable as they travelled. They joked and laughed and seemed unruffled by the terrifying nature of the fungi. And at each junction, they would stop and think, searching their feelings for the urging of their gods. Ree didn't know whether they really could feel their gods in their guts, but it certainly *felt* like they had direction, which was more than Ree and Andomerys had. Nonetheless, with no sign of Emberlon and the ever-increasing fungi, a seed of despair planted in her belly. Remembering Andomerys' advice, she did her best not to let it sprout.

Finally, they came to a black door at the end of a passage. All of the rooms they'd encountered thus far had been doorless, featureless in all ways.

An architectural shell. But this door stood stark and imposing against the white.

Ree wondered if the way her stomach kicked was Morrin's way of telling her she was on the right path.

No. She didn't need divine intervention to see that this was something new. And probably didn't lead anywhere good.

Tabris tried the handle. 'Locked tight,' they said. 'No give or jiggle at all.' They turned to Ree, their green hair swishing. 'You have any experience of this? Is it some kind of...I don't know, necromancer door?'

Ree frowned and strode forward. 'Maybe...' She placed her hand flat against the door. It was just as warm as the rest of this cursed place. 'I don't think so,' she said.

Tabris rubbed the back of their head. 'Well, shit. I was hoping you had one of your tricks for getting around it.'

Ree frowned. She started feeling around at the edges of the door. The gap between door and wall was only a hair-line, impossibly narrow. There weren't many locked doors in the crypt, unless they were also puzzles of some kind. But here in these corridors, devoid of any features or objects, it was hard to imagine she'd missed a trick lever or crystal or engraved password. 'No tricks,' she said. 'It's...weird. Like the rest of this place.'

'You can say that again,' said Tabris. They looked at Persephone. 'Shall we?'

'Of course.'

'Shall we what?' said Andomerys.

The paladin took three long strides back in unison. 'There's a trick they taught us back at Paladur-Ez,' said Tabris.

'We call it "the paladin's lockpick",' added Persephone.

Andomerys seized Larry by the elbow and dragged him back. Ree quickly followed suit. The paladins charged, thundering forward in a clatter of metal, to slam into the door. It didn't move.

'Shit,' said Tabris.

'Again,' said Persephone.

The second time there was a crack.

The third, the door split down the middle. The paladins kicked aside the pieces.

'Subtle,' said Andomerys.

'*Effective,*' said Tabris.

Ree stepped over the shattered remains of the black door, her lip curling. Given the choice, she'd prefer a real lockpick.

The room was thick with crimson fungi, which clung to the walls and ceiling and made piles on the floor. Among them were several undead, standing perfectly, uncannily still. All stared at the door where they'd entered. The undead were pocked with fungi, which grew straight out of their skin, poking between whatever rags they might be wearing. Some even had it growing out of their eyes.

Tabris drew their sickle and started forward, but Persephone grabbed their arm and jerked their head at Ree.

Tabris sighed. 'Friends of yours? Or may I kill the mushroom abominations?'

Ree frowned. Technically, feral undead didn't seem to be...*people*...the same way that minions did. They were mindless and hungry. But she wondered sometimes whether that was just her own bias as to what being a person meant. She didn't see the point in killing them, either way.

'No, but I can deal with this,' she said. A little doubtfully, in all honesty; the undead seemed very still, fixated on the door they'd destroyed. Not normal behaviour for the restless dead.

She unhooked her pouch of herbs from her belt. 'Remember this?'

Tabris rolled their eyes. 'Sure, go season them.'

Ree strode forward, picking her way across the floor. Her skin crawled to find her bare feet so close to the fungi. At one point, the top of her foot brushed a mushroom cap and her stomach actually heaved at the sense that it had pressed lips to her skin.

The undead only continued to stare fixedly at the door. They paid no mind to her at all.

As she approached the nearest, which was heavily covered, she took a pinch of herbs and threw it into its face. 'Morrin give you peace,' she said. 'Your time is over and your rest begins.'

Nothing. Not so much as a blink.

For a moment, she wondered whether these were really undead. Perhaps they were just corpses propped up by fungi as some kind of bizarre statues. But then she heard the rattling inhale of breath from the one she was staring at. An icy shiver ran down her spine.

'Something's wrong,' she said, glancing back at the others. 'They aren't responding.'

'And that's bad?' said Persephone.

'That's bad,' said Andomerys. 'I've got Larry!' she called down, and seized the minion by his elbow. He immediately gargled a protest and tried to pull away.

'Good.'

She considered the figures before her. None of the others moved any more than the one in front of her, but she was willing to bet they were just as undead. 'Put his hood up,' she called up to the healer. 'Some of these fungi piles are quite tall.' Almost like stalactites and stalagmites, reaching for each other from above and below. Like the fungi had been dripping from the ceiling like liquid. An unsettling thought.

Persephone was the first to step out. The moment she stepped between the fungi, the undead lurched into motion. All at once, all of the undead issued a high-pitched, hissing scream and began to charge.

'Stop!' Ree yelled. 'Rest now!' She threw another cloud of herbs into the face of the nearest one and it barged past her, knocking her into a pile of fungi. She felt it crunch beneath her. She coughed as a cloud of spores went up in a cloud of red mist. Not good.

She scrambled to her feet, shedding mushrooms and spore dust.

Persephone unslung her spear and hefted her shield, as smoothly as if she were opening her pack. Just in time for the first undead to crash against it. She yelled and shoved, sending it flying with one powerful bash. It hit the undead behind it and both fell into a pile of fungi, releasing even more spores.

'Be careful!' Ree yelled between coughs. 'Watch out for spores!'

She didn't like to think about what the spores might do inside her lungs. Regular mushrooms might have toxic spores, but nothing Andomerys couldn't deal with. But the crimson fungi? It didn't bear thinking about.

Larry howled from the doorway. A hand pulled her to her feet and she was surrounded in a cloud of sunlight and warmth energy; Andomerys grimly purged the spores from the air around them. 'You're clear,' she said.

The paladins flashed with bright light as well now. Where Andomerys' magic was like a glimpse of the sun, Persephone's was like the moon, cool silver filling the area. Tabris' healing was sunlight but weaker, the sun on a winter day rather than Andomerys' summer blaze. The fungal undead hissed and drew back from the sudden flare, but didn't flee or crumble as might a regular undead. Tabris cut an undead across the middle with two quick slashes of their scythe, only for the undead's midriff to release dozens of crimson tendrils that reached for them, forcing them back.

'Is this normal?!' they yelled.

Ree couldn't say that it was. The undead throwing themselves at the paladins still showed no interest in her. Andomerys motioned for her to fall back to the doorway with Larry, then strode forward to join the paladins, magic flaring around her so brightly that Ree had to avert her eyes as if from the sun itself.

'Purge the fungi first,' she said. 'The parameters are *elthinia loritis valethi sul*,' she said, and began casting very quickly in *iyad-anar*, words too quick for Ree to catch. She had only a passing knowledge of iyadi, having focused instead on Old Antherian, the language favoured by necromancers.

Andomerys held up a palm as if asking the undead before her to halt and a beam of focused sunlight shot out from it. It wrapped around the undead, leaving the flesh untouched but shrivelling up the fungi like raisins in the sun. The undead shook and twitched. The fungi crumbled; ash fell from the undead's open mouth and eyes. And then it collapsed, an inert corpse.

Persephone and Tabris mimicked her, dropping their weapons to free their hands to cast. Their lights were neither as bright nor as controlled as Andomerys' spell, but when the flare cleared enough for Ree to see, another three undead fell limp at their feet.

They cleared the room quickly after that. The crimson fungi around them scuttled away, insect-like, toward the walls with a sound like skin rubbing against skin. The speed and dexterity of its movement terrified

Ree. Thus far, its movement had been rare and restrained. The thought that it might be able to cross a room within the space of a breath was terrifying.

Ree grabbed Larry's hand, which was terribly clammy. 'Quickly,' she said. 'We should go now!'

Larry resisted, cowering away from where all the light had flared. And no wonder, when healing magic and sunlight both were normally the undoing of undead.

'Larry, come now or you have to go back on your own,' Ree snapped. He allowed her to tow him along after that.

They got to the other end of the room where another door of black stood. The paladins made quick work of it, with Persephone handing Ree an extremely heavy and now thoroughly dented shield to hold. Ree noticed she was favouring her shield arm, slamming into the door with her other shoulder instead.

The paladins stumbled through to find a lace-cloaked figure on the other side, their hood misshapen where it rested against their horn-shaped hair. Before they could do anything foolish, Ree yelled, 'Wait!'

She stepped through after them. The young person on the other side watching them with cautious eyes was vaguely familiar. 'Ellenil?' She vaguely remembered them running with a cabal of other teen necromancers and younger aspirants. They always returned their library books on time, so while Ree had had little to do with them, she'd always held warm feelings for them.

'The Lord and Lady have been expecting you,' said Ellenil. 'Follow me.'

CHAPTER TWENTY-ONE

Usther

The idea that everything they said and did in this awful place was monitored by the Many-That-Hungers was not a comforting thought. In fact, it rather put a hole in Usther's bright shining plan to shake the truth out of her fellow denizens in a dark corner, and maybe drag Ellenil home to their parents while she was at it.

She strode down the hall, her steps heavy with frustration. Smythe and Misery had to pick up the pace just to keep up.

'Where do we go first?' asked Smythe. 'I don't know any denizens, so I don't know who would be good to ask. Not that I think anyone is going to be particularly keen to open up to me...'

'Oh excellent,' Usther snapped. 'Very astute. Please do keep on about how nobody likes you because you tried to kill them and their families, it's really earning you sympathy points.'

'I wasn't—I'm not—' Smythe stopped, and sighed, and almost against her will, Usther turned on her heel to face him. 'Just tell me what to do,' he said. 'I'm at your service. If you want me to leave, I'll leave.'

Usther breathed out hard through her nose. 'Of course I don't want you to *leave*! I'm sure being abandoned in this place will go *very* well for me indeed. What I *want* is immaterial, anyway. I'm stuck here with you, the very last person I would ever choose, and I have no direction or idea what to do at all!'

She clenched her fists. Her eyes stung and she gritted her teeth and promised to curse herself seven different ways if a single tear fell.

Smythe hesitated, in that hateful, goofy way that he had. He looked for a moment like he might take her hand, or pat her shoulder, and he would have found himself on the wrong side of a length of cursed intestine if he had. But, he let his hands fall. Finally, he said, 'I have some ideas, if...if that would help?'

Usther breathed out hard through her nose. 'Let's hear them.'

It wasn't as bad as she'd expected. He wanted to start with the guarded black doors they'd passed on their way in, and that seemed as good a place to start as any. Even if they weren't allowed inside, perhaps the necromancers guarding it would have something enlightening to say.

He also wanted to return to their room and secure it. Begrudgingly, Usther agreed. They spent an hour chalking runes onto the borders of the floor and along the inside of the door, which would harm and repel visitors, with specific exclusions for those in their company. 'There's no fungi in here,' Smythe said as they surveyed their work. 'And we don't know what danger we might be going into. I think you should consider leaving Dichotomy and Misery here, in the safety of the spells.'

'No.'

'Your cat needs to stretch her legs and just have time to be a cat. And anyone can see Misery hates all the fungi we've encountered. I'm willing to bet there will be more of it—'

'No!' Usther shocked herself with the bark to her words.

'But—it's—' Smythe stopped, took a deep breath, and asked, 'Why is it so important that they go with you wherever you go?'

Usther flopped onto the bed she'd claimed earlier. Dichotomy hopped up beside her and boffed her hand, begging for attention. 'That woman who escorted us to Mykol and Celia earlier? Years ago, she was angry that I wouldn't do what she wanted, so she set my house on fire while I was out. I barely got back in time to get Misery and Dichotomy out. So I'm not going to leave them *anywhere* alone, but certainly not here, in a place where she seemingly has power and influence.' Usther's lip curled. 'Everything she's always wanted, I'm sure, and how amusing for her that I wandered in for her to toy with.'

'She set your house on fire,' Smythe repeated. His eyes were wide behind his glasses. 'She set your *house* on *fire*...'

'That's what I said.'

'Festering rats,' he said, and he sat down across from her. 'Well...is she strong, this Symphona?'

'Stronger than I am,' Usther said. 'And twice as nasty, loathe though I am to admit it.'

'Stronger than me?'

Usther sat up and frowned at him. She didn't want to say it, but she didn't *know* of any necromancers stronger than him. Ree had told her he'd seemed to absorb the Lich's powers as well, during the ritual to destroy the town. If that was true, she couldn't fathom the kind of necromancy he was capable of.

'I only mean,' said Smythe, 'that if she wants to hurt your family, she'll have to get through our wards. And it doesn't sound like she's strong enough to take on both of us.'

'No,' said Usther. 'I...I suppose she isn't.'

But that wasn't the point! She wanted to scream. The point was that Misery and Dichotomy had to be *here* where she could see them and make sure they were safe. That Ree and Arthura and even awful old Igneus needed to be where she could watch them, but they weren't and the hurt of them wandering around unprotected was almost too much for her to bear sometimes. But Misery and Dichotomy: she could watch them. She could take them with her. She could *know* they were safe, because they were with *her.*

But those rules no longer applied, did they? If they ever had. This wasn't the town, where overt acts of aggression would be met with harsh punishments from the council. This wasn't the crypt she knew, where the biggest threats were crotchety dead queens and the mild man sitting across from her.

Taking them with her *was* more dangerous. Mykol had said the Many-That-Hungers *knew* her. And Symphona would certainly want to harm her.

And the fungi was everywhere. Everywhere but here, a privacy the Lord and Lady had afforded her that she didn't entirely trust, but was surely too valuable to shun entirely.

Smythe was watching her. He didn't press his point. He'd said his piece. He was waiting for her to decide.

'You're different than you were,' she said, though she hadn't really meant to.

'Not as much as I should be, probably,' he replied, and shrugged.

Usther stood up and surveyed their wards. 'These are good,' she said. 'I like what you did with the *eztorka vitz nav* there, especially.' She sniffed. 'We...we could leave them here, if you helped me power it. To make sure sh—nobody can get in.'

Smythe nodded. 'I can do that,' he said.

His eyes filled with ink as he summoned his magic around him. It was a blast of chill energy so strong that she could imagine it riming her bones and she could feel the echo of it vibrating in her blood. Oddly, she found she wasn't afraid of it.

Usther said her goodbyes, trying to put on an encouraging smile in spite of the turmoil in her chest. Misery laid flat on the floor, face-down, with a sigh of utter relief. Dichotomy walked up and down Misery's back, purring and kneading on her borrowed clothes, then curled up on the back of her neck. Misery made a second, significantly less relieved sigh.

For a moment, Usther just looked at them there. Her closest minion and her only pet. 'Don't leave, be safe, look after each other,' she whispered. Then she followed Smythe out the door, feeling that her heart was tearing out of her chest and being left behind. When the door closed behind them, there was a ripple of icy energy as the curses and wards took effect. It was something of a comfort that even untriggered, the wards were so powerful they stung.

The corridor outside their room was oddly devoid of denizens compared to the bustle of earlier. No fungal minions marched past, no denizens hurried about their tasks. Usther might have suspected Mykol of ordering everyone out of sight, if not for when they turned the corner. In a room with the door still open, two denizens spoke in low voices. They sat on two beds identical to the ones Smythe and Usther had been offered. She was surprised to see two denizens who'd had nothing to do with each other before so comfortable in each other's presence.

'Etherea,' Usther said. 'Passacath. Do you have a moment?'

Their chatter immediately stopped. Passacath, a man with long locs beaded with knucklebones, nodded. 'Sure,' he said. His voice was deep and mellow.

Etherea smiled. She was a little older than Usther, and Usther had had a terrible crush on her when she'd first arrived in the town as a teenager loose amongst practitioners her own age for the first time. Her skin had leeched entirely white instead of becoming ashen and grey the way most practitioners' did. And her eyes were a shocking blood red, likely the result of additional sight rituals beyond the traditional darksight. 'It's good to see you,' she said. 'Where're your shadows?' She gestured for her to sit on the bed beside her.

Usther's cheeks heated. She tucked a braid behind her ear. 'Oh, I don't actually take them *everywhere,*' Usther said, which was true as of today. 'They're having a rest.' She sat beside Etherea, suddenly feeling self-conscious. While travelling, she'd not been able to check her appearance in a mirror. Her robes were probably very dusty. And was her kohl smudged? She straightened her skirts and resisted the urge to inspect them. 'How are you liking your new lodgings?'

'Well enough,' said Etherea. 'Though I'm looking forward to getting my own room. No offense, Passacath.'

'None taken. You snore loud enough to wake the dead. Literally! I saw a spirit jump out of a passing minion when you exhaled.'

Etherea's smile became forced. 'There's no need to exaggerate.'

Passacath raised his eyebrows. 'Who's exaggerating? I had to dispel it before the scream could wake anyone.'

Etherea glared at Passacath. Passacath's smile took on a snarling edge.

'Uh...I hope you don't mind the intrusion,' said Smythe. 'We're just trying to—we're looking—we're new here.'

The denizens broke their stare. Passacath frowned at Smythe. 'Who are you?' he asked. 'I don't recognise you from around town.'

'Oh! Chandrian Smythe, historian.' He offered Passacath his hand. 'Pleased to meet you.'

Oh no.

Passacath's expression turned blank. He shook Smythe's hand limply, expression unreadable.

'Smythe?' Etherea leaned forward, fingers-steepling. Her red eyes gleamed. 'Surely not the same Smythe who was exiled?'

'Uh. Well...'

'The Smythe who attacked the town?'

Smythe rubbed the back of his neck. 'That isn't quite how—'

'The one who killed the Lich?'

Smythe's shoulders slumped. He leaned his back against the door, as if he could no longer bear to hold himself up.

'That's the one,' said Usther. 'But he's assisting me right now.'

Etherea cackled and clapped her hands together. 'Wonderful! So you really have been living alone in the crypt this whole time?'

Smythe smiled like his teeth hurt. 'Afraid so.'

'Passacath, you've heard of him, right? I don't know if you were here before.'

'I've heard of him,' said Passacath quietly.

Etherea pressed on, 'Most upstart practitioners have a go at taking over the town but this kid—no necromantic background, a historian, if you'll believe it—damn well nearly does it. Absolutely wild stuff. Was it difficult?' she asked Smythe. She fiddled with the thick red ribbon tied around her wrist. Like the other denizens here, she and Passccath both wore one.

Smythe took off his glasses and wiped them on his shirt hem. 'I'd...rather not discuss it, really.'

'That's a no, then!' Etherea nearly howled in delight, rocking in her seat.

'He nearly killed you,' said Usther. 'Aren't you upset?'

Etherea shrugged. 'Well, he didn't. And it was a long time ago. It's not like he's going around destroying necromantic settlements now.' This last she said almost too casually, not meeting anyone's eyes.

Usher frowned and studied her more closely. That aversion wasn't fear, was it?

Was it...

Could it be hope?

Passacath stretched his arms up and put them behind his head, leaning back against the wall. Oddly casual himself. 'Did my lord and lady send you?' he asked.

Etherea's red gaze turned on Usther. There was nothing casual about that stare.

'No,' said Usther. 'They didn't.'

'I hope you don't mind the intrusion?' asked Smythe.

There was something almost studied about their laughter. 'No, no, not at all.'

'We could close the door...' Usther ventured, looking between the two.

Etherea shrugged.

Usther's gaze swept the room. There didn't *seem* to be any fungi in here...

She shut the door. Etherea's shoulders slumped. Passacath lips formed a tight line.

'What are you doing here?' Etherea asked in a tight whisper. Her entire countenance changed. 'Everyone knows you're close with the council.'

If only *that* were true. Usther was friends with one of the founding members' daughter, but a fat lot of good that had done her.

Just thinking that made her feel guilty, actually. She wouldn't trade Ree for any amount of power. Not...not these days, anyway.

'I was investigating the crimson fungi,' Usther said. 'I didn't expect to find a whole other town down here, with a King and Queen, no less.'

'Does Igneus know you're here?' she asked. 'Or Kylath?'

Usther's eyes narrowed. Why those council members in particular? She shook her head. 'Arthura sent me. I doubt the council is even aware. I'm not as close with them as you think.'

Etherea stood up and strode to the door. She opened and peered outside, tension written into the hard lines of her shoulders. Then she closed it. 'We're not all here by choice,' Etherea said.

'So I've gathered.'

'Passacath was just fishing in this part of the crypt when the fungal minions took him. There was nothing he could do; they're immune to necromancy.' Passacath bowed his head while she spoke, shrinking in on himself. 'I was tricked into this part of the crypt. I went on Tarantur's damn field trip. When Celia appeared, I've never seen him look more afraid...and he *knew* she was coming.'

Tarantur? She thought of the last town meeting and Tarantur's vague promises of power and favour.

Would a council member betray the town he'd helped found? Had he even had a choice?

She thought of his smug announcement, the way he'd puffed himself up when so many denizens crowded around him to ask more.

He hadn't seemed like a man under duress.

'What do you mean he *knew* she was coming?' she asked, though she feared she already knew the answer.

'I mean exactly what I said. He lured us out here on purpose. The siblings love him; credit him with establishing their kingdom.'

'Well, why don't you leave?' said Usther. 'Go back to town, tell the rest of the council!'

'Some have tried,' Etherea said darkly. 'The Many-That-Hungers sees everything. There's nowhere in this crypt we can go that it won't notice. It is too spread out.' She shook her head. 'I heard Mazerin say it'll reach Tombtown next month, if it keeps getting fed.'

'Fed?' asked Smythe.

Etherea stared at him for a long moment, her lips pressing into a thin line, before she pulled at the ribbon wrapped around her wrist, revealing a long, thin cut, barely healed. She fumbled to put it back on.

Smythe stepped forward to help. She flinched and he stopped, uncertain, but she held out her arm. Carefully, he tied it into a loose bow.

'Dead flesh and living blood,' Usther whispered.

Etherea nodded. 'It prefers minions to corpses. I don't know why, except that it lets them control them. That's one reason they need us; we raise the dead for it to eat.'

'A fungus that feeds on necromancy,' Smythe mused. He glanced at Usther. 'Maybe it lets it access the memories. Our host seemed quite keen on that.'

Cataloguing, he'd said.

'He was particularly interested in us,' said Usther. 'Do you know why?'

Etherea shook her head. 'No-one else is called "honoured guest". We're all servants. You have more freedom than we do, too. There are others who might know more, but...'

'But?'

Etherea smoothed her robes with shaking hands as she sat down. 'Their favourite servants are loyal. They are taken into their confidence, but I can't see them betraying them.'

'Who?' asked Smythe.

Etherea bit her lip. 'Symphona. Tarantur. And Ellenil.'

The world spun. Usther braced herself against the wall, thinking hard. Symphona was no surprise. It was clear what she was getting out of loyalty to them. A new Tombtown where she was not only welcome, but empowered.

Tarantur was a council member. How long had he been working for Mykol and Celia? What did it mean, that one of the town's most powerful practitioners had not only sided with these invaders, but was a double-agent against the town he'd helped found?

But it was Ellenil that gave her the most pause. Little Ellenil, shrieking and laughing when the rat minion's whiskers tickled their face. Little Ellenil, balancing along a sarcophagus and trying to jump to the next one.

Little Ellenil, with a red ribbon at their wrist.

Finally, Passacath spoke. His voice was a rasping whisper. 'Is it true?' he asked. 'Are you really him? Smythe Townslayer?'

She couldn't quite read Smythe's expression. Was that shock? Hurt? Pride?

'You...' He cleared his throat. 'You could say that.'

Passacath looked up for the first time, meeting Smythe's surprised gaze. 'Good,' he said. 'Good.'

He seemed relieved.

And wasn't that a terrifying thought.

CHAPTER TWENTY-TWO

Ree

They followed Ellenil down more stark white corridors. These held doors; not black ones, like the ones the paladins had kicked in, but white doors that almost completely blended in with the walls. Patches of crimson fungi were everywhere, clinging to the walls, the ceiling, clustered at the foot of a door, but not in the same terrifying mass they'd seen in the room with the undead queen.

They passed denizens, too—necromancers Ree recognised from town, walking with heads lowered and purposeful speed..

'More necros?' Tabris muttered. 'Just how many are there?'

Ree waved away their question. 'Ellenil, what are you doing out here? What is this place?'

Ellenil didn't glance back, their face obscured by their lace hood. 'The lord and lady will answer all of your questions,' they said.

A flash of red. A pack of fungal minions headed toward them.

'You know what? No.' There was a sound of steel on leather as Tabris drew their sickles. 'Those things nearly punched a hole through Sef. Give us some answers, kid.'

Ellenil stopped. They waved to the distant fungal minions, who paused. Persephone frowned to see it. She still had not drawn her spear, instead cradling her injured arm.

'The Lord and Lady request only the presence of Reanima,' said Ellenil. 'You witchkillers are not required. You may attend, or you may go back the way you came. Those are the only options.'

'Reanima?' Persephone asked quietly. Andomerys snorted.

'No,' said Tabris. 'I'm not in the habit of taking orders from necros.'
They took a half-step back, falling into a fighting stance.

The tunnel suddenly felt very cold. Power emanated from Ellenil.

Andomerys slapped Tabris in the back of the head.

'Ow!'

'That's enough,' she said. 'This is the way your gods were sending you,
right? Then find some fucking manners.'

Tabris gritted their teeth as if to argue.

'Tab,' Persephone said wearily.

They lowered their sickles. 'Fine.'

Ellenil's expression flickered. Ree wondered if they, too, were surprised
by Tabris' desire for violence. Ree had surely been not much older than
Ellenil when she'd ended up on the wrong end of an adventurer's knife. And
Ellenil, like Ree, would have grown up with stories of the upworld, but not
witnessed it themself. Witchkillers who hunted good honest practitioners,
and the greedy adventurers who sometimes found the crypt and tried to
take its treasures for themselves.

But Ellenil was controlled. More controlled than Ree was at that age.
Perhaps being a practitioner did that; Ree, at least, had never had to engage
in necromancer politics.

'I don't think they'll hurt you if you don't hurt them,' said Ree quietly as
they resumed their walk.

Ellenil glanced at Ree, a flash of dark eyes in a pale face. 'I'm not
worried about them,' they said. There was a bleakness to their tone that
made Ree shudder.

The fungal minions parted to let them pass, their unseeing eyes fixed on
their faces. Persephone kept a hand on Tabris' elbow. Larry hugged close to
Andomerys, who for once didn't protest.

'Where did all this come from?' Ree asked. 'It's...it's like it's replaced a
whole section of the crypt.'

'My lord and my lady are very resourceful,' was all Ellenil replied.

Ree narrowed her eyes. She didn't know Ellenil especially well, but
Tombtown children were known neither for their manners nor for their
subservience. She found this courtly behaviour extremely odd.

Ahead at a crossroads, a lady in white and a woman with cherry blossom-pink hair bid farewell. Ree frowned as the pink-haired woman retreated. Surely that couldn't be...?

The woman in white greeted them with arms spread. Her hair was the colour of fresh blood, her eyes a shocking fuschia pink. Her warm brown skin was perfectly smooth and unblemished, her smile perfectly even and white. 'Honoured guests,' she said. 'We've been waiting for you for so long!' Her voice was almost girlish with excitement, save for the oddly deliberate pace of her speech.

Ree stared at her uneasily, as one might stare at a snake about to strike. She was the most beautiful woman Ree had ever seen. In Ree's experience, beautiful people were more prone to cruelty. Usther herself was testament to that.

But perhaps she was being unfair. After all, Persephone was also extremely beautiful and seemed thoughtful. And Usther might be cruel at times, but she could also be very kind.

'I don't know you,' Ree said. She didn't keep the guardedness out of her tone. This whole situation was incredibly strange.

'But I know you,' said Celia. 'And I owe you a great deal. And in return for that debt, your friends will not be killed for their crimes.' Her smile never faltered.

Ree went cold. She looked back at her companions. 'What crimes?'

Tabris hefted their weapons again. 'You know what? Fuck this!' They leapt at Celia, knocking Ree aside.

Celia didn't so much as blink. Red tendrils burst from the walls on all sides, catching Tabris in the air. They wrapped around their throat, their arms, their legs constricting so tightly that Tabris started to choke.

Persephone unleashed a blast of healing light, burning the tendrils to a crisp, but more came. Andomerys seized Ree by the elbow and pulled her aside. Together, they sheltered a cowering Larry with their bodies.

Tabris hit the ground and swiped at Celia, who moved aside so quickly Ree didn't even *see* her move. It was as if she had teleported, still with that even smile fixed on her face, as if this was just more pleasant conversation.

Persephone turned on Celia as red tendrils lashed Tabris up to the ceiling again, jabbing out with her spear more quickly than Ree had thought she could move. Celia again flickered out of the way, turning aside the spear with a gentle push of her hand and catching Persephone by the throat.

'My patience only runs so far,' she said. And then in a great sucking rush, more tendrils shot out, criss-crossing the room. Mushrooms bloomed from them and covered the struggling paladins, rising up in a great roiling wave of red with the horrible sliding sound of flesh on flesh. It covered their legs, their torsos, their faces. Their cries were choked by mouthfuls of fungi. The paladins struggled beneath the mounds, then went still.

The mushrooms died away until there were only the same small, innocuous clusters of fungi there had been originally. There was no sign of the paladins at all.

Ree turned her face into Andomerys' shoulder, choking on a sob. It was too quick to properly process. They were just...gone?

'The Many-That-Hungers is not to be trifled with,' said Celia. 'You, healer. You also burned it. Don't forget that it suffers your survival only at my pleasure.'

'I understand,' said Andomerys. She gently nudged Ree aside and bowed stiffly. Ree mimicked her, feeling like the world was falling apart.

Tabris and Persephone were just...gone.

And then a feeling came over her she had only experienced once before. Of the earth shifting beneath her feet even as she stood perfectly still. Of the nausea rising up as she realised the world she had known was gone.

CHAPTER TWENTY-THREE

Usther

Usther stared at the black door guarded by necromancers, arms crossed and tapping her lip. It was the only such door she could find that was guarded by people and not by fungal minions. Even the room where the Many-That-Hungers fed on the remains of the ancient queen was guarded by fungal minions.

That meant this room was something different. Something special. Perhaps something she could use to gain leverage over Mykol, Celia, and their horrifying fungi.

Etherea had warned her she wouldn't be able to get in. That nobody went in except the lord and lady themselves. Usther wasn't so convinced.

'Do you know how to mind-snare? On purpose?' she asked Smythe, straightening the sleeves of her black dress.

Smythe shrugged. 'Not properly. I've been focused on soul summoning and wards. Not much headspace to spare for curses.'

Usther nodded. 'You caught me in one accidentally, or so you claimed, when I first came to visit you.'

Smythe frowned and nodded.

'You're strong enough that I'm not sure someone could break your snare. Let me tell you how to do it properly.'

She talked him through the act of catching another's eyes and trapping them in a box made of your own will. The words to be held in your mind to keep it fixed. The shapes to be envisioned that acted as a maze for the other mind.

Smythe listened intently, asking only a few incisive questions, before nodding. 'I think I can do that.'

Usther considered the guards. She didn't know them personally, but she'd seen them around town. A denizen with wavy dark blue hair and jewel-brown skin. Another so pale and dry-skinned he looked like he'd been powdered with chalk. They were talking easily, leaning against the walls to either side of the door. The pale one guffawed at something the other said, making them blush.

She considered asking Smythe to practise on her, but she didn't want to give either the necromancers or the Many any warning. She shoved him toward the necromancers. 'Go do it, then!'

She fell into step behind him. The necromancers straightened as they approached, looking nervous.

'Uh, hi,' said the pale one.

'Hello,' said Smythe.

The one with blue hair bowed and elbowed their companion, who bowed as well. 'Honoured guests,' they said. 'You aren't allowed in this room, by order of my lord and my lady.'

'Are you sure?' asked Smythe.

'Yeah,' said the pale one. He rubbed his hands nervously and white dust fell off him—he actually *was* dusted with chalk.

They didn't seem to be the sharpest denizens she'd ever met...and were none too sure of themselves. Perhaps she could use that to her advantage.

'Don't be ridiculous,' she snapped. She drew herself up and let her eyes flash; she was taller than both of these denizens. '*Mykol* and *Celia* gave us freedom to explore wherever we choose. You are directly working against their order.' She places special emphasis on their names, since everyone seemed to be too submissive to use them.

'We are?' said the one with blue hair.

'We're not! They were very specific!' said the pale one. 'I'm sorry but you'll have to go somewhere else.'

Usther noted the way he twisted his hands as he said it. 'Well,' she said. 'I suppose I'll have to let Mykol know that you obstructed us in our work.'

'Obstructed?'

'Work?'

Usther shrugged as regretfully as she could. 'There's no other option.'

The blue-haired denizen leaned toward their companion. 'Greef, maybe we should just—'

'No!' Greef said sharply. 'Better to get in trouble for following an order than ignoring one.'

The blue-haired denizen nodded, then peered closely at Smythe. 'Are you Smythe Townslayer?'

'I'm afraid I am,' he said. He drummed his fingers below his eyes, drawing the denizens' attention. The air became bitingly cold. Usther shielded her face against a blast of chill wind; frost rimed the front of her dress. The necromancers both froze, slack-jawed, and stared at Smythe as the mind-snare went into effect, easily over-powering whatever mental shields and wards they'd placed on themselves.

'Morrin's *fucking* teeth,' she muttered. 'Show some restraint!'

'Usther!' Smythe flailed toward her without turning his head. His hand brushed her face; she scoffed and slapped it away.

'Stop it!'

'I think I've got them. They're struggling. *Really* struggling,' he said. 'I don't think I'll have them for long.'

Well, she'd best get going then. The idea of leaving Smythe behind did *not* appeal, but she didn't have any other options. 'Just don't look away.'

'What?' Smythe glanced at her and the denizens started to blink and wake, their expressions morphing into confusion.

'Don't look away!' she snapped.

'Right! Sorry.' He caught them again, his will locking them back down immediately.

Gods, that was terrifying.

She pushed past them to try the door. It was locked. She looked at the necromancers, wondering if perhaps one held the key, but she couldn't see Mykol or Celia trusting them with something that important. After all, Etherea had made it clear which denizens held their confidence, and these two were not the ones.

She unwrapped a rubbery rope of treated intestine from her waist. '*Lithz kahz,*' she said, and it became a rope of shadow edged with red light, hovering above her hands. She moved her hands through the air, directing it. It shot at the lock and wriggled in, stretching itself until it was long and thin. The handle jiggled, but when she tried it, it was still locked fast.

'Oh to hell with it,' she said. She clenched her fists and drew them apart. The lock cracked as the intestine expanded inside it. When she tried it again, with a little push from her shoulder, it opened. The intestine wrapped itself neatly around her waist again and went still, nothing more than a hideously textured belt.

The door swung open, revealing another stark white room with a single bed and three occupants, two of whom appeared to be bound up to the neck by a thick coating of crimson fungi.

The man on the bed sat up. An older man, appearing in his fifties, though she knew he was much older. Dark-skinned but with ice-chip grey eyes. He wore a threadbare brown cassock and his dark curls were touched with white at the temples. 'Usther?' said Emberlon. 'Don't tell me you're wrapped up in this as well.'

He looked...sad. He always did. But his cheeks were unusually gaunt and he was so bony, she could see the points of his shoulders through his cassock. A red ribbon hung filthy and ragged from his wrist.

'I...Emberlon?' Usther hesitated in the doorway. 'Why are you here? Why did they lock you up?'

'All in good time,' said Emberlon. 'Will you help me up? I'm afraid I can't stand.'

Usther hurried to do so, her thoughts spinning. What possible reason could there be to keep Emberlon of all people under locked guard? Everyone knew he could barely raise a rat. He was a librarian, for gods' sake!

When she put her arm under his shoulder, he lifted far, far too easily. Usther was hardly stocky herself, but she was pretty sure a man of his age ought to weigh more than a heavy blanket.

'Hello,' said one of the mushroomed people. Usther looked at them again; their skin was flush and clear, with not a hint of shadow about their eyes. One was a person with bright green hair and a smirk she instantly hated. The other was silver-haired and beautiful, in a broad, healthy way, and watched her with weighing eyes.

'I don't have time to save upworlders, even if I knew how to get those mushrooms off of you,' said Usther. 'You're on your own.'

She headed for the door, supporting Emberlon.

'Necros,' said the green-haired person darkly.

'If you see Ree, tell her we found Emberlon,' said the woman.

Usther stopped and looked back. 'How do you know Ree?'

'We were travelling together.' The woman struggled against the mushrooms restraining her, but seemed unable to make any impact. 'She was looking for her friend, we were looking for trouble.'

'We found it,' added her companion.

Usther let Emberlon rest against the doorway for a moment. 'Do you know these people?'

'Not at all,' said Emberlon. 'They just arrived. Prisoners like me.'

'Let us out,' said the woman again. Her voice was low and calm. 'We can help.'

'Oh, hello Emberlon!' Smythe said, his cheery voice strained. 'Lovely to see you again if not under these...ah...circumstances...' he trailed off. Sweat poured down his face and soaked through his copper-buttoned coat. Usther ignored him.

'They'll be here soon,' said Emberlon. He leaned against the doorway and closed his eyes. 'They see too much.'

'Quite slippery, these two,' said Smythe conversationally. 'Like...their minds...are oiled...'

Usther approached the trapped figures. 'Who are you?'

'My name is Persephone Owl-and-Spear of Paladur-Ez,' said the silver-haired woman.

Usther was used to the outrageous titles of the denizens, but upworlders tended to use family names instead. She frowned as the word tickled her memory, bringing things up from a long time ago. 'You're paladins.' Her lip curled as she said the word.

Persephone inclined her head, watching Usther for her reaction.

'Usther,' Emberlon said pleadingly, his voice weak.

'This is really quite—I don't think I can—!'

Even if she wanted to set them free, how would she remove the fungi? It was immune to necromancy. Was she supposed to scoop it off with her hands?

As if she could read her mind, Persephone said, 'Just tell your friend we found him.'

The message infuriated her. This paladin thought Ree would come storming into the heart of this nightmare kingdom to try and rescue them. She was probably right. Better not to tell her, then.

She opened her mouth to lie, but instead she said, 'Smythe, take Emberlon back to our room. As quickly as you can.'

'What? I'm not—I can't—'

The necromancers guarding the door groaned. She glanced at them; they were clutching their heads, swaying on the spot. They'd get their bearings soon enough.

'Go!' she said, and shunted Emberlon into his surprised arms. She closed the door behind her and started to search the room. It was so barren...there was little more than the bed and a used chamberpot in the corner. She couldn't bring herself to try the chamberpot, so she took the pillow and ripped it open, sending feathers flying across the room.

Persephone said, 'What're you—?'

'Shut up,' Usther snapped.

Shouts from outside. Smythe was powerful enough to protect Emberlon. They would make it back.

She wrapped the pillow case around her hands. It was so ridiculously soft. Right now, she'd rather it was as coarse as burlap. Anything to dull the sensation of what she was about to attempt.

She started to scrape the fungi from Persephone, aiming around the middle, where she hoped the hands would be. The mushrooms ripped away, some of them lighting up, some even emitting a tiny, barely perceptible squeak that made her toes curl. She gritted her teeth and kept working.

'Me as well!' the green-haired one said. They began struggling against their fungal bindings.

'I'm working as quickly as I can!' she said. 'You'd better not try to stab me for it, either.'

'Wouldn't dream of it,' Persephone said firmly. 'One moment, Tabris.'

The fungi was trying to plug the gaps, red tendrils spreading across the holes Usther made, but it moved lazily and without the fast, decided purpose it had when Mykol was nearby. The paladin got one gauntleted fist free.

'*Isthera,*' she said, and her voice sounded like clear bells. Sunlight formed on her palm. She clenched her fist.

The fungi over her was subsumed in silver moonlight and crumbled to ash. She stumbled free and repeated the gesture. Her companion hit the ground with a thump and the jangle of metal.

And suddenly Usther was alone in a small cell with two paladins. Persephone rolled her shoulders. Her companion, Tabris, flexed their hands and pressed fist into palm. She was unprepared for how *large* they were. She had thought the mounds binding them were mostly mushroom, but looking at them now, they were both taller and broader than she was ready for. She felt like Persephone could lift her one-handed and not break a sweat.

Which was not, Usther was surprised to find, an unattractive trait in a woman. If that woman wasn't a festering *paladin.*

That paladin clenched and raised her fist. Usther flinched back, hands crooking into a casting shape, only for the woman to press her fist to her chest and bow. 'Thank you,' Persephone said.

After a moment, the other paladin repeated the gesture.

Usther hardly knew what to make of any of this. She didn't know why she'd even *done* it, except that the thought of leaving anyone in a pile of crimson fungi like the old undead queen was utterly repulsive to her.

She tried to say something scathing but for once the words wouldn't come.

Outside, there were voices and shuffling feet. The paladins picked their weapons up off the floor and moved to either side of the door. Usther had no idea whether that was a sensible thing to do. Everything that was happening right now seemed utterly beyond her.

She'd broken the lock and slightly cracked the door to get in here. Any close examination would quickly reveal that. And there was nowhere from here that they could run.

Could she mind-snare another necromancer? Perhaps, if they were particularly weak-willed. She'd just never had the kind of power that someone like Smythe had. She was always second-guessing herself, always uncertain.

Always regretting.

Footsteps receding, and then quiet.

The paladins nodded to each other. Tabris cracked the door open, then drew it closed again.

'Nobody there,' they said. 'They must not realise you broke in.'

'Or they have more pressing concerns,' she said, her stomach sinking. Why had she stayed to release these witchkillers when Emberlon needed her protection? She still couldn't get her head around the idea that they'd seen fit to have him under locked guard.

'Well,' said Tabris. 'I guess we know what the "great evil" we were sent to find is?'

'We do,' said Persephone. She frowned at Usther.

Usther took a half-step back, rage and panic making her blood pound. 'You *cannot* be serious—'

'The fungi,' she interrupted. 'The woman, Celia.'

Usther lowered her hands. She hadn't even realised she'd gotten them ready to cast. 'She has a brother just as worrying,' she said. 'You know Ree?'

'We've been travelling together,' Persephone confirmed again.

'Then—' she couldn't believe she was asking this. 'Then maybe you can help save our friend. Emberlon. Mykol and Celia want him; I have no idea why.'

And they wanted her. And Smythe and Ree. A particular trio that raised more questions than it answered.

Tabris looked to Persephone. 'We should find the source of the fungi. Ree said it was new.'

Persephone nodded and closed her eyes, breathing out through her nose. A wrinkle appeared between her eyebrows, as if she had a headache going on. 'We should,' she said at length. 'You go. Look around. We'll scry each other when we get the chance.'

'You can't be serious,' said Tabris.

'I'm completely serious. We're paired up for a reason. Two can go where one cannot.'

'Don't quote Ez-Thandar at us,' Tabris said disgustedly. They rolled their eyes at the ceiling. 'Ah. Fine! We'll go. Find the others if you can. We can't let the world's only beastmage fall to darkness.'

We? Us? Was this green-haired paladin plural?

Persephone nodded and Tabris swiftly left, the heavy clank of their bootsteps fading into the distance.

Usther didn't know what to say. Smythe and Emberlon were gone, Ree was in unknown danger, and Usther was left alone with a woman with heavier armour than she had known existed. She wanted to say something commanding, but what came out was, '"Fall into darkness"?'

Persephone gave a pained smile. 'Paladin-speak for "get herself killed".'

Usther shook herself. There were things to do. She opened the door. 'My friends went this way,' she said. 'If you see Mykol or Celia, run the other way. Somehow I doubt our status as 'honoured guests' is going to last much longer.'

'After you,' said Persephone, courtly as a knight.

Usther made a face and ran out into the corridor. Persephone stomped along behind her, surprisingly swift for one so heavy. Usther glanced at her; she had her spear slung over her shoulder as casually as a satchel.

When they hit the corridor, there was nobody around. The bustle and rush of earlier was gone. It was almost eerily quiet.

She led Persephone down the corridor, taking lefts and rights as she wove her way back to their room. They should have run into Emberlon and Smythe by now, shouldn't they? Or anyone at all? Emberlon had been incredibly slow, he couldn't possibly have moved that quickly.

Her anxiety grew as she approached their room. The wards lay dormant and broken and she choked back a sob. When she opened it, Mykol sat on her bed, his legs crossed. He had a teacup and saucer in his hands.

He smiled. 'Usther.'

The world spun. Misery and Dichotomy were not here. Smythe and Emberlon were not here. She choked out the words, 'Where are they?' Persephone hovered behind her, tense but not leaping to the attack.

Mykol took a sip from his teacup.

CHAPTER TWENTY-FOUR

Ree

Celia led them down the corridors toward a set of double-doors. 'You'll find us gracious hosts,' said Celia. 'We have a kingdom any ruler would be proud of. And you...you are our most honoured guest.'

Ree said nothing, watching Ellenil. The young practitioner followed their Lady with their head bowed. Ree thought perhaps they would give her some signal, some sign that they wanted to escape this, but they seemed every bit the obedient servant.

Celia placed a hand on the door and then paused. Her head cocked, as if listening to something far away. Her dark lips pursed. 'No,' she said and turned. Her skirts swirled, briefly flashing her perfectly smooth thighs in what Ree thought was a deliberate fashion. Ree, who could acknowledge beauty without feeling drawn to it, was unmoved.

'There's been a change of plans,' Celia continued. 'Ellenil, show them to the grand suite.' She looked not at Ellenil, but at Ree, her fuschia eyes boring into her so strongly Ree felt almost mind-snared. 'It's finally time for the welcome feast.'

Celia waved them away, and disappeared through the double doors without a backwards glance.

Ree immediately turned to Ellenil. 'What's happening? Who was that? What happened to our companions?'

Ellenil didn't look at her, just gestured and strode away at a fast pace. 'Lady Celia is a master of this kingdom. You are her honoured guests. And I don't know what happened to your friends.' They paused. 'Though they're probably dead.' The words were delivered flatly, devoid of emotion, but they rocked Ree to her core.

She clasped shaking hands in front of her, her thoughts spinning. She could still picture the fungi rising up, their tendrils strangling Tabris, then both of them being melted down to nothing. Consumed.

They weren't her friends. They were barely her allies. They'd terrified her on first meeting. But she didn't wish them dead, and now they were.

Morrin guide their souls, Ree thought. *Or...I suppose they'd prefer Allariel and the Rootfather.* She hoped Morrin wouldn't mind passing along the prayer.

Dead...

'Larry,' she said. 'Stay close. I don't like—Larry?' She spun. The masterless minion was nowhere to be seen. Ree went cold. 'Andomerys—'

'I don't know.' She shook her head.

Ellenil made a sound in their throat that sounded frustrated. 'If you will come with me—' they said tensely.

'We have to find Larry,' Ree said. 'He can't just—just run around here on his own!' He'd get eaten by the fungi. Or he'd offend Celia and she'd order him to be executed, or whatever it was that ladies did.

Ellenil's hand went to their chest, fidgeting with an amulet.

Ree spun on her heels and started walking back the way they'd come. She couldn't let Larry wander here. She wasn't losing anyone else.

'Stop.'

A blast of cold air from behind. When Ree looked back, Ellenil was spinning their amulet in their hand. It caught the light so strangely...

Her amulet burned cold against her chest. 'Festering rats,' Ree breathed. She wrenched her eyes away. Without her amulet, Ellenil would surely have caught her. It was some kind of modified mind-snare.

And Andomerys stared directly at them, unmoving. Ree grabbed her arm and made to pull her away.

'I'll knock her out,' Ellenil said. 'You know I can do it. And then you'll be another friend down. I don't think you want that.'

Ree averted her eyes, staring at Ellenil's feet. 'Why are you doing this?' Her voice was hoarse. 'We didn't come here to hurt anyone. We're just looking for Emberlon.'

'I am my masters' servant,' said Ellenil coldly. 'Blame the wielder, not the weapon.' They exhaled through their nose, like they were bored of this.

'Now follow me. Lady Celia has invited you to a feast. And wouldn't that be so much nicer than the alternative?' There was a sneer in Ellenil's voice. Genuine dislike. Genuine pleasure in what they were doing. Ree couldn't look at their face but she could *hear* it.

'I'll do whatever you want.'

'You will.'

What Ellenil wanted was to take them to a large white suite behind a black door, which Ree was beginning to recognise as a rarity among the swathes of white doors they passed. This opened onto a large suite with three interconnected rooms and what looked like a washroom behind. It was lavishly furnished with intricate old rugs and hanging tapestries. It was the kind of finery Ree had rarely seen, except rolled up as the tribute to long dead kings. There was some kind of long chair with embroidered cushions and a blanket folded on the back that Ree found particularly unnerving. Were you supposed to sit on it or sleep on it?

'Your outfits have been prepared,' Ellenil said. 'Clean yourselves up. You have the rest of the day.' They dropped their amulet and shut the door. Ree immediately pressed her ear to it. She couldn't hear them walking away—they must be standing guard outside.

'Ree?' Andomerys said groggily.

Ree glanced at her. She looked very out of sorts, her grimace far deeper than usual as she rubbed her face. 'You were mind-snared.'

'That doesn't sound like me.'

'I know.'

Andomerys was one of the most powerful mages Ree had ever heard of. It was hard to snare someone who had that much power to bring to bear against you. 'Ellenil had some kind of amulet that enhanced their snare.'

Andomerys pulled a face. 'I really do hate kids.'

'They're eighteen. Did you hate me when I was eighteen?'

'Do you really want me to answer that?'

A loud sigh drifted into the room. Ree startled and looked around. Surely it couldn't be...

A woman with a bandaged face hovered at a bedside in one of the other rooms. It took her a second to realise that this was, in fact, Misery—though Misery was wearing an unfamiliar shirt, trousers, and even boots over her rags. Ree hurried forward and took the arm of the house-minion. 'What are you doing here? Where's—' She looked down at the figure sprawled unconscious on the bed, then released Misery and backed up so fast she hit the doorframe.

Because curled up on the bed was not Misery's sarcastic mistress.

Heart-pounding, Ree hissed, 'Get away from him!' She motioned for Misery to follow her out of the room.

Misery turned her head to one side, mouth lolling and revealing the black void of her mouth. She looked down at Smythe again and didn't leave.

'Misery!'

Andomerys appeared at her shoulder. 'What's all—oh.' She took in the figure on the bed then put her head in her hand. 'I hate this place.'

Ree motioned sharply to Misery again, but Ree had no power to command her and Misery seemed to prefer where she was.

'Isn't that Usther's houseminion?' said Andomerys quietly. She paused. 'And cat?'

Cat?

Ree forced herself to look at the figure on the bed, with his curly hair and glasses askew. Curled up under his chin and against his chest was a familiar black-and-white cat.

'Where's Usther?' she whispered. She couldn't fathom what Misery and Dichotomy would be doing out of the house without her. She'd never leave them alone, certainly not in a place like this. Her stomach kicked anxiously; perhaps Smythe had done something to her. But, if so, then why would Misery and Dichotomy watch over him?

At her master's name, Misery immediately started moaning. She hurried to Ree, clutching at her robes and babbling in the grunts and gargles of a minion.

'I don't know where she is! Misery, shhh, I don't know! You're going to wake—'

Smythe stirred on the bed. First he stretched, dislodging the sleeping Dichotomy, then he sat bolt upright. His eyes widened with alarm; the temperature in the room plunged. 'Misery, are you—!' He stopped, panting hard as he took in the scene. 'Oh. Uh. H-hello.' He scooted to the back of the bed, putting his back to the wall. He stared at the floor.

He'd aged. Not that that should be a surprise. Where Ree had become plump and strong, Smythe had wasted. He was thinner, sharper. Greyer. Sadder.

Good.

Dichotomy bit his arm, making him yelp, then climbed into his lap and curled up again. He pet her absently. 'So, they got you too?' he said. 'She—Usther—was afraid of that.'

Ree wanted to demand where Usther was, wanted to hiss how *dare* he touch her cat, but something about his skittish demeanour and the cat and minions' clear acceptance of him deflated her rage and she could find no words at all.

Andomerys leaned against the doorframe. '"They" being that woman Celia?'

Smythe nodded. 'Well, her brother, actually. Though honestly they seem to form rather a unit. They took Emberlon—'

'Emberlon?' Andomerys said breathlessly.

'We'd only just found him. They had him...locked up, I suppose. Two denizens were guarding him. He was so weak...' Smythe shook his head. 'I was quite planning to summon every spirit out of every damn one of their minions, but those crimson fungi grabbed Misery and Dichotomy and Mykol told me that if I didn't comply, they'd infest them just like the minions we've seen about.' He shook his head. 'What could I do? He'd smashed straight through the wards we set on our room, and I put everything I had into those. And the damn mushrooms are unkillable by necromantic means. I said I'd do whatever they wanted. Then something hit me in the back of the head and...well, you can surmise the rest.'

'About *Emberlon,*' Andomerys said firmly.

'I don't know. I assume they've taken him back to his cell—though they'll have a repair job on their hands, as Usther really did a marvellous job destroying the lock. But Andomerys, he wasn't well at all. I don't know what they're doing to him, but he looked one foot in the grave already, and he struggled to walk. Weakness, I think. I don't know from what.'

The temperature in the room, which had plunged during Smythe's panicked awakening, now raised a few degrees so quickly that Ree began to sweat. 'Andomerys,' Ree said warningly.

Andomerys' fist was clenched. Her skin took on a faint haze, as if she was illuminated from within. Misery cried out and scrambled away, pulling at Smythe as if begging for defence. He sheltered her with his arms, a red glow suffusing him in response. 'Andomerys, please,' he said quietly.

Her nostrils flared, but she nodded tightly. The glow subsided.

'I'm sorry,' Andomerys said stiffly to Misery.

Misery hid her face in Smythe's shoulder.

Ree had no idea what to do with this sight. She only knew she hated it.

Smythe gave Misery a reassuring pat and nudged her away. Misery went to stand in the corner, as she always did when she wanted the comfort of isolation. That, at least, was familiar.

'Usther stayed behind,' Smythe said. 'At the cell. There were other people in there—I don't know who, I didn't recognise them—and she said to get Emberlon to our room. To safety.'

Andomerys crossed her arms. 'You failed at that.'

Smythe nodded once, tense. 'I did.'

He spoke only to Andomerys, still not looking at either of them. She couldn't decide whether she was relieved or furious that he didn't address her.

CHAPTER TWENTY-FIVE

Usther

Persephone returned from her survey of the rooms. 'All clear,' she said. Her armour was gone, as was her spear, but even in the padded cloth pyjamas she wore under them, she looked fierce. *A killer is a killer, no matter how they're dressed,* Usther thought to herself. She still had her magic, after all, and everyone in Tombtown knew the story of Andomerys defeating the founding council. Healers were just as capable of killing as necromancers. More, even. And she was willing to bet that most of the healing a paladin was taught was the killing kind.

'No fungi?' Usther asked, because that seemed important to be clear on.

'No fungi.' Persephone found a sofa and sat down heavily. She ran a hand through her silver hair, which had come loose from its plait and hung sweaty around her face. 'Not that I can see, anyway. I wouldn't put it past them to be invisible, or for there to be, I don't know, a coating of spores on the walls.'

A horrifying thought. Gingerly, Usther took a chair across from her. Mykol had sent them to an extended suite. Three bedrooms and a sort of washroom, as well—if a washroom with a narrow waterfall plunging down it counted. She didn't like to think how washing in *that* would feel. Like having your skin stripped off with ice, no doubt.

On the little table between them were two folded outfits, one bright red, the other soft brown and yellow. Usther didn't have to guess which was intended for her; the difference in the size of them, even folded, was stark. Much as she loved dresses, though, she didn't pick hers up. It was galling to think that Mykol intended to dress them up like dolls. More galling still that they likely had no choice but to let him.

'How do you know Ree?' Persephone asked in the quiet. She had her elbow on her knee and her chin pillowed in her hand, somehow looking strong even when at rest, even with worry wrinkling her eyes.

Mykol had said they had a day to themselves before the feast. She supposed there was time enough to talk.

'I suppose there's no point hiding it, after all you've seen,' said Usther. 'We live in the same town. We've been friends since we were children, or near enough. We share a house now, on the rare occasion she isn't off scribbling her little maps or collecting books, or whatever it is she does all day.' Usther sniffed.

'Oh. I hadn't realised—'

'Not like that,' Usther said quickly. 'We're just friends. And I don't like to live alone.'

Persephone nodded. 'It's like that with me and Tabris. Important to have a good friend, someone you can trust.'

'Someone you can trust,' Usther agreed, though she felt a little bewildered by the conversation. Too normal and domestic, surely, to be had by a necromancer and a paladin held prisoner in a subterranean fungi kingdom. Silence fell between them.

After a moment, Persephone picked up the brown outfit. It fell open, revealing its shape. Fitted at the bust and waist and then flaring out to a knee-length skirt cut into ribbons of brown and yellow.

She made a face. 'I don't think this is going to suit me,' she confided, and sighed. 'Though it's probably not worth the non-compliance.'

'Not worth it?'

Persephone shrugged a shoulder and carefully refolded the dress, placing it back on the table. 'If I'm going to attract their suspicion, I'd rather it was for something that has a chance of getting you out of here.' She paused. 'Or my spear through their chest. Either works.'

There was too much there to work through. 'Me? Why getting me out of here?'

'You're an innocent,' Persephone said. 'You shouldn't be caught up in all this. Nor should your friend, Ree. Or anyone else I've encountered here so far.'

'We're necromancers,' Usther said, and could hardly believe she was arguing this point. She certainly didn't want Persephone to *kill* her, but this went against everything she understood about the world and she was nothing if not argumentative. 'The entire reason you exist is to kill necromancers.'

Persephone looked uncomfortable, shifting in her seat. 'It's a little more complicated than that.'

Usther ran her hands through her hair, tossing her braids over her shoulder. 'Well, tell that to the ones that chased me out of my village.'

'What did you do?' she said, then made a face, but it was too late.

Usther's blood went cold with the familiar feeling of old rage. 'I didn't *do* anything,' she said, voice low. 'I was ten. I accidentally raised a taxidermied animal while I was playing. It happens like that, sometimes. Some people just have the knack. Especially children.' She breathed in deeply through her nose and exhaled. 'I had to run from my family, my village, everything I'd ever known, knowing that if I stopped for even a second, someone who looked just like you with shiny armour and a huge sword was going to kill me for the mistake.'

It hadn't been a paladin, actually, though she'd been warned one was on the way. It had been ordinary villagers that had chased her away from her home. Adults who'd given her sweets. Children who'd played with her in the long grass. Neighbours. Friends. Pitchforks and torches.

But it didn't matter that it hadn't been a paladin for her. Because it had been a paladin for so many other denizens. And for so many young necromancers who hadn't been lucky enough to make it to a haven like Tombtown and had instead found themselves on the end of a sword.

Persephone's lips were pressed into a tight line while Usther spoke. No doubt resisting the urge to berate her for her sins. At length, she said, 'It shouldn't have happened.'

'Well, I didn't have any control over it!'

'No—no, I mean...' she trailed off, breathing hard through her nose. She reminded Usther of a bull at rest. A beautiful, terrifying bull. 'I meant that you shouldn't have had to run. That paladin should have helped you, if they could. Not threatened you.'

'Well you don't have to tell me that,' Usther said stiffly. 'Tell your siblings-in-arms, if you ever see them again. Maybe you can ruin one or two fewer lives.'

Persephone stared into her hands and said nothing for a long time. Usther was content to sit in her seat and fume over the entire situation. Then quietly, Persephone said, 'I never imagined this would go this way.'

'Of course not,' Usther said, irritated. 'I didn't expect to be imprisoned by fungi-wielding weirdos, either.'

'Not—not this.' Persephone shook her head. 'Stuff like *this* happens to me all the time. Well, perhaps not so bad as this, but...' She shook her head. 'Nevermind.'

Usther was quite willing not to. She leaned forward, hands clasped in front of her. Persephone's eyes widened at her nearness, but she didn't pull back.

'We have some time,' Usther said quietly. 'Before they take us to this...this farce of a feast. We can find a way out.'

Persephone nodded, her mouth curving in the smallest of smiles. 'I like the way you think.'

'Yes. Well.' Usther's cheeks heated. She cleared her throat. 'You'll find I'm rather clever.' She stood up and strode quickly away. On a cursory examination, the bedrooms had nothing of interest, simply being larger, more lavish versions of the room she'd briefly shared with Smythe. She discounted their usefulness immediately, though she supposed it would be nice to have more blankets, should she need to slough off any more fungi by hand.

The washroom, though...

There was a Tombhome-style drop privy, unused. She couldn't see the bottom, and she had the horrible thought that perhaps there was more crimson fungi down there awaiting fertiliser. She kept the door to it firmly closed.

The wash facilities were more promising, if overwhelming. Even with so small a waterfall, there was a loud roar as it fell, no doubt echoing all the way down. With no tub in sight and a clear platform beneath the water, it was unfortunately clear what was expected; one had to stand beneath the shower, where a filter above reduced the spray, and the platform below allowed the remaining water to rejoin the fall. Usther shivered as she approached it. Even a gentle mist from it was freezing, and she didn't often feel the cold. She didn't fancy washing in it, and much preferred the solution at home where they boiled water and filled a tub.

She peered closer to the edge, where there seemed to be a vast void below. Ree would probably like this, she thought as her stomach dropped. She often bathed in the subterranean rivers and minor falls just like this while on her travels, because she was a wild thing incapable of appreciating civilised comfort. She thought of her friend encountering the feather-soft beds of the Many's kingdom. No doubt she would find them repulsive, much preferring her thin straw bedroll and a hard stone floor.

She hoped Ree would never need to form an opinion, that she'd make it out of this place before Mykol or Celia could trap her in a lavish prison. It was a small, flickering hope.

She edged a bit closer to the shower, keeping a hand on the wall beside the gap. The water fell into a yawning hole, noticeably dark. Not the shining white marble of the Many, but good, water-eroded mountain rock. She wanted to lean closer, to see how far the opening went, but her breath was coming fast and sharp and her chest felt painfully tight. She backed away, gasping, and rested the back of her hand against her forehead.

'Everything all right?'

'Gah!' Usther spun, glaring. Her heart-rate had spiked painfully. 'Don't—*do* that!' She got her breathing under control. Persephone raised her hands in apologetic surrender.

'The waterfall,' Usther said at length, when she no longer had the sensation she was running for her life. 'I was looking at the waterfall. I thought perhaps it might make a useful avenue for escape, or for hiding objects, or *something*.'

'And is it?'

'I don't know!' Usther snapped. 'I was getting up the courage to try again when you scared me out of my wits!'

Persephone frowned and tapped her lip. 'I'll go.'

'You'll—?' But Usther was rendered speechless as Persephone unbuttoned her padded top and handed it to her. The muscles slid beneath her forearms as she did so. Usther spluttered, absolutely lost for words.

Persephone didn't seem to notice. Clad only in her padded trousers and a narrow breast-band, she edged out over the gap. She had cobweb stretch-marks below her breastband, marks of gender transition. They were beautiful, like threads of silver.

It's rude to stare, Usther reminded herself, and did not stop staring.

She'd known Persephone was large. A bulky, round person even in her padded armour. She hadn't really registered that she was also shapely, the roundness of her belly contrasting with the hard muscles of her arms, her round shoulders suddenly planed when she tensed. Persephone stuck her head into the waterfall and rivulets of water cascaded down her back, following the interesting hollow of her spine toward her ample—

That was enough of that. Usther tore her eyes away, flushed from head to toe and mortified.

Persephone swore and trotted back. She snatched up a towel folded on the floor and started to dry her sopping silver hair, pulling it from the remains of its plait. 'It goes deep,' she confirmed. Her hair, which Usther had thought to be straight, had begun to curl from the touch of water. 'Wide enough to climb down, if you were brave or stupid.' Some of her hair got stuck in her breastband, which had a far-too interesting water-pattern on it.

Usther closed her eyes and pinched her nose between her fingers, disgusted with herself. 'I am neither of those things, but I might be desperate enough to try, if worst comes to worst.'

'B-brave t-then,' Persephone stuttered.

Usther opened her eyes. The paladin had wrapped herself in the towel, hair a mess of wavy silver. Her shoulders were hunched, her skin oddly wan.

'Was it that cold?' Usther asked, surprised. She'd forgotten upworlders were sensitive to the cold. Were healers even more so? She'd never thought to ask Andomerys or Arthura, the only healers in town.

'Yes. B-but it's not that.'

Usther raised her eyebrows, irritation rising. 'Well, what is it then?'

Persephone took a long, shuddering breath, followed by another. The sound of it was oddly soothing, and the sight of her bundled in towels and shivering like a chick in a rainstorm was unfortunately endearing. Her irritation eased a little.

'I hate heights,' she said, the stutter banished. 'Absolutely despise them.'

'Then why would you do it?'

Persephone shrugged. 'You seemed scared, too.'

She held out her hand for the padded doublet, and a stunned Usther handed it over wordlessly.

CHAPTER TWENTY-SIX

Ree

Smythe and Andomerys filled each other in on all they'd discovered. It sounded like Smythe and Usther had been through quite a lot, but Ree felt like she was hearing the words underwater, like their meaning was dulled and couldn't quite reach her ears.

He looked different. Older, obviously. He'd grown sharper; planed cheekbones and eyes that were less innocent and more shrewd. Instead of the khaki travelling clothes she remembered, he wore a blue coat with copper buttons and fitted brown trousers. A shabby scholar now, rather than an expensive burial historian. The glasses were the same, though significantly more scratched. His hair was longer and pulled into a messy, curly tail.

But the biggest change was necromantic. His sepia skin was tinged grey, and there were shadows under his eyes. His irises, once brown, now seemed an inky black. As teenagers, she'd had to smuggle him into town. Now, he could walk in and nobody would throw him a second glance. He was a necromancer through and through.

She stared at her lap, petting Misery's head absently as the minion huddled beside the sofa. As happy as she was to see Ree, she looked often to Smythe. Dichotomy, too, curled around his legs, purring and begging for scritches. They trusted him. She wanted to tell them not to make that mistake.

It was hard to believe that Usther had. But Misery would not trust anyone Usther didn't. She was unusually in-tune with her mistress, perhaps thanks to her role as a house-minion. If Smythe did anything to hurt Usther, Misery would turn on him without question.

'You nearly mauled me when I lost Usther's hairbrush,' she murmured to the minion now. 'Do you think maybe that was a little unfair?'

Misery sighed and leaned her head against the arm of the sofa.

Well, nevermind then.

'Honestly,' said Andomerys, 'I think our best bet is to go to their feast. If we're their special prisoners, and Emberlon is as well, then surely we'll find him there.'

'I haven't been to a feast in a while,' Smythe said, a little anxiously. 'But whatever you think is best.'

'Neither have I,' Andomerys replied. 'But this doesn't sound so different from any other court dinner. Powerful dictators and a room full of people where you don't know whether they're friends or enemies, and cannot safely ask...yeah, that's court.'

'I was never very good at court,' Smythe said in a small voice. 'My elder sibling took to politics like an undead hippo takes to swamps, but I was always much more comfortable with books.'

'It's good to be uncomfortable,' Andomerys said. 'Mykol and Celia don't seem like people you can let your guard down around.'

'I—' Ree cleared her throat. 'I don't know what a feast is like.'

Smythe's brows furrowed. 'You don't have feasts in Tombtown?'

Ree shrugged, not meeting his eyes.

'Not so much,' Andomerys said. 'It's not like they're keen on dinner parties, either. Or remember to keep themselves fed. I've got Mortana sneaking vitamin supplements into their drinks.' She shook her head. 'Ree, it's just a big dinner.'

Ree shrugged. 'I gathered that.'

'Well...everyone sits at a long table and eats a fancy meal and talks about nothing at all. Then usually there's dancing, though gods only know what to expect from these people.'

'I don't know how to do any of that.'

'Well, don't let it worry you,' Andomerys said. 'Our escape isn't going to hinge on your ability to small talk convincingly. Look for opportunities to escape and try to get messages to each other if we can.'

She inspected the clothes that had been left for them. 'I think that one's for you,' she said. And she was surely right, given that it looked a perfect match for her size.

Ree stared at the proffered outfit. 'It's orange.'

Andomerys sighed. 'It's just for now.'

Ree took the stack of clothes into the washroom. This room was unexpected. What looked like a small natural waterfall rushed down a gap in the wall, with a little platform of white marble reaching into it.

Well, if she was changing clothes soon anyway...

She crept toward the shower, fully-dressed, and peered inside. The water hit her hard, icy cold, but not with enough force to unbalance her. She gritted her teeth and examined the stone of the shower wall. Wet and worn smooth by the passage of water, it was simple mountain stone. This had probably already been here long before Celia had converted this part of the crypt into a marble nightmare. Perhaps it had been here even before the crypt. Ignoring the cold soak down her back and the water sticking her hair to her face, she reached further in, patting around for handholds. She felt certain she could climb it as a rat, but she had no intention of leaving Andomerys behind.

She flexed her bare feet on the marble, considering. She hadn't climbed barefoot since she was a child, and she hadn't climbed anything this wet before successfully. She'd have to take it slowly.

She eased out onto a narrow lip of stone, toes hooking on as best as they could, her fingers digging into the only faint grooves she could find. The water splashed at her unevenly, its rush wild and erratic. She forced herself to ignore it. She needed only focus on the stone.

There was a bulbous bump there she could perhaps rest on, though it looked slippery. She stretched out to it and got a foot on. Slowly, she shifted her weight, reaching for a handhold above it. Her foot slipped and she shifted back. Tried again. Slipped again.

She gritted her teeth and tried one more time. This time she transferred properly, though her muscles shook with the effort of keeping most of her weight on her arms, rather than her legs. Morrin's teeth, she wished she was still as scrawny as she'd been as a teenager. She had so much damn weight to hold up these days. She reached for the next one across and a little ways up. She was coming around the falls now.

And she realised as she got there that there was another room. Another ledge and doorway, obscured by the fall of the water. She eyed the gap to the other ledge. She could maybe reach it, if she pushed off just right...

Her foot slipped; her knee hit rock and then she plunged into the falling water. She half-screamed the song that spelled her into her skin, and then she was a rat tumbling into darkness and swept away by the falls. She twisted as she fell and managed to get her little claws onto the rock, finding purchase as a rat where a human would find none. She clung there for a few minutes, panting heavily, her entire little rat-body shivering. And then she began the climb back up to her room.

When she got there, she paused, shivering, and collapsed onto the floor. A moment later, she released the ratskin and pressed her human cheek to the oddly warm marble floor.

A knock at the door. 'Ree?' Andomerys' voice was muffled. 'Is everything all right? I heard a shout.'

'I'm fine!' Ree's reply was hoarse. She got onto her knees, her sopping wet robes nearly tripping her as she did. 'I, uh, I just need to shower.'

And she did, though she felt more nervous standing in the shower than she might have been before. Hard to enjoy the refreshing cold of it when the memory of falling was still so fresh. When she was done, she wrung out her hair and pulled it into a simple high bun.

She spread out her now soaked travel robes and trousers and made herself pull on the new robes. They were long and loose with a hood. The material was extremely soft, almost fur-like, and the colour was orange at the hood gradually fading to yellow at the bottom. She'd never seen such seamless dye-work, nor such luscious materials. Even Andomerys, who wore loud patterns and silks regularly, had never worn something so delicately made. It reminded her of flames.

Beneath it went a long-sleeved orange top and matching trousers, and soft brown boots of better make than the ones she'd given Larry. Everything fit perfectly, even the smallclothes. She found that incredibly uncomfortable to think about. Who were these people, and how did they know so much about them?

When Ree emerged, fidgeting nervously, it was to find Smythe petting Dichotomy while Andomerys stared silently at the wall.

Andomerys looked over and raised her eyebrows. 'I've never seen you in colours before,' she said. 'It suits you.'

Ree pulled at the robes. They ended at the knees and didn't restrict her movement too badly. They were, essentially, the kind of thing she might normally wear, though brighter, plusher, and more expensive. 'I prefer black,' she confessed. She felt...visible. Horribly visible. Hard to imagine scrambling up crumbling stone walls in this. Or watching intruders pass below as she balanced on a beam. She would shine like a lantern in this, even for those without darksight.

She glanced at Smythe. He was staring with eyes wide behind his spectacles. At her look, he cleared his throat and focused his attention on the cat in his lap. Just as well, as Dichotomy's ears had flattened to find him distracted. He made no comment about her appearance, and for that, she was relieved.

'I saw something. In the washroom.' She took the seat next to Andomerys. 'There's some kind of mountain waterfall to wash in. The hole it falls through falls very far—down to the river, I'd guess. Wide enough to climb down, but not safely. But there's another room across from it using the same waterfall.

Andomerys frowned. 'Another washroom?'

Ree shrugged. 'I tried to climb over to it but I slipped. I could try again in my ratskin.'

'You don't think we could make it in human shape?'

She stroked her bun and flicked water from her hands. 'I could maybe do it.'

Andomerys sighed. 'And if you can't do it for certain, we have no chance at all.'

Ree inclined her head apologetically. 'Unless you can magically make yourself good at climbing?'

She shook her head. 'I could make myself stronger, maybe. But I can't create skill.'

It had been worth a try, Ree supposed. She promised to try again later.

Andomerys went next. She came out looking more formal than Ree had ever seen her in a purple wrap-around dress embroidered in gold. Unlike Ree's robes, it looked quite different from what Andomerys normally wore, even if the colours weren't so out of place.

'You look nice,' Ree offered.

Andomerys made a face. 'I feel like I'm back at court,' she said.

Smythe went next, leaving behind a very annoyed Dichotomy. She suffered through Ree petting her, clearly biding her time until her preferred human returned.

Smythe emerged, looking sheepish. His curls were wet, and instead of a tail, he'd pulled his hair into a half-bun. Instead of his blue jacket with copper buttons, he wore elaborate dark robes befitting an affluent necromancer, embroidered with silver moons and stars as well as runes in a language she recognised only from the outside of the rooms in the crypt. Older than Old Antherian. The robes split around his legs, revealing dark trousers and a flash of ankle before elaborately embroidered black slippers.

He looked powerful. A future lich at the height of his influence.

'This is...rather more grand than I'm used to,' he said nervously. He tucked a stray curl behind his ear. Her vision of him as a lich faded, and he was only a man again. 'And disturbingly well-tailored, considering I don't remember going to a fitting.'

'I find that interesting,' Andomerys said. 'Mine wasn't. I had to pull the dress quite tight to make it fit. And Celia did say that I was being suffered as a guest only because of Ree. She said you and Usther were honoured guests as well, yes?'

Smythe nodded reluctantly. 'Mykol seemed very keen to earn us to his side. He knew about us, somehow.' He shook his head. 'I confess I don't know why. What the three of us have in common.'

Ree looked away from him, her thoughts churning. It was hard to look into their shared past. She couldn't see past the dais surrounded by spirits, the sight of Usther and her parents sprawled, still and weak, on the stairs.

But there had been time before that. Her eyes stung; she wiped away a tear, though she didn't feel at all like crying. She felt empty, dispassionate. She had found Smythe. They'd saved each other. Usther had trained him in necromancy, with Ree's help. Smythe had helped her with her therianthropy research. And then he'd—

No. There was more to it. She closed her eyes.

The Lich had found them. Used a spell they didn't understand and sent them back in time to the days of the Old King and his necromancer kingdom. Before Tombtown, before the founding council. That had been only Ree and Smythe. Only they had suffered the Black Oath to be carved into their skin.

But Usther...

Usther had scried to them.

Usther had pulled them back.

It was the single most significant thing she could think of in which they'd all had a part.

'We meddled with time,' she whispered.

CHAPTER TWENTY-SEVEN

Usther

U sther wrung her hands and paced the lounge.

'Are you sure you don't want to just hold hands and jump down the washroom abyss?' Persephone said. 'You look a little wan.'

Usther snorted. 'Well, that's hardly unusual for me.'

Persephone said nothing, and Usther warmed under her observant gaze. They'd only spent a few hours together and already Usther felt altogether too seen around her. It made her want to crawl under the bed like she'd done as a little girl, hiding under a blanket until her nightmares had subsided.

'There are monsters under the bed,' her mother had told her. *'That's what most children think.'* On reflection, Usther thought she'd been desperate to get her daughter to act more normal. To behave in the way she expected. But Usther had only told her, very solemnly, that it was the monsters that made her feel safe.

The foolish fancies of a child who would accidentally implode her own life only a handful of years later...

'I've never been to a feast,' Usther confessed. 'I've been to a few dinners, I suppose, but only with Ree's family and they don't stand much on tradition.'

Persephone's mouth twitched, though whether in a frown or a smile, Usther couldn't tell. 'You're being held prisoner and forced to dine for the entertainment of evil mages and your concern is that you don't know the etiquette?'

Usther paused and considered, twisting her hands in front of her. She nodded. 'Yes. Yes, I think that sums it up. I'm already a prisoner; I don't want to be an *unfashionable* one.'

Persephone said, very quietly, 'I think there's little risk of that.'

Usther flushed and studied Persephone. The other woman had changed into the outfit given her by their captors. Though it was not as perfectly tailored as Usther's own dress, it suited her very well. A brown dress in a very soft material, the skirt cut into ribbons of brown and yellow. When she walked, her long, full legs were visible, bare up to mid-thigh. Usther had had no notion, on meeting her, that Persephone could look so soft and lady-like, but exchanging armour and boots for a dress and embroidered slippers had really shown her the truth of it.

Persephone's cheeks brightened, and Usther realised she'd been staring. She quickly turned away, cursing herself for rudeness. Anyone would think she was a mannerless teenager, the way she gawped, and not the grown woman of poise she worked to be.

And she had better things to think about than some paladin's legs, for Morrin's sake. She belligerently wiped the image of Persephone topless and wringing out her hair from her mind.

A knock came at the door and then it swung open. Symphona stood there, wearing a dress of fuschia lace with a matching velvet capelet. Bracelets banded her wrists and arms and a delicate choker with a red gem rested at her throat. She smiled sweetly at Usther.

'The lord and lady will see you now,' she said. Her eyes swept Usther up and down, taking in her fitted dress. 'You look positively delicious,' she said. She bit her lip, grinned, and turned to lead them out.

Looks like that had once made Usther swoon, but now she only felt sick. The world danced around her, narrowing in on Symphona's receding back.

A touch at her shoulder, firm. She looked up at Persephone, surprised.

'You okay?' the paladin asked.

Usther nodded, not trusting herself to words, and followed Symphona down the corridor.

She led them into the same grand hall the siblings had held court in before. Now the thrones sat empty at one end and in the centre of the hall, a long table had been laid. Several denizens were already seated at it, most dressed up, but none wearing the kind of finery Usther and Persephone had been given—none except for Ellenil, Symphona, and Tarantur.

Usther hesitated, unsure where to sit that would place her the farthest from the siblings and their 'beloved' servants.

Symphona waited until she made a move and then tsked. 'The lord and lady were very particular that you would sit here.' She gestured to an empty seat in the middle of the table.

Usther shuddered. She moved to take her seat and froze as Symphona started to pull out the seat beside her.

'Thank you,' Persephone said, shunting her out of the way easily and sliding into the open seat.

Symphona's expression darkened and her lip started to curl. 'You—!'

'Symphona!' Tarantur clicked his fingers and waved her over to one end of the table. 'Ellenil has an interesting proposition.'

Symphona hovered a moment, her hands shaped into claws at her side. Then her hands relaxed and she exchanged her grimace for an apologetic smile. 'If you'll excuse me,' she said.

Usther pressed shaking hands to the edge of the table. 'Thank you,' she whispered.

Persephone frowned at Symphona's retreating back. 'Who is she to you?'

Usther shook her head. She wasn't supposed to be anything at all.

More denizens arrived—how many willingly, she didn't know. She didn't like to look at them and wonder whether those smiles were fixed, whether their shoulders were a little too tense.

She focused on the feast table instead. Plates, glasses, and cutlery were regimented down the table, all in the same positions, but there seemed to be more of each assigned to each guest than surely anyone could need. Down the middle of the table were various trays with silver lids, presumably keeping everything fresh. Jugs of juice and bottles of wine were plentiful. And the tablecloth was an impractical, plush red velvet. Another display of wealth and profligacy Usther found distasteful. It would be a waste of good velvet for this to be splashed and stained with food and drink.

'I hope there aren't any mushrooms on the menu,' Persephone murmured, following her gaze.

In spite of everything, Usther smiled, then made a face. 'Don't even joke about that.'

Movement across the table as someone sat down. 'Usther?'

Ree. For a moment, the world narrowed only to her and her friend. It had been weeks since they had last seen each other. Anger and relief warred in her, that it had taken this for them to finally meet.

Ree's eyes were shadowed and brimming with worry. She tried to lean across the table but there was too much in the way.

The anger fell away. 'I'm here,' said Usther. 'I'm safe.'

Andomerys and Smythe took the seats to either side of her. Usther followed Andomerys' wide-eyed stare; Emberlon was seated to the right of one end of the table, emaciated and drooping where he sat.

'I've seen Misery and Dichotomy,' said Ree. 'Smythe said—'

There was a mass scraping of chairs as everyone stood up. Usther rushed to follow, her heart pounding. The doors flew open; Mykol and Celia glided in. Unlike everyone else, their outfits were unchanged. Ragged white dresses, perfectly white. Their crimson hair unstyled, their heads uncrowned. But they glided down either side of the feast table as regal as monarchs. Celia took the seat nearest the door. Symphona sat on her right, Ellenil on her left. Mykol took the seat at the far end, with Emberlon on his right hand and Tarantur on his left. As one, they gestured for everyone to sit, and once again, Usther followed the lead of the entire room.

Mykol bestowed an approving smile on her. 'The dress suits you,' he said. 'Celia chose yours herself.' He nodded to his sister at the other end of the long table.

Usther glanced at her and caught the edge of a perfectly wicked smile that chilled her to her core. She quickly moved her gaze to her plate, saying nothing.

'You may begin,' Celia called from the other end.

Platters were uncovered, revealing food the likes of which Usther had never seen. Whole roast pigs and garnished roast chickens. Vegetables and fruit aplenty. Chutneys and sauces and even fresh-baked bread.

Not quite believing what was in front of her, she reached for a steaming roll. It was warm enough to sting her hands, and when she broke it, the smell of hot bread was heady and overwhelming.

Persephone paused in filling her plate to look at her. 'You look like you've never seen bread before,' she said.

Usther mentally shook herself and placed the bread on the larger of her three plates. 'It's been a while, is all,' she said.

Where had they baked it, that it was still so fresh? Was there a white marble kitchen in here with a chimney to release the smoke? The bread they made in town was a hardy, long-life mushroom loaf cooked in a specialist kitchen. Wheat couldn't be farmed reliably in the crypt and they had to ration out what they traded from the Dead Marsh villages and passing tinkers.

All of this food was impossible. There were no pigs in Tombtown that weren't already salted and dried before arrival. There were no cabbages to steam, no leafy greens to boil. There were minion-laboured farms, she knew, that worked at night or in the crypt itself, which did a good business in potatoes, mushrooms, and various root vegetables. But this kind of colour and bounty was beyond anything the crypt ought to be able to provide.

'We have a great many bounties,' Mykol said from the head of the table. 'Our methods of production far outstrip the crude farms of that failing town.'

She stared, unnerved by his observation. He smiled and returned to his conversation with Tarantur.

She could feel Ree's eyes on her and looked over. She thought her friend might be trying to tell her something by the way she raised her eyebrows and pulled faces, but Usther couldn't for the life of her work out what.

'At least the food is good,' said a voice to her left. It was old Mazerin, who sold bones at the town market. Without his stall and his ebullient patter, he looked small and a little lost. He pushed some vegetables around his plate then cast something wordlessly over what was left of his meat. The meat immediately sloughed off and the little bones flew up and into his hand. He got a knife out of his pocket and started carving, heedless of the mess the shavings made.

Usther found she couldn't be mad. He had a haunted look about him, and she got the sense he needed this. There was a tattered red ribbon tied around his wrist.

'When did you get here?' she asked quietly.

'Oh, a few days ago,' he said. 'Little Ellenil said they needed my help, and I wasn't going to say no. I'm no powerful practitioner, but I know a few tricks with bones most don't, and the young'uns know they can trust me.' He smiled a little at that.

Ellenil. Usther's eyes went to the young necromancer. They were resplendent in a high-collared night-blue robe with silver trim. Their hair had been teased into two small antlers; she was amazed they'd gotten it to keep the shape.

'Shame you couldn't trust them,' she said quietly.

Mazerin went still.

He set aside his carving and speared some meat on his fork. His eyes went wide as he tasted it. 'Amazing stuff,' he said. 'Thought I might never taste fresh pork again! I'm not spry enough to travel.'

Usther leaned toward him. 'Mazerin,' she said. 'Are you here by—?'

Mazerin thrust the bone he was carving under her nose. 'I reckon I can make an ocarina out of this if I'm careful with the shaping. Might take a little extra Craft to nudge the bone into the right shape. And how's your little cat?'

She made a vague noise and turned back to her plate. Did Mazerin know that Dichotomy had been taken hostage? Was he threatening her, or warning her? Or was he just trying to change the subject?

She took a tentative bite of the chicken. Hot, moist, and fresh. The flavour flooded her tastebuds. She had no idea how they'd managed to acquire and cook it. There were loose chickens on the mountain, she supposed, but...

A gentle touch at her elbow. Persephone nodded toward Ellenil. 'Who are they?'

Ellenil nodded attentively while Symphona talked and laughed.

Usther shrugged and returned to her meal. 'Someone I used to know,' she said. She hated the way her voice quavered as she said it.

Persephone said nothing, but she felt the paladin's gaze on her for a moment longer.

'Do you miss your family, when you're off looking for necromancers to kill?' Usther asked, spearing a sprout with her fork.

Persephone wiped her lips with a napkin. 'I'm rarely looking to kill anyone,' she said. 'But I do miss my family. In a dull kind of way. I haven't seen them since I was a child.'

That was unexpected. Startled, Usther looked up and into the paladin's grim face. 'You haven't?'

'They give us up to the gods when we're young,' she said. 'I've seen them a few times since, but it's like meeting strangers. They remember a little boy with bad dreams. They don't know the woman who is the spear of a goddess. I guess I miss my memory of them. What it was like to know them.'

Usther nodded at that, her throat tight. Her final memories of her parents were not particularly warm. When she missed them, she missed when things had been less complicated. She missed the feeling of being loved more than the actual parents, she supposed.

'I have a cat,' she told Persephone. 'I found her hunting cave rats. A tiny thing, fierce as you like, and about to run right into giant spider territory and get herself eaten. I took her home and tried to make a safe place for her to live.' She smiled a little at the memory. 'She hated me to begin with. I let her hide as much as she wanted, but she'd still scratch me bloody any time I chanced to get too near. I decided I was going to love her anyway, even if she was a cruel little beast. Even if I collected a few scars for doing it. Sometimes I wish someone had done the same for me.'

Pressure behind her eyes; she forced herself to calm down. 'She's very sweet now. Well. Mostly.'

'What kind of cat is she?'

Usther smiled. 'Black-and-white. Almost exactly split down the middle of her face, actually. Her name is Dichotomy.'

'She sounds very special,' Persephone said. 'I hope you see her again soon.'

'Me too,' said Usther, her heart falling. She looked to her right, where Mykol was in deep conversation with Tarantur once more. She wondered what kind of person held a cat hostage to control their carer.

Mykol's gaze slid to hers. He smiled.

CHAPTER TWENTY-EIGHT

Ree

She was seated in-between Andomerys and Smythe. Ellenil had insisted, with a little too much relish for Ree's taste. She was really starting to dislike that kid. But the discomfort of Smythe's nearness was utterly eclipsed by the sight of Mykol's right hand.

Because seated there in honour was Emberlon. She almost hadn't recognised him; might even have looked past him, if not for following Andomerys' intense stare. Gone was his brown cassock and unassuming hemp belt. Now, he was resplendent in royal blue velvet which looked plusher and softer even than the fabric of her own robes. And it wasn't a royal blue robe, either, but a tunic with fine detailing and sharp shoulders. Instead of his usual anti-scry amulet, he wore a large gold chain with a ruby pendant. And on his head was a gold circlet, also picked out with rubies.

But the biggest change was to his face. He looked terribly gaunt, malnourished rather than necromantic. And his eyes were dull and distant, staring at his untouched plate, though it was heaped with food.

Andomerys stared fixedly, her hands digging into the table and scrunching up the tablecloth. 'How *dare* they?' she said.

Ree frowned. 'He doesn't look like himself,' she said.

'That's because he isn't. They're making him into what they want him to be.' A muscle twitched in her cheek. 'That was never him.'

Except it *did* suit him. It unnerved her, how much it suited him. How her mild, somewhat melancholy mentor who had taught her how to index books and spent hours teaching her to read *iyad-anar* could look so natural in a crown. This was a man who had slipped into the town without fuss. In spite of the rumours surrounding him. In spite of the way people felt the urge to bow or kneel under his regard.

It suited him. But it didn't look like *him*.

It looked like another man. And that man wasn't quietly sad, like the one she knew. Wasn't brightened only by his historical writings of the town. That man was deeply, painfully miserable.

'It's true, isn't it?' she whispered, her heart squeezing in her chest. 'He really is a lost King.'

Andomerys turned to look at her. Her eyes were red and angry. Like she was about to cry. Like she was about to scream. 'Not anymore.'

A shift at her other side. She looked side-long at Smythe. He watched Emberlon not with awe or excitement, but with sorrow. When he caught her eye, he said nothing. Only looked down at his plate and took another bite of pork.

Celia stood up abruptly. Ree perched on her seat, poised to follow suit, but as Mykol remained seated, it seemed so would everyone else.

'A dance,' she said. 'A dance should be had now. Wouldn't that be perfect, my dear Symphona?' She bestowed a smile upon the woman seated on her right hand.

'Of course, my Lady.'

Celia gestured for everyone to stand up, then strode out onto the floor. As Mykol and the others stood, Ree hurried to follow. Fungal minions entered the hall from two of the doors and bore away the table and chairs with a most un-minionly efficiency. Ree watched them go, her skin crawling. There was a reason house-minions like Usther were uncommon. Minions were not known for either their grace or their manners.

Her mind turned again to Larry, but she barely had a moment to fret over him before the first chord of a song was struck. She looked to the corner, where a cluster of musicians stood. One held a bone-lyre, another a bone flute, and three others more traditional instruments in the form of a drum, a trap-horn, and a lute. They had all played at the *Bone & Brew* at some point, though not all together as far as she could remember. The tune they ran was slow and melancholic.

Necromancers began to pair up. Mykol danced with Ellenil and Celia danced with Symphona. Both of those pairs moved with courtly concert and correctness, while the necromancer pairs danced rough and awkward around them.

Ree and Smythe stood to one side while Andomerys rushed to Emberlon, who alone had been left a chair. Ree made to follow her when a woman danced past and hissed at her, 'Dance!' It was Etherea Eversworn, who had cared for Ree as a child when her parents were away on council business, and who had always had a smile for her. She didn't have a smile now; her eyes were full of warning. She danced with a young man Ree didn't recognise.

Immediately, Ree thought she needed to warn Andomerys, but Emberlon was standing and bowing stiffly to the healer, who propped him up so that they could sway together.

Across the room, Mykol caught Ree's eye. He separated from Ellenil and began to glide toward her.

Ree spun and seized Smythe by the hands. 'You know how to dance, right?' she asked breathlessly.

Smythe sputtered a moment, but then his eyes went over her shoulder and his mouth formed a grim line. 'Of course,' he said smoothly. He moved her hand to his shoulder. His hand went high on her waist, feather-light, and with that he spun her away.

Ree could only shuffle after him, unprepared for the rhythm and speed of this movement. She'd never been clumsy, but this unfamiliar mode of travel nearly had her tripping. 'It's okay,' Smythe said. 'Just step where I step. Nobody really needs to be good at dancing.'

She focused on the steps. When they turned, she could see Mykol watching them with a hard-to-read expression before being swallowed up by the crowd of dancers. That was a relief, at least. Smythe moved more slowly, always waiting for her steps to follow his before moving on. She started to feel the rhythm of it, the way it followed the rise and fall of the music. That, at least, she could follow. She started to move more in time.

'You're a quick learner,' he said. 'Far faster than I was. I don't know why I'm surprised.'

She glanced at his face but he wasn't looking at her. In spite of their closeness, he had his gaze fixed just over her shoulder. He looked...uncomfortable. Nervous, perhaps. Safe in the knowledge it wouldn't be observed, she allowed herself to take in his face. How it had changed. Age had sharpened the lines of his cheeks and jaw. He had a dusting of stubble, though she didn't remember him shaving in the weeks they'd known each other in the past.

She looked away again, not sure how she felt about any of this. About him protecting Misery. About Dichotomy choosing him for comfort. About him existing in her life at all.

'Ree!' someone hissed.

Ree looked around in surprise; Usther and Persephone danced near to them. Like Ree and Smythe, they seemed to dance in the courtly style, hands on waist and shoulder, bodies close. The song was winding down, the last long throe of the bone harp fading. 'Switch partners!' said Usther.

Persephone released her and bowed to Smythe. 'May I, sir?' she asked formally.

Smythe bowed in return. He let her take the lead and the pair disappeared as the next tune was struck, this one much more fast-paced.

Usther seized her friend's hands and started to spin away with her. There was none of the grace of dancing with Smythe, but a lot of urgency. 'Misery is safe?' she asked. A few other dancers stopped and clapped at the beat. Ree and Usther followed suit, half a beat behind. 'And Dichotomy?'

'Smythe has them,' Ree replied in a low voice. 'Apparently Mykol threatened them if he didn't comply and hand over Emberlon.' She didn't try to hide her scepticism, but Usther nodded.

'I thought he'd protect them if he could,' she said. 'I've been quartered with that paladin, Persephone. Her friend got away. There's a waterfall in the washroom—'

'In ours as well!' Ree said.

'—so I thought that—what?'

They stopped and clapped again, somewhat clumsily, but now partners were changing with alarming speed. Hands took Ree's wrist; Persephone led her away, and now the pair of them danced while Smythe and Usther spun away across the floor. Persephone had none of Usther's awkwardness, but she leaned close on the off-beat. 'There's a waterfall in our room,' she said. 'We're not sure how far it goes.'

'I was just saying the same to Usther,' Ree said. 'I think it's actually the same waterfall connecting both our rooms.'

They clapped again. 'If that's so, then we can—'

Partners were changing. A necromancer Ree didn't recognise seemed to be angling for them, but Andomerys blocked the way. 'With me, paladin,' Andomerys said, and an exhausted Emberlon took Ree's hand.

'You're going to have to lead,' he said. 'I barely have the strength to stand.'

She let him lean on her, as strange as that was. They'd rarely so much as touched hands when handing each other books. He was terrifyingly light. Pity and relief warred in her. She hated to see him like this, but she was so deeply, *deeply* relieved to find him alive.

'Everyone is plotting, I think,' he said. 'I was never one much for plots, myself.'

'Me either,' Ree replied. 'A book is better company.'

He almost smiled, which from Emberlon was a volley of laughter from someone else. He slipped a little on their next step; Ree caught him firmly.

'What did they do to you?' she asked.

'Beware the red ribbon,' he said grimly. 'I don't doubt they want you to wear one, too. In fact, they seem bent on it.'

'Why me?' Ree said.

Emberlon shook his head. 'My mother once said to me, "Powerful men collect powerful people".'

'I'm not powerful,' Ree said. And that was true. She had resurrected a long dead magic and still all she could do was turn into a bird, a rat, and a blind slimy fish. And a few other tricks, here and there.

'I wouldn't say that,' Emberlon said. 'I think more accurately, you don't try to be. But the power remains, all the same.' He got a familiar distant look as he said it.

She needed to get him out of here. Even if not for his clearly failing health, it was never good when he got all reminiscent like this. 'The past is in the past,' she said fiercely. 'And this will be soon.'

He shook his head. 'Not for me.'

They changed partners again, this time Smythe taking her waist again. 'We have a bit of a plan,' he said. 'Usther seems quite determined.'

'We'll meet in our rooms, I suppose,' Ree said. She didn't like how easy it was to dance with him. It wasn't just that he was good at it—Persephone was just as good, maybe better—but, there was a rhythm between *them* that felt natural. Normal.

'Yes,' he said. He seemed troubled. 'In our rooms.'

The song wound down. A woman appeared at their side. 'If I might have this dance?' said Celia, curtsying to Ree with perfect grace.

Mykol broke from the crowd to bow to Smythe. 'And I yours,' he said. 'Since your partner denied me the last?'

Smythe's cheeks flushed. He nodded and bowed back to Mykol, but his eyes slid to Ree. Concerned.

She was plenty concerned enough for herself.

She half-wanted to give Smythe some reassurance, but that warred with their history and with the watching eyes of their shared enemies. So she only took Celia's hand and let herself be led away.

As the next tune was struck, wailing and fast, Celia pulled her close, pressing her body along Ree's. It was a move, Ree thought dispassionately, designed to arouse and unbalance. Celia's body was firm and shapely, her breasts pressing into Ree's collarbone.

Ree felt no such stirrings. Celia was beautiful, but she was a beautiful stranger. To Ree, this was only an unpleasant invasion of her privacy. She tried to put some space between them, but Celia's hand on her waist held her fast with unexpected strength.

As Celia led them in a circle, Ree took no special care to match her steps. She stomped on the lady's bare feet more than once, but Celia did not so much as flinch. Her feet were oddly pliant, a sensation that made Ree shudder.

'Are you going to tell me what you want with us?' Ree asked.

Celia laughed, a tinkling, coquettish sound. 'I would think my brother and I have been most clear on that point. The Many-That-Hungers wishes to honour you. To lavish luxury upon you.'

'Why?'

Celia spun Ree out, keeping her tethered to her locked hand, then pulled her back in tight. She leaned close to Ree, almost cheek to cheek. Her breath tickled Ree's ear as she whispered, 'To thank you.'

CHAPTER TWENTY-NINE

Usther

Usther found herself once again dancing with Persephone. She was unprepared for the smoothness of Persephone's steps. Even Smythe, who was so posh Usther wouldn't be surprised to learn he wiped his ass with gold leaf, didn't have the grace of the paladin.

'May I hold you closer?' Persephone asked as the next tune started up.

A flutter in Usther's belly. 'You may,' she said.

The transition was smooth. Persephone held her so gently that she almost felt cradled. Traitorously, she wished she were held harder. In spite of her strength, Persephone's body was incredibly soft and part of her wanted to know what the muscles beneath felt like.

They were almost of a height, too. Usther was very tall and it was a shock to meet a woman slightly taller. Surprisingly intimate for their eyes to meet on the same level.

This was...not where she wanted her thoughts to be going.

Persephone leaned close. 'We have a plan, then?'

Usther nodded, letting Persephone guide her between the other dancers. 'Tonight.'

They continued. Persephone and Usther chose not to separate for the next song. Emberlon had returned to his seat, drenched in sweat, and Andomerys, Smythe, and Ree mixed with other dancers and each other. Once or twice she saw Mykol or Celia move as if to join them, but Persephone always guided them into the throng.

As yet another song started up and Usther was thinking longingly of the soft beds in their chambers, Symphona appeared beside them and curtsied. 'May I have this dance?' she asked, holding out her hand to Usther, her lips curved in a cruel smile.

Usther stiffened and tried to find the words to repel her but found she didn't have the breath.

Persephone looked from Usther to Symphona and said simply, 'No,' and steered Usther away.

It was a relief when Celia announced the end of the festivities. They returned to their room under a watchful guard of fungal minions.

Once the door closed behind her, Usther went to the sofa and draped herself across it. 'What a disaster that was,' she muttered, resting the back of her hand against her forehead.

Persephone took the seat opposite her. 'It could have been much worse,' she said. 'I confess, I don't really understand these villains of yours. They threaten and they control, but then they throw us a party?'

'A party where we'd be punished for lack of participation,' Usther reminded her.

'Even so.' She rested her cheek in her hand. 'I wonder what their ultimate goal is. You say they're kidnapping townsfolk from some other settlement in the crypt—'

'The *only* settlement in the crypt,' Usther said, still wondering how this woman had gained her trust so quickly. She supposed she had no other option; there was no hiding that this was a great gathering place of necromancers now. 'This marble monstrosity didn't exist a year ago. Or even a few months ago!'

'But why build their own? Why not take over what already exists? And what exactly are they gaining from demanding the devotion of all your neighbours?'

'They're just playing at being King and Queen,' Usther said. She pushed herself up until she was sitting upright. 'Surely they don't need any more reason than that.'

'It's a small kingdom,' Persephone said 'with little to reward them.' She sighed and rubbed her eyes. 'But perhaps you're right. It's not like I know this place. How long do you think it'll be before your friend Ree arrives?'

Usther waved a lazy hand. 'Oh, she's probably already here. She's a chronic eavesdropper and has no respect for personal boundaries. Isn't that right, Ree?' She raised her voice, calling out to the room at large.

Persephone raised her eyebrows.

Usther shrugged. 'It was worth a try. One should never miss the opportunity to aggravate one's friends.'

A burst of cold and a swirl of shadows. Ree stood up behind the sofa; Persephone lurched forward, as if to attack, and then caught herself. 'Allariel give me strength,' she said, pressing a hand to her chest. 'You don't half know how to sneak up on someone.'

'Alarming, isn't it?' Usther agreed fondly. She scooted over on the sofa, allowing Ree the seat beside her, which Ree took. 'So what's the plan?'

Ree shrugged, a little helplessly. 'It's not much of one. Both our doors are watched, as is the entire compound. The only way out is down, and it's a long, long fall into water. Dangerous, for sure. Not sure how much air there will be down there. Some parts of the river are completely encased in stone, with no breathing room. I can turn into a fish and I *might* be able to give someone else gills, perhaps, but...well, it'll be an experiment. And I can't do it for everyone.'

'Gills?' Usther repeated, pressing her hands to her own neck. She imagined the hideous, slimy slits in it that Ree had in her slime fish form. The idea made her skin crawl.

'Does Andomerys know how to give longer breath?' Persephone asked. 'I can do that for a handful of people, if it's not for too long. She could probably do it for much longer.'

'You can give people the ability to breathe underwater?' Ree asked, surprised.

Persephone shook her head. 'It's more like...I can make one breathful of air last a very long time. Tabris never got the hang of it, so I always had to cast it for them. Our masters speculate it's the Owl's influence that gives me a knack for it. One of her domains is water.'

Usther nodded uncertainly, remembering the symbol of the owl with river wings that had marked her shield and armour. She didn't remember much about the goddess Allariel. She didn't have a presence in Usther's home village, nor a shrine in the Tombtown Altar of Many Gods.

'Well, the trick now is to get you to our room so we can get the spells going,' Ree said. 'I have to make the climb in my ratskin. It's too slippery for me.'

Usther snorted. 'Too slippery for a cockroach like you? Then we're doomed.'

'How far is the other platform?' Persephone asked.

Ree frowned. 'About twelve feet across, maybe?'

'Higher? Lower?'

'Exactly the same height.' She said it like it was distasteful to her. Perhaps it was; the crypt was not ordinarily straightforward or symmetrical. It was a mess of extra steps, slanted floors, and odd angles.

Persephone pursed her lips. 'Let's get a look at it.'

The roaring falls in the washroom was much the same as it had been before. An awful wall of icy water. 'I don't particularly relish jumping down that,' Usther said.

Persephone examined it. 'You really can't see through to the other side, can you?'

Ree shook her head. 'The water's too fast-moving, I think.'

'Hmm.' She stepped back, then took several more steps.

Alarmed, Usther said, 'What are you—?'

She sprinted at the falls and leapt, disappearing into the water.

'Morrin's teeth!' Usther ran to the falls. 'Persephone? Persephone!'

Ree tugged at her elbow. 'Might want to step back.'

'Step—?'

Ree pulled her back just in time for Persephone to land on their side. She skidded, then slipped, hitting the ground hard.

'Ow! Well, that hurts a lot more than it used to.' She stood up, rubbing her lower back.

She was absolutely drenched. Soaked head to toe, her dress clinging to every curve, the ribbons of her skirt stuck to her thick legs in a very revealing sort of way. 'Jumpable!' she said to Usther cheerfully. 'Gave the little man on the other side quite the shock, though.'

'He didn't...uh...attack you?' Ree asked.

Persephone shrugged. 'Squeaked a little and introduced himself. I didn't hang around, though. Can you make it? It's less than six feet, I think, but the water definitely obstructs the jump.'

'Can I jump *six feet?*' Usther asked in tones of utter disbelief.

'So I should take that as a no...?' She sighed at Usther's glare. 'Fine. You can make it back all right, Ree? Good. You go. Usther and I will follow.'

'Usther is going to jump?' Ree said. She actually *smiled*. 'I don't mind hanging around—'

'Better to go now, I think. We may take a minute,' said Persephone.

Her friend gave her a look that wasn't nearly apologetic enough and transformed back into her nasty little cave rat. She skittered away, disappearing over the lip of the washroom platform.

'I can't jump that far,' Usther said. 'I'm not sure I could jump a *quarter* of that. Ree once laughed herself sick because I had spectres carry me across a three foot gap. It was a very long fall and I didn't want to trip! But spectres won't survive a waterfall. Or that distance, for that matter.' She loved spectres; considered herself a specialist, really. But she knew their limitations and physical strength was their biggest one.

'I could spell you to have stronger legs,' Persephone offered. 'You'd be able to make the jump.'

Usther imagining leaping blindly into the waterfall, the icy cold of it, forced to trust that she would touch down on the other side. She took a half-step back, raising a hand to stay the paladin, though she'd made no move toward casting. 'No, no I couldn't.'

'All right,' Persephone said. She took her folded clothes from before the feast and handed them to Usther. 'Could you put these in your pack, please?'

Usther did as she asked, though they didn't quite fit. She supposed she ought to be glad Misery didn't have the strength to carry her belongings as most minions did. Or that she feigned not having the strength. Else Usther would have none of her things right now.

'All packed?'

'Yes?' Usther eyed the paladin suspiciously.

Persephone approached, arms loose at her sides.

'What're you doing?'

'I'm going to pick you up. If you'll let me.'

When Usther didn't protest, Peresephone put one hand between her shoulders and half-crouched to put the other at the back of her thighs. In one smooth motion, she lifted Usther to cradle her against her chest.

'You're wet,' was all Usther could say, because every nerve in her body had lit up all at once and there was no thought in her left to say something clever.

'We're about to get a lot wetter.' Usther could feel Persephone's muscles bunch, the soft roundness of her arms and belly suddenly hard and toned. Persephone muttered under her breath; the paladin's entire body heated in a burst of healing.

Then she took three running steps and sprang into the waterfall. Usther screamed and huddled against her chest, eyes squeezed shut.

A heavy thump, a swooping sensation, and a blast of icy cold, quickly vanished.

Persephone laughed, her entire body rumbling. Usther dared to open her eyes.

They were on the floor of a washroom identical to their own, but now the rushing falls were behind them and water puddled on the floor. Ree, Smythe, and Andomerys stood in the doorway. Persephone's legs were outstretched in front of her, one knee half-raised, holding Usther tight to her chest. As she laughed, she gently set Usther aside.

'The Owl must be punishing me,' she said. 'Gods...my tailbone has been bruised on top of bruises.' She stood up, wincing, and placed a silver-glowing hand to her backside.

Usther's heart was still beating far too fast. Her eyes went from Ree to Smythe. 'Where are they?'

A small, relieved sigh, followed by a loud yowl. Misery knocked Ree aside and stumbled into the room, reaching for Usther.

'Misery!' She threw her arms around her minion, stroking the tangled mess of her plait. 'Oh darling, I'm so glad you're all right! Did he look after you? Do I need to curse him?' She pulled back, looking her minion over. She was still clothed in a protective layer of Smythe's clothing and she seemed uninjured even with a cursory brush of necromancy to check. She wrinkled her nose. 'Your hair is a *mess*, Misery. Did nobody brush it?'

Misery sighed.

Usther crouched to scoop up the cat curling frantically around her legs. 'Well *you* look in good order,' she said. Dichotomy purred and drooled with a desperate intensity, and reached up to press a velvet paw against her cheek with only the smallest touch of claws. Misery leaned in, bumping her shoulder against Usther's.

Usther's vision blurred. She blinked away tears. Her chest was tight and full, hours of constant anxiety lifted and leaving a rush of panic in their wake. 'I'm so glad you're okay,' she said, and pressed a kiss between her cat's ears.

After a moment, she composed herself. She put her cat on the floor and strode over to Smythe.

'I ought to slap you,' she said calmly.

He looked startled. 'I—?'

'"The wards will keep them safe"?' she said.

Smythe's skin turned a paler shade of grey. 'Oh.'

She glared at him a moment. 'But they are safe,' she said. 'And I hear you protected them. And you wouldn't even be in this mess if you weren't trying to help me.'

Smythe sighed. 'Well, it's not like I don't owe you the help.'

'True. But I suppose I won't slap you just yet.'

She looked to Ree. Her friend had changed out of her flame-coloured robes and back into her dusty blacks.

'We need to go,' she said. 'We don't know how long it'll be before they check on us.'

Usther felt a stab of anxiety. 'We can't possibly get down there.'

'We can,' Ree said firmly. 'The healers can give you strength for the climb. There's a few shelves on the way down where we can rest. At least for the first fifty feet or so. We can make it.'

Persephone nodded, but Andomerys said, 'I'm not going.'

'What?'

She raised her chin. 'Emberlon is still here somewhere. He's hurt. He needs my help. I'm not going to abandon him.'

Ree's brow furrowed. 'Then we'll all—'

'No. It's important that you get back to town. Warn whoever remains. Get help if you can.'

'Andomerys...' Ree stared at the healer helplessly.

Usther remained silent. She didn't think it was wise to stay in this place, but neither did she blame Andomerys for wanting to stay for her friend. If the siblings had locked Misery away somewhere, Usther would have no choice but to remain as well.

'Go,' Andomerys said. She stayed in the doorway, watching, as their group approached the falls.

'How many of us can you give extra breath?' Smythe asked Persephone nervously.

'Ahhh...Owl's wings.' She rubbed the back of her head. 'Myself and two others almost indefinitely. It's not the most draining spell. Any more than that and we might run into problems. And I daren't do anything for your undead friend; I might accidentally undo the magic animating her.'

'Misery?' Usther asked. She patted her minion's shoulder. 'Are you all right under water, darling?'

Misery shook her head, looking panicked.

'She can,' Ree said. 'Larry fell into a lake once. He couldn't swim but he was down there for ten minutes with no problem. I don't think either he or Misery breathe.'

'No, I suppose not,' Usther said.

Misery shook her head again.

'It's the only option, darling,' Usther said quietly.

She wasn't keen on the plunge into damp and darkness, herself.

CHAPTER THIRTY

Ree

A plan was made, though Ree felt it might fray in their hands. Persephone would spell breath into Usther and Dichotomy. Usther and Smythe would spell strength into Misery. And Ree would sing gills into Smythe.

Now, she took out her travel journal. The one she took with her was a distillation of several years worth of work, meant to hold only her completed spells. Over time, it had accumulated loose pages and additional notes, nearly bursting from its binding. She flipped through the pages until she found the one she needed. A spell modified from one of Wylandriah Witch-feather's, to emulate stories told of therianthropes. The page was a mess of scribbles and crossings-out even in its finished form, so she read it through a few times before she tried to sing it.

'Ell-an ellerra,' she sang, her voice hoarse and low. She could feel her magic like water on her skin, and drew strength from the waters of her belly. A song of something deep and unknowable. *'Ell-an kur-la terr, durro, durro...'*

As she continued the song, she walked up to Smythe. One hand went to the pouch on her belt holding her fishskin. Smythe watched her nervously, his face familiar beneath its new sharpness, his eyes kinder than she remembered.

She touched her other hand lightly to his neck, still singing, and brushed her thumb across the skin.

They were very close like this, Ree realised. Close enough that he was breathing her breath, while she touched him as one might a lover.

Smythe visibly swallowed. 'Will it hurt?' he asked in a small voice. He didn't pull away.

Sympathy bloomed. She shook her head. Energy flowed from pouch through her arms, belly, and out again through her hand, sparkling along his skin in shades of blue and black. She turned his face with a light touch to his chin, and repeated the motion on the other side of his neck, leaving energy sparkling there.

She stepped back, letting the song die on her lips.

Smythe reached up and touched his neck with a trembling hand. 'The skin is normal,' he said. 'But I can feel something there. Cold, but not like necromancy.'

And no surprise. Necromancy felt like wind and ice. To Ree, therianthropy had always felt like smoke and water.

She might never have learned that, if not for him. The thought was intrusive and unwanted. She also might not dream of her friends and family dying in a storm of spirits, if not for him. She might not feel so suffocated by Usther if not for him. But the man who had done those things seemed increasingly far away, whereas the man before her, who had risked himself for Usther's minion and cat, who had followed Usther into danger, felt almost different entirely.

Was it wrong that she wanted to ascribe him the good and not the bad? It felt like naivety. And she had promised herself never to be naive again.

She turned away, clearing her throat. 'It'll trigger if you submerge in water,' she said. Or certainly, she hoped it would. If not, Persephone would have to spell breath into him as well, and she seemed uncertain whether she could hold so many spells at once.

She looked back at Andomerys. The healer smiled. 'Go,' she said. 'I'll be fine. I'll turn their damn mushrooms into ash if it comes to it.'

'Keep him safe?' she said.

'Of course.' She looked almost like she might say something else, but then she shook her head and walked into the other room.

Now it was just their group. The three honoured guests and their sworn enemy-turned-ally.

'I'll go first,' Ree said. 'Follow my steps. If we get down to the first ledge, it's a clear fall.'

She eased herself over the edge of the platform, wincing at the icy blast of the waterfall. But she was able to get enough of a grip to begin picking her way down. Persephone followed her, her bare feet sure and steady. Misery clung to her neck, moaning miserably.

'It's not as bad as all that,' Persephone said. Hard to imagine she'd drawn her spear on Larry only a little while ago. She watched each of Ree's movements carefully before copying them. Usther and Smythe followed. When Ree got down to the small ledge about twenty feet below, she hovered anxiously. Neither Smythe nor Usther were particularly strong or agile. Indeed, quite the opposite. Quintessential necromancers, both, with toothpick arms and noodle legs.

Usther slipped, and Ree sprang to the wall, ready to climb up to her, but Usther's feet landed on Persephone's shoulders. 'It's fine,' Persephone said soothingly. 'You're doing great. Take all the time you need.'

It must have required a level of strength that Ree could barely conceive of, but Persephone bore it with gentle patience. She did regularly wear thick sheets of metal, so perhaps the weight of a scarecrow minion and her necromancer compared favourably.

When Persephone dropped down onto the platform beside Ree, though, she looked tired. Ree wondered how much of the moisture on her face was from the fall, and how much was sweat. She gave Ree a brief smile, though, and tried to prise Misery from her neck. 'Could you give me a hand? She doesn't want to let go.'

Misery gave a coughing cry of protest.

'Aren't you scared?' Ree asked her.

Persephone's smile was wan. 'Haven't looked down.'

When Misery was detached and Smythe and Usther were crowded onto the ledge, Ree said, 'It's a wide fall from here. I flew down once there was room. We should be able to hit the river. And from there, it'll get us to town, or near it.'

'Is this definitely the same river that runs near town?' Usther stared down at the hole like it might reach up and bite her.

Ree shrugged. 'I think so. As far as I know, there's only one river in the crypt, and a few fast-flowing streams. But—'

'—nobody knows for sure,' Usther finished. She frowned at Ree. 'For a cartographer, you are rather lacking in useful directions.'

She was more useful than anyone else, but she didn't want to have that argument. Usther was just scared. She always got sharp when she was scared.

'How far?' Smythe asked.

Ree hesitated. 'About thirty feet.'

Usther scoffed; Smythe spluttered.

'It's that or we go back to the Many,' Ree said.

'Climbable?' Persephone said.

Ree shook her head. 'We'll have to jump.'

Persephone clenched her fists. 'All right. Fine. Good. Great.' She flexed her hands and muttered something, touching silver light to Usther's chest, and again to the cat snuggled against her back. 'Breath. And it ought to help a little with the impact as well, I hope,' she said.

She turned to Smythe and Ree and repeated the gesture. 'Impact only.' Her touch was gently warm, sunshine on a winter's day, and Ree felt that warmth spread throughout her body. 'Should last a few minutes.'

'Well then,' Smythe said. He rubbed his hands together, his eyes wide and worried. He tucked away his glasses in his pack. 'I suppose there's nothing for it but to go.'

'Arms crossed like this,' she said, demonstrating. 'Feet together. Try to hit feet first.'

He nodded grimly. 'Delightful.' He looked to Usther. 'I'll see you on the other side.'

'Don't die,' Usther replied.

Ree watched their interaction uneasily. Something had passed between them these last few days. Usther's concern seemed genuine, though Ree could not imagine her ever reconciling with him. It once again gave her the feeling that she wasn't looking at the same person.

People changed. Ree knew that. She herself was not exactly the same person she'd been as a teenager. She was more weary, and, she hoped, more wise. But the kind of change Smythe had made...she didn't know that she could really believe it.

Smythe had his back to them now, contemplating the edge. His shoulders were tight. She couldn't see his face. Then wordlessly, he crossed his arms and stepped off the edge.

Misery gasped. Usther pat her consolingly.

Ree went to the edge. 'He made it,' she said. 'Who's next?'

Persephone shook herself. 'I suppose it had better be me.' She flashed Ree a pained smile. 'I can't go last. I don't think I'd go through with it.'

Ree nodded, remembering Persephone's fear of the crumbling chasm. She walked to the edge, shaking out her hands and stretching her neck. 'It's just water,' she said. She had taken Dichotomy, now strapped to her chest; Persephone wrapped her arms protectively around the little bundle, and Ree saw her hands glow as she did so. Additional protections, no doubt.

She glanced at Usther, then jumped.

Ree watched her hit the water below and be swept away.

Misery was already backing away from the edge. She couldn't be carried safely; she might drag someone else down in the water. So Ree went to her and said, very gently, 'Sorry, Misery.' And shoved her over the edge.

Usther stared at her, mouth agape. 'You *pushed* her!'

'She wasn't going to go,' Ree said. A small part of her recognised that the act had been ruthless, even if it had been necessary. 'She can't stay here, Usther.'

'No, I know, I know...' Usther pushed back her braids, her eyes full of worry. She stared at the ledge. Her mouth trembled. 'I don't think I can do it,' she said. She turned to Ree, her eyes pleading.

Ree took her hand. It was something she'd rarely ever done. She walked to the edge with her. 'You just need to keep your feet together,' she said. She let go of Usther's hand and reached up to squeeze her shoulder.

Usther closed her eyes, knowing it was coming.

And Ree shoved her off the edge as well.

Usther screamed, a high-pitched, throat-tearing sound, then was swept away.

Ree ignored the tight feeling in her chest, the churning in her gut. The jump wouldn't haunt her/ But that push certainly would.

No time to waste on it now. She took first to her crowskin to glide down, and then dropped into the rushing water as a small blind fish and was swept away.

CHAPTER THIRTY-ONE

Usther

She wanted her to do it. She hoped she wouldn't. She feared she would. And then she was falling and she barely had time to register betrayal or relief before she hit the water with a bone-jarring splash and then everything was a quick-flailing disaster.

She couldn't sense the others. Couldn't see in the fast-flowing water except for distant hazy blobs and the black rock that enclosed on all sides. She tried to swim but it was hard to hit her stride. Her robes tangled around her legs and when she kicked, she lost a boot.

But she could *breathe.* Or at least, she didn't feel the need to. Her lungs were full and comfortable, beating with the ease of natural breath, though her mouth was closed and she did not inhale. Her chest felt warm, as if touched by sunlight. It was only that which reduced her panic enough that she could begin to orientate herself and strike out along with the current.

She reached out with her senses. Misery was ahead, floundering but fine. Unalive and confused was better than dead and at peace, but her heart still ached for the panic her minion must be feeling. There was another necromancy on her, too; Smythe must be pouring strength into her, as he'd promised. It seemed likely that he was all right as well, in spite of Ree's dubiously safe therianthropy.

The river was swift, but not gentle. It banged her against rocks when she wasn't careful, or scraped her against the cave wall. She had to try to keep herself near the middle, where the flow was strong and the banks couldn't touch her. She quickly grew tired, her strokes growing weaker, and then failing entirely. The river didn't care, and carried her regardless.

She became aware of something small paddling at her side. She could just make out the somewhat amorphous shape of Ree's eyeless slimefish. The fish darted around her, concerned, then swam ahead with surprising speed. No doubt to check on the others with similar prods and bumps.

Light flooded in. The roof of the river fell away to a far distant ceiling cracked with moonlight. There was a bank, too. Good, familiar stone pocked with green moss. She could see figures lying on the bank.

She emerged, gasping, and clawed her way onto the stone. Strong hands took her arms and hauled her out properly. She blinked blearily up at Persephone, who held her in a light embrace.

'You okay?' the paladin asked.

Usther nodded mutely and the paladin released her. She was still too dazed to be frightened.

'Ree?' she looked around.

A fish flopped out of the water and bounced on the bank, gasping, before Ree unspooled from the skin and onto her knees. 'Still not used to that,' she said.

'Well, why don't you change back *before* you climb on land?' Usther asked, irritated.

Ree shook her head. 'Too disoriented. Might get swept away.'

'So you'd rather suffocate for a few seconds?'

Her friend nodded and Usther threw up her hands in defeat. 'There's no help for you,' she said.

Smythe and Misery lay side-by-side on the bank, Misery curled up while Smythe gave her a reassuring pat. 'You did wonderfully, old girl,' he said. 'The bravest minion anyone's ever heard of. The bards will write ballads in your name!'

Misery groaned and rolled away from him, which seemed to express her opinion on bravery, bards, or ballads.

Dichotomy ran over to her and curled against her chest. The little cat was soaked to the bone and looked positively skeletal. She growled as she did so, throwing a flat-eared glare toward the unnoticing Persephone.

Usther went to comfort her family, accepting a few swipes from Dichotomy as her due. 'At least we'll be home soon,' she said soothingly. 'It's almost over now.' And she'd have to re-evaluate the risks of leaving her cat and minion at home versus taking them with her. Perhaps she could train Misery to open the wards on the door safely.

Ree wrung out her hair and started digging in her pack.

'Where are we?' Usther asked.

'Give me a minute!' her friend snapped.

Usther rolled her eyes. 'So testy after a bit of suffocation,' Usther said, earning her a glare she was glad to accept.

Truthfully, it was nice to have Ree annoyed at her. It made everything feel a lot more normal than it had these last few days.

Ree opened about three different layers of oilskin and unfolded a carefully wrapped map from her pack. She was silent for a few moments, eyes and fingers tracing the lines of the map and then looking around at the space around them.

'I think this could be here,' she said, showing a page a level down from the town. 'Below and a bit to the east. Less than a day from town.'

'Less than a day!' Usther said. They'd travelled for days to get to the Many's kingdom.

Ree shrugged. 'I *think* so. It's hard to say. The white marble tunnels really made me lose all sense of place. But the river moves more directly than any path to that side of the crypt I can think of and it moved fast as well.'

She rolled up the map, resealed it, and packed it away. 'We should get going. The first place they'll look for us is the river.'

'Fat chance they'll get any denizens down those falls,' Usther said.

'I'd still rather not be here if any fungal minions wash up,' her friend replied, and Usther made a face. No, she'd rather not be there for that either.

'This town,' Persephone said, following Usther up the rocks. Usther followed Ree.

'Mm?'

'It's not...not like a nice, bright surface town, is it?' she asked.

Usther laughed bitterly. 'Not at all, no.'

'And is it safe to say that they will not be happy to see a paladin?'

'Extremely safe,' Usther said. 'Which is to say, it will be extremely unsafe for you.'

'We're not letting anybody attack you,' Ree said. She glanced back over her shoulder, looking past Persephone. 'We've had enough trouble with that sort of thing.'

Smythe said, 'They aren't going to be happy to see me, either.'

'No,' said Ree. 'But you deserve it.'

Smythe didn't reply, and when Usther cast a look back at him, he looked sad. 'I won't let anyone attack you either,' she told him firmly. Then, feeling a little awkward about it, she added quickly, 'It would upset Misery, and she's been through quite enough recently.'

Smythe gave the smallest smile. 'No, it wouldn't do to upset her. Thank you.'

They moved on.

Disoriented or not, Ree had an uncanny ability to find her way through the crypt and it wasn't long before they were on a nice uneven stone brick path again.

It wasn't a terribly long journey from there. Ree had estimated their distance very well. A few hours later, they appeared at the top of the Central Mausoleum, gazing down at the many-tiered collection of converted tombhomes that made up Tombtown.

Usther gazed down at it with a kind of weak-kneed relief. Misery cried out and tried to push past, rushing down the steps toward home, and Usther let her go, and put Dichotomy down so that the cat could race after her. 'We're finally home,' Usther said quietly. She looked sidelong at Ree, but her housemate did not seem to share her joy. She looked terribly weary.

'If there's anyone left to welcome us,' she said.

CHAPTER THIRTY-TWO

Ree

It was all wrong. The town was all wrong. No torches lit the tombhome entrances. The *Bone & Brew*'s doors stood closed. And all of the noise and bustle she had come to expect from her town—the necromancers bickering on street corners, the children playing in the streets with their undead rats—were absent.

Transplanted elsewhere.

'Stay close,' Ree said to Smythe and Persephone, and started down the stairs.

'Are we in danger?' Persephone asked.

Ree shrugged. It was very unlikely that anyone would attack people in her company. Even a paladin. Even Smythe. But with the town standing empty, anyone left would be on edge. And necromancers did not, as a rule, handle nerves with grace.

Assuming that there *was* anyone left.

They descended the steps in silence. Behind her, Persephone radiated tension and a touch of unnatural warmth. Smythe seemed almost a void of conversation, so far had he withdrawn into himself. She wondered if he was remembering these steps being ripped away in the wind and replaced with unworn cut stone. If he remembered the howl of hundreds of spirits at once encircling him in a vast tornado. There were days when it was all she could remember. She hoped it pained him the way it did her. She hoped it hurt him more.

As they passed tombhomes, it became clear the town was not as abandoned as it first appeared. Denizens peered through cracked doors and hid when Ree caught their eyes, or stood in the streets surrounded by bags and baskets, gesturing for their families to follow.

Ree trotted up to one such family. She didn't recognise this denizen, with her white hair and high-collared robes, but she'd seen her son around many times playing with the other children. 'Pardon,' Ree said, raising her hands palm out to show she meant no harm. The denizen looked tightly-wound, and her lips were pressed into a thin line. Her fingers twitched, as if she were ready to cast at any moment. 'Where is everyone?'

'Mortana's, most like,' said the necromancer. 'Those that mean to stay.' She shook her head. 'I can't risk it. Venlana's little girls were just took. I'm not letting them get my Chestofer as well.'

Ree thanked her and led the group on. The mother watched them pass with narrowed eyes, saying nothing else.

'Mortana's?' Usther said quietly. 'Not the town hall?'

'Perhaps there aren't enough people for the town hall,' Ree said.

Misery and Dichotomy returned to them as they went, their exuberance overcome by impatience with the closed door. Ree looked around the town, hopeful of the return of her own minion companion, but there were no gargling cries to be heard and no masterless minion to be found.

'Looking for someone?' Smythe asked quietly.

Ree startled at the sudden sound of his voice. He'd been terribly quiet the entire journey. 'Larry was with us,' she said in a low voice. 'Before we met Celia. I tried to send him home when we entered the marble tunnels, but he wouldn't go. Then when Celia appeared, he vanished.'

'You're worried she took him?'

Ree shrugged, not trusting herself to words.

Smythe nodded. He seemed to search for words for a moment, before saying, 'Larry isn't like other minions. He's smart, and he's strong. Maybe he left to avoid being captured.'

'Maybe,' Ree agreed, though she didn't feel it. It was true that Larry was stronger than other minions, though it was hard to believe when he was chomping ineffectually on your arm with his blunt teeth. He'd survived an arrow to the head, something fatal to all other minions. He was some kind of experiment of the Lich that used to haunt the town.

But if anything, that would just make him more appealing to Mykol and Celia. They seemed very keen to collect people of power. And whatever it was that bound Smythe, Ree, and Usther in their eyes, surely Larry would be part of that. Because everything they'd done back then, Larry had been part of.

They made it to the town square. Ree went for *The Bone & Brew,* which stood sober as a fortress with its heavy doors pulled shut. Light flickered beneath the door, the only sign of life in the eerily desolate square.

Ree tried the door but it wouldn't budge. She waved her friends back and knocked heavily on it. 'Mortana? It's Ree. And...friends.'

For a moment, nothing. Then the sound of lots of shuffling and quick footsteps on stone. The door creaked open. Mortana peered around, her wyrdling horns scraping the wood. She held a red curse in her hand, a cruel orb of light waiting to be released. 'What are you doing here?' she asked. Her gaze went to the others, and her eyes narrowed. 'Who are they?'

'Usther, Persephone, and...Smythe.' She said the last name with reticence, knowing the reaction it would get.

But instead of fear or anger, Mortana's brows lifted. 'Smythe Townslayer? Come in, come in.' She pulled the door open wider.

It was dimly lit. The torch sconces were left dark, and instead a handful of candles were scattered across the in-use tables clustered near the bar. Mortana marched back there, her feather-tipped tail brushing the floor as she walked, but instead of going behind the bar to work on her potions, as she usually did, instead she hopped up to sit on it, looking more subdued than Ree had ever seen her.

The crowd was small. She recognised a few of them. Kylath, youngest of the town council, now sitting with her head in her hands while another woman rubbed her shoulder. Bald-headed Veritas with goggles around his neck, hunched over to whisper to a skull that chattered its teeth in return. Pontifar, a practitioner who always wore red and appeared to be in his thirties, hugged his bonehound, scratching its non-existent ears while it wiggled in delight, oblivious to its master's worry. There were others: neighbours, shopkeepers, and—

'Reanima!' Her mother rushed forward to throw her arms around her with none of her usual grace. Ree was startled by the touch but instinctually hugged back, tears burning in her eyes.

'You're okay,' she said.

Her mother nodded, eyes shining. She looked different. Gone was her cassock and fur cloak. So, too, was the otherworldly air that always seemed to surround her. She wore a simple linen shirt and loose trousers. She looked smaller than Ree had ever seen her. Her mother released her, immediately embracing Usther as well.

Her father took her place. He reached out and squeezed her shoulder, giving her a shaky smile. 'I thought you were gone,' he said. She'd never heard his voice so tremulous. 'Every night, we said to each other, "She knows the crypt. She'll come back." But when you didn't...' He took a deep breath. 'I'm glad you're back.'

'I am, too,' she said.

Her father patted her on the shoulder again and joined her mother at Kylath's table. Usther waved her over to another table. Persephone sat beside her, looking around with interest. There was a tinkle of glass as Dichotomy knocked a small pot onto the floor, then looked startled.

Ree glanced at Smythe. He was frozen in place, his mouth set in an uncertain line. She hesitated, then tugged at his sleeve. When he looked around, she jerked her head toward Usther's table, and left without waiting for his response. But when she slid into the seat beside Usther, Smythe took the seat on her other side a moment later.

'What's happening?' Ree said, looking from her father to Mortana. 'Why are you all here?'

'We're all that's left,' said Mortana. She crossed her arms, her shoulders high and tense.

'We check in here every day,' said Igneus. 'Nobody wants to go missing.'

'Mortana's even letting some stay in the rooms,' said Arthura. 'Better that than people disappear unnoticed in their disparate towers.'

'They wouldn't get into *my* tower,' said Veritas. He wiggled his fingers at his little skull minion, which snapped at him. 'I'm just here because my assistant was nervous.'

Persephone said, 'You're assis—? Oh.' She looked surprised and glanced at Usther. Ree was willing to bet that Usther had kicked her. She'd been on the receiving end of those kicks many times herself.

The room went very still. Kylath looked up from her hands, her eyes narrowed. 'Just *who* are you?' she asked. 'Not a friend of the Townslayer, I hope.'

'The Towns—? Uh, no. We're recent acquaintances.'

There was a clattering sound as Veritas' skull minion hopped from his table to theirs, bouncing by means of opening and closing its jaw. Dichotomy hit it on the dome as it went by, but it seemed not to notice. Persephone leaned back a bit as it bounced in front of her, chattering.

'I quite agree,' said Veritas. He put on his goggles and leaned between the tables, fixed on her. 'There's something wrong with her. Her skin is almost...*glowing.*'

'Rather big to be a healer,' said Mortana.

'Oh, I don't agree with that,' said Persephone. 'You need to hold people down rather a lot in the healing arts.'

'And the Craft as well,' someone muttered.

'Last minion I raised had a little too much juice,' someone else added. 'Woulda had my nose off it, if I hadn't strapped it down.'

'But you're not a healer, are you?' said Arthura. She might not be wearing her robes and fur, but her eyes were still piercing, and her voice still carried.

'No,' Persephone agreed. 'I'm not.'

The temperature in the room dropped.

Smythe raised his hands. 'Woah, woah!' he said. 'There's no need for that!'

A few people flinched at his voice, and Ree saw some eyes clear of shadow or blood, but there was still a sense of poised curses, a chill edged with electricity that made the hair on her arms stand on end.

'She saved my life,' Usther said tartly. She leaned forward, glaring down at the skull in front of her. 'And I should think that, after what happened the last time you took issue with an upworlder, you might have learned your lesson.'

'She's right,' said Arthura. 'Calm yourselves. Morrin's law is as true today as it was at the founding.'

'Morrin's law?' Ree saw Persephone mouth to Usther.

Usther mouthed back, 'Play nice.'

Persephone raised her eyebrows, but made no comment.

'Do you know where people are going?' Ree asked, looking from face to face. 'Do you know anything at all about what's been happening?'

'It's the white city,' Veritas said. He slammed his leather-gloved fist on the table. 'I've been saying it for years now. There's a white city full of terrible ghosts, and they're coming for our souls.'

'Nobody cares about your latest ravings,' Mortana said, rolling her eyes. 'This is serious business.'

Ree said, 'He's not wrong.' And with every eye on her, she recounted their experiences as clearly as she could, talking around the fact that Persephone and Tabris were paladins. Her listeners were not silent, interjecting with scoffs of disbelief or gasps of recognition. All the while, her mother's eyes were fixed on Persephone, her expression utterly unreadable, while her father watched Smythe with obvious dislike.

'Fungi that can resist necromancy,' Kylath murmured when Ree was finished. 'I've never heard of anything of the sort.'

'Well, that's not a surprise,' Veritas scoffed.

Ree raised her eyebrows at the experimental necromancer. 'Have you heard of it before?'

Veritas hesitated. 'Well...no. But I've heard of a great deal more than Kylath!'

Kylath waved a bored hand in his direction. 'Yes, we're all very impressed by your worldliness,' she said.

Usther snorted and Kylath threw her an approving look.

Persephone shifted uncomfortably. 'Could it have been created by necromancy?' she asked.

'It's possible,' said Igneus. 'Every year, new discoveries are being made.'

'But unlikely,' said Mortana. Everyone looked at her. 'Well, for one, necromantic creations can also be destroyed by necromancy. That's a core tenant of the Craft. But for another, I've been experimenting with fungi for the last five years and not seen any success.'

Usther leaned forward. 'Well, it's not surprising. You can hardly raise plants from the dead.'

'You can!' Veritas insisted. 'Only those of small vision and smaller minds—'

'Fungi aren't plants,' said Arthura.

Mortana's tail thumped the bar loudly. 'That's neither here nor there. The problem isn't that you can't raise it. The problem is that you can't kill it in the first place.'

The arguments immediately stopped. After a moment, Ree said, 'I don't know what you mean. Surely you can sterilise it with a targeted curse?'

Mortana shook her head. 'Some of it, sure. We can kill spores. You can even kill the—the plant, I suppose—itself. But fungi is more complex than that. Killing part of it isn't the same as killing the thing itself. If I cut off my arm and someone tried to raise it, they would fail. Because the arm is still attached to a living soul, yes? You'd have to kill *me* first.'

'But surely if you kill the mushroom, you've killed the creature,' said Igneus.

Mortana shook her head. 'Only a piece of it.'

'So you're suggesting that all that red fungi you encountered—it was all one being?' said Kylath.

Ree and Usther exchanged a look. She knew what her friend was thinking. 'It's called the Many-That-Hungers,' Ree said.

'And it's intelligent,' Usther added. 'It can move. Act. Think.'

'When directed by Mykol or Celia,' Ree said.

Smythe shook his head. 'Uh...actually, I'm fairly certain it can act independently. If that's the right way to put it. They don't need to be present for it to act. But it seems to act...better...more cleverly, in their presence.'

'That's interesting,' said Persephone. 'Because I'm not entirely sure they're human.'

This caused a burst of heated arguing, which Kylath waved down.

'What makes you say that? You think they're undead?'

'Not undead,' she said. 'They seem worlds apart from, say, Misery here.' She gestured to Usther's house-minion, who stood in the corner of the room with shoulders sagging in what Ree interpreted as absolute bliss.

'They just don't seem human to me. I have a sense for these things, and there are some essential things missing.'

'Like what?' Usther asked.

'Like pores,' she replied. 'Like hair on their skin. And as long as I watched them, I don't think I ever saw them draw a breath.'

That stilled the room more powerfully than anything before.

'You *are* a healer, then,' said Pontifar, hopefully.

Persephone inclined her head slightly. Ree supposed it wasn't quite a lie. She herself had no strong desire to warn everyone of the paladin in their midst. It would only complicate matters.

'This...we need to think about this,' Igneus said.

'We do,' Kylath agreed. 'But before we get to that, we need to deal with a more immediate threat.'

'Oh?' said Ree, glancing nervously at Persephone.

'Indeed.' She stood up, and placed her hands flat on the table as she considered their group. 'Smythe Townslayer. You have broken your exile.'

'Oh,' said Smythe. He took off his glasses and cleaned them on his shirt. 'I did think that might come up.'

THE BEAUTIFUL DECAY

CHAPTER THIRTY-THREE

Usther

'You can't be serious,' said Usther, letting her disdain positively *drip* from her voice. Disdain was a powerful weapon, especially against other necromancers. They absolutely could not bear to be thought less of. 'We're beyond the point of exile. You can't keep any denizens *in!'*

'The law is the law,' said Kylath, rising. Igneus rose from his seat as well. The vaunted town council, now reduced to two people wallowing in sorrow in a poorly-lit tavern.

'The *law* is fucking made up,' Usther said. 'You council members decide a different law every day.' She stood up and went to stand behind Smythe, gripping the back of his chair so hard her knuckles hurt.

'It's okay,' said Smythe. He looked nervously between Kylath and Igneus. 'I'll leave, if you want. Or take your punishment.'

'No you won't,' Usther hissed. 'The punishment for breaking exile is death!'

'Oh.' Smythe paused, and said in a small voice, 'Well, I'd rather not do that, then.'

She knew he could rival at least one of the council members for power. Maybe both of them. Maybe everyone in the room. Her understanding of his power was tenuous; only that he was stronger than anyone she'd yet encountered. If he wanted to, he could mind-snare them and hold them in their place, as he'd accidentally done to her on their first meeting. But there was no cold radiating from Smythe, and his hands were folded on the table in front of him. He kept his eyes lowered—perhaps even to avoid any mindsnaring accidents.

Kylath and Igneus stood in front of their table now, Igneus' arms crossed, Kylath leaning forward with both palms flat on the surface.

Usther wanted to scream at them. She wanted to point at them and tell them exactly what she thought about their laws—laws which had nearly killed Smythe as a teenager, laws which had given him no love of the town and no help when he was frightened. She had been blaming him for years for what had happened, and while that blame was justified, it wasn't justified to blame him alone. He'd been a teenager, no older than she had been. He'd been frightened and threatened with death and blood sacrifice. Was it any wonder that in his fear he'd seen fit to sacrifice the people who'd tried to kill him?

She could blame him for hurting *her*. She'd never done anything to hurt him. But the town?

No, she couldn't blame him for that.

Truthfully, there were days when she wished she could burn it all down herself.

Misery sensed her nerves and started to whine. Dichotomy boffed Smythe's chin with her head and stared at the council with wide eyes.

'*He saved my life*,' Usther said again, an accidental death echo colouring her voice.

'You nearly destroyed our town,' said Igneus.

'You can help us destroy another,' said Kylath.

A sharp intake of air from Smythe. Usther could only stare. Everyone else in the room had gone quiet, their gazes fixed on Smythe. Mortana inclined her head toward him, just barely. Pontifar hugged his bonehound, eyes desperate.

'I don't know if I can,' Smythe said quietly. 'I don't know if I *want* to. I don't want to hurt anyone.'

'Not the people, then,' said Kylath. 'Just the ones running things. Just the fungi. Can you do that thing again? That ritual?'

'I can't,' Smythe said, though he didn't sound apologetic. 'The tablet that described the ritual was destroyed, and I made no attempt to remember it. I'll help you, if you want my help. There are people trapped by Mykol and Celia. Many more than serve them willingly, perhaps. But I'm not killing anyone.'

'And if they try to kill you?' demanded Kylath.

'They can try,' Smythe said bleakly.

That hovered in the air a moment, a tension broken only by Dichotomy gently patting Smythe's cheek to ask for more attention.

'That'll have to do,' Igneus said. 'Mortana, do you have a room to spare for the guests?'

'Only one room,' she said. 'And only if they don't mind sleeping in the cellar.'

'Cellar's fine,' said Smythe.

'I don't have a problem with that,' Persephone added.

Ree frowned. 'You can stay with us,' she told the paladin.

'Uh,' said Usther.

Persephone looked surprised. 'Thank you.' She looked to Usther for confirmation, and Usther could only nod.

'Then we'll gather again in the morning,' said Igneus, wiping his face tiredly. 'Don't go anywhere alone.'

'Yeah, yeah,' said Mortana, waving a dismissive hand.

Gradually, the group dispersed. Mortana waved Smythe over, but he paused as he stood up. 'Thank you,' he whispered.

Usther avoided his eyes, her face heating. 'Sure,' she replied, and then he disappeared behind the bar.

Arthura approached them, looking worriedly between her and Ree. 'You've been through a lot,' she said. 'We need to talk about it.'

'In the morning,' Ree said, rubbing her eyes. 'I miss my bed.'

'In the morning,' Igneus agreed. 'We'll come knocking.'

It was strange to go home after everything they'd been through. Stranger still to cross the threshold with Persephone in tow. They rarely had visitors, truthfully. And never had anyone *stay*. It had always just been Usther and Ree. It was a small, comfortable world that sometimes included Ree's parents. But now that world was expanding at a frightening speed, and included people Usther had never imagined.

Home looked exactly the same as they'd left it. There was a coating of dust Usther would take pleasure in cleaning away. A bit of normalcy to look forward to. But it felt...empty, too. All the clutter and familiarity could do nothing to change the airlessness of it. The emptiness. There had been no one here for days. No Ree to leave her books strewn across the floor. No Dichotomy to scratch on Usther's armchair. No Misery standing in the corner and refusing her chores.

It was good to be home. But it was strange, too. She wondered if Ree felt this after all of her many trips out into the crypt. If she had come back feeling changed, while the tombhome had remained static. While Usther had remained static.

Ree came out of her room with a stack of blankets and a travel bedroll. 'Sorry we don't have better,' she said, handing them to the paladin.

'No, this is more than I could have asked. Thank you both for welcoming me into your home.' She bowed and accepted the stack of blankets.

Usther hesitated, watching for set up on the floor. She rolled out the bedroll with a smooth motion and laid the blankets atop it. She seemed to sense Usther's gaze on her. 'Something on your mind?' she asked.

'Does it bother you?' Usther asked. 'Sleeping in a necromancer's home?'

She paused and looked up at Usther, her expression thoughtful. Even with her hair dried into a frizzy mess and her clothes still a little damp, she was beautiful. 'If you'd asked me a few weeks ago, I think it would have,' she said. 'But I've learned a lot since then. And anyway, this isn't just any necromancer's house.'

'Oh?'

'It's yours,' she said, and gave Usther a gentle smile. 'Goodnight, Usther.'

Usther murmured goodnight as well and fled to her room. Thankfully, she was too exhausted to dwell on the way her heart pounded, or the warm feeling spreading in her belly. She curled up on her hard, familiar bed, and passed quickly from waking into dreams.

When she woke, she had to take a minute to berate herself. She'd been having a quite pleasant dream about joining Persephone in a waterfall and it was only on waking that the shame of it really struck her.

She had no business thinking that way about a paladin, or a woman she'd just met, or a guest in her festering house. It had just been a long time since she'd gotten to enjoy the company of another woman, that was all.

She went to the washroom and stoked the fire, filled a thin tin cauldron, and let the water heat. She put Misery in the room with strict instructions not to touch the fire or cauldron and to call for her when the water boiled.

Then she went to the kitchen and saw about making breakfast. She had no rations that weren't soggy and disgusting after their dive into the subterranean river, and there was little in the house that was still good after a few weeks away, but she found some serviceable flat bread and cut off the mould, and a pot of stewed apples that had been kept very fresh inside her icebox, as well as a good bit of dried and salted rat. There were mushrooms, too, that looked okay, but though they were just inert brown caps, she couldn't bring herself to do anything with them, and chucked them out into the street for the rats to enjoy.

When Ree emerged from her room with an armful of parchment and scrolls (which she dumped on the table, heedless of the fact they'd soon need it to dine on), she considered the fare Usther was setting out and returned to her room, bringing back some very hard cheese and a bottle of juice. It looked unharmed by their watery adventures. Either the fishskin had kept her dry, or Ree waterproofed all her rations. Probably both. She wouldn't put it past her adventurous friend to take the odd swim in the service of mapping out the crypt.

The three of them had a quiet breakfast while Ree buried herself in reading and Dichotomy assaulted her legs out of desperation for food. She got up and went out with her cat to beg something from Mortana, since she had no fresh fish or meat to be found. The innkeeper was quick enough to hand over some off-cuts of rat, which Dichotomy gobbled up while growling the whole time. The rest, she put away in her icebox for later.

She felt…numb. Out of place. Nothing right now felt right, and not just because they had a muscular guest doing stretches in their sitting room. Home was too domestic after everything they'd just faced. And she had the creeping, awful sensation that this wasn't over yet.

'What're you reading?' she asked Ree, out of desperation more than anything. Anything to break the awful, liminal sensation of an oncoming storm which had not yet struck.

Ree didn't look up, turning a page. 'Looking through my references so I know which libraries to search.'

'Search for what?'

Ree did look at her now, frowning so hard her eyebrows pinched. 'The Many-That-Hungers. The...time spell.' She lowered her voice. 'Why the siblings and the Many are so interested in you, me, and Smythe.'

'Why would it have anything to do with the time spell?'

'Why wouldn't it?' Ree frowned at her. 'What else links the three of us, and only us?'

'It's not just us! They favour Symphona, Ellenil, and Tarantur as well.' But even as she said it, she remembered. Those three were 'beloved servants'. Perhaps more beloved than the others, but even so. But the three of *them*? They were 'honoured guests'.

There *was* something different about them. Not just in how they were named, but also how they were treated. The other denizens were coerced into service. But neither Mykol nor Celia seemed inclined to harm them.

She didn't want to think about that. She excused herself and went to her room, where none of this would be a problem. As she closed the door, Persephone caught her eye. The paladin watched her with a thoughtful frown.

CHAPTER THIRTY-FOUR

Ree

What remained of the town made a plan to get their people away from the Many. The morning they were to gather for it, Ree found Persephone sitting with legs crossed in front of a bowl of water. The entire room was gently warm, as if by sunlight streaming through a non-existent window.

'Did you find Tabris?' Ree asked as Persephone opened her eyes.

Persephone nodded. 'They're safe. They've found…I don't know how to describe it. A room full of fungi, but far larger than the one we saw before. They'll need my help to deal with it.'

'Is it necessary?' Ree mixed boiled water with oats and stirred it around. 'We could use your help, too. It's going to be difficult to get our people out.'

'I know, I know. But I have to consider what Allariel sent me to do.'

Usther swept into the room. 'I thought she sent you here to help people.' Her braids were pulled up into a large bun with a few hanging artfully loose, and she wore the most practical robes Ree had ever seen her in. Thick material, pitch black, and split around the legs for ease of movement. Even the sleeves were tight. Still far less dusty and faded than anything Ree owned. Ree wasn't entirely sure she'd ever seen her wear them before.

How like Usther to get a new wardrobe for a town emergency.

Persephone turned her steady gaze on Usther. 'She did,' Persephone said. 'But I need to consider where I will be of the most use.'

'With us,' Usther said sharply.

Persephone looked away and did not reply.

They gathered again in *The Bone & Brew*. It struck Ree how awful it was that this was all that remained of her home. This lonely cluster. The rest were either gone or taken. They discussed tactics and handed out supplies, but the overwhelming agreement was that they should stay together.

'And necromancy cannot kill them?' her father asked again, for what felt like the hundredth time.

'It can't,' said Ree.

'Even Smythe couldn't kill them,' said Usther.

'Then we're relying on you, Persephone,' said Arthura. 'I can heal, but my strength is not in my power.'

'I'll do what I can while I'm with you,' said Persephone. 'If we find Andomerys and my partner, that will make it easier.'

Ree hesitated. 'One last thing before we go,' said Ree. She motioned to Usther, and the pair of them went behind the counter and heaved out a thick cloth sack and a long wrapped pole, and dumped them on the table in front of Persephone with a clatter.

'We got permission,' Ree said, glancing at her father, who nodded.

'You shouldn't go unarmed,' Usther added.

Persephone started to take pieces from the sack. Out came pauldrons and armguards and tangled buckles; a mess of silver-white armour, lightly dulled. She unwrapped the pole as well; a burnished spear, the metal almost black. It seemed to be made of a single piece, shaped. Old antherian script circled the butt.

'What does this say?' she asked, brushing the script with her fingers.

Usther cleared her throat. 'To protect,' she said.

Persephone stared down at it for a long time, hefting a gauntlet between her hands. Finally, she looked up at Usther. 'Will you help arm me?'

Usther got a very odd expression. 'You'll have to show me what to do,' she said.

The two retreated to the back room.

After a moment, Ree's mother raised her eyebrows. 'Armour?' she said.

Ree could hear her true question behind it. Could read it in the suddenly anxious eyes of everyone in the room. 'She's here to help,' Ree said. 'She'll help better in armour.'

Veritas started to say, 'But she's—!'

'We can hardly be choosy,' Mortana cut in. She gave Ree a curt nod, warming Ree's heart a little, before adding, 'We can always kill her if it looks like she's turning on us.'

A relieved murmur of assent rippled around the room.

Ree put her head in her hands. 'This is why everyone hates us, isn't it?'

Igneus put a hand on her shoulder, the weight a surprise. 'They hated us first,' he said softly. 'Besides, they aren't really planning anything. It just makes them feel safer to imagine they could.'

'Do you ever think that's...wrong?' Ree asked. 'That maybe there's a better way?'

Igneus shrugged. 'The world is as it is.'

Ree said nothing. She didn't accept that.

When they set off, with Ree in the lead, she realised Smythe was not far behind. He didn't complain, as many of the rest of their party did—loudly and often—instead following in complete silence. She shortened her stride so that they could walk beside each other.

He blinked at her, eyes wide behind his glasses, but didn't try to engage her in conversation. She was glad of it. She wasn't certain she had worked out the puzzle of him yet, of this older, kinder Smythe. Of what secrets he must be hiding. She watched him surreptitiously as they travelled, but learned nothing of him beyond that his footing was more sure than she remembered.

Travelling through the crypt with a pack of necromancers was like nothing she'd ever experienced before. Sure, she and Usther had made some journeys together, and certainly she'd travelled with the supply caravan to the dead marshes villages before. But the journey to the villages was overland, where the travel was straightforward as soon as they found the road. And Usther might be a complaining, difficult, troublesome necromancer, but she was just *one* complaining, difficult, troublesome necromancer. Now Ree was travelling with a dozen of them.

Even her father, who was as stoic a parent as Ree could ever have asked for, struggled with the physical toll of the journey and somewhat loudly made his struggle known. She helped him up short climbs and did her best to reassure him that they were taking the best paths available. Her mother and Persephone tended to as many wounds and scrapes for him as for any of the necromancers.

Her mother, at least, did not complain. If anything, she seemed rejuvenated. She'd put on her cassock and furs again, and though she travelled barefoot, she never seemed to tire or complain of the uneven terrain. She had a quiver of arrows on her belt and an unstrung bow on her back—relics of her life before Tombtown, which Ree was surprised to see her willing to use. She hunted for them as they travelled, shooting rats and spearing small fish, and, on one impressive occasion, shot a spider the size of Dichotomy straight dead, consulting with Mortana on how best to cook it.

'Is your mother feral?' Usther had asked her while the spider was folded into a pot on a fire.

'Your mother is amazing,' Persephone had told her while tentatively biting into a hunk of cooked spider.

Ree, who knew her best, thought both were true but was much more likely to describe her as embarrassing.

As they travelled, they discussed strategies for fighting the Many, if it came to it. All flesh minions were left at home and none were raised on the journey, though it was rare for necromancers to travel without a shambling entourage. Even Misery and Dichotomy had been left behind by a tearful Usther, with enough food to last a few weeks and strict instructions that they protect each other.

But that didn't mean they travelled unaccompanied. They took their time collecting gravemould and residue from the various tombs, as spectres seemed unlikely to be infestable. Usther often debated spectre summoning practices with others of the group. None were as specialised as her, but that didn't stop everyone from offering their critique. She looked, by turn, elated and murderous.

Veritas brought his assistant, Anders, with him, and Pontifar brought his bonehound. Since nothing could grow easily on bone, skeleton minions were seriously considered. Normally considered expensive and ostentatious to raise compared to the more practical fleshy minions, nobody but Pontifar troubled over them. Now, though, they collected what bones they could. They angered a few skeletal guardians in the process, but it was nothing a group of necromancers of this size couldn't handle.

Of course, *carrying* the bones was annoying for most involved, but nobody wanted to permanently raise the skeletons so they could carry themselves, since they were so costly and awkward to maintain. So the complaints increased and Ree somehow ended up carrying a sack of bones herself,. She clattered with every step and quickly grew to hate the sound.

All the while, Ree kept an eye out for a certain shambling shape, kept an ear out for the familiar excitable howls. She told herself that Larry was smart, that he'd gotten far away from all of this, but she couldn't shake the feeling that something terrible had happened to him.

One evening, when they made camp on the edge of the white marble territory overlooking a large chasm, she found Smythe gazing down into the abyss, leaning up against a large rock. A faint crypt-breeze rippled his hair, making the curls of his ponytail dance.

'Something on your mind?' she asked him, coming to stand beside him. They had traded few words on their journey, but strangely the less they spoke the more comfortable she felt around him. He didn't seem invested in convincing her of anything, of persuading her of anything. Like Persephone, he was here to help.

'Oh. Well, yes.' He glanced at her sidelong, seeming surprised by her company. 'I was thinking about how nice it is to be travelling in company. I'm not—not great with people. I don't think I ever really was, but I wasn't aware of it then. But now, after so long with no one but Larry for company...' He trailed off. 'Well, I'm just glad of it. It's nice to hear people talking—'

'*Complaining*.'

'Well, yes, that too.' He smiled as he stared down into the chasm. 'Sometimes people even talk to me, if you'll believe it. Ask me how I'm doing. I never thought I would have that again.'

'I'm not sure you deserve to have it,' Ree said.

Smythe inclined his head. 'I'm not sure I deserve it either. But still, I'm glad for it.'

Ree considered him. She still couldn't shake the feeling that this was an act. That he might betray these people as suddenly as he had when they were young. It had been a long time, but how much could people really change?

She'd brought up those fears to Usther back in town, and Usther had grown irritated with her. *'He was a scared child, then,'* she'd said. *'We all were. Just let it rest.'*

The trouble was, Ree *had* let it rest. For eight years, she'd tried to put it from her mind and let her wounds heal. But now that Smythe was here, it felt like they were all open again and the bleeding wouldn't stop.

Except that the person she wanted to blame for that was a lot harder to blame now that he was in front of her.

'Why did you stay?' she asked him. 'You could have gone home.'

'Oh, I couldn't have,' he said. 'The Grand University doesn't actually accept knowledge gained through necromantic means. And if I'd gone home, I'd put my family's reputation at risk. Even if I never practised again, I bore the mark of necromancy. There would have been rumours. It would have ruined my sibling's political career, and everything they'd been working so hard toward.

'So you see, I would have been an exile no matter where I went. And that's my own fault, of course. I'm not asking for sympathy.' He shook his head. 'And there's something about this crypt. Ever since I first set foot in it, it just...called to me. I think this place is special.'

'It is special,' Ree said, hating that she was agreeing with him. Her mother had often reminded her that she didn't need to stay in Tombtown just because she'd been born there. That the upworld was vast, and that it was only natural she would want to see it one day.

And while Ree didn't mind the idea of going on a trip someday—of seeing a landscape dominated not by stone but by trees, of seeing the ocean, or the ancient ruins scattered across Ilyad and Paladur—she was also utterly in love with the crypt, which was still largely unmapped and undiscovered.

She lived in a place where Emberlon was its first historian and she was its first cartographer. Here she had discovered a magic long thought dead, and made friends with a creature that had died hundreds of years previously. It was hard to imagine she would ever be done with it.

'Well, I chose to live here alone rather than live alone anywhere else,' he said. 'I don't know whether that was wise—in fact, I suspect it was rather foolish of me. But it was what I chose.'

'What have you been doing, anyway?' she asked him, curiosity getting the better of him.

He shrugged. 'Historical research, mostly. I'm still a burial scholar, somewhere deep down. I study and I make notes, even though it might be that nobody ever sees them. That was pretty much how I spent all my time, until Usther appeared in my library, full of questions.'

It sounded lonely. Even Ree was glad to return home in-between excursions. To argue with Usther, or have dinner with her parents.

'I don't know what to make of you,' Ree said.

His mouth pulled to one side. He glanced at her, then away. 'Make nothing of me at all. I'll be gone soon enough.'

He stretched and walked away. Ree took his place leaning against the rock and gazed down into the chasm. Perhaps it would illuminate for her what he'd seen.

CHAPTER THIRTY-FIVE

Usther

Usther glared down the white marble corridors with their many doors and labyrinthine layout. 'Just as ugly as ever,' she said.

Beside her, Arthura strung her bow, taking out a long bowstring made of gut and looping it over the bottom of the bow, before stepping in, bending the bow, and looping the other side over the top. Usther eyed her uneasily; the priestess was stronger than she looked. The bow was hard enamelled wood, and Usther doubted she could have bent it even if she'd jumped up and down on top of it.

'You don't really intend to shoot anyone, do you?' she asked quietly.

Arthura shrugged and hefted the bow, testing the draw by pulling the string back to her cheek. The sleeves of her cassock fell back as she did so, revealing muscular forearms. 'People die every day,' she said. 'I feel no shame in adding an enemy to that number before they add me.'

'Is that one of Morrin's precepts?'

'No. One of mine.' She nodded to Usther. 'Stay close to me or your paladin friend, if you can.'

Usther nodded, repressing a shudder. She hated to be so helpless. She wondered if the other necromancers realised just how vulnerable they would be.

They moved ahead as a herd, a rare cluster of necromancers. The clinking of Persephone's mail was now accompanied by the hollow clatter of bones. Pontifar's bonehound, as well as a dozen human skeletons, also travelled with the group. As one clattered past Usther, it turned its head toward her and waved its bony fingers. She rolled her eyes, repressing a smile. As stressed as she was, it was hard not to be charmed by a skeleton minion. Perhaps it was something about how they were always smiling, but they were very jolly minions.

'Which way from here?' Igneus asked, looking to his daughter.

Usther almost complained that she and Smythe had spent more time in the Many's kingdom, but stopped herself just in time. Ree *would* remember better. Memorising directions was her main skill, apart from impersonating animals.

'Their main hall is much further in,' Ree said.

'We should try to get out who we can along the way,' said Kylath, and Igneus nodded his agreement.

'What if they don't want to go?' said Pontifar.

'Then we tie them up good and tight until we have time to decide what to do with them,' said Kylath archly. 'There is no room for traitors in Tombtown.'

They moved in, pairs of necromancers going to each room, flanked by a skeleton or two. It went smoothly enough; the council members, especially, were quick and ruthless, mindsnaring those who sought to fight back or sound the alarm, sending the rest to the back of the group. Arthura saw to the red sashes, which concealed barely-healed red scars and even open wounds.

'They make us do it,' said one denizen. A teenager, hardly out of childhood. They'd probably only started practising that year. 'To feed—' They stopped, looking nervously to their friend.

'We can't talk about it,' said the other teen. 'They'll punish us.'

'Then don't,' Arthura assured them. 'Nobody expects you to put yourselves in harm's way.'

The adults, too, were wary of saying too much.

'It's clear enough what they're feeding,' Usther said to Persephone. 'Mykol simply *told* us that his pets will only eat undead flesh and fresh blood.'

'Undead flesh,' Persephone mused. She shifted and crossed her arms, armour clinking. 'This still doesn't add up.'

'Well, Ree's been doing nothing but researching it for the last week,' said Usther. 'If there was even a hint of what to look for, she'd have found it. We're dealing with something new here.'

Persephone nodded, her expression distant. She took a few steps away from the group, staring at something Usther couldn't see.

'Persephone?'

She looked around, her expression clearing. 'Sorry,' she said. 'Just an odd feeling, that's all.'

Usther rolled her eyes. 'Paladins,' she said with all the disdain she could muster.

Persephone smiled, and she couldn't help but smile back.

They moved on, picking up more denizens as they went. They kept more than they left tied up. Most were overwhelmed with relief to see Igneus and Kylath. Some even cried. The more they met, the more furious Usther was that this had been allowed to happen. How could the Many have been allowed to spread and kidnap so many denizens without repercussion? Was Tombtown really that insular, that divided, that all of their neighbours could disappear over the course of a few weeks and all anyone had done about it was mutter ominously or pack up and leave?

But then, had she done much better? She'd been suspicious of Tarantur's grand quest but had simply scoffed at those foolish enough to sign up for it.

Many denizens stared at Smythe with wide eyes as they passed. Some even murmured 'Townslayer' in tones of hope and awe. Smythe seemed alarmed every time. She fell into step beside him as Ursula the Underqueen gripped his hands in her gnarled claws and gave him the same greeting before moving on.

'I can't do what they want me to,' he said. 'It was never my intention to make a second attempt.'

Usther watched Ursula as Arthura examined her wound. It was very fresh and still bleeding, the blood cracked and dry on her wrinkled skin. 'Maybe some towns were never meant to exist in the first place.'

Smythe shook his head. 'I don't have the power to do that. You and I both know it was more the ritual than me, and that ritual is gone. But even if I could...Usther, who are *we* to decide?'

'They came into *our* home,' Usther said. 'They've hurt and oppressed *our* people. Many civilisations have fought and died to protect themselves from just that.'

Smythe opened his mouth to reply, stuttered a moment, then said, 'I can't say you're wrong. But I will not personally be slaying anyone.'

Usther nodded, because what could she say to that? She was glad he wasn't keen to go murdering. She was glad that he never had been, and relieved that part of him that had been willing to risk the deaths of others seemed to have been purged from him.

She didn't want to kill anyone, either. Just the sight of Arthura's bow made her slightly nauseated. But she wouldn't stand still and let someone kill her.

She hadn't let Symphona do it. And she certainly wouldn't let Mykol and Celia do it. They now had dozens of their people together, enough to send back. Some asked to stay with their group, but most were keen to leave. They were given instructions: don't raise flesh minions, call spectres and raise skeletons if they must. Ree spoke to each group, giving instructions on the fastest way out of the Many's kingdom and handing out sketchy maps of the nearby area.

'Do you think I should go with them?' Ree asked worriedly as the first group left. 'Some of them ended up here because they got lost. Without a proper guide, they could get lost again.'

'They have young Nightshade with them,' Usther said, pointing out a young person maybe eight years their junior. 'They do almost as much exploring around the crypt as you do.'

'They're quite a good cartographer, too,' Ree admitted. 'They showed me their work a few months ago. I've been trying to decide whether I could bear to take on an apprentice.'

'Then they'll be fine,' said Usther. 'But you *could* go. What's really on your mind?'

Ree rubbed the back of her neck and didn't say anything for a long time. Usther, who was used to her friend's long, thoughtful silences, waited with as much patience as she could muster. At length, Ree said, 'I don't understand why they're just letting us evacuate people. The Many melted Persephone and Tabris away like it was nothing and stuck them in a prison. All the denizens here say that Mykol and Celia know everything, are always watching. So why let us do this?' She shook her head. 'There has to be something more going on. And I don't want to think of all those denizens going alone into danger.'

It was a reasonable concern. Truthfully, Usther was worried about how smoothly it seemed to be going, as well. And she had no idea how many of the denizens they'd evacuated truly wanted to return home, and how many just knew better than to protest when confronted with a cabal of the most powerful necromancers in town.

'Persephone?' Usther called. The paladin was ahead of the group, frowning down a corridor. 'Could you come here a moment?'

Persephone visibly shook herself and came to join them. The silver-white of her armour gleamed oddly in the scant torchlight, making her look almost as if flames danced over her. A woman of silver flame.

'You okay?' Ree asked. 'You seem distracted.'

'Can you even see that far without a torch?' Usther added. Persephone had refused her offer of a darksight ritual, which still rankled. For all her big talk about not judging necromancers, she'd balked at a tiny, useful necromancy which would have made her job here a hundred times easier.

And honestly, it was a little hard not to take it personally.

'I'm fine,' said Persephone. 'How can I help?'

But prejudiced or not, she was a powerful protector. 'We're worried that Mykol and Celia haven't tried to stop us,' said Usther. 'I was wondering if you'd be able to escort the denizens back to town?'

Persephone was already looking back over her shoulder. 'What? No, I'm sorry.' She shook her head. 'I think...I think I have to go.'

'Go?' said Ree.

'You can't be serious.' Usther said.

Persephone turned back and focused on Usther's face. 'I'll come back.' Her words were fierce, her eyes hard. 'I promise I'll come back. But...' She gritted her teeth, shook her head and stomped away. She disappeared around the corner.

'No...no, that's unacceptable.' Usther clenched her fists. To Ree, she said, 'Get Smythe. He can go back with the others.'

'Usther!'

'I'm going after her,' Usther said. 'Don't worry, I'll be fine!'

She ran off, puffing, to chase after the paladin. Her mind was awhirl with too many things. Too many problems. The Many. Mykol and Celia. Smythe. The denizens. But rising above it all was an absolute fury at the injustice of Persephone abandoning them now.

When she got around the corner, the paladin was gone, the sound of her clanking bootsteps already fading into the distance.

Morrin's teeth, she was quick. Usther picked up the pace.

CHAPTER THIRTY-SIX

Ree

'Usther!'

Ree watched her friend go with the horrible sense that everything was unravelling. She hesitated. Should she go after her? Drag her back?

But it was true that she was as safe with Persephone as anywhere else. And that they *needed* Persephone to have any chance of getting out safely. She growled under her breath and spun away, fists clenching.

And bumped into Smythe, her forehead almost hitting his. He caught her easily, gently stopping her and then stepping away. His eyes were on the corridor where Usther and Persephone had just run off. 'Where are they going?' he asked.

Ree's cheeks heated, embarrassed to have been so clumsy. 'Persephone ran off. Usther...I don't know. Wants to drag her back, or something.'

Smythe shook his head. 'We should be sticking together.'

'You don't have to tell me that!' Ree snapped. She breathed out hard through her nose, closed her eyes a moment, and tried again. 'I'm worried about the denizens going home. I don't know why Mykol and Celia are letting this happen.'

Smythe nodded, biting his lip in thought. Ree despised how endearing she found that. 'The fungi have been mostly inert,' he said. 'Perhaps whatever does the thinking for them is busy elsewhere?'

'Busy with what?'

Smythe shrugged helplessly, but his words had ignited something in Ree's brain. 'There's still one paladin unaccounted for,' she said. 'And Persephone said the gods pull them wherever they're needed.'

'That must be...convenient?'

'That must be where she ran off to. To Tabris! But she couldn't explain, because—'

'Because she doesn't know that,' Smythe said. 'She just has a feeling.'

'Yes.'

Ree tapped her foot, overwhelmed with restless energy as she followed the thought. 'If that's true, then stealth has meant nothing. We have a limited time to do this.' She looked around for her father. 'We've got to move fast.'

Igneus and Kylath were standing outside another room, ushering a pair of older denizens out. Ree rushed over. She relayed her concerns as quickly as she could.

Kylath and Igneus exchanged a look. 'You take the first room,' said Kylath. 'I'll take the next. You *can* handle a few denizens alone, can't you?'

'See that *you* can,' he replied curtly, but Ree could sense a hint of a smile hidden in his frown.

She wished she had his good humour. But then, he hadn't yet met Mykol and Celia, or seen what the Many could really do.

'Come on.' She gestured to Smythe. 'We'll take the next room.'

They took the next room, and the next. Ree did all the talking but all eyes were fixed on Smythe, and they weren't forced to tie anyone up or mind-snare. Ree could believe their intimidation. She *knew* Smythe, and had known him at the time of the ritual, and he still frightened her. But for the other denizens, it must have seemed that they had voted for his death and then he'd returned to kill them all, and nearly succeeded. To see him now must be like staring down your executioner, caught up to you at last.

They started to hit empty rooms. Rooms with perfectly made red beds and no sign of habitation. Rooms with no furniture at all, just blank marble cubes. Thinking it must be time to turn back, they tried one more room.

The inhabitants startled. A woman not much older than Ree stood up and raised her hands palm-out in a gesture of surrender. There were tired bags under her eyes. 'Etherea?' Ree took a few steps forward, not quite believing she was seeing the other woman. 'They got you, too?'

'Ree!' Etherea dropped her hands. She looked like she might go to Ree but stopped herself as her eyes fell on Smythe. 'What are you doing here?' she asked. 'Where's Usther?'

'We're getting people out,' Smythe said. 'The council is here.'

'Mykol and Celia won't stand for that,' Etherea said. She rubbed the ribbon at her wrist and Ree's stomach lurched to think of her being cut and bled to feed the hideous mushrooms.

'We're not waiting around to find out,' Ree said. 'One group has already left. You're the last to join the second.'

Etherea's companion stood up, shoulders hunched, and nodded to Smythe. He headed for the door.

'Don't raise any flesh minions,' Ree said. 'Skeletons and spectres only. Stick with the group.'

Etherea dipped her head in acknowledgement. She hesitated as she passed Ree, and clasped her arm. 'You're coming with us, right?' she asked. Her eyes were full of worry. 'You shouldn't be mixed up in any of this either.'

Ree gave her a shaky smile, though she meant it to be reassuring. 'I can't help it. I am mixed up. I'll follow you when I'm sure everything is clear.'

'They want you the most,' she said urgently. 'You and him and Usther. You can't let them—after what they did to Emberlon—!'

'I'll follow you soon,' Ree said again. Etherea searched her face, Ree wasn't sure what for, then released her and followed her companion out the door.

'Well,' said Smythe. 'That was ominous.'

'She's just worried about me,' Ree said, though she felt shaken by Etherea's intensity. 'She was my nanny, you know. When I was a kid. She used to watch me, sometimes, and take me for hikes outside town.'

Ree still remembered the sense of freedom Etherea had given her, that when she'd asked, 'Can we go outside town?', Etherea would always answer, 'Yes.' She'd only been a teenager herself at the time, but she'd been strong enough in the Craft to protect herself and a small child. She'd encouraged Ree to collect rat bones for Mazerin to make into necklaces, and quiz Ree on the various undead they encountered; what they were called, how they were raised, and what their abilities were. It had been those walks that had ignited Ree's desire to explore further, to see and learn more of the crypt beyond the town.

When Ree got older, she'd had little to do with Etherea, but the older woman had always had a kind word for her when they met, and Ree had never forgotten her.

'She sounds kind,' Smythe said.

Ree shrugged. 'She cursed her former lover with boils and spectres a few years ago. People are complicated.'

And she'd confronted Ree with that uncomfortable truth she still didn't fully understand. That Mykol and Celia wanted Ree, Smythe, and Usther *specifically*. She still believed it had to be something to do with Usther pulling them back into their own time after the Lich had banished them, but she just didn't understand *what*. How could Mykol or Celia possibly know about what had happened then? Not even her parents knew the full details. Were Mykol and Celia from that strange and violent past of the Old King's court? Was that why their necromancy was so bizarre, so far from anything any of them had experienced?

But they didn't *seem* like those necromancers. Their speech was modern enough, whereas the Old King's court had all spoken Old Antherian. They didn't seem to have an interest in the Old King's tomb, or in reclaiming the heart of that old kingdom, now modern Tombtown.

There was still something she was missing.

They searched a few more rooms that came up empty, then returned to her father and Kylath. 'All clear,' she said.

'For us as well. There may be more people. We can take a survey when we get back to town, and regroup from there,' said Kylath.

Her father nodded his agreement. 'Better to get out with who we've got now, before the siblings return. Let's go.'

He frowned as Ree held her ground.

'I need to stay,' she said.

'Reanima.' His voice was a warning, but it had been a long time since she'd sought his permission for anything at all.

'Usther is still out here. We need to find her,' Ree said. 'And Andomerys. And Emberlon. And we still don't know what Mykol and Celia want with us.' She shook her head. 'Mykol and Celia seemed loathe to hurt any of the three of us. We're the least at risk. And we have to stay.'

'I'm not leaving you here among these...usurpers!' he said. 'You're my daughter. I knew ever since you were born that you were at risk for this sort of thing. Kylath, I knew, wouldn't betray me, but everyone else...'

Ree shook her head. 'This isn't about the council, or the town. It's about me, and Usther, and Smythe. And I'm not leaving until I lay it to rest.'

Even as the words left her mouth, she wondered at the sense of it.

She only needed to find Persephone and Usther.

She turned to Kylath. 'Do you have a scry-bowl?'

The councillor nodded and took a small bowl from her pack. 'Bring it back,' she said. Which Ree understood to mean, 'be careful'.

'I will,' she promised.

Igneus hesitated.

'You need to protect our people,' Ree said.

Smythe cleared his throat. 'They seem particularly keen on collecting people of station,' he said. 'I would hazard a guess that you and Kylath might make particular targets.'

'Go,' Ree said again.

They went, leaving Ree with a mix of emotions. There was a time when her parents would have refused to leave her, fearing what might happen to her without their protection. Now, she worried about *them* going alone.

She brushed aside her worry; there was plenty enough to be concerned about without borrowing trouble. 'Do you know how to scry?' she asked Smythe.

'A bit,' he said. 'I've checked on my family a few times.'

Ree nodded and placed the bowl on the floor, pouring in a shallow pool of water from her waterskin. 'Get to it,' she said.

Scrying tended to work better with certain foci—typically a treated eye, similar to a suneye. Blood helped, too. But it was perfectly manageable with nothing more than a reflective surface and a concentrated will. Smythe knelt beside the bowl and hesitated. 'I'm not in Usther's exclusion,' he said. 'I won't be able to find her.'

Ree frowned. 'Well, I can't scry. You might be able to override her amulet if you focus your will.' Surely, that was the only thing he was good for, with such an excess of power.

Smythe looked pained. 'I'm not going to do that. It's a breach of trust.'

Ree growled in frustration. 'I think the circumstances call for it!'

He shook his head. 'Maybe you're right. But if I do that, it might break her amulet and *anyone* will be able to scry for her. I don't think that's a risk we should be taking. You're an exception, right? You should scry.'

'Smythe, I'm a therianthrope. I can't scry.'

He frowned. 'I don't see why that would be a problem. Healers and necromancers can both scry. Why shouldn't a therianthrope?'

Ree gawped at him. Because her magic was about squishing herself into animal skins and borrowing the senses of animals, not about her strength of will or anything like that. Because her magic was *different*. It was songs and skin and nothing at all like any magic she had known before.

But then again, she'd been guarding her mind against mind-snares since she was a child. Anyone could do that, whether they practised magic or not. And Persephone had claimed her magic *felt* like necromancy.

She knelt in front of the bowl, placing her hand to either side of it and staring down. 'What's the incantation for scrying?' she asked.

Smythe frowned. 'Well, for necromancy, it's *krizt vas* and then the name of the person you're scrying on. You hold them in your mind. It's not complicated magic but...I don't know what it would be for therianthropy.'

A song, certainly. *Krizt vas* essentially just translated to 'Show me', with a certain amount of Antherian command flavour. The songs she sang were in the language of the beasts, and she was sure she could translate so simple a phrase and work out the tune it required.

But at the same time...what if therianthropy *wasn't* so different from necromancy? Wylandriah had been part of the Old King's necromancer court, afterall. And healing magic had nearly destroyed Ree's therianskin.

They were short on time.

She stared down into the water, imagining it like a window with Usther on the other side. '*Krizt vas Usther,*' she intoned in a low hum.

A bubble rose in the water, burst, and was still.

Was this a waste of time?

She rubbed her eyes tiredly and sat back a moment. Of course she couldn't use necromancy. That wasn't how magic worked. Magic was so discreet that you couldn't even learn another magic if you'd already cast a spell in another. Therianthropy was no different, whatever superficial similarities it might share with necromancy. Necromancy and healing had some similarities, too, and yet they were each other's antitheses.

'You okay?' asked Smythe.

Ree nodded. She leaned back over the bowl, taking a deep breath. She felt the water in her belly, the source from which all therianthropy was drawn. Then she sang *Ilath lor tu Ustheri,'* the makeshift tune rough. She stared hard at the bowl, thinking of Usther, thinking of how desperately she needed to find her.

Two bubbles, then nothing.

'Ree,' said Smythe quietly. 'I think—'

She didn't look away. And then the water rippled and changed, lit by a blue glow that showed around the edges. It was a vision as if she were flying down white corridors and down a long spiralling stair. There, at the base of a hole in the floor, was Usther. Her braids were askew and she stared up at someone Ree couldn't see, her face set in a snarl.

'I know where she is,' Ree whispered. She blinked and the image dissipated, the blue light becoming black smoke that wisped away.

When she looked up at Smythe, he was staring at her with something like awe.

CHAPTER THIRTY-SEVEN

Usther

'You are out of your mind!' Usther snarled. She backed away from the hideous gaping mouth in the floor and pointed a shaky finger at Persephone. 'Find another way around!'

Persephone sighed. 'You don't have to come,' she said. 'You can go back to your friends. But Tabris came this way, look.' She nodded at the dangling rope staked into the floor and slipping over the edge into the hole. 'So I must go.'

'I'm not leaving you here alone.'

'Then you'll have to go down the hole.'

'I'm *not* jumping down that hole!'

Persephone rubbed her eyes, looking more tired than Usther had yet seen her. A dim part of her mind recognised that she was being unreasonable; irrational, even. That Persephone had not asked her to accompany her. That her people were behind, not ahead.

But a much larger part of her couldn't reconcile with the idea of letting Persephone vanish into this vast, evil place alone.

'You jumped into the waterfall,' Persephone said, a little desperately.

Usther shook her head, her cheeks heating. 'Actually, Ree pushed me. I couldn't do it.'

'She *pushed* you.' Persephone whistled.

'Yeah, she can be really rotten when she needs to be,' Usther said, though privately she was grateful that Ree had done it and not just left Usther languishing in the Many's kingdom.

'Look,' said Persephone. She rubbed the back of her head. 'If you refuse to go back...we could go down together.'

'Together?' Usther repeated.

Persephone looked a little flustered. 'Well, I'm not keen on heights myself. I could carry you down.'

'Carry me,' Usther echoed. She mentally berated herself for being so slack-witted, but there seemed to be nothing she could do to get her mouth to say something meaningful. She forced herself to ask, 'How would that work?'

Persephone stepped toward her, as she had when she'd carried Usther through the waterfall. 'You'd put your arms around my neck,' she said. She was very close and Usther was struck again by how nice it was that their eyes were on the same level. Without really thinking about it, she wrapped her arms around the paladin's neck.

'Then I would hold you around the waist, like this,' she said, gently pulling Usther closer. In spite of her armour, she was incredibly light-touched. And in spite of her armour, Usther was feeling decidedly warm and flustered by her nearness.

'And then,' she said, her breath warm on Usther's face. 'We scoot down the hole very carefully and with very little dignity.'

The mention of the hole brought Usther back to her senses. 'How are you going to hold onto the rope and me at the same time?'

'I have two hands,' said Persephone with such genuine confidence that it honestly made Usther feel a little breathless.

Usther put her trust in Persephone. Part of her mind screeched that this was foolishness, part of her marvelled at how easy it was to do. The paladin gently eased them both to the floor, placing Usther in her lap in a way Usther would have found thrilling, if there wasn't a fifty-foot fall at her back. She pressed her face into Persephone's armoured shoulder, the coldness of the metal giving her a small amount of comfort.

Persephone scooted forward, wrapping the rope around her gauntlet a few times. And then there was a sudden shift, and the bottom fell out of Usther's stomach. She clung to Persephone's neck. Persephone's arm around her waist was solid as an iron bar, and yet she felt utterly helpless.

Slowly, Persephone began to slide them down, shifting her legs in a way Usther found strange but daren't look to find out. She must have had the rope wrapped around her feet as well for better grip.

'It's okay,' Persephone whispered against her hair. There was the barest hint of strain in her voice. 'I've got you.'

They slid down further. Usther turned her head, staring sidelong at Persephone's face. The paladin looked determined. Sweat dripped down her face, and her jaw was clenched, but she didn't seem as exhausted or panicked as Usther had feared. Behind her, white walls slowly slid past in the distance. If Usther looked down, she could get a better look at the room. But she didn't look down, instead turning her face back into Persephone's shoulder.

There was a brief drop and then a thump as Persephone landed, holding Usther well enough that her feet didn't even touch the ground. The paladin patted Usther's back. 'We're here,' she said, stepping away.

Usther ignored the feelings of being exposed and bereft and looked around. The chamber they were in was more impressive than she had realised. The ceiling was a vast prism of marble, and from that point spiralled down a column of crimson fungi. At the base, trails of fungi spider-webbed out in frighteningly symmetrical design, destroying any illusion that this was a natural or undirected growth.

As they stared, the column pulsed, purple and red light rippling up and down it, and then fading.

'Where's Tabris?' asked Usther.

Persephone didn't reply. Instead, she stepped carefully toward the column, stepping over the many spidery trails of crimson fungi. She unslung her spear from her back, hefting it in both hands.

She thought there was danger here. Usther took a pinch of gravemould from her pouch. Her magic was icy in her veins, keeping her on edge. She wished she'd thought to grab a sack of bones before she'd chased after Persephone. A skeleton would be incredibly draining for her to maintain, but it seemed a rather more substantial defence than her spectres, however much she loved them.

She hurried after Persephone, skipping over the strands of fungi, praying desperately that Morrin would prevent her from tripping and landing in a bed of the stuff. When she finally caught up with Persephone, the paladin stood at the base of the enormous column. At Usther's approach, it pulsed again, rippling with movement and light.

Usther repressed a shudder, but still tried to take it in. This column seemed important. Different from the other rooms of fungi they'd encountered. There were no fungal minions here, and no bodies being decomposed.

'Persephone?' Usther asked again. The lack of response from the paladin was starting to worry her. 'Why are we here?'

Persephone said something Usther couldn't quite catch. The column pulsed again, light rippling up and down it, the entire column flexing.

She reached for her. 'Persephone—!'

Red tendrils wrapped around her hand, fixing it to Persephone's shoulder. She screamed and pulled back, dragging Persephone with her. As the paladin twisted, it became clear; the tendrils trussed her up tightly, mushrooms clustered across her armour and pulsing against it with a faint sucking sound, as if they possessed mouths and were eating it. Mushrooms also gagged her open mouth, spilling free.

'No!' Usther made to blow on her gravemould but the tendrils spread and seized her other hand as well. She sent a burst of panicked necromantic energy out and it washed harmlessly over the fungi.

More tendrils around her waist, pulling themselves tight with a sound of squeaking tension like leather against leather.

She tried to struggle free, but with her arms and legs pinned, there was nothing she could do. Persephone was still gagged and was much stronger than Usther, yet her struggles were almost imperceptible. Was she even trying to get free, or was she just held too fast to move?

'Usther! Darling.' A voice trilled toward them. Usther stared as a figure stepped languidly from around the column of crimson fungi, her red skirt trailing along the marble floor. She crushed the fungi beneath her delicate slippers, sending up glittering clouds of spores with every step, unconcerned by the shining coat it gave her feet and skirts. 'My Lady said you would be along soon enough,' said Symphona. 'She'd observed uncanny navigation from this brute's partner and set the trap accordingly.'

'Let us go, Symphona,' Usther said in a low voice.

Symphona tapped her lips. 'Do you know? I don't think I will.' She smiled, perfectly wicked. 'Honestly, darling, I thought you'd be happy to see me. But then you *did* seem to be rather cosy with this horrible thug on the way down.' She paused at Persephone, considering her. She reached up to touch the back of her hand to the paladin's cheek. Persephone said something unintelligible, choking on the mushrooms.

'She's very fat,' Symphona observed disappointedly. 'I knew you'd move on eventually, but I can't say I admire your taste.'

Usther spat the nastiest curse she knew at her, putting all her hate behind it, but Symphona lifted a hand and a wall of fungi rose up to take the brunt of it.

Symphona gestured for the fungi to lower. 'Honestly,' she said, tsking. 'You ought to know better than that. You don't even have your hands free. What, were you hoping to give me a nosebleed?'

'What are you even doing here?' Usther said. 'You can do better than to be the pet of a pretend queen.'

Symphona's eyes flashed. She flew to Usther and grabbed her face in her clawed fingers, the nails cutting into Usther's cheeks. 'I am here,' she snarled, 'because *you* and that slut Reanima drove me from my home. Don't you dare tell me what is and isn't good enough for me when you are at *my* fucking mercy.' The tendrils around Usther squeezed tightly, her ribs pressed so hard that she could feel them bruise.

'Celia...won't like it...if you kill me,' Usther wheezed.

'You? No. I suppose she wouldn't. She isn't quite done with you yet,' said Symphona. 'But your chubby lover over there?' She gestured at Persephone without looking back.

Usther screamed as Persephone was ripped away from her. Fungi climbed up her, consuming her, then collapsed back down leaving nothing behind.

Not dead, Usther told herself, though she heard ringing in her ears and felt utterly struck dumb. Not dead, only moved. They did this before, Ree told you about it.

But seeing it for herself...where had she *gone*? How was it possible to just...melt a person like that?

'Oh, don't *worry*,' said Symphona. 'You'll be reunited with all your little friends soon. Ellenil and Tarantur are seeing to that.'

CHAPTER THIRTY-EIGHT

Ree

Ree raced down the corridor, with Smythe scrambling to keep up. 'Where is she?'

'A hole,' Ree said. 'A hole in the floor, like a giant mouth. It's...this way!' She turned the corner without missing a step.

'Ree! Ree.' Smythe's voice was pleading. 'We need to think about this. We need to prepare.'

'They aren't far,' Ree retorted.

And then she could see it. Beyond the grand hall, an arched alcove with a wide, grinning hole in the floor. A rope and piton were staked into the ground there. 'They must already have—'

Two figures stepped out from the side corridors, one bare-chested and covered in tattoos, the other in a cloak of trailing lace.

Ree didn't hesitate. She thrust her hand into her crow-pouch and trilled the first few notes of the song, flashing forward in a cloud of smoke and feathers.

'I don't think so,' said Tarantur, raising one tattooed hand.

A wall of fungi surged up in front of her. She beat her wings frantically back, trying to stop herself, but her momentum was too great and she slammed into the fungi only for grasping tendrils to seize her, digging into her feathers. She squirmed, cawing frantically, while Smythe shouted and a blizzard of icy air blasted the fungi. She could feel the tendrils squirming under her feathers, trying to pierce the skin.

She released the spell, unspooling out of the crowskin and onto the floor and ripping it free from the fungi's grasp, but more tendrils were reaching. A gap appeared in the crimson wall and Ellenil stepped through, face shadowed beneath their hood.

'That's enough,' they said, and crooked their fingers in a spell-casting shape. Ree rolled aside just as a red dart of a curse hit the ground where she'd been.

'Hold on!' Smythe said. 'We don't need to fight!'

'Oh, but we'd *like* to,' said Tarantur. He reached for something in his pouch. Ellenil started to cast again.

'*Find her,*' Smythe said, his voice transformed to be grotesque with a death echo. '*Go!*' His eyes filled with ink and his veins stood out black against his fast-greying skin. He locked eyes with Ellenil.

Ree didn't need to be told twice. She sang herself into her crowskin and soared past Smythe. The fungal wall was already half-crumbled, having lost its direction. She glanced at Ellenil, expecting to find the young acolyte paralysed in a mind-snare.

They smiled. And there was a choking sound from behind Ree.

She half-turned on the wing; Smythe's gaze was locked with Ellenil, but sweat poured down him, riming as frost on his clothes.

Ree hesitated, treading air. A burst of cold behind her and a sound like howling wind caught her attention. She spun, and dropped out of the air just in time to avoid the mottled, grasping hands of a greywraith.

As she hit the ground, she gasped at a sudden flash of pain in her chest. She felt, in a horrible, squirmy sort of way, that there was something embedded there. Something foreign. Something *moving*.

Tarantur laughed. 'Feeling weak, are you? I expect nothing better from Igneus' whelp. The pathetic spawn of a pathetic family.'

His greywraith reached for her where she lay wings-splayed on the ground. It was a hideous thing of twisted green arms and a fluttering black cloak, a spectre given terrifying physicality. Under its hood, she could see the toothed hole of its mouth, round and utterly inhuman. Its breath howled and rattled like a gale wind rushing through a ramshackle shed.

She couldn't move fast enough as a crow. She cawed her anger and unspooled from her crowskin, but the greywraith grasped only at smoke as she immediately poured herself into a ratskin and raced for the rope leading down the hole.

She slid down it head-first, little rat-hands clinging and sliding, tail wrapped around it behind her. She could hear the horrifying sucking wind of the Greywraith as it followed her, unhindered by gravity. She barely had time to register the vast and horrible chamber, its prism-like ceiling, or the horrifying column of crimson fungi. All she could do was *run*. And all the while, she could feel that wrongness in her chest. Pulsing like a second heartbeat.

When she hit the ground, she took three fast leaps before red tendrils snaked out to catch her. Fungi started to grow along it, to grow on her fur, to trap her paws. Her vision narrowed to a fast-closing hole in a casing of fungi.

And from a carpet of red ahead, something formed of red tendrils suddenly rose, split, and bloomed into stark colour. Red muscle and sinew knitting and spreading, then plumping out into smooth skin. Fluttering white skirts. Fuschia eyes.

Mykol and Celia smiled. 'At last,' they said in unison. And then fungi closed over her eyes and Ree's thoughts went dark.

REE WOKE BLEARILY. Her eyes gradually adjusted, turning the hazy blacks into a riot of reds, pinks, and purples. When she realised, she startled awake. she was in human shape again, her ratskin gone, her pouches all removed. Her back hit a pliant, flesh-like wall of fungi and she scooted forward again as it creaked and scritched against itself, as if in delight.

A figure emerged from the wall, materialising just as horrifically as she had before; Celia, her lovely face set in an eager smile. 'You're awake! Good, good.' She stepped lightly toward Ree, barefeet silent on the marble floor. Ree flinched, but didn't dare back away. Her chest twinged painfully and she gasped, grasping at it.

Celia crouched in front of her, so that their eyes were almost level. 'Yes, that was a welcome surprise. We cannot normally pierce living flesh. But you aren't always wearing your living flesh, are you?' She smiled. 'We're delighted to live inside you. You are not just an honoured guest. You are a fascinating creature, worthy of cataloguing.'

Oh Morrin. There was some part of the fungi living inside her? She scratched at her chest and she had a fleeting, panicked thought of trying to dig it out. As if it could hear her thoughts, something inside her *flexed* and she gasped at the sudden hot pain of it. Her heart beat felt *sharp*, like it was beating against a cage.

Celia only watched her while she panicked. Slowly, Ree got a grip on her own thoughts. She couldn't rip the fungi out, and Celia certainly wasn't going to help her. But there was something else wrong with her statement.

She hadn't said 'The Many'. She'd said 'We'.

'*You* are the Many-That-Hungers,' Ree whispered. 'You don't control it; you *are* it.'

Celia laughed. 'We are, and we aren't. When we emerged here and began to grow, we lost our connection to the Many-That-Came-Before. We needed to shape ourselves into something new. Something that could harness the strange power that exists in this world of stone and death. So, we created Mykol and Celia. Mykol and *me*.' She smiled. 'It is strange to be a person. To be an individual, as well as a whole. But I like it, and we are glad of the new opportunities it has afforded us.'

It had *created* Mykol and Celia. Ree remembered Persephone's observation—that their skin didn't have hair, or pores. That they didn't seem to breathe. The way she'd put specificity to the uncanniness that the siblings portrayed. She'd been right. Mykol and Celia had never been human.

'How did you learn to act like us?' Ree asked.

Celia smiled and shrugged, too sharply to quite resemble a human motion, Ree noticed, now that she knew to look. 'We observed. And we found tutors, in exchange for power. Power for power. They told us that though there are humans who think with many minds, we'd do better to speak of ourselves as individuals. To hide the truth of our connection to the Many-That-Hungers. It was a small thing for us. For me.'

But this made even less sense than what had come before. All along, Ree had been working on the assumption that Mykol and Celia had something to do with the Old King's kingdom and the time before Tombtown. It was the only thing she could come up with that linked Smythe, Usther, and her together. She wracked her brain, but couldn't remember *any* mushrooms from that time, nor any white marble. The crypt had been the crypt she knew, but bright and new and unworn. Everything that Celia and Mykol had created here was utterly different. It wasn't regenerating the tomb; it was replacing it entirely.

The thing in her chest flexed again and she choked on the sudden burst of pain it caused.

'Sorry about that,' Celia said. 'We're still not sure how to navigate your living tissue. Growth is...awkward.'

Ree wanted to ask her what she meant by that, but she was sure she already knew the answer. The Many intended to infest her, as surely as it had infested the crypt and its undead. How far did it need to spread before it controlled her? Did it need to cover her heart? Her brain?

But she couldn't think about that. Andomerys could burn it out of her if she ever found the healer, she was sure of it. Or so she stubbornly told herself. There were more pressing matters, however.

'Where's Usther?' she asked, her voice strained.

CHAPTER THIRTY-NINE

Usther

Smythe was pushed out of the fungus wall and landed on the floor in a heap. Usther walked over and crouched beside him. His eyes were closed, his jaw slack. She slapped his cheek. 'Hey. Hey!' She slapped him again.

He blinked at her a few times, then scrambled upright, nearly smacking his forehead against hers. 'Oh no. Where are we? Where's Ree?'

'Where are we? I don't know. At a guess, we're in that fucking enormous pillar of fungi. I think it's important to them, somehow. As for, "where's Ree"? What by Morrin's bloody hole do you mean, "where's Ree"? Weren't you with her?'

Smythe shook his head. 'We went after you. We were attacked by...that teenager with the sharp hair and the tattooed councillor. I told her to go on without me.'

So Ree might still be free? Usther's spirits lifted a little, feeling the first tingling of hope since she'd woken up in this horrifying fungi prison. 'And did she?'

'If I'm quite honest, I don't know.' He frowned and pressed a hand to his head. 'I tried to mind-snare the teenager. That's the last thing I remember. Their eyes...their eyes were red like blood.' He shook his head.

'Well, shit.' Usther stood up and paced the edge of their prison. 'Ellenil mind-snared *you*? Little Ellenil?'

'I think they must've,' Smythe said. 'The closest feeling to it I've ever had is when the Lich mind-snared me and tried to kill me.'

Usther pulled a narrow ribbon from her wrist and tied up her braids into a large knot, thinking hard. 'It was a mind-snare. They probably did it just long enough for the fungi to get you—they can control it, did you know? Morrin only knows what sick bargains they had to make to get *that* power.'

The idea that Ellenil possessed that kind of power was startling. Even more so that they would use it to attack Ree and Smythe. They thought of the headstrong child they'd looked after years before and the intense, self-possessed young person they'd become.

People changed, Usther reminded herself, and not always for the better.

At least Tarantur wasn't surprising. She'd always hated him the most of all the council. Obsequious, patronising little man—quite a feat of weaselling, to be both. Of course he'd leapt at the chance to curry favour with a greater power.

'We need to find a way out,' said Usther. 'Smythe, if you got snared, there's no way to know if she made it out. And Persephone was taken as well, and who *knows* what's happened to the evacuated denizens.'

'And why are you so keen to leave?' Came a silken voice. Mykol materialised from the fungal wall, first in veiny flesh made of tendrils that then quickly plumped and coloured to form the man. It was a horrifyingly anatomical construction, like watching someone be skinned and gutted, but in reverse. Smythe actually retched; Usther's stomach lurched, but she was made of sterner stuff.

She drew herself up as tall as she could and said imperiously, 'I hate to say it, Mykol, but you've been a terrible host.'

Mykol's expression was at first puzzled, then broke into a radiant smile. 'Humour,' he said. 'Our beloved servants said humans are prone to it.'

'Why are you doing this?' Usther asked. She swept a hand, as if to encompass the whole tomb. 'Any of this? Just let us go.'

'We?' Mykol was puzzled again. 'We did not create this situation. It was you, Usther of the Ashes. It was always you.'

She and Smythe exchanged a look. 'How?' she asked.

Mykol smiled widely. 'A question on our mind as well. We can find out together. All your knowledge, all that you have achieved, can be catalogued and examined. Learned. Absorbed. All it requires is a little blood.' He held out his hand. His perfectly shaped fingernails lengthened into talons, his fingertips turning lurid red. 'Just one little scratch,' he said. 'And we can discover such things as have never been imagined in any world. Together.'

Usther remembered the red ribbons and the long cuts they concealed, and shuddered. 'No, thank you,' she said.

'You say we're your honoured guests,' Smythe said. 'Please, just let us go. We don't want anything to do with this.'

Mykol's smile didn't falter. 'But you brought us here. Everything we have done, we have done because of you.' His voice darkened on the last word, his fuschia eyes taking on a strangely matte look.

Usther shuddered. Her hands went to her waist, feeling the ropy intestine belted there. A spark of necromancy went from her fingertips to the belt.

Mykol's voice darkened further. His body took on a strangely oily appearance, as if something oozed from his non-existent pores. 'We thought you would be happy. We thought we would work together to make this place into something new and beautiful. But that's no matter.' He seemed almost to stretch, the strange flesh splitting and revealing chorded mycelia beneath. 'Blood doesn't have to be willingly given. It only has to be consumed.'

Usther clenched her hands, screaming a curse. The intestine around her waist unwrapped itself, becoming a squirming rope of wriggling shadow, and snaked through the air toward Mykol. He swiped at Usther with a suddenly enlarged hand, his perfect fingernails reshaped into long red claws. She twisted her arms, and the intestine looped around his wrist and yanked it back and away, giving her just enough space to dodge back.

'Smythe!' Usther yelled. Mykol's arm started to sprout red tendrils that buried into the intestine, trying to rip it apart, and Mykol struggled against it with teeth bared—teeth which were no longer white and even, but were now red and fanged.

'Uh...right!' Smythe threw himself at Mykol, throwing his arms wildly around the man's neck. Mykol snarled, and as he did so the fungal walls seemed to flex and grow, light rippling up and down them. The walls started to close in. Usther gritted her teeth and yanked the intestine free of Mykol's grip. Red tendrils filled the air like slimy confetti.

'We need an exit!'

'But how will I—oh!' Smythe reached into his pocket and pulled out a handful of gravemould—Usther's gravemould. He summoned a spectre with a blast of cool air. It gasped into existence, a faded thing of ghostly rags and the barest hint of a human form. 'Make an exit,' he ordered. 'But don't let the fungi get you!'

The spectre rushed like an icy wind at the fungal wall, reaching out with translucent hands to dig at it. The fungi extended its tendrils, gasping for the spectre, but they passed through slowly as if through treacle, unable to find purchase.

Mykol opened his mouth, the face splitting far too wide. More red tendrils extended from the fleshy red inside, reaching for Usther's face. She yelled and threw up her hands; the intestine unwound from Mykol's arms to shield her face, immediately being seized by dozens more tendrils. Mykol's clawed hand swung wide but Usther fell flat on the floor and scooted back, her cursed intestine straining to return.

Mykol panted, mouth closing up. He seized her intestine in one hand and tossed it aside; with the other, enlarged red one he reached for her.

'Usther!' Smythe threw a pinch of gravemould at her. It scattered in the air, so many motes of dirt and healthy decay. She reached out, with her hand and with her mind, and gathered the pieces of it, drawing them together. Mykol's claws almost met her throat when a gasp of wind and insubstantial hands shunted her aside. Her side hit a wall of fleshy fungus. Tendrils immediately spread and wrapped around her, each thick chord sprouting multi-coloured caps. Her spectre dug at the tendrils with ghostly fingers, but for every thread it managed to break, another sprang up in its place. She tried to voice a curse, but the tendrils constricted around her throat, cutting off the airflow, almost as soon as she had the thought. She choked, her vision going spotty. The tendrils relaxed the barest few millimetres, keeping up just enough pressure to keep her panicking.

Across the room, Smythe's spectre had made some progress. She could see white walls through a small gap and the spectre was still digging, but it was slow going as it fought off the tendrils. For all they could only briefly get a grip on it, it was still enough to slow it down. Smythe fought off a storm of tendrils himself; they spun and lashed at him, leaving angry red welts on his skin.

Mykol staggered over to her. His balance was all wrong. Too much of his weight had been thrown into his over-sized, clawed hand. But he looked perfectly calm.

'Once you are catalogued, we will understand you,' he said. He touched a claw to her chin, the sharpness of it enough to snick the skin but not yet draw blood. Usther's heart pounded frantically in her chest, but the tendrils around her neck still prevented her from moving, speaking.

'And then, perhaps, you will also understand us,' he said. 'This is what it was all *for,* you see? This is what it was all about!'

He flexed his hand and the claw sunk a fraction deeper. He leaned close, fuschia eyes aglow. 'You'll thank us,' he said. He paused, thoughtful. 'Or you'll die.'

A wild howl split the air. Usther's eyes darted to the hole Smythe's spectre had made. A helmeted grey face appeared there, mouth agape, and then the entire wall burst open, sending fungi flying across the narrow chamber.

As the fungi scattered in the air, it was surrounded by golden light and shrivelled into dust, squeaking like panicked mice.

An armoured figure scrambled in. Clad in midnight blue that hung from his skeletal frame, he panted and locked eyes on Mykol.

Two other figures stepped in behind. One in a brilliant purple wrap dress, her black hair a stormcloud about her face. Golden light flared at her hands. The other wore a brown cassock and heavy fur. She held a strung bow loosely at her side.

Hope flared, brilliant as Andomerys' sunlight magic.

Mykol snarled and lunged for them. An arrow struck his shoulder the moment he moved.

The entire fungal chamber, all at once, lit up like a thousand lanterns and started to shriek.

CHAPTER FORTY

Ree

Celia circled her, her movements perfectly fluid; too perfect, uncanny in her precision. As she walked, tendrils extended from the fungal walls of this red prison to gently stroke her hair, her skin, her trailing skirts.

Ree clutched her chest, panting. She needed to find a way out but she couldn't see past her revulsion for the thing burrowed in her chest, couldn't see past her fear of its next agonising flex.

'Usther is safe, of course,' said Celia. 'Our beloved servant requested that no harm come to her, but from the servant's own hand, and we want to reward her for her service. Mykol is keeping her company, and your companion Smythe as well. Oh...I wouldn't grow hopeful about that.' Celia smiled. 'Mykol can more than handle the two of them together. Their magic is, after all, of no consequence to us.'

'People are more than their magic,' Ree said.

'Maybe some people are,' said Celia. She stopped and crouched in front of Ree, arms circling her knees. 'But that's not true of you, is it? You made magic your whole identity. Shaped your entire life around what you would and wouldn't do with it. And now that you have the magic you crave, there is nothing else of interest about you.' She leaned close, and Ree pulled her head back, gasping at the sudden wriggle in her chest.

Celia's fuschia eyes took on a horrible glow. 'No love, no desire. No ambition. An empty vessel, our beloved servant called you, and as we draw closer to the heart of you, we can only agree.'

It wasn't true. Ree held on to the thought amid her pain and panic. It wasn't true.

But how many times had she wondered about the richness of the lives of others? How many times had Usther complained that the only thing she cared about was her damn books? How many times had she feared that she was lacking something fundamental that made others whole and left her with a hole?

'But your magic *is* interesting, isn't it?' Celia breathed. 'These necromancers resurrect bodies but you resurrected magic itself. You alone in this world can change your shape, can be more than flesh and blood. Alone, apart from Mykol and myself.' She held out her hand, turning it this way and that. 'I created this shape, you know. Created Celia. We are still the Many-That-Hungers, but I am myself as well. I know what it is to be both plural and singular. And *I* have discovered passions such as *we* had never imagined. Human passions.' She smiled. 'But you don't know anything about that, do you?'

Stricken, Ree whispered, 'You don't know me.'

How many times had she wondered if she was fundamentally broken? Incapable of the sort of desire others seemed to have.

But she wasn't broken. She was only different. She had learned the word asexual and wore it like a badge. Like a shield.

She shouldn't *need* a shield.

'Feeling misunderstood, are you? You could *show* me I am wrong. You could show everyone they are wrong. All I need is your blood. The Many-That-Hungers will catalogue every part of you, understand you on the level you so desperately crave.' Celia reached out slowly, putting a fingertip to Ree's chest.

Ree stared with wide eyes and didn't pull away.

'And we would understand your body better,' she said quietly. 'The pain you are feeling...it is unnecessary. The Many would prefer to rest peacefully inside you.'

The tendril in her chest vibrated gently, as if purring. Utterly repulsive.

'Why convince me?' Ree said. 'You could just take my blood.'

Celia sighed and stood up. 'I could,' she said. She sounded disappointed. 'I will, if I must. But that's no way to start a friendship, is it?' She frowned. 'You still don't understand why we love you, do you? Why you are so important to us? Do you really not remember, Ree?' She leaned forward, hands on her knees. 'You brought us here. You, Chandrian Smythe, and Usther of the Ashes reached across the cosmos, straight through us. In that brief moment, we knew you. We recognised you. The first thing that wasn't us, in our long memory. We followed the trail you left behind and *oh* what a world it led us to.'

Ree froze as Celia's words struck her.

Mykol and Celia hadn't followed them from the past.

They'd followed them from the spell itself. Whatever strange magic the Lich had used to send them into the Old Kingdom of the crypt, it had brushed up against The Many-That-Hungers.

They really *had* brought the Many here.

Celia stiffened as all the fungi burst into a flare of angry colour, flickering and flashing like leaping flame. 'No,' she said. 'Not now!' She walked over to the wall and melted into it, deconstructing into red tendrils and fungi and then vanishing from sight.

Ree pushed up into a crouch, staring at the place where she'd disappeared. She spared no thought for the unnerving sight of Celia disintegrating into fungal sinew, and instead got cautiously to her feet. The crimson fungi, which had been so animated in Celia's presence, was suddenly inert, except for the occasional lazy luminesce or twitching mushroom cap.

She went to the wall. She steeled herself and grabbed a mushroom cap. The fungi around it twitched and reached for her with searching tendrils, but with none of the focus and strength it showed when Celia was present. She ripped a mushroom away and tossed it on the floor, then started to dig with both hands. The crimson fungi lit up and began to twitch and scritch in protest, but she ignored its movements, digging more and more frantically. She already had a piece of it lodged in her chest. What more could it do to her?

The fungi was unpleasantly fleshy to touch. She felt like she was digging through raw meat, warm and cloying, but she carried on. When the tendrils tried to seize her, she swatted them away, breaking their tenuous filaments. She was making progress. She could just make out a hole in the wall through which she could see distant white marble.

She ripped away more and more fungi, wincing against the faint pulse of pain in her chest, until there was a hole large enough to climb through. She heaved herself up and through it, snapping the web of tendrils that grew desperately to close the space, and tumbled out onto the floor amid a scattering of crushed mushrooms.

Ree scanned the area around her. She was still in the large, prism-roofed chamber into which she'd followed Usther. The column behind her was much larger than it had seemed from the inside; perhaps she'd been in only one chamber of it. To either side of her, long trails of fungi snaked away from the column like the tentacles of some giant fungal squid.

She stood up and dusted off her robes; bits of fungi fell, and clouds of glittering red spores rose in a worrying cloud. She pushed that worry aside. She already had fungi in her chest. Things were hardly going to get worse if she inhaled a few stray spores.

She considered the column; towering, twitching, *alive*. If she had been imprisoned in only one part of it, perhaps Usther had been trapped in another? She started to circle the column, only to come up short as a narrow figure stepped out to meet her.

Ellenil looked every bit as composed as they had on their last meeting, their hood still pinned perfectly into place, the lace trail of their cloak unsullied by dirt and unstained by spores.

On seeing Ree, they rolled their eyes. 'Of *course* you got out,' they said. 'You really are a nuisance, did you know that?' The air went cold; they raised their hands to cast, the fungi at their feet starting to roil and twitch like disturbed water.

Ree didn't hesitate. She threw herself forward, too rushed even to sing herself into a skin, and drove her fist into Ellenil's face.

Ellenil reeled back, their spell forgotten. 'Oh, you absolute *rat!*' They put their hands to their nose, now bleeding profusely. Their lip looked split as well. Ree hadn't pulled the punch at all. 'How *dare* you?'

Before they could do anything else, Ree seized them around their middle and knocked them to the floor. She registered the jarring sensation of hitting the ground as bruising on her arms, but it would be much worse for Ellenil, who had largely broken their fall. Ellenil scrabbled at her back but couldn't get their hands free enough to cast, and whenever they tried to say something, Ree jammed her shoulder into their mouth, just to make sure it wasn't a curse.

'Ellenil,' Ree said, pulling her arm free from underneath them. 'I am older than you, I am bigger than you, and I am fast running out of patience with you. I don't like violence any more than you do, but I like being kidnapped by mushroom monsters even less.'

Ellenil licked the inside of her hand, perhaps in an attempt to disgust her into pulling back, but Ree had grown up with Wandering Larry and a living human tongue held no horrors for her.

Now was the question of what to do with them. Ree didn't doubt for a second that Ellenil would curse her the moment they had the chance. Questioning them would certainly give them that chance. But Ree didn't see an easy way to bind them without getting cursed in the process.

'So, I guess we're just stuck like this,' she said, glaring at the teenaged practitioner. 'I can't let you go, and I don't know what to do with you.'

Ellenil squirmed, trying to kick or dislodge Ree, but Ree was easily twice the size of the scrawny youth and had them well and truly pinned. She raised her eyebrows at Ellenil; Ellenil's eyes burned with frustration, though Ree dared not meet them directly.

This wasn't going to work. Ree wished she had the ability to mind-snare, but though she'd been trained to guard her own mind, she'd never learned necromancy.

Ellenil started to wiggle their eyebrows, furrowing and unfurrowing them. Ree paused. 'Are you...trying to mind-snare me?'

Ellenil said something muffled against Ree's hand.

'I'm not meeting your eyes,' said Ree. 'Maybe it looks like I am, but I'm not. I almost never do.'

Ellenil licked Ree's hand again.

'Enjoying the taste?'

Ellenil gave a muffled scream, eyes squeezing shut.

If Ree was honest, she'd quite like to scream herself. But it didn't seem like it would accomplish much.

Morrin's teeth, what she wouldn't give for a gag and a bit of rope right now...adventurers who came to the tomb always seemed to have rope. For the first time, she was seeing the use of it.

She felt a tickle against her legs. She ignored it at first, until it became more insistent. She glanced back just in time to be yanked away from Ellenil by her ankles. Fungal tendrils wrapped around her legs more tightly, binding her.

A short bald man, skin covered in tattoos, strode toward them. His fine silk robes swished around his legs. 'Ah, Reanima,' said Tarantur. His lip curled with distaste. 'I see you've been causing problems. Hardly a surprise, given your history.' He stretched a finger out toward her and gently twirled it. The tendrils grew up her body more quickly, trying to pin her arms.

Ree quickly sang a spell to sharpen her nails into crow's talons and swiped at the creeping threads. Though crow talons were not particularly sharp, they were more than enough to cut through the lazy fungal flesh. Tarantur didn't have Ellenil's skill in commanding the fungi.

As her nails shrunk back to their normal size, Ellenil shoved her aside.

'Took you long enough,' Ellenil griped. A wall of fungi rose up as Ree severed the last of Tarantur's tendrils, and seized her all the way up to her chin. She tried to sing herself into her ratskin, but the fungi climbed higher, until she was choking on it. It tasted foul in her mouth; a powerfully metallic taste against the horrible spongy flesh. No matter how she squirmed, she couldn't break free; could barely move, in fact, so tightly did the fungi hold her.

Ellenil stood up and straightened their robes, turning their little lace capelet back around the right way, and patted their hair. Some of their elaborate buns had come loose, revealing rough horn. For a moment, all Ree could do was stare. Ellenil was a wyrdling, a person born with strange traits, like scales, feathers, and horns. She had only known one other, and had no idea that the little Ellenil, who had grown up in town, had been a wyrdling this whole time.

'Send her back to the chamber to await the Lord and Lady,' said Tarantur, nose wrinkling in disgust. 'And fix your hair, for gods' sakes.'

Ree expected Ellenil, so quick and proud, to respond sharply to that, but she let it pass, her expression oddly still. 'She escaped once; there's no reason to think she won't escape again. We hold her here.'

'That was an order,' Tarantur said. 'I won't argue strategy with a horn-headed teenager.'

Ellenil paused for a long moment. 'And I don't answer to you,' they said. 'Move her yourself, if you are so sure of it, and let the responsibility lie with you.'

'How *dare*—!' Tarantur stopped, choking on his words. The air took on a chill quality as the pair locked gazes. Tarantur's expression was one of utter shock, while Ellenil only looked bored. After a moment, Tarantur's eyes rolled back into his head and he collapsed.

'I never liked him,' Ellenil said. Ree wondered whether they were speaking to her, or to themself. 'He is all pride and no practice.'

Ree crunched down on the fungi in her mouth, though her jaw creaked and protested the action. The mushrooms burst into a flood of iron-tasting liquid and grit. Ree wretched and spat, then tried to sing a spell, but the mushrooms were already reforming and she could feel the spores trickling down her throat.

'Do you feel clever?' Ellenil rolled their eyes. 'Fungi are not fragile enough that merely shattering them will kill them. Certainly not *these* fungi.' They strode over to Ree and considered them, tapping their lips. 'The Lord and Lady will be impressed that I detained you after your escape. Maybe I should display you more prettily for them.'

Ree stared at them, feeling like they didn't recognise them. How had a child raised in Tombtown ended up like this? So lacking in empathy, so willing to do whatever it took to gain power? She had always known that the town's focus on power dynamics and hierarchy was a weakness, but had never dreamed that it would lead to this level of ruthlessness.

A shadowed figure rose up behind them and placed a glowing hand to their temple. Ellenil's eyes closed and they slumped. Strong, armoured arms caught them and lowered them to the ground.

'Well,' said Tabris, straightening. 'I take it things did not go well after I left?'

CHAPTER FORTY-ONE

Usther

Mykol hissed, his entire face shifting into a mask of flexing red mycelia and long, curved fangs. He lunged for Arthura, only to throw himself back, flesh steaming, as Andomerys blasted him with another wave of hot golden light.

Usther didn't wait to be asked. She grabbed Smythe's arm and dragged him toward the opening, across which thin cobwebs of fungi were already growing.

'No!' Mykol splayed his clawed hand toward the opening. Thicker filaments latticed across it, the hole fast sealing.

'Andomerys, the exit!'

Andomerys didn't turn around, throwing up another wall of light as Mykol made to lunge forward again. 'Deal with it!'

Smythe went to the tendrils and started ripping at them. They wriggled and curled around his hands like snakes, reforming with his hands trapped. 'Uh?'

Usther whistled her spectre back over and together, they ripped through the tendrils. 'We need to move,' she said as her spectre gasped and dissipated in a cloud of dust.

'What about—?'

'Go!' yelled Arthura.

Usther went, rushing through the exit. Behind her, the entire chamber pulsed and rippled with light, every single mushroom cap suddenly a tiny lantern, every mushroom cap suddenly screaming.

'No. No!' Mykol's voice had become distorted, inhuman. He lunged for her with his clawed hand, which had nearly tripled in size, only for an arrow to strike the palm and pin it to the fungal wall.

Usther didn't hang around to see what happened next, stumbling out into the wider chamber with Smythe dragging behind her. Larry crashed into them, rattling around in his oversized armour.

Smythe yelped. 'Careful, old chap!' he said. 'You weigh a lot more right now.'

Larry gargled a war-cry and tried to bite a protesting Smythe.

Usther looked around, thinking fast. The rope they'd descended still hung through a hole in the ceiling, and the thick pillar of fungi still pulsed and shrieked. Mykol might be busy, but surely his sister would get here soon.

They needed to get Ree. They needed to get out. They needed to find a way to stop the Many's terrible spread.

And honestly, she was pretty bloody tired and needed a sit-down and something to eat.

Muffled shouts from the pillar. Usther tensed, but restrained herself from running back.

Smythe looked at her with worried eyes. 'Shouldn't we go back to help?'

The question pulled at her. Her friends were in there, fighting so that *she* could escape. Risking their lives for her.

The pillar of fungi continued to flash and screech.

'There's nothing we can do,' Usther said. She locked her hands in front of her. 'We were useless in there.' Besides, as long as the fungi were still shrieking the alarm, their rescuers must still be up and causing trouble.

Focus. Look ahead, not behind.

She studied the fungal tower. 'What we need to do is find Ree.'

'You think she's in there somewhere?'

'I do.'

This place...the domed ceiling, the bizarre cluster and spiral of fungi...it seemed special somehow. Almost religious. A temple to the Many-That-Hungers. A temple *of* the Many-That-Hungers.

If Morrin had really chosen her to deal with all this...did that mean Morrin wanted her to see this? To stop it? The Undying One was not a jealous goddess, but she had blessed the founding of the town with her own presence, and was said to be fiercely protective of it.

Was there some way that here, at the heart of the Many's power, Usther could stop them? If there was, she couldn't see it.

Usther bit her lip. Ree first. The Many later. Somehow she doubted the goddess would resent her saving her priestess' daughter. 'There must be more in here than just the part we were imprisoned in. She'll be making trouble, so we look for—'

Larry knocked her aside, howling. He shambled as quickly as he could, armour clacking, to where a woman in black was being helped out of the crumbling remains of a mound of crimson fungi by a green paladin.

'I think you underestimated her capacity for trouble,' Smythe said.

Usther rushed for her friend, shoving past the paladin.. 'Are you all right? Why the hell did you let them capture you?'

'No, and I could ask you the same thing,' Ree said. Her wry tone was underwritten with breathlessness, and even for her she was shockingly pale.

'Guess I'll just stand here, then,' said Tabris.

'Chandrian Smythe, historian.' Smythe extended his hand to the paladin.

Tabris looked Smythe up and down. 'Tabris Root-and-Sickle of Paladur-Ez.'

'I did sort of guess, from the armour. You're a friend of Persephone?'

'In increasing company, it seems. By the way, why is your undead wearing her armour?'

'Haven't the foggiest, honestly, but she has new armour anyway—'

'Smythe—shut up, would you?'

Smythe fell silent.

Usther took her friend's hands and shuddered at their unnatural warmth. Ree was normally nearly as cold as a necromancer, with none of this cloying, sweaty heat. Ree's hair hung damp and tangled, sticking to her face. Her dark eyes were dull but for the faint golden gleam of darksight.

'What did they do to you?' Usther asked quietly.

Ree shook her head. 'They put...they put something inside me.' She placed a trembling hand over her heart. 'They seemed surprised to have done it, honestly. Something about my therianskin caused it, maybe...I don't know.'

Usther stared at her, momentarily frozen by horror. Finally, she found the word: 'Something?'

'There are fungi growing around my heart,' said Ree. She stared at the floor, her mouth trembling. 'It hurts.'

Usther had never seen her friend look so vulnerable as this, and they had known each other since Usther was barely a teenager and Ree was a little girl sneaking her books. Ree had always been cold, distant, unreadable. Untouchable. To see her now, ashen-skinned and on the verge of tears, sent an icy finger of fear down Usther's spine.

'Andomerys will get it out,' Usther said. She transferred her grip to Ree's wrist and started to tow her away. 'But first, we need to get out of here. Smythe, how good are you at climbing up ropes?'

'Significantly worse than I am at climbing down them,' said Smythe.

And Usther had only gotten down in the first place because Persephone had carried her.

Persephone...no, she had to still be here. Tabris would know if she wasn't. And the Many was still at full-alert.

Usther looked around the chamber. There were other exits. Slim doorways through which the fungi crawled in snaking trails. But they would have no idea where they were.

Not that they had a lot of options.

'Smythe, you and Larry get Ree out of here,' she said. 'Hopefully Ree will find familiar territory and be able to navigate you out.' She released her friend, who gave her a worried look. Larry gargled a question.

'I'm going to stay with *you*,' Usther said, turning to Tabris.

The paladin raised their eyebrows, and Usther fought her own misgivings. Unlike Persephone, she had no reason to trust this paladin. But they'd saved Ree from the Many, so she hoped that they weren't likely to stab her, at least.

Tabris scratched the back of their head. 'Shouldn't you get out of here? I thought the fungi ate necros, or something.'

Usther managed to hold back a flinch at the derogatory term for practitioners. 'I think Persephone is still here somewhere.'

Tabris nodded. 'All right. Let's go find her.'

They turned, and Usther made to follow.

'Come with us,' Ree pleaded quietly.

Usther paused and shook her head. She couldn't quite bring herself to meet her friend's eyes. 'I'll find you,' she said. She hurried after Tabris.

When she looked over her shoulder, they were headed for one of the exits, Larry clanking after them.

She glanced at Tabris. 'Can you do the thing to find her?' she asked.

Tabris raised their eyebrows. 'The "thing"?'

'The god-compass thing,' Usther said. 'Persephone said the gods pull at your guts.'

'Oh that.' Tabris shrugged. 'Well, I don't turn it on or off, but it's brought me this far.'

Usther digested that as she considered the fungal tower Tabris was leading them around. She had never much trusted her own intuition. After all, it was her intuition that had led her to play so imaginatively with her grandfather's hunting trophies that she'd been branded a witch and chased from her village.

But if Morrin had chosen her for this task—and it seemed increasingly likely that she had, given how tied up in it all Usther had become—might she have some godly intuition, too? Some way of the goddess guiding her actions?

She tried to empty her mind and go with her gut, while Tabris poked at the tower with their sickles, shook their head, and stomped on ahead, but she couldn't seem to find any gut instinct. She felt tired and afraid, that was all.

Tabris suddenly stood stock still, so suddenly that Usther bumped into their back, knocking her forehead against the hard armour. 'What is it?'

'Do you hear whistling?' Tabris asked.

Usther shook her head. She couldn't hear anything but the unnatural crying of the crimson fungi.

Tabris stared at the wall of fungi, then started to tear into it with their curved sickles, sending severed caps flying. Usther shielded their face and stepped to the side, trying to avoid the spray.

'Sef?' they called into the growing gap. 'Sef, we're coming!' They kept digging. 'You! I've got a space about big enough for a person. I'll pause a second and you jump in. I'll follow.'

Usther nodded, steeling herself. The gap Tabris had sliced seemed terribly narrow, and thin filaments of crimson were already regrowing across the gap, veiny and glistening.

Tabris sliced one more time and stepped aside. Usther didn't wait for their say-so; she plunged through, narrowing her shoulders and trying to ignore the awful feeling that she was brushing shoulders with a flesh monster. She stumbled into another fungal chamber, with Tabris thumping down behind her.

Usther considered the chamber; it was indistinguishable from the one in which she and Smythe had been held. A white marble floor walled in by pulsing, twitching fungi. There was a mound of it at one side, but the room was otherwise empty.

'She's not here,' Usther said, and tried to force down the panic that tightened her chest. Andomerys and Arthura had risked their lives to free her from a chamber just like this, and she had blindly trapped herself again. She started back to the gap through which they'd come, but it was already closing. 'Paladin?'

Tabris strode over to the pile of fungi. It twitched with a sound a little bit like a whistle.

Tabris sheathed one of their scythes and reached out with a hand burning with green-gold light. 'Let's just clear this up.'

The fungi crumbled into dust, sloughing from the shoulders of the hunched figure beneath.

Usther's breath caught in her chest.

Persephone wiped the fungal dust from her eyes and made a face. 'That was not the most welcoming prison I've ever been held in,' she said. She grinned at Tabris, who grinned back and clasped her arm to heave her to her feet. 'Where've you been?'

'Oh, you know, making ourselves a thorn in the side of evil, the usual,' they replied lightly. 'How'd they get you?'

Persephone shrugged. 'Just not that good, I guess.' Her eyes moved to Usther and she immediately released her friend to approach her. The fungal dust slid off her armour, leaving it again gleaming and gold. 'Are you all right?' she asked. 'Did they hurt you?'

Usther shook her head, not really sure to which question she was responding. 'Friends got me out,' she said. 'Smythe and Ree have already fled, but—' She stopped herself from saying the words, *I didn't want to leave you.* They felt, somehow, weightier than the sum of their meaning.

And right now, in her golden armour, standing beside her companion, she looked more a paladin than ever. A gleaming holy vision, where Usther was a ragged necromancer, her dress shredded by the angry tendrils of so many fungi. She looked away, pressing her lips into a thin line.

Persephone took a half-step closer, gauntleted hands hovering beneath the elbow's of Usther's crossed arms, as if she intended to support them. 'Hey,' she said quietly. 'I'm glad you're alright.'

The sincerity in her voice made Usther shiver, but she still couldn't bring herself to meet the paladin's eyes.

Usther had always prided herself on not being a fool. In this moment, it was hard to ignore just how much of a fool she really was. She'd thought it was simple attraction, easily dismissed, but...

'Usther?' asked Persephone.

Usther met her eyes and felt her stomach swoop. A mistake. She should never have looked. Should have known better than to trust her ridiculous self.

'I'm fine,' she said, and tried to mean it.

Tabris cut free a hole in the fungal wall again, and this time Persephone unslung the spear from her shoulder and helped, tearing a long slice through it. 'Time to leave,' Tabris said. 'We've hung around here long enough.'

After they squeezed through, Persephone took stock of the bodies of Ellenil and Tarantur lying on the ground not far away. 'They're not—?'

'Just unconscious,' said Tabris. 'You told me not to kill any necros; I haven't killed any necros.'

A pause.

Persephone said, 'Necromancers, Tab.'

Tabris shrugged.

Usther gestured for them to follow her. 'Ree and Smythe ran this way,' she said, pointing out the passage they'd gone through. 'I think if we hurry—'

There was a shout; a woman's voice, incoherent. Both paladins stiffened and then ran for the source. Usther barely hesitated to follow.

They were running toward the chamber in which she'd been imprisoned.

Which meant that shout had either come from Arthura or Andomerys.

THE BEAUTIFUL DECAY

CHAPTER FORTY-TWO

Ree

Ree hurried down an unfamiliar white marble corridor with Smythe at her heels and Larry lumbering after them. Trails of crimson fungi snaked ahead of them and behind, still flashing, still crying out in their strange not-voices. She felt chased, certain that at any moment Celia would materialise as an anatomical nightmare and bury her in mushrooms.

She skidded to a halt at a crossroads, thinking hard. Her heart pounded in her chest, the fungi curled there making each beat barbed. She did not know which way to go. Each corridor was the same as the others, a long blank stretch of marble studded with red. She needed to go up, she knew, needed to reach the levels she'd already navigated, and hopefully from there, find her way into the familiar crypt. But she could see no stairs, no doors. Nothing to ground her, or provide direction.

'You okay?' Smythe asked. He looked at her with concern in his spectacled eyes. His hair was springing loose from his ponytail, with curls hanging down around his face.

She knew he'd heard her confession to Usther, of the fungi in her heart, but she couldn't bear to talk about that. 'I don't know where to go,' she said, and she couldn't keep the roughness from her voice. 'I've lived here all my life, but this place...it's completely foreign to me. It's been so long since I've ever been lost.' Her voice broke on the last word.

Lost. That's what she was now. In so many ways.

Smythe frowned. She thought he might bubble with positivity, as he had when they were teenagers, or else offer some encouragement. Instead, he said, 'Could I see your maps?'

Ree froze, not quite comprehending. Then slowly, she reached into her pack and handed him a rolled up map of what had been the area now occupied by the crimson fungi.

He crouched down, unrolling the map on the floor. 'We came in...here, maybe?' He circled an area of the map far east of the town.

Almost unwillingly, Ree said, 'More like here,' and pointed to a series of tunnels. 'We took the lower passages beneath the amphitheatre.'

'Ah. Of course.' His cheeks flushed a little. 'So then we travelled...roughly in this direction, right? Getting the denizens out. Then followed Usther this way...' He traced a path directly across several chambers and passages, heedless of the walls and paths marked there.

'None of that is there anymore,' said Ree.

'I know, I just thought...it's not like they've changed the cardinal directions. How far this way would you say we travelled before we went down into the heart chamber?'

Ree stared at him. This was futile. This part of the crypt had shifted under her feet, and maybe was still shifting. None of her painstaking work mapping this area could help her.

And yet she could still feel the drum of her steps as she'd run down the marble corridors. And she knew that rhythm intimately. 'We'll have travelled about here,' she said, pointing to a non-existent storage room.

She frowned. 'And then...we'll have travelled almost a hundred feet below.' She started to shuffle to other pages of the map. 'So the heart chamber is...somewhere here? And then we travelled through...a southern tunnel, I think. So we must be...' She stopped, her finger hovering over the map. 'I know where we are,' she breathed.

She lifted her eyes to meet Smythe's, her chest fluttery and light for the first time in weeks.

His smile warmed her. 'So where next?'

She scanned the map a moment, then rolled it up. 'We keep travelling south, and take our first chance to reach a higher level.' She studied the junction and pointed in a direction. 'That way.'

Was it just her, or did these tunnels look...unfinished? Like when they'd first approached the edges of the Many's domain, these walls were utterly devoid of features. No doors or rooms.

She started to move, slowly at first and then picking up speed. Larry howled a complaint, struggling to keep up in his ill-fitting armour, and she felt a rush of cold as Smythe augmented the minion's abilities, followed by the increased speed of Larry's clanking footsteps. She tried not to focus on what she could see, on the endless red and white, but instead on where she was headed, southwest and higher. The specifics didn't have to matter; she only needed to get out to familiar territory.

As they travelled, the fungi stopped flashing and went inert. Ree hoped that didn't mean anything terrible had happened to Usther or anyone else caught in the Many's heart chamber, but put those thoughts from her mind. The paladins and healers were better equipped to escape the Many than they were; there was little she'd be able to do to help them now.

No, what she needed to find was a way to deal with the Many permanently, and for *that* she needed her libraries.

The tunnels changed. White marble gave way to bored stone, like a great worm had dug it out. Ree's spirits lifted. Though this was not the crypt she knew, it also meant the Many's influence was leaving. Indeed, the fungi became more sparse, clumps and speckles of red rather than the spiralling tentacles they'd faced so far. She kept true to her direction, careful not to take a turning that would send her the wrong way. Southwest and higher. If only they could find some stairs, some pathway back to the crypt proper.

And there it was. A marr in the odd stone tunnel. She slowed and approached it, running her hand around the edges of the narrow crack. It was a little too tight for her, but Smythe and Larry would be able to squeeze through. There weren't even many fungi growing inside it; a single splash on the ground, easily over-stepped. She couldn't quite make out what was at the other end, but she could tell it wasn't white marble. All to the good, then.

'Here,' she said. 'You go through. I'll get Larry's things.' She reached for the minion and started unbuckling his pauldrons. It was only a moment before the entire arm's worth of armour slid off to clatter on the ground. 'Are these even fixed on?' Ree asked him. 'Who's idea was it to put you in armour, anyway?'

Larry gargled confusedly and picked up the fallen gauntlet. He gave it an experimental bite.

'Can you make it through?' Smythe asked, concerned.

Ree touched a hand to her heart. 'I think so,' she said, though she felt a pang of anxiety. She hadn't attempted to shapeshift since the Many had infested her heart. She wasn't sure what it would mean.

But it was already *inside* her. How much worse could it get?

Smythe and Larry made their way through, with much complaining from Larry and lots of encouragement from Smythe. Ree reached into the pouch containing her ratskin, her fingers brushing the coarse fur there.

It didn't *feel* infested. It wasn't gritty with spores or new growth. It was only her ratskin.

She took a moment to centre herself and began to sing.

The magic swirled around her and sucked her into the skin. Her chest screamed as the magic took hold, the fungi around her heart pulsing as if in excitement. But the pain was not unbearable, as it had been when the fungi first took hold. She adjusted to her new low-to-the-ground viewpoint and skittered after Smythe and Larry, her movements swift and easy.

On the other side, she unspooled from her therianskin to step beside Smythe. Together, they looked around; walls of stone brick, a floor that had probably once been cobble and was now worn almost entirely smooth. A wooden beam stretched overhead, dust falling from it, shaken loose by their arrival.

'We're in the crypt again,' said Ree. Her knees shook and she clenched her hands at her sides. The wave of relief breaking over her was almost enough to drown her. Larry bumped into her shoulder, nibbling her encouragingly.

'We are,' said Smythe. 'Where to next?'

Next? It had been so long since she'd been able to really plan ahead beyond the immediate need to escape the Many. Since she'd had any fear more pressing than the threat of mushrooms filling her mouth and crushing her heart.

She unslung her pack and studied the maps. She thought she knew vaguely where they were, but without any specific landmarks in their immediate surroundings, she couldn't pinpoint them.

But she didn't need to. She had found her way out of the Many's kingdom, and she could find her way anywhere within her own.

'Next we need to find books,' she said. 'Celia told me that the Many came here via the time travel spell, somehow. When Usther pulled us back from the Old King's crypt. We need to find some way to recreate that spell. Modify it, I suppose. Perhaps we can send them back.' She looked at the map, finding the Lich's Wing—or rather, Smythe's Wing—to the east. 'Usther said you destroyed the book that held the spell that transported us the first time, but is there anything in the Lich's library that might help us reconstruct it?'

'Ah. About that.' Smythe shifted uncomfortably.

Ree's eyebrows pinched together. 'You didn't destroy the book.' Emotions warred within her. Relief that she wouldn't have to waste time digging through related titles hoping to find the necessary knowledge to recreate the magic. Disgust that, after all Smythe's talk of having changed, he'd still kept a terrible magic for himself.

'I did,' he said. 'But it's not what you think.'

Ree rolled up her map, slung her pack over her shoulder, and shrugged. 'You have no idea what I'm thinking,' she said coldly. She brushed past him, knocking him slightly aside. 'Come on. It's this way.'

What she was thinking was that she was a fool for trusting Chandrian Smythe twice.

CHAPTER FORTY-THREE

Usther

They found Arthura panting and standing over Andomerys, an arrow knocked to a bow held lowered. In front of them was a burnt crater of crimson fungi, little more than ash.

'Morrin help us, are you all right?' Usther hovered beside them, her eyes shifting between them and the burnt remains of the fungi, half-expecting it to regrow at any moment.

Arthura turned to look at her. Her face was lacerated from several deep cuts. Blood ran down her face in sticky rivers. Her cassock was similarly torn and spotted with blood, but she stood as tall as ever, even panting from exertion. 'We're fine,' she said.

Andomerys groaned from the floor. 'Speak for yourself.' Though she had no tears in her robes or visible wounds, her normally bright and healthy skin had an almost necromantic ashen-ness to it that instantly made Usther worry.

'You'd be a lot worse off if I hadn't taken the hits for you.'

'And you'd be dead if I hadn't blasted those damn mushroom people. You're welcome.'

Persephone went to Arthura and, after a murmured request for consent, healed Arthura's wounds in a gentle burst of silver moonlight. After a moment's hesitation, Tabris offered Andomerys a hand up, and, with a similar pulse of energy, brought some of the colour back to Andomerys' cheeks.

'Thanks,' Andomerys said, and patted the paladin on their armoured shoulder. Tabris shrugged.

Usther was still trying to take in this scene. 'You killed Mykol and Celia?'

'We killed their bodies,' said Andomerys. 'I think we're all starting to get the impression that that doesn't mean as much as it would with you or me.'

Usther remembered the way they seemed to travel among the fungi, reconstructing themselves from fungal fibres and tendrils. Andomerys was right. They were part of the Many-That-Hungers. Those bodies were a trick to fool people into thinking they were human, nothing more. There was nothing to say they couldn't create new ones.

'Then we have a limited time to get out of here,' said Usther. 'Before they...regroup.' She couldn't quite bring herself to say 'reconstruct'. The image was too awful.

Arthura rolled her shoulders. 'I think I can get back up the rope, long though it is; I'm not sure about any of you.' She cast a worried look at Usther and Andomerys, neither of whom were particularly fit, to the paladins in their heavy armour.

Persephone and Tabris exchanged a look. 'Up is definitely harder than down,' said Tabris. 'We'd need magic to support it. It'll be costly.'

'I don't want to go up, anyway,' Usther said. 'We need to find Ree! She and Smythe ran that way.'

But when she pointed, she could see their misgiving.

Arthura in particular looked pained. 'We don't know this place,' she said. 'We have no idea which path they might have taken out, and have no way to track them in this sterile hole. But if anyone can find their way out of here, it's my daughter.'

'So you want to...what? Just let her run off into danger, with nobody but Smythe and Larry to protect her?'

'I've been "letting" her do that her whole life,' said Arthura. 'And she always comes home safe.' There was a mixture of bitterness and pride in her voice.

'No,' said Usther. 'No! I'm not leaving her.'

None of them understood the danger Ree was in. None of them knew that Mykol and Celia had chosen them specifically. Nobody was more at risk from the Many than Ree, Usther, and Smythe.

Persephone said, 'I'll go with you.'

There was a faint scoff of disbelief from Tabris, but Usther had eyes only for Persephone. The paladin's expression was serious. She looked more tired than Usther had ever seen her. No doubt her time buried beneath the crimson fungi had not been kind to her.

She continued, 'I don't know the way, and I doubt I can track in this place, but I'll go with you, if that's what you think is best.'

Did she think it was best? Faced with Persephone's solemn support, she suddenly wasn't sure. It was true that she had never known Ree to get lost in the crypt, whereas Usther dared not wander far from the town without her. Even here in the Many's kingdom, she had somehow tracked Usther to the Many's heart chamber and made her own exit from it.

But to Usther, this was all so much blank parchment in the tiny, scribbled map in her mind. She was neither an explorer nor a cartographer; she was not entirely sure, at any given time, which way was north and which south. And while Persephone was certainly more of an explorer than she, the paladin was guided not by her sense of direction but by her goddess' will, which Usther had no assurance aligned with her desire to find her friend.

If even Arthura believed it was futile to follow her daughter, was Usther being foolish yet again?

She looked at Persephone, who met her gaze levelly and without judgement. She really would go with her.

Usther lowered her eyes and clasped her hands in front of her. 'No,' she said. 'You're right. I shouldn't chase after her. She'll have to find her own way out.'

'She will,' said Arthura, and Usther heard in her voice that she believed it. She remembered when they were younger, how Arthura had fussed and worried over Ree. How both parents had insisted that Ree learn some means of defending herself. How they fretted when she travelled further and further, taking up mentorship from Emberlon as an archivist, fearless of the dangers of the crypt.

Well, Ree had magic now to defend herself from the old dangers of the crypt. And Usther supposed none of them were well protected from the Many. Ree would just have to do what she could.

As a group, they made their way back to the rope that dangled from the ceiling. The Many no longer flashed in warning; perhaps having lost the guiding force of Mykol and Celia, they struggled to make sense of the actions of humans. Usther stopped beside the unconscious forms of Tarantur and Ellenil, gazing down at her one-time charge. Ellenil looked troubled even in sleep, their brow slightly furrowed, their hands in loose claws, as if they reached for a spell, even now. Their normally immaculate hair was mussed, revealing two small horns from the decorative buns on their head.

Usther hadn't known Ellenil was a wyrdling. Perhaps their horns had been small enough as a child to avoid notice. She felt it was a failing, somehow. That Ellenil's parents hadn't thought they could trust her with the knowledge. That she had thought she had known that child, yet it was becoming increasingly clear that she had known nothing at all.

Arthura looked back over her shoulder, seeing Usther paused above them. 'We have little time,' she reminded Usther.

And they'd spent much of it deliberating with Usther over what to do already. And yet...

'We shouldn't leave them here,' she said.

Arthura's expression was unreadable. Her dark eyes were cold and murky as the deepest lake, but then they always were. 'Tarantur and Ellenil chose their fate. They thought nothing of sacrificing you to their false gods.'

Usther nodded, looking down at Ellenil again. The young necromancer wore so much lace and velvet. Few in town bothered with such fancies. Just the two of them, perhaps. She remembered a young Ellenil leaping from stone to stone, Usther's lace cloak dragging behind them.

'They're only a teenager,' Usther said. 'No older than Ree and I were when we met Smythe.'

'And look what that led to,' Arthura pointed out. When Usther didn't budge, she sighed.

She felt a hand on her shoulder, firm, and back into Persephone's face.

Wordless, Persephone moved past her and knelt to scoop up the unconscious practitioner. They looked weightless and loose-limbed as a ragdoll in the paladin's arms, but Persephone took care to cradle their head against her chest.

Arthura pursed her lips as Persephone passed them with her burden. She turned her gaze on Usther. Usther wasn't sure what to make of the thoughtfulness in the priestess' eyes. The evaluation there.

The journey back up the rope was not one Usther wanted to dwell on. Arthura, it seemed, could climb up ably enough, even pausing to glance back down at those below with a casual air Usther found almost galling. As she hung there, one-handed, surveying all below before continuing her journey, Usther could see her daughter in her clearly for perhaps the first time in all the years she'd known them.

Andomerys did not have the priestess' wily strength and agility. When asked how she'd made it down the first time, she'd simply shrugged and said, 'Magic can compensate.' But it was clear, as weary and ashen as she was now, that that would not be the solution for her now. 'And down is a lot easier than up, with one hand.'

Tabris sighed. 'Well...I can get you up, probably. And strap that girl to me as well, Sef. No, don't look at me like that. We're a lot less tired than you are.'

Tabris blessed themself with glowing light and did the same to Persephone, and then followed Arthura with Ellenil strapped to their back and Andomerys clinging to their front.

It would never cease to amaze Usther how *strong* these paladins were. Even with magic to help them.

'Why did you need the blessing?' Usther asked Persephone. 'You found the journey down smooth enough?'

'Up is harder than down,' she said. 'Especially in armour. Especially with a passenger.' She tried the rope. 'But I feel strong enough for the next ten minutes or so. We'll be fine.'

Again, she asked Usther's consent and pulled her snugly to her armoured body. And again, she wrapped the rope about her arm and lifted them up. It was certainly not as smooth as the way down, and in a panic, Usther wrapped her legs around the paladin's waist for better grip. Hardly dignified, but then hardly scandalous either, when there was a thick sheet of metal between them. She was glad she'd chosen a tasteless but practical outfit, for these leggings were far better for her dignity than her trailing skirts.

She didn't dare look down or unwrap her aching legs until Persephone said gently, 'Take Tabris' hand. They'll pull you up the rest of the way.'

And though she didn't want to do it, she trusted that gentle voice and, in moments, she was standing unsteadily between the priestess and the healer, and Tabris was helping Persephone up through the hole as well.

'Well,' said Tabris. 'What next?'

'Isn't your god guiding you?'

'Oh, probably,' said Persephone. 'But the Owl seems quiet right now.'

'And the Rootfather,' said Tabris.

'If you do not hear from yours, then perhaps you should listen to mine,' said Arthura. 'We are not done with the Many-That-Hungers. We need to find a way to destroy it.'

'They can't be destroyed,' came a whispered voice. Ellenil stirred on the ground where they lay. Though the paladins raised their weapons, Ellenil did nothing more than press a hand to their forehead. 'They're not like us,' they said tiredly. For the first time since Usther had first met them, they sounded young and scared. 'They showed me, many times. What is not an individual cannot be destroyed. To crush a mushroom only releases its spores. Destruction only makes them stronger.'

'They seemed to die pretty easily to a blast of holy fire,' said Tabris.

Ellenil shrugged. 'So it seemed.'

Their agreement brought Usther no comfort.

CHAPTER FORTY-FOUR

Ree

She didn't speak to Smythe as they travelled, except to give basic directions. Not even when they camped in a small tomb shelved with dead did she speak to him. For his part, he seemed to have lost the will to explain himself. Good. She didn't want to listen to any more lies.

They had lain like this before, across a stone floor with nothing more than travel rolls between them and the stone floor. She remembered falling asleep gazing into his eyes. She'd been younger and stupider then. Now, she slept with her back turned to him and willed her dreams away from him and the anxiety and betrayal he filled her with.

They found their way to the Lich's Wing quickly enough, given she'd entirely lost her bearings before. It helped that they could travel the more dangerous paths; Smythe could turn any undead that came for them, and could even help Larry overcome obstacles he was normally too clumsy to face.

When at last, they stood at the top of the stairs overlooking Smythe's library, Ree felt relief mixed with her resentment. At least this was familiar territory.

Familiar territory, but still unfamiliar in its way. When the Lich had lived here, this had been a very different environment. Blood and books scattered everywhere and no sign of any human needs.

But now the books were stacked neatly in piles about the place and the desk against the wall was covered in notes and writing implements. A discarded coat hung over an open box; a loose shirt mounded on the floor. There was an armchair at one end of the library, and Ree could see a crocheted blanket there, the undyed yarn still wrapped around the hook.

Smythe's shoulders slumped at the sight of it all. 'We're home, old chap.' He gave Larry a clap on the shoulder. The minion gargled almost mutinously, but followed him down the steps. After a moment's hesitation, Ree followed.

Smythe picked up his coat and shirt and quickly folded them away into the box and pushed them aside, giving Ree a quick look Ree couldn't read but assumed was embarrassment. 'Make yourself comfortable,' Smythe said. It was the first thing he'd said to her since his admission that he hadn't destroyed the time travel spell. 'I'll be just a moment.'

She frowned, expecting him to leave, but he only went to his desk and pulled something out from one of the drawers. A long bit of metal with a thin, hooked tip. 'Crowbar,' he said conversationally. 'The tinker charged me quite a bit for it. They're not very valuable in the upworld, but I suppose anything that requires smithy is valuable here.'

Ree went to the armchair, carefully set the crochet on the floor, and sat down, leaning forward and clasping her hands as she watched.

First, Smythe searched the floor for a certain brick. He did so quickly; she suspected he had magically marked it in some way, a suspicion that was confirmed when he murmured an incantation and disabled a hidden curse attached to it. Then, he wedged the crowbar between the brick and its fellows and levered it up and aside. He reached into the new hole, his arm disappearing far further than she had expected. She couldn't help but stand up and draw near to peer inside, her curiosity too strong to resist.

He'd created a deep hollow beneath the brick. There were a few books there, and, shockingly, a long sword that practically hummed with necromancy. He removed the bottom-most book and looked at it a moment, mouth twisting into a frown, then offered it to Ree.

Wordlessly, Ree took it. She could feel from the weight of it that it was very old; the parchment was incredibly thick and it crinkled beneath her fingers. The cover was worn and cracked leather, unmarked save for what appeared to be two knife cuts across the front creating an X of blistered leather.

As she turned to the first page, she studied the writing there. It was cramped and incredibly difficult to read, but she thought she recognised Old Antherian. Much of it was written in some kind of shorthand that would take her a little time to decrypt. As she turned the pages, she saw diagrams, sketches of hand shapes and human anatomy. The style was strange, but the diagrams were shocking in their detail.

'What is this?' she asked Smythe.

Smythe breathed out through his nose. 'That,' he said. 'Is the Lich's tome of knowledge. He had others, but this contains his most precious discoveries. It was hard to find and once I did, harder to hide.'

The Lich's tome. The accumulated knowledge of the oldest necromancer she had ever heard of, a man so powerful he had been able to bend time itself when stirred. She nodded toward the other book in the hole. 'And that?'

'His journal.' He paused. 'There is no danger in it, I don't think.'

'You read it?'

Smythe nodded, not meeting her eyes. 'I felt...compelled to. To know and remember him.'

Ree almost said, 'Because you killed him,' but she kept the words inside. The Lich had almost killed him on their first meeting for no reason other than that he was in the way. The Lich had sent him back in time to suffer on their second meeting, and on their third, had arrived to kill him because of the threat he posed to the crypt.

Whatever terrible things Smythe had done, killing the Lich had been the least of his crimes. Even if it was the greatest of his horrors.

Ree turned her attention back to the book in her hands. The Lich's grimoire, the pick of his most valuable invented spells. Most necromancers made one at some point, if they were adventurous enough to push the boundaries of the Craft. It was their legacy, proof that they had been powerful. That they had mattered.

Now that she thought about it, Wylandriah Witch-feather, the therianthrope whose work she studied, had done much the same. And then there was Ree's own journal...

She brushed her fingers over the cover, feeling the rough edges of the cut cross.

'The time travel spell is in there,' Smythe said. 'I have notes on the short hand, so there's no decryption to be done.'

Ree nodded. Smythe gestured to his desk, and cleared her a space, moving all of his notes and books to be stacked on the floor beside it. He went and got the armchair for himself and set it beside the existing chair. After a moment's hesitation, Ree took the offered seat at the desk. She opened the book in front of her, and got parchment, ink and other supplies from her pack. Then together, they looked for the spell and discussed what it meant.

The mechanics of the spell made no sense to Ree. Her knowledge of necromancy was basic, having resolutely refused to study it herself. What she was looking at here, diagrammed out in strange symbols and sketches, was complicated beyond anything she had encountered. Even the ritual to bring the Old Kingdom into the present had been deceptively simple; a trigger activating some greater magic, rather than the magic itself.

She worked at it anyway, while Smythe made his own notes from the seat beside her, unaware of her growing frustration. At last, she said, 'I don't know what any of this means.'

Smythe looked up in surprise. 'Truthfully, I don't have a clear idea myself. I'd hoped your greater experience might clarify.'

'I live among necromancers,' said Ree. 'I'm not a necromancer myself.'

'No, of course not.' Smythe fell silent a moment, then drew the book nearer to him and started to point out sections of it. 'Here, we can see that this is a spell based on principles of soul summoning—soul summoning involves transferring souls across the realms, from the spirit realm to the living realm and back—and this particular spell uses those principles to shift a soul from this world back into this world, but at a different time.'

Ree rubbed her forehead. 'Where does time play into it?'

'Well, the spirit realm is said to exist outside of our time. Similarly, the Lich's spell is designed to push the soul and body to a realm outside of time before drawing it back in. The actual realm is not specified.'

Ree pressed her lips into a thin line. She thought she knew at least one thing about the realm this spell passed through.

'How does it move the body instead?' she asked.

Smythe shrugged helplessly. 'There's something here about binding living corpses and living souls...I don't completely understand it, honestly. The diagram is...very complex.' He pointed out one with so many overlapping shapes and tiny symbols labelling the outside that Ree thought she'd need a magnifying glass to read.

'So...we don't know how he did it?'

'We know the *basics* of how he did it,' Smythe said anxiously. 'It's possible I could recreate his spell even without knowing it. But that would only serve to send us through time. What we want is a way to send Mykol and Celia back to their original realm. Do you know anyone who could make sense of this?'

Ree chewed her lip. 'My father and Kylath, maybe. Veritas, possibly.' She made a face, thinking of the experimental necromancer and what he might attempt once he got his hands on this kind of magic. Truthfully, she didn't like to think of *anyone* having access to this spell. 'Usther,' she said quietly. Usther was the most intelligent necromancer she knew, with the most broad knowledge base. For someone who had learned largely through spying on other necromancers rather than through books, she was surprisingly thorough.

And Usther had improvised this magic before with nothing more than the knowledge of where they'd gone. She'd never attempted anything like it again.

Usther could be trusted.

But the issue of trust raised another. She turned a considering gaze on Smythe. 'Why did you tell Usther you'd destroyed it?' she asked.

Smythe shook his head. 'I thought...well, I thought someone might try to use it. And I was frightened of what that might mean. It is dangerous.' He smiled wanly. 'And look at us now. We *are* thinking about using it.'

'But why not destroy it, as you said you had?'

'I've been asking myself that, honestly. To begin with, it seemed too dangerous a thing to be allowed to fall into anyone's hands, least of all mine. But I was little more than a boy then, and still working through what I had been willing to do. What I had almost done. I didn't trust my own judgement, and I had no one to turn to. I was exiled from town. And you had told me personally that you wanted nothing more to do with me.'

Ree remembered that day. The first day she'd truly tried out her wings, in front of all her friends and family. She remembered swooping through the long halls and retracing her steps to the precious library. Only for her heart to stop on finding her enemy already ensconced there.

Just the memory of it made her blood burn. A library of the crypt, perhaps the greatest curated necromantic collection in the entire crypt, in the hands of the man who had tried to destroy her town. All that knowledge, lost to her and hers.

He'd offered to share it with the town archive. But he'd also refused to leave, and that was intolerable.

'At first,' he said. 'I hid it away, to deal with at a later time. And then later. And then later still. When I got it out and studied it, I realised how dangerous it was. I hid it again, not sure if it would be better to destroy it and hope we never needed the knowledge or keep it in case we did. I felt...a pull toward it, too. As I feel the pull toward all foolish things.' His voice turned bitter. 'But I had learned better to resist that, so I put it from my mind. A problem for later.' He shook his head. 'Truthfully, until Usther came knocking on my door, I hadn't thought of it in years. And when she asked about it, I was afraid of what she might do. And I realised in that moment that I *should* have destroyed it. So I told her that I had, and hoped that would avert the danger.'

She glared at him, but he only looked back at her with an open honesty, and she felt her anger leak out of her.

He had possessed all the knowledge of the Lich all this time, and he had done nothing with it.

Perhaps he really had changed.

'Well,' she said, looking away. 'I'm glad it wasn't destroyed, I suppose. We're going to have enough trouble undoing whatever the Lich did even with his tome.'

'So you aren't angry?' Smythe asked.

Ree rubbed her eyes. 'I'm angry with you all the time,' Ree said. 'Sometimes I think I haven't spent a single day without anger since you performed the ritual. But I'm not angry about this.'

With a nod, they returned to their work. Ree didn't doubt that they'd need to find an experienced necromancer to study it for them, but they'd do what they could while they were here.

She tried not to wonder what it would mean if they could not find a way to banish the Many-That-Hungers back to their realm.

CHAPTER FORTY-FIVE

Usther

In spite of everything, Usther sat straight and proud in her seat at the front row of the town hall. She had exchanged her dirty travel clothes for a dress of red so dark, it was almost black, embroidered at the bodice, hems, and sleeves with tiny black skeletons, almost too dark to see. She'd washed her hair and styled her braids so that half made a knot atop her head, while the rest fell loose about her shoulders. She'd done her make-up carefully, applying paint to her lips and kohl around her eyes, accenting the hollowness of her cheeks with dark powder to increase her necromantic airs.

This was an important moment for her. And for the town. She needed every advantage, every authority she could muster, when she addressed them.

She glanced around at the hall. While many seats were empty, the town was livelier than she'd seen it in weeks. Denizens stood at the ends of aisles to talk, or leaned over the backs of their seats. A few children that ran down the aisles in the first real play they'd likely had in a long time. Her heart jumped to her throat at the sight of all this life. *Home*. This was home. She hadn't realised how much she missed it; not the tombhomes and the central mausoleum, but the people.

Beside her, Persephone murmured, 'When you said there was a settlement, I had no idea there were so many of you.' Her gaze, like Usther's, roamed around the room. She and Tabris had left their armour and weapons behind in Usther's house, though Tabris had protested heavily. It was believed that the denizens would accept them better, and with less of a reaction borne of fear, if they didn't face them equipped for war.

There were certainly uneasy glances thrown their way. There was no hiding their size and strength, nor the healthy upworlder glow of their skin, but so far nobody had challenged their presence. Since they sat between Usther, Andomerys, and Emberlon, that was small wonder. And though not everyone in town had been personally rescued by Persephone, the word had spread that a paladin had agreed to fight the Many to help them escape.

'There used to be a lot more of us,' Usther said. 'A lot of people fled when denizens started disappearing. Especially the families.'

'I had no notion necromancers raised families,' Persephone said quietly. 'I was wrong about so many things. I'm ashamed to think of how many.'

Usther shifted uncomfortably. She knew Persephone didn't think of necromancers as mindless evils to be destroyed, as some did, but it still bothered her how surprised she was every time she discovered proof of that.

Though if she'd been here at the last town meeting where an upworlder had been present, she might not feel so warmly toward Tombtown. Smythe, whose only crime had been that he wasn't a necromancer, had been marked to be blood sacrificed for the good of the town, the strength of his life and blood to enter Namura's Ward, the great magic around the central mausoleum that kept it safe.

She used to think back on that time with a bitter conviction that they shouldn't have let him escape and wreak the havoc that he had. But now she couldn't help but think that perhaps they had brought that doom down on themselves. He would not have been so quick to sacrifice the town if they had not been so quick to sacrifice *him*.

An amplified boom of a staff hitting the ground. Beside her, Persephone didn't jump but did turn her eyes curiously to the necromancers now entering the hall. The council here was much diminished; with Bahamut retired to lichdom and Tarantur a traitor, only Igneus and Kylath remained.

The chatter in the hall quieted down, somewhat grudgingly. Usther had always liked that. Tombtown denizens were too independent to be easily hushed, but too curious to properly interrupt.

Igneus and Kylath made their way up the tall staircase to the raised dais on which the sarcophagus of the old king rested. Since hearing from Ree years ago what the Old King was like and the ruin his curse had nearly brought down upon the town, she had often fantasised about raising his body and having it march itself out into the sun. But that would be a petty and worthless revenge. The Old King did not reside in his old bones any more than the soul that had once lived inside Misery lived there any longer. Using a corpse on frivolous magic was wasteful; condemning a minion to death because of the actions of the body's former inhabitant was cruel. So she put those thoughts from her mind and instead focused on the council.

Kylath and Igneus stood side by side at the front. As usual, Igneus cast the spell that amplified their voices, like a particularly impressive death echo.

'We gather here at a time where we teeter on the edge of tragedy,' said Kylath. Her voice boomed across the hall, echoing off the walls. In spite of its loudness, it seemed accompanied by the whispers of many gasping voices. 'Our crypt has been invaded, its people enslaved. Those of you we have rescued bear the marks of your forced servitude.' At her word, Emberlon stood up and walked to the front. He rolled back his sleeve and raised his hand; where once there had been a crimson ribbon, there was now bare flesh marked with a still-healing, jagged scab.

Many nodded at the sight of it, while others murmured in shock. Emberlon bowed and returned to his seat.

'We have been forced into an unlikely alliance with these...adventurers,' she continued, not quite daring to voice the word 'paladin' in front of so many denizens, 'to free our people and take back our crypt. Thus far, our efforts have been rewarded. A great many denizens have been returned home—we believe all who were brave enough or willing enough to leave. The masters of this parasitic kingdom, Mykol and Celia, have similarly been dealt with. Permanently, is our hope.'

This raised further conversation—murmurs of disbelief, exclamations of joy, and arguments between the two. Usther shifted uncomfortably in her seat. She herself doubted Mykol and Celia were really gone, but she didn't know how one went about explaining that the lord and lady of the Many's kingdom were made of mushroom and not meat.

Igneus stomped his staff on the dais, sending out another loud cracking boom. Slowly, the crowd subsided. 'But it isn't over,' he said. 'Many of our number have already evacuated the town for fear of their lives, before we

knew anything of the Many-That-Hungers. And more still remain within
the Many's kingdom, whether by choice or cowardice. The mushrooms that
Mykol and Celia were feeding seem to have some intelligence of their own,
and *they* are not destroyed. We will need to be wary if we are to stand
against them, using all of our wiles and all of our cunning. But we will
also need to be *united*.' The last word echoed around the chamber with a
necromantic gasp. Beside her, Persephone flinched, but Usther knew that
the death echo was no barrier to the other listeners.

'The council proposes we gather knowledge on how best to defeat them
or, failing that, how best to defend ourselves. Anyone with information
on the Many-That-Hungers is encouraged to come forward to the council
room at *The Bone & Brew,* where we will be discussing strategy. In the
meantime: do not leave the safety of the town. While travelling through
town, go nowhere without a fellow denizen to accompany you. We believe
they lured denizens away in the past; do not be fooled again. Nobody is to
leave the town until this threat has been addressed.'

There was instant chaos as people stood up and made their disgust with
this policy clear. Usther groaned and slumped in her seat, fed up with her
fellow denizens.

'I don't understand,' said Persephone. 'Why are they so angry?'

'They're fools, the lot of them,' said Tabris, only to yelp as Andomerys
elbowed them in the side.

Emberlon leaned over from the end of the aisle. 'They are angry because
they do not wish to be ruled,' he said. 'And it is important to them that
the council remember that. I doubt any of them are in any rush to leave
the central mausoleum, given what they've been through, but to be assigned
partners and have their movement restricted grates for each and every one
of them.'

'But it's for their own good, surely?' said Persephone.

Emberlon shrugged. 'People are quite bad at judging what is and isn't
in their best interests. And it matters that they have a say in it. That always
matters.'

'You mean necromancers,' said Tabris.

'I mean people,' said Emberlon, and his voice held an edge Usther had
never heard before. Tabris sat up straight at the sound of it, then seemed

314

surprised at themself. They gave Emberlon an appraising look, which Emberlon ignored.

Eventually, Igneus and Kylath called the town hall back into order and the arguments subsided into private grumbling. Kylath addressed the room once more, 'Finally, we have word from Usther of the Ashes, who risked much investigating the missing denizens, and who has unique insight into the nature of the Many-That-Hungers.'

Usther straightened. This was what she'd come for. She stood up proudly, chin raised, and made her way up the dais. Igneus and Kylath both nodded politely to her, acknowledging her authority in a way that gave her chills.

She turned to address the room. Though she'd told herself she'd given up on the ambition of being a council member, years of fantasising about just this situation—about her importance, about every eye in town being fixed on her, every ear straining for her voice—took over. She wet her lips, mentally running over every line she'd practised. The grave tone. The stirring call to arms. The humble recounting of dangers she'd faced such that it actually raised her in their esteem.

And then she really *looked* at them. Not as 'the denizens'. But as her neighbours. Etherea Eversworn rested her head on Mazerin the Bold's shoulder. Pontifar sent his bonehound to comfort a teenager crying silently in the corner, the teen's long sleeves not quite covering the thick scar the siblings had left. He laughed in surprise as the skeleton licked him with a spectral tongue and smiled when the hound clattered its hind paw on the ground while it enjoyed being scratched. Everywhere she looked, it was haunted eyes and drooping shoulders. A few brave souls seeking comfort, while the rest looked in dire need of it nonetheless.

She sighed. Nobody needed her long-faded ambition right now. Least of all her.

'The Many-That-Hungers do not belong here,' she said. 'This is our home, given to us by Morrin the Undying. A place where centuries of necromancers have flourished, even before the time of Tombtown. The Many-That-Hungers, and the creatures it created, known as Mykol and Celia, do not belong here. They do not answer to Morrin or any god of this world. They do not raise the dead; they consume them. And seek to use us to fatten the Many-That-Hungers with minimal effort, having us walk the dead right into their hungry mouths.'

Usther rubbed her eyes tiredly. 'Maybe they could have lived here in peace. But that's not what they want. They are here to dominate, not to live alongside us. We are tools to them; vehicles for their food. Carriers of knowledge.'

The silence that met her words was not the baited breath of a captivated audience, but the tired quiet of people well-ready to go home. She tried not to begrudge it.

'A lot of us came to dominate.' Odalia stood up and looked around the room. She had no scars, and had likely never left her home. Usther wasn't sure she'd ever seen her except at town meetings. 'What makes them so different?'

'They succeeded,' said Usther. A murmur went around the room at this. She hesitated. Her eyes found Arthura in the crowd. The priestess watched, impassive. 'Morrin the Undying decreed that we should play nice. Well, they haven't, and that's dangerous. They resist necromancy. They kidnap people. Trap them in pillars of mushroom. Drink their blood. Infest their minions.' She shook her head. 'All we can do is keep ourselves safe until we have some way to get rid of them. That's what I'm going to do. I suggest you do the same.'

She folded her hands in front of her to resist the urge to twitch and twist her fingers. She had always craved this attention, and yet now she felt utterly underwhelmed by it, even betrayed by her own disappointment. When no further questions were raised, she quietly returned to her seat.

The town meeting went on, with denizens making arrangements for travelling partners among their neighbours and discussing whether evacuation was the only option.

Her contribution to the meeting was swiftly pushed into the past, irrelevant to the denizens she'd addressed.

After the meeting, Usther returned home and took the paladins with her. With the town returned to its previous state of activity, there was room at the *Bone & Brew*, but she didn't trust Mortana with their safety. She liked having Persephone nearby, little as she wanted to admit it. The paladin was quick to help prepare food or clean and was soft-spoken and comfortable company. Sometimes, living with Ree had felt worse than living alone. Ree was rarely home, and when she was, she'd lock herself in her room and have little to say to her housemate. Persephone was actively attentive.

Tabris she was less comfortable with. They didn't hide their instant dislike of Usther's home, their disapproval of the skulls and bones Usther had decorated the shelves with, and had complained loudly that they had never imagined they would be sleeping in a stolen tomb.

'It's hardly stolen,' Usther said shortly. 'The dead are dead. This space better serves the living.'

Tabris had shaken their head in disgust, and Persephone had drawn them away to talk quietly, no doubt sensing that her partner planned to insult their host further.

She felt no sense of relief on dumping her things in her house. With paladin armour and bedrolls covering the floor, it didn't *feel* like home. She needed to do something about her growing unease. About the desperate sense of things growing beyond her. But she didn't know what.

At length, while Persephone stirred a simple rat and mushroom soup, Usther said, 'I'm going out. I won't be long.'

'Wait!' Persephone set aside her spoon and strode after Usther. 'You shouldn't go alone. Didn't your council say as much?'

'I'm not leaving town,' Usther said. 'It hardly matters.'

It *did* matter, though she didn't want to think of it. She already knew, in no uncertain terms, that she was a primary target for the Many. If Mykol and Celia had reconstructed themselves, as she was uncomfortably sure they had, they would be keen to trap her again and steal the knowledge in her blood.

'I'll come with you. Tab, don't let the soup burn.'

Tabris made a face and trudged toward the pot boiling over the fire. 'Fine.'

Usther wanted to protest that she didn't need company. That this was her town, full of people she had known since she was a teenager. But she didn't. The last few weeks had shown the lie to that. And Persephone didn't look likely to change her position.

For a mercy, she didn't don her armour or pick up her spear, so they were quickly out the door. 'So where are we going?' Persephone asked.

Usther shrugged. 'To pray.'

Persephone's eyebrows raised, but she didn't ask any questions.

The Altar of Many Gods was the most beautiful structure in town. Instead of modifying an existing tomb, it had been built out of the ruins of many structures throughout the tomb, showing columns and archways of a variety of kinds of stone and brick work, or even marble, though thankfully, none that was stark white. Ensconced in the columns or at their feet were shrines to various gods, nearly all of them gods of death or dying.

'What is this place?' Persephone asked, following her in.

'This is where we keep our religions. All of them,' she said, a little wryly. 'That there is The Great Wraith, patron of souls that have not departed. And there is Lorr, God of lost knowledge. And Mercur, god of good fortune. You get the idea.'

She'd picked out some deities she knew were worshipped in the upworld as well. If Persephone thought anything of that, Usther's sidelong glance wasn't enough to discern it.

'Is there a particular god you pray to?' Persephone asked.

'Yes.' Usther chose not to elaborate, and Persephone did not push her to. Instead she made her way to the small altar to Morrin the Undying. In spite of her priestess setting up the Altar of Many Gods, it was no larger nor better cared for than any of the other altars. Usther knelt before the little skull with a hole through its forehead and picked up the small velvet pouch of human teeth, feeling them in her hands.

Behind her, Persephone was so silent as to not exist. Usther didn't look around to see if she had left; instead, she emptied her mind of Persephone, of the town meeting, of Ree lost somewhere in the crypt, of everything weighing on her mind.

'Why did you choose me?' she asked the skull. 'Did you choose me, really? Or was this all some big coincidence?' She dropped her gaze to the pouch of teeth, which she rolled around in her palm. The teeth clacked faintly. 'This is all so far beyond me. The Many. Mykol and Celia. Everything that is happening in the tomb. And the only thing that has kept me going was the idea that you had *chosen* me for this. That I might have some part to play. But I have only been stumbling from one danger into the next and I feel no closer to a solution. I could use some guidance.'

She waited, the echo of her voice in this columned place fading. She tried to let her mind go still, to open herself to the divine. Arthura had once spoken of communing with the goddess in such terms, and Usther had never forgotten.

Time passed. She wasn't sure how long, was *trying* not to be aware. She didn't feel any stirring of the divine in her heart. Didn't hear the whisper of a voice in the still air. Tears pricked at her eyes, and she clenched the teeth more tightly.

'Why don't you speak to me? If I'm chosen?' she whispered. 'Or did Arthura make that up?'

Because she *knew* the goddess was real. They had all seen her work through Arthura at one time or another. Heard the visions she gave Arthura every Toothday. Festering rats, she'd *possessed* Arthura at the founding of the town. All of the council had borne witness to it.

'Why don't you answer me!' she shouted. She stood up and thrust the tooth pouch back onto the altar, where a few teeth spilled out across the stone surface. She strode angrily away, brushing past Persephone, who had watched the entire thing in perfect stillness behind her.

Later that evening, when Persephone had gone to bed, Usther glared down, unseeing, at the embroidery hoop in her lap. She'd been hoping to embellish the hem of her travel cloak but had barely managed a few stitches before her hands stilled.

'Hey. Hey!'

She raised her glare to the paladin sitting across from her. They had a notebook open in their lap and had been sketching with charcoal, their fingertips blackened with dust.

Tabris said, 'Sef said you went to speak to your goddess.'

'Yes.' Usther said the word crisply and with finality, having no desire to share confidences, least of all with Tabris.

Tabris studied them a moment then went back to their sketching. Usther thought that had been the end of it, but then: 'Sometimes I think I'm angry at the Rootfather for not making things clear to me. But eventually, I realise I'm angry at myself for not living up to my own expectations.'

'That sounds like a "you" problem,' Usther said sharply.

Tabris shrugged. 'Maybe it is.'

After a long silence, Usther said, 'The gods don't speak to me, anyway. I'm not a paladin. I don't have a magical connection for what I'm supposed to do.'

'Don't you?' Tabris raised their eyebrows. They closed their sketchbook and stood up, stretching. 'I'm going to bed now.' They stomped over to the other side of the room, where Persephone had been gently snoring for the last hour, and stretched out on the vacant bedroll there.

Usther went to bed soon after, fuming at Tabris and everything they'd said.

CHAPTER FORTY-SIX

Ree

It was a few days before they made it home—longer than Ree had intended the journey to take. The Many had spread further, its red fungi springing up along their path. Though it seemed dormant, and neither lit up nor screeched at their approach, Ree decided it was safest to give it a wide berth. She didn't want to risk either of the siblings materialising from among a small cluster and trapping them once more.

They'd made little progress with the Lich's grimoire. Smythe carried it now. In spite of Ree's misgivings, he'd had it for years and never used it, and he was certainly better able to defend it than Ree was. Larry himself seemed subdued. He didn't like to see the tome, and would yell and flee whenever they got it out, only to creep back later when it had been put away. Larry had been the Lich's minion, once. His fear and dislike of all things Lich worried Ree sometimes. She wondered what the Lich had done to him, or had him do, that inspired such a powerful aversion in her normally cheerful undead friend.

She was surprised to find the town inhabited again. Necromancers travelled around in small pairs or cabals, an unusual sight among the normally solitary denizens. She recognised many of the faces they'd freed from the Many's kingdom and felt a powerful rush of relief; they had made it back, then. She'd been very worried that the siblings had thwarted their escape while she had been imprisoned.

She went first to her own tombhome, where she found the paladins drilling their weapons outside. A small cabal of children watched them from across the street, their eyes wide, gasping at every blow the paladins struck. Weapons were beyond uncommon in Tombtown; necromancers had no need of them and often had aversions to them from past experience.

'Archivist Ree!' one of them gasped. She couldn't remember his name, but he was one of Allogrim Angerwake's children, and had been born in the town.

Larry gave a great howl and ran at the children. Tabris shouted and leapt out to meet him, but Ree imposed herself between them. 'Don't you *dare,*' she said in a low voice. She made her eyes flash, a trick she had learned from her father, and Tabris seemed momentarily stunned.

The children shrieked as Larry plunged into their midst. He picked up the smallest one, a little girl in black robes, and swung her around. The other children grabbed his legs, laughing and yelling, and dragged him to the ground.

'They don't seem to be in any danger, Tab,' said Persephone. She leaned on her spear, sweat glistening on her forehead. She had made no move to intercept Larry. 'The opposite, I'd say.'

Tabris hesitated, then swore quite foully and barged into the tombhome. Ree almost tried to stop them, but the tombhome's wards didn't activate. Usther must have modified them to make an exception. Interesting.

'I'm glad to see you made it back safe,' Ree offered. 'Is Usther home?'

'Gladder that you have,' Persephone said. 'Your friend has been worried sick. And yes, she's home.' She inclined her head to Ree in a semi-formal way that almost felt like a salute, and continued her drills without her partner, moving now in rote patterns against an imaginary foe.

It looked a little like make-believe to Ree, but she decided not to remark on the foolishness of it. Besides, she knew nothing of a paladin's training; perhaps the make-believe was useful, like a child learning to strengthen their mental wards against mind-snares by imagining a mental intruder.

She followed Tabris inside, tension easing from her shoulders as she felt the familiar cold rush of passing through the wards. Usther froze, halfway to the door herself. She wore a dress of dark blue, with silk on the back that trailed like wings. 'Ree,' she whispered.

Ree braced herself. 'Hi, Usther.'

Her friend rushed forward and threw her arms around her in a hug. She smelled of incense and a floral perfume she rarely used. Her boxbraids had been redone and were slightly thicker now. She'd pulled them into a tail over one shoulder.

'I'm so glad you made it home all right,' Ree said, and patted her back as comfortingly as she could. Normally, she resisted physical affection. Neither of her parents were particularly prone to it and Ree had always found it stifling. But she knew it was important to Usther.

'What happened to you?' Usther said. 'Where are Smythe and Larry?'

'We got away,' Ree said simply. 'I'll tell you it all properly when we have a moment to sit down. Smythe is outside, watching Persephone train. Larry is greeting the children.'

'Oh, they're still out there, are they?' Usther said with distaste. 'I can't convince them to go and do something useful with their time.'

'I expect their parents are glad they have somewhere to play within sight of the paladins, given the greater threats,' Ree said. 'Will you modify the ward so Smythe can get in?'

Usther agreed without hesitation. When she returned with Smythe, Usther greeted him with warm relief that he had survived. They had become friends, Ree realised, and it was shocking to think of it. Usther had far more reason to hate Smythe than she did.

Ree settled in, uncomfortable with the small space their new guests led to. There was no room for Smythe at all, and Ree suggested that he, at least, go to Mortana's. 'If that's what he wants,' Usther had replied. 'He can have a spot on the floor in my room, if not.'

It was a level of generosity that left Ree frankly stunned. She was not entirely convinced that Usther would have offered *her* a spot on her bedroom floor if she'd needed it. 'What's changed?' she asked Usther suspiciously.

Usther only looked tired. 'We all did,' she said. 'All of us.'

She would not be drawn further on the subject.

Smythe thanked Usther for the offer, but went to take a room at Mortana's, once he was sure Ree was settled. In spite of her desire for more space, she felt oddly bereft when he left.

She ignored the feeling and went to call on her parents. She found only her mother, who did not embrace her but offered her a watery smile. 'I knew you would return,' she said, though her conviction was underwritten by the faint tremble in her voice.

Moved, Ree clasped her mother's hands. The physical touch was still jarring, even though she found she craved it this time. 'I'm glad you're safe, too,' she said.

Her mother's smile faltered. 'None of us are safe,' she said quietly. 'But enough of that. Meet your father and me in *The Bone & Brew* this evening. It's important that we catch up, and I suspect Kylath should hear of your journey as well.'

'And more than Kylath,' Ree said. 'I'll bring the others. I think...I think I may have found a way to stop the Many.'

Arthura's eyes widened, but she didn't question her further.

THE BONE & BREW was the busiest she'd seen it in weeks. Denizens gathered in small cabals around tables, talking in quiet voices. To Ree's shock, papers were also changing hands. Notes for spells and wards, discussed openly and in public.

'Are they really so eager to part with their knowledge?' Ree said. Having grown up in the town, and a daughter of a council member no less, she was well-familiar with how jealously practitioners guarded their magic. Indeed, it was one of the reasons it was often so difficult to get books back from them when they were 'borrowed' from the many libraries; nobody wanted anyone else to discover the same secrets they had. Apprenticeships were also rare—hence why acolytes tended to gather in young cabals, sharing what they dared and keeping the best of their knowledge for themselves.

'People are frightened,' Usther said. 'There is nobody to protect them but each other.'

'But that was always the case,' said Ree.

Usther shrugged. 'Perhaps it has become more real to them.'

'In times of great strife, communities either come together or fall apart entirely,' said Persephone. Ree glanced at her, surprised she was listening.

'Your town already came very close to total destruction—more than once, as I understand it. Perhaps a lesson has been learned.'

Ree nodded, unsure what to think. She had always wished for more community feeling among her neighbours, but the lesson had come with a high price. She rubbed her chest.

Mortana waved them through to the back. She and another denizen seemed to be discussing potion recipes, and Mortana waved a handful of dried herbs emphatically while she spoke.

In the backroom, Igneus and Kylath were seated, speaking quietly, while Arthura paced barefoot around the back. Ree noticed she had her bow and quiver to hand. Though the bow was unstrung, she knew her mother could string it quickly and smoothly in a matter of seconds.

In all her life, her mother had never gone armed in the town and rarely in the crypt unless word of adventurers came to her. She'd always saved it for their rare visits to the mountain top, or travelling to the local villages for supplies.

Ree shivered at the thought her town was really that unsafe. Though what a bow and arrow could do against Mykol and Celia, she couldn't guess.

Kylath nodded to Usther, who inclined her head graciously and took a seat at their table. Ree and Smythe followed suit. When Ree cast a nervous glance at the paladins, they merely stood by the door, flanking it like sentinels. Persephone gave her a small smile; Tabris frowned at the gathering in front of them.

'I'm told you have relevant information on the siblings,' said Kylath. 'I'd be happy to hear anything that might help us defend against them.'

Ree nodded and spoke of everything that had happened since she left the rescue mission. She spoke of Tarantur and Ellenil controlling the crimson fungi, of the strange temple-like heart chamber, of being imprisoned in a room of fungal walls, and of Mykol and Celia's ability to deconstruct and reconstruct themselves via the Many. Usther and Smythe interjected with their own experiences when relevant. Ree was horrified to hear of Mykol transforming his hand into a claw and attempting to rip the blood from her, and though she'd heard of her mother and Andomerys rescuing them already, it was still frightening to imagine the danger they had been in.

She felt the absence of Andomerys and Emberlon now; they could really use the knowledge of those friends who had seen and risked so much. But Emberlon was still ill, and Andomerys convalesced in a healing sleep from her own exhausting efforts. Both were staying at Andomerys' cottage at the top of town, and Emberlon had passed on his regrets that he couldn't be there to help.

'So these...beings are here because of...the Lich?' Kylath asked. Ree could hear the words she almost said in her hesitation. *'So they're here because of you?'*

She appreciated that Kylath chose a less accusatory tone. She'd never really known where she stood with the council, though they were obviously all close with her father and had been fixtures in her life ever since she was born. Kylath had always been a cold and distant authority figure, never someone she had expected empathy from.

But then, she supposed she'd been a fixture in Kylath's life as well. And Kylath was the last loyal member of the council beside her father. She had not been tempted by the power of the Many-That-Hungers.

'It's all tied to what happened eight years ago,' said Usther. 'The magic used to send Ree and Smythe to the crypt's old kingdom is the same magic that drew the Many here. They've as much as admitted that.'

'But what's their interest with you?' said Igneus. 'Why should they want anything to do with the three of you, now you're here?'

Smythe said, 'It seems...well, almost like...like an infatuation. They're curious not just about us, but about how they came to be. Mykol and Celia did not exist before they arrived in the crypt. I honestly believe it's as much about self-discovery and whatever fantasies they've made up about us as about whatever they might have planned for us.'

'But you said you had a plan to get rid of them?' said Igneus.

Ree and Smythe looked at each other. Smythe said, 'We think...perhaps it would be possible to create a spell banishing them back to where they came from, using the same principles as the spell that first attracted them.'

Kylath frowned. 'For that, you would need the original spell. The Lich is dead.'

Ree cleared her throat. 'The Lich is dead. But we have his grimoire'

Kylath and Igneus stared at her in shock. Arthura paused in her bare-footed pacing to consider her daughter, her expression unreadable.

'You have it?' Igneus said. 'Well, let's see it!'

Ree shifted uncomfortably in her seat. She glanced at Smythe, who made no move to hand over the tome. 'No,' she said. 'The Lich meddled with things that have put the entire crypt at risk. We don't want that knowledge to spread further than it has to.'

Kylath folded her hands in front of her, her mouth shifting to one side. 'I quite agree, but we are your town councillors. We are the most experienced practitioners in town, and the only people you can trust to undo whatever has been done.'

'Oldest doesn't mean best,' Usther muttered under her breath, not quite too quietly for the rest of the table to hear.

'Reanima.' Igneus appealed to his daughter in a gentle tone.

Ree loved her father. She trusted him, to a certain extent. He was not as greedy for power as many. After all, he already possessed more of it than anyone but Kylath. But she had stopped being able to trust him wholly years ago, when he had tried to shape her future to his liking, and not her own. He would abuse power if he thought it was his right.

She raised her chin and put her shoulders back. 'Whatever is happening here, it started with us three, and we will finish it. We've held the secret of what happened to us for years and never experimented with the magic, knowing what it might cost. Even,' and she looked at Smythe, 'when there was no-one to know if we did it.' As she said the words, she felt their truth like a kick in the guts.

'The Lich was hundreds of years old,' said Igneus. 'You need a necromancer of incredible skill to be able to unravel that kind of complexity of magic.'

'We have one,' said Smythe. 'After all, she did it once before with nothing more than the knowledge of what had happened to us.'

Usther's eyes widened. One hand crept to her throat.

CHAPTER FORTY-SEVEN

Usther

U sther could hardly believe the words her friend had just uttered.
'It's the natural choice,' said Smythe. 'You've dealt with this magic
before. You're an extremely capable practitioner. And you are more at risk
than anyone else, as the siblings want you in particular. You have all the
motivation others might lack.'

'Usther is a child,' Kylath said.

'I'm twenty-seven years old,' Usther said. 'I haven't been a child for a
long time now.'

'Trust us when we say that twenty-seven is a drop in the lake,' said
Igneus, and when she looked at him, his eyes suddenly seemed far more
ancient, deep and unfathomable.

She glared and put an otherwordly light into her own eyes. She was not
intimidated by cheap tricks.

'It doesn't matter what you think,' said Ree. 'We aren't trusting the book
to anyone else.'

'Be serious,' said Kylath.

'I'm always serious,' Ree replied flatly.

'If I may speak?' said Tabris.

The denizens startled.

'Speak,' said Igneus.

'There is no need to drag magic better left dead into this,' they said.
'Healing magic is incredibly effective against both the Many-That-Hungers
and the creatures Mykol and Celia, if they even still live. We know where to
find the heart of their power. We need only to burn them out.'

'It was my understanding that the effort of fighting them caused considerable exhaustion of your magical resources, and particularly of Andomerys', said Igneus. 'She is recovering in her cottage even now.'

'We won't be able to do it all at once,' said Tabris. 'But we could do it. Persephone and I have deep reserves of power, and your healer has greater reserves than anyone I've ever met.'

Ree frowned. 'You're dealing with fungi,' she said. 'You can't just burn some of it and hope that it won't come back before you're done. Killing it just produces more spores. And even ignoring that, it spreads more quickly than I believe you are capable of killing it. If you'd seen the way even Ellenil and Tarantur could control it, I think you'd be a lot more wary.'

'We're healers,' Persephone said quietly. 'Truly, we can kill the spores. It's a natural part of our skillset. The Many we burn do not come back.'

'But are easily replaced by others,' Ree replied.

'I can do it,' Usther said quietly. The argument stopped and everyone looked at her. 'I've done something similar before, as Smythe says. I'm certain I can modify the Lich's spell.'

In fact, learning and building upon the spells of others was how she had done almost all of her learning as a young necromancer. With no mentor or books to learn from, she had learned through spying and her own trial-and-error. While she was hardly above using the odd book to learn her way, she had never valued book learning as highly as Ree did when there was so much to be gleaned through simple practice and observation. It was one reason she had nearly perfected the art of spectre summoning; she'd needed to use the spectres as her eyes and ears many times.

She'd expected protest, but there was only a long pause, broken by Igneus asking, 'Are you sure?'

Something about the lack of resistance shook her. Was she really going to take on the burden of defeating the Many-That-Hungers, a being from another realm that had almost destroyed the town? She'd always craved the opportunity to prove herself, but surely this was a step too far. She should leave this to someone more capable than she was.

She looked around at the table, ready to say as much, when she saw Smythe looking at her with shining belief, and Ree giving her the smallest encouraging smile. And for a moment, she forgot about the paladins, and the council, and the pressures that weighed on her from Arthura and Morrin the Undying and Symphona, somewhere out there, waiting for her chance to kill her. Because her decision wasn't about any of them. It was about her, and Ree, and Smythe. It had been about them eight years ago, and fate had made it about them once again.

Last time, she hadn't been strong enough. She'd tried to teach Smythe, but had failed to teach him anything truly important. She had failed to make any attempt to sway the town in his favour, though she had known in her heart that killing him would be wrong. And she had failed to withstand the power of his ritual and climb the stairs to stop him, though she had put everything she had into trying.

This time was different. This time, she wouldn't fail.

She nodded to Igneus, sitting up straighter in her chair.

'This is a mistake,' Tabris said. 'Better to kill it, and have done with it.'

Usther looked at them now, in their shining armour, with their weapons gleaming at their belt. 'Killing is never better,' she said, and meant it.

After that, there was a little discussion. A few more protests, a few more alternatives offered. But there was no better plan than to use the magic that had brought them here to banish them, and there was no better candidate than Usther, as Ree and Smythe refused to surrender the tome of knowledge to anyone else.

The group dispersed, and Usther, Ree, and Smythe returned to their home. It was time to discover how the Lich had created a spell to displace someone from their time, and from there, how to send something back to the realm it came from.

REE POURED TEA FOR Usther and Smythe, then sat down with a glass of water for herself. Usther glanced at the tea uneasily. Did it look a little pale? She decided not to ask whether Ree had allowed it to steep properly this time. Her housemate was a joyless bore who didn't drink tea, so it was kind of her to make it up—even if she always made it rather unpleasant.

She added a sugar to her own and took a sip, making a face. It was indeed weak, which made the sugar far too sweet in comparison.

She had the tome of knowledge open in front of her, and Smythe and Ree's notes spread out beside. The other two were crowded around the small table, but made no move to read the book. They'd had their time with it and deemed it beyond their understanding. They'd put all their hope in her.

She could only hope she'd live up to it.

She started to sift through their notes, comparing them to the pages they referenced. Removing the target from the living realm...realms without time...non-specific physical translation with specific temporal co-ordinates...

She stopped and pinched her brow between her fingers and took another sip of her sweet and watery tea. She didn't want to say that this was beyond her, but it was certainly a lot to take in.

How had she done this before? She had scried Ree and somehow seen her outside of time. That shouldn't have been possible—people could not scry on the past or future, whatever fairytales might say—but she'd theorised that it was because Ree was still *of this time,* though the specifics now escaped her, if she'd ever had them. Hard to pick up where you left off when you'd spent the last half a decade deliberately forgetting it.

She wished she'd kept notes, but she was not a great note-taker, and at the time, she'd been too distracted by the news of Ree's curse to really digest the magic she'd done. She closed her eyes and rested her head on her arms, slumping forward over the table.

'I say, are you all right?' Smythe asked.

'Just shut up a moment?' Usther mumbled back, and for a mercy, he did.

She remembered the pool of water, glowing with a scry-light, and Ree's face inside of it. She remembered the tight-chested panic as she wracked her brain for how to bring her back. She had sketched spells in the air and murmured incantations, none of which quite seemed to take. And then, she had been seized by the conviction that she didn't need to recreate what had been created. She needed only to right what had been wronged.

And a spell had come together in her mind, and she had reached into the bowl of water, hand to hand, soul to soul, and dragged Ree back into her own time, and Smythe with her.

She put aside the notes her friends had made and tugged the grimoire closer, smoothing the pages with her fingertips. It crackled slightly beneath her touch. The diagrams and notations here were intimidatingly dense, but she felt certain that she could work through it, given the time. Here, wasn't this just a more detailed depiction of the realms-as-spheres theory, where each of the realms was an overlapping sphere surrounding the central sphere of the living realm? And the bands of notes around them seemed to be specific incantations...

She delved deeper into it, musing under her breath. Beside her, Ree's quill scratched against paper as she made some notes of her own. Dimly, Usther was aware that Ree was noting down the things Usther was saying, but she was too focused to be irritated.

Eventually, she blinked and rubbed her eyes, finally taking in the room. The paladins were asleep on the floor. She didn't remember them coming in. Smythe, she could just make out on the floor of her bedroom, the door still ajar. And Ree was slumped over the table, the smeared ink of her sleepy collapse already long dry. Usther's body was sore, especially her back and legs; she was vaguely aware that she must have been at this for hours, though she had been too focused to keep track.

But there was a glowing ember of knowledge inside her. 'Ree,' she whispered. She poked her friend in the shoulder. 'Ree!'

Ree stirred and lifted her head. A piece of paper was sealed to her cheek, presumably by drool. She plucked it off and glared at Usther. 'What?'

Usther smiled. 'I think I know how to reverse the magic that brought them here.'

THE NEXT MORNING, THE three of them gathered again in the main room, surrounded by loose notes and quills. Persephone leaned against the kitchen counter, sipping a cup of tea. She'd made up a lovely strong pot from her own stores which had a wonderful citrusy scent. Usther held it now, enjoying the scent and the way it warmed her hands. She tried not to look at Persephone, who had bought a sleeping robe of dark silk from another denizen, which made her silver hair all the more stark, and which was just open enough at the chest to reveal the barest curve of one breast.

She scolded herself for even noticing it. She needed to focus.

She watched Ree and Smythe as they looked through her notes. Ree chewed her lip; Smythe rubbed his chin. They had identical expressions of perplexed concentration. Did her notes not make sense? Ree wasn't a necromancer, but Smythe at least ought to be able to follow her line of thought, surely?

Tabris headed for the door. They wore their armour, but didn't have their sickles. Usther raised her eyebrows at them. 'Meeting someone?'

The paladin glared at her. 'It's not any of your business if I am.'

Persephone said, 'They're walking some of the local kids around town so they can play safely and keep out of your parents' way.'

That was unexpected. Any attempt at focus vanished. 'Tombtown kids?'

'They're children,' said Tabris shortly. They left, slamming the door behind them.

Usther glanced at Persephone, who shrugged. 'We heard their parents complaining that their children were going mad stuck inside,' she said. 'Tab has always liked kids.'

'Most of them are going to be necromancers one day, you know,' said Usther.

'You don't know that,' Ree said idly, turning to a new page.

'Town law is that they can't practise until they're at least sixteen,' Usther continued, 'But that doesn't always stop them from trying.' And she knew very well that even if it did, accidents could still happen.

'Yes, they're very terrifying witches,' Persephone said. 'However will Tabris hold their own?' She settled herself on the kitchen floor with one of Usther's many cushions to read an extremely worn novel. It was the only one in the house; Ree didn't approve of fiction.

Usther returned her attention to her friends. Ree had finished the notes and was drumming her fingers against the table thoughtfully. Smythe finished a moment later, blinking and rubbing his eyes behind his glasses.

'Well?'

Ree folded her hands in front of her. 'You've made more sense of the theory for me—I hadn't realised that was a diagram of the realms-as-spheres. But in practice, I still don't understand. How can necromancy move something from one realm to another?'

'Well, for starters, I don't necessarily need to know how—I already know that it *can* be done. But in fact, necromancy moves things between realms all the time, even with our most basic spells.'

'Soul summoning,' Smythe said quietly.

'Soul summoning,' Usther agreed.

Ree's hands started to twitch on the table. 'Necromancy's domain is death, not time,' she said.

Smythe took off his glasses and gave them a hasty clean. 'One might argue that the two are closely related,' he said.

'Besides which, we already know magic is capable of far more than a simple description can provide,' she said. 'Why can therianthropy give the ability to breathe underwater, or increase your reflexes, when it is the domain of shapeshifting? Why can healing and necromancy both scry, though it has nothing to do with either life or death? Magic is larger than we believe it is...sometimes, I think on Veritas' assertion that books have souls. Not because I agree with him—he's certainly very mad, and annoying besides—but because he is doing what all of us should be doing. He is pushing the boundaries of what we think magic can do and searching for the actual boundaries of what magic *is*. Who is to say that time is *not* the domain of necromancy? The only way to be sure is to try.

'And I think,' she tapped the grimoire, 'the Lich tried a great deal, and here we hold the results. This isn't a work journal full of disjointed thoughts and musings—this is a proper grimoire, a complete and curated collection of everything the Lich thought was worth writing down.'

She realised she'd been lecturing and stopped, but her friends looked thoughtful rather than irritated.

'Well, how are we to test it, then?' Smythe asked. 'We can hardly banish a human to another realm. They are anchored here as surely as we are.'

'Not to mention we don't want to risk anyone ending up outside their own time,' Ree murmured, and Usther was forced to agree. They still didn't know the full risks of sending someone through time, but they knew it had worked out very poorly the last time.

'We need some crimson fungi,' Usther said. 'Not a lot of it—even one cap would do. Just enough that I can cast the spell on it.'

Ree frowned. 'That's a big risk. We know Celia and Mykol can travel via the Many.'

'And that the Many can multiply rapidly when it chooses.'

'Celia and Mykol were turned to ash by healing fire,' Usther said. 'We'll have to hope they're still recovering from that, if they still live.'

Ree's mouth pressed into a thin line, and Usther could almost hear her protest: that had been days ago. If they were still alive, they would surely have reconstructed themselves by now.

But the siblings didn't have perfect awareness of all that the Many experienced. She'd seen that many times already, like when she'd freed Emberlon, Persephone, and Tabris from their prison.

'We'll need to distract them,' she said. 'I don't know how best to go about it.'

'And we'll need a way to defend ourselves,' said Ree.

Persephone cleared her throat. 'I'll join you,' Perspehone said. 'If you'll wait for me to don my armour.'

Usther nodded, feeling warmed to her core. 'That would be...helpful,' she said, not quite able to bring herself to say 'kind of you' to a paladin; even one as beautiful and gentle-spirited as Persephone.

Ree said, 'We'll go somewhere the crimson fungi is sparse, on the outskirts of the Many's territory. The further we are from the white marble, the better.' She tapped her lips, then nodded to herself, clearly already having a location in mind.

They got ready in a flurry from there. Usther didn't change into her plain travel clothes; if she was going to face Mykol and Celia, she wanted to do so with as much pride and intimidation as she could muster.

It was time to be rid of the Many-That-Hungers once and for all.

CHAPTER FORTY-EIGHT

Ree

Ree waited in the main room. Knowing Usther, it could be some time before she was ready. She never had a travel bag packed, as Ree did, and was very likely donning her face paints and best dress ready for facing whatever lay ahead. It made her smile wryly to think of her friend's strange ways. She might not understand them, but she liked how uniquely Usther it was.

Now, Persephone approached her and took another seat at the table. Though she sat down heavily—hard not to, Ree supposed, when you were wearing so much metal—she didn't so much as ruffle the many notes laid out in front of her. 'Feeling all right about this?' she asked quietly. 'I know you went through quite a lot out there.'

Ree shrugged. 'No more than you did.'

'I am a paladin—it's my job to get myself into horrible and bleak situations. But that's not at all the case for you. Aren't you some kind of librarian?'

Ree surprised herself by smiling. 'I'm an archivist. Though I've had my share of horrible and bleak situations, too.'

Persephone studied her and nodded slowly. 'I believe you.'

In the corner, Misery sighed loudly and shuffled off with a broom to begin sweeping the floor.

'Once I would have thought living with an undead minion would be nightmarish,' she said. 'I was...unprepared for the reality.'

Misery gave a few listless sweeps of the broom and then returned to her corner.

'Is she forced to do that? The cleaning and such?'

Ree considered. 'Yes and no. Necromancers can use magic to command undead. But minions like Misery, who've been around a long time, can resist commands if they choose to. And Usther rarely uses necromancy to enforce her to do anything but stay safe.'

'She's...like a pet?' Persephone ventured.

Ree's eyes narrowed. 'She's family,' she said. She rubbed her chest unthinkingly, and Persephone's eyes followed the movement.

'Are you still having trouble with that?' she asked.

Ree shrugged. 'Andomerys isn't well enough to look at it, but it's been still since she turned Mykol and Celia to ash.'

She dared to hope that meant Mykol and Celia had not put themselves back together again.

Persephone considered. 'Would you like me to have a look at it?'

Ree hesitated. 'If you think you can?' Though the paladins practised healing magic, they seemed to be trained more in the destruction of undead and the augmentation of their own bodies than in the actual science of healing. They were powerful, certainly, but power alone wasn't why Andomerys was an incredible healer. She was knowledgeable beyond any healer Ree had ever heard of, and had spent her long life studying human anatomy and healing techniques. Even when she used non-magical methods of healing, such as mundane potions or surgery, she worked with an efficiency and precision that invited complete confidence from her patients.

Persephone reached a hand toward Ree's chest. 'If you don't mind?' she asked, and at Ree's quick nod, she pressed her hand to Ree's chest, right over her heart. Warmth immediately flooded Ree, surprising in its lack of familiarity; Andomerys' healing was a humid summer heat, while Persephone's magic was much cooler and more gentle by comparison. A silver glow suffused her hand.

The fungi around Ree's heart twitched for the first time in days; pain flared, small but sharp, and Ree couldn't repress her gasp. Immediately, Persephone's magic reduced to the barest glimmer of warmth. 'Sorry,' she murmured, her brow pinching together.

Ree nodded wordlessly, resisting the urge to shove the paladin away. This pain was how the fungi defended itself, how it aimed to control her.

She needed to be strong enough to withstand it. She closed her eyes and focused on her breathing, long and deep, as her mother had taught her to do when praying to Morrin.

Eventually, Persephone drew back. 'This is beyond me,' Persephone said. 'I cannot purge it without damaging the tissue it clings to. There are more spores growing on your heart, so it needs to be purged soon. But, I don't have the subtlety necessary to remove only it and heal the hurts it leaves behind as well.

Spreading? Ree nodded and said around a lump in her throat, 'Andomerys will be able to remove it.' She tried to believe that was true.

Persephone nodded. 'I'm certain that she will.' Her words held a conviction that Ree lacked, and it comforted her.

Surprised by the emotion, Ree said, 'I'm glad you're here, strange as that sounds.'

'I'm glad to be here, strange though it sounds,' she replied with a small smile.

Usther came sweeping out of her bedroom with braids pulled into a loose tail over her shoulder and with sweepingly dramatic paint lining her eyes. Her dress was thickly embroidered but looked more hardy than her silk and velvets. Her only real nod to practicality was that she wore sensible boots instead of her preferred embroidered slippers, though even those were polished to a shine that would quickly dull. 'Smythe?' she asked as she came out.

'He's outside with Larry,' Ree said.

She nodded. 'Good. Misery? Go and get Dichotomy, would you? We're going for a walk.'

Misery whimpered and gave her master a dramatically sagging frown, her mouth a black hole.

'That's quite enough of that. A walk will do you good and I'll keep you quite away from anything dangerous. Honestly, *Larry* never complains of coming with us.'

At Larry's name, Misery...Ree would almost describe it as a glare. Her eyes narrowed and took on the faintest gleam, and she shuffled off to collect Usther's contrary cat without so much as another sigh.

Ree raised her eyebrows at Usther.

'I know,' Usther replied in a low voice. 'It turns out they quite dislike each other. Which is not ideal, I grant you, but I'm not above exploiting the knowledge...'

THEY JOURNEYED OVERNIGHT, heading for the Lich's Wing in the eastern tunnels, but keeping an eye out for any sign of the crimson fungi along the way. At first, it was a relief to travel near the town and see no sign of them; for a while, it felt like all was well in the crypt. No lesser dead bore the marks of fungal infestation. There were no strange cracks in the walls or bored tunnels, and certainly no white marble. They made camp and Ree dared not to fear that there would be creeping fungi in the night, or that they would wake with a sibling standing over them with their uncannily white smiles.

But that feeling of safety didn't last. They didn't make it even as far as the eastern tunnels before Persephone spied a clump of unnaturally bright red, as lurid as freshly spilled blood. It hung from an outcropping of crumbling stairs.

'Well, that'll be it, then,' Ree said quietly. There seemed to be no further trail of it, but Ree didn't trust for a second that what she couldn't see didn't exist. It had to have spread here somehow, whether by invisible spores or the wandering of some infested minion.

'Stay back,' Usther warned Larry and Misery. She picked up Dichotomy from the floor. The cat yowled her protest, but Usther put her in her sling and hung the sling around Misery. 'And don't let Larry bite her,' she said.

Ree snorted. Dichotomy was far more likely to bite Larry, who had a natural fear of the fierce little cat.

She followed Usther nearer to the fungi, where it clustered on the stairs. She wondered if she imagined the fungi in her chest shifting at the nearness; she felt no pain, but couldn't shake the sense that it was stirring in some way.

'So what do we do?' she asked.

'We don't do anything,' Usther said. 'I have to do this myself.' She paused. 'But I'd prefer it if you were near, anyway.'

'I'm not going anywhere,' Ree said.

Smythe strode up on her other side. 'And I'll be here as well, if you wish.'

Usther nodded and gave him a grim smile of thanks.

The three of them faced this little cluster together. Then, Usther took a step forward and got to work.

The temperature plummeted as she worked, necromantic energy so thick in the air that the world seemed darker and tinted red. She cast with a speed and precision Ree found stunning, making incantations and sweeping gestures in the air and forming spell-shapes with her hands in rapid succession. Her voice took on a death echo as she incanted the spell—no simple chant or utterance, but a long string of Old Antherian so quickly spoken that Ree struggled to discern its meaning. The Lich had done none of this when it had cast Ree and Smythe back into his own past—but then, he'd been a necromancer many centuries older than Usther was now. As she worked, her hair started to rise, floating around her in trails of shining black. Her dress too became almost weightless. Ree wondered if even her feet would lift from the ground, as the Lich had at the height of his powers, like a spectre given physical form.

Ree glanced sidelong at Smythe, who watched Usther with open awe. He caught her eye and smiled a little.

Usther worked on, and the temperature dropped further. A chill wind rushed through the crypt, and frost rimed the floor around Usther in a perfect fractal with her at its origin. Finally, with a cry, she sketched a circle in the air over the fungi; there was a pulse of energy so forceful, it sent Ree skidding backwards with her arms raised to guard herself, with Smythe hitting the ground beside her.

Green light gathered around the fungi, startling in its strangeness. There was a sense of reaching and pulling; the mushrooms were drawn toward the glowing circle as if sucked at by a powerful current.

Usther stood before it, hands outstretched, sweat darkening the back of her dress and hanging in the air around her like shining crystals. She screamed, her voice booming with death echo, and shoved her hands forward as if pushing the fungi from afar.

The circle flickered, then went out. The ice around her melted. The fungi, which had been nearly pulled from its perch, reached out with red tendrils to re-anchor itself and went still.

Usther collapsed to her knees and Ree ran to her side. Moments later, with a gasping cry, Misery hurried over and pawed at her mistress' back.

'I'm...I'm fine,' Usther panted. She gave her minion a pat. 'Go back, darling. I...don't want...you near it.'

Misery obeyed, and Ree pulled her friend to her feet.

'What happened?'

Usther shook her head. 'It should have worked. I had the parameters correct. I had it all planned to the finest detail. I could feel the spell catch, like it was getting its hooks into the fungi. But then it just...didn't go. I could feel pressure in my brain. Resistance. I wonder if its will was stronger than mine, or if there is some key component I'm missing.'

'And you have no idea what went wrong?' Smythe asked nervously. 'Nowhere to start?'

Usther shook her head. 'Nothing. I've never controlled such a powerful spell...perhaps I'm just not strong enough.' Her tone rang with long-held bitterness.

Ree wasn't sure what to say to that. Usther had long struggled with a lack of inherent power. Power reserves of necromancers seemed to lean heavily toward natural ability, though practice could increase it. It was one reason she'd become so skilled with spectres, which required the least power to summon of any minion.

Ree had no idea whether the kind of magic Usther was attempting required lots of power. It was completely new and too complex for her to discern much about. But before she could console Usther that they'd have to find another way, Smythe said, 'Well, that's nonsense. You're plenty powerful.'

Ree frowned. It was surely particularly galling to hear that from Smythe, a man for whom necromantic power had come almost without trying, but Usther said, 'You think so?' very quietly and Ree's heart almost broke to hear it.

'I'm certain,' Smythe said. 'And clever enough to work around any limitations, I'm sure. More likely there is something here that we're missing. Perhaps we need a knowledgeable perspective.'

From behind them, Persephone said, 'Are you going to dig up your Lich and ask him?' Her voice was heavy with sarcasm.

'Well, we can't because...there isn't, uh, a body.'

For a moment, they all remembered the sight of the Lich tumbling into the swirling portal in the town hall, before Smythe ploughed on, 'But we have the next best thing.'

Ree's eyebrows pinched together. 'We do?'

Smythe nodded. 'We have the body of the Lich's lover.'

'You have what now?' Persephone followed their gazes and made a face. 'You can't be serious. How does that...even happen?'

Larry, startled by the sudden attention, ceased trying to pet Dichotomy through Misery's half-hearted defence and gargled a question.

'Come here, old chap,' said Smythe, striding forward and gesturing. 'This won't take a moment.'

Larry took three steps back, looking from Smythe to Ree.

'He isn't going to like this,' Ree murmured.

'It's unnecessary,' said Usther. 'Smythe, I don't see how it could possibly help.'

Smythe was trying to encourage Larry over and Larry wasn't having it. Finally, Ree said, 'Larry. Please,' as gently as she could.

Larry paused, mid-way through turning to flee. He studied her a moment, with his dull eyes. His shoulders slumped. He shuffled over to stand beside her, bumping into her shoulder.

She gave him a pat. 'Just be quick,' Ree said. 'It can't be pleasant for him.' She knew he could handle it. He was an ancient creature, and braver than anyone she knew. If not for Larry, the Lich might have killed Ree. If not for Larry, Smythe might have destroyed the town. And he'd tried to save her from adventurers as a teenager as well, before she had any magic of her own to defend herself with.

Smythe nodded. At his direction, Larry laid down on the ground. In that position, flat as a plank, eyes staring blankly at the distant rock ceiling, he looked almost like a true corpse. His chest didn't rise and fall with breaths. He had none of the shambling, swaying movement that so animated him when standing up. It occurred to Ree that she'd never seen Larry lay down—never seen *any* active minion lay down, except for Misery. Perhaps there was something about the position that disturbed them. Perhaps it reminded them too much of what they had once been.

Persephone came to stand beside her. 'What is he doing?' she asked in a low voice.

'Soul summoning,' she said. 'To speak with the soul of the dead. It's rarely that useful; the dead do not care to be brought back to the world of the living. It can cause...' she hesitated. 'Discomfort. But Smythe is very good at it.'

'I'd heard it was the darkest of magics,' she said. 'That it can harm or even destroy the souls of the dead. That to kill a living person is evil, but to kill an immortal soul is a crime against the gods.'

Ree hesitated. 'You know, it's fine if you want to go back—'

'No. I want to see this.'

Ree looked at her sidelong. Her expression had settled into its usual unreadable mask. Ree wondered if there was a tension in her shoulders, or if she was imagining it. She almost asked, but managed to hold it inside. If she let anxiety rule her in her dealings with the paladin now, it would undo the trust they had built. Persephone had done well by them so far; she would continue to. Necromancy was *not* evil, whatever her paladin school might have said.

If only she could silence the guilt in her own heart over soul summoning, perhaps she could believe it.

She expected the icy chill of Smythe's magic to break over them like a glacial wave, but instead there was only a mild drop in temperature as he gently placed his hand on Larry's chest and murmured something she didn't catch.

Red light burst from Larry's chest; Ree braced herself for the scream. But the featureless figure of red light that rose from Larry's chest wasn't screaming or clutching its head in pain.

Instead, it hovered there, ghostly legs fading into Larry's chest, and said in a perfectly cultured voice, 'And to whom do I owe the pleasure of being returned to this mortal coil?'

Ree was torn between horror and intrigue. No spirit ever summoned had been this calm. Though this spirit had no more definition than any other, the coolness of the voice immediately drew her back in time to when she'd been a teenager lost in time and trapped in the clutches of this violent man and the young Lich.

'Well?' prompted Lazarin, the former inhabitant of Larry's body.

Larry gargled a protest and swiped at the spirit emerging from his chest. His frantic hands passed through the spirit's immaterial form, creating wisps of red smoke that then reformed. The soul of Lazarin gave no sign that he noticed.

Smythe said, 'We are attempting to return something to a realm outside the living one which was brought here by Evanert's spell. What do you know of such magic?'

The spirit paused. 'Who are you, that you ask the King's torturer, for advice on necromancy?'

Beside Ree, Persephone stiffened.

Larry howled and swatted ineffectually at the spirit again. He tried to sit up, but Smythe pressed a hand to his shoulder, holding him down. 'I would ask Evanert's lover,' he said.

The spirit laughed. 'And wise of you to do so, for I was there when the spell was made. I cannot speak to the specifics of necromancy, nor would I care to, but I can tell you this. To walk between the realms, or to force another to do the same, a sacrifice in life and will must be made. Somehow, I doubt you are willing to die to play with magic far beyond your ken. Trick another into doing it for you.'

The spirit's mood changed. He leaned shapelessly toward Smythe. 'Who are you?' he asked. 'I cannot see your face. The world is all of shadow. *Who are you?*'

Smythe dismissed the spirit with a wave of his hand. He dissipated like red smoke. 'It never goes well once they start trying to learn your identity,' he said wearily.

'Someone needs to die to cast the spell,' said Usther. 'I had never thought...is it hopeless, then? We'll truly have to leave Tombtown?'

'Nobody will have to leave,' Persephone said. 'Tabris and I will handle it.'

'It's not hopeless,' said Smythe quietly. 'One death is nothing held against the good of the crypt.'

Ree felt ice run down her spine. 'You can't mean that,' she said. 'After *everything,* you cannot mean to kill—'

'The sacrifice is life and *will*,' said Smythe. 'You're right, I don't mean to kill anyone. But I am willing to die.'

CHAPTER FORTY-NINE

Usther

U sther felt the world shift under her feet too many times. She hardly knew which way she was supposed to look. 'Be serious,' she said, as witheringly as she could.

'What other choice do we have?' Smythe said.

Usther looked around at Ree for support, but Ree was silent. Her eyes were full of a pain Usther couldn't quite read. 'Do you remember what Veritas said about the Black Oath?' asked Ree. 'About magic and...and intent?'

'Sometimes I feel like it's all I think about,' Smythe said. 'You are welcome to try to save me. But if a sacrifice is required, I have to mean to die.' He shook his head. 'It makes a kind of symmetry, doesn't it? Perhaps this is the only penance I can do.'

'Dying isn't penance,' Usther snapped. 'It's escapism. If you want to make amends for what you've done, then you should bloody well work at it.'

But he had, she realised. He'd been doing nothing but that since she turned up in his library. Perhaps for much longer. How had he summoned Lazarin's spirit without damaging it? She had never heard of a spirit able to answer so calmly. Never known them to have such clarity of mind. It was the truest black mark of necromancy, all the worse because it was the simplest kind to learn. And he had wiped it away as if it was nothing.

'Tell him, Ree,' Usther said desperately, glaring at her friend. But Ree remained silent as a sack of wheat, and said nothing at all. 'Ree!'

Ree turned on her heel and left, singing herself into a rat and vanishing over the side of the chasm.

'Wonderful,' Usther muttered. 'Delightful. I can always count on you.' She turned to Persephone. 'Do you really think you can kill the Many-That-Hungers? All of it?'

'It has to be worth trying.'

Usther studied her face. Persephone met her eyes levelly.

'Sacrifices are powerful,' said Smythe. 'Willing sacrifices all the more. You should at least put the spell together. See if you think it will work.'

'It will,' Usther said dully. 'As soon as he said it, I knew it would. There was a hole in the centre of the spell I designed. Now I know what was meant to fill it.'

All her life, she had believed necromancy was *good*. That those who persecuted necromancers were wrong. Necromancy took something dark and terrible and turned it into something good and useful. It turned corpses into people. It created life from death. It took untapped energy and from it created ingenuity; darksight, scrying, even purification. People thought necromancy was the magic of killing, but she knew it was the magic of undeath instead. One was destructive; the other was *recycling*.

She couldn't look at her darling Misery, protectively carrying their cat in her sling, and not see that necromancy was full of goodness. Surely, *surely* it brought more to the world than it could ever take away.

But there were things she couldn't, or shouldn't, look away from as well. Greywraiths. The Black Oath. And ritual sacrifice. Necromancy could be done without them. It frequently was. But those were always available to those who reached for them. To those who cared more about power than what was right.

She had never killed. Never even entertained killing—though, if she was honest, she was quite willing to knock people around if she had to.

She wouldn't kill her friend to save her town. Nevermind that he had once been willing to do the reverse.

'The paladins and healers should deal with it,' she said.

Smythe gave her a look of disbelief. 'If it doesn't work—'

'It will work,' Usther said harshly. She snapped the grimoire shut, with her own notes inside it, and thrust it into her pack. 'Let's go home.'

The journey back was solemn. Smythe kept trying to meet her eyes, which she refused. Ree didn't reappear, and Usther tried to hold her nerves for her in check until they made it back to town. Persephone seemed to sense some of it. She would meet her eyes and nod in sympathy, or gently brush her arm as she passed. How she understood that Usther could not bear to speak right now, Usther couldn't guess. That was just Persephone, wasn't it?

When she got back to the tombhome, there were some books scattered in the main room and a note from Ree that she'd gone to visit her parents. Usther scrunched it up in disgust and tossed it into the wastebasket.

It took the healers a few days to prepare. Andomerys needed a few days to recover, and the paladins wanted to discuss strategy with Arthura, who, in spite of being priestess to a goddess they were trained to oppose, Tabris seemed delighted to spend time with.

'You don't see many traditional hunters these days,' said Tabris. 'Raised in the old ways. Your Morrin priestess knows things about the balance of nature the priests of the Rootfather never learned.'

'So?' said Usther.

Tabris frowned at her. 'So she's *excellent*.'

Usther rolled her eyes and left them to it.

Smythe came by often to see her. She avoided him, and gave the paladins instructions to tell him she wasn't home. She doubted he believed them—the paladins were terrible liars—but she couldn't face him. She couldn't sit quietly and nod along while her friend explained why she should kill him.

When the healers and paladins finally set out—without fanfare, and only quiet goodbyes from those near them—Usther wordlessly opened the door to Smythe. He took the armchair opposite Usther, while Ree perched on the edge of the table, rereading the same page over and over again with a blank expression. Usther couldn't bear to leave her hands idle, so she picked up her lace, only to make such a mess of it that she shunted it aside in disgust, with no care for her carefully laid bobbins.

Smythe glanced at her. Unlike her and her housemate, Smythe had made no pretence of keeping busy. 'They'll be okay,' he said. 'The Many couldn't hold them even when Mykol and Celia were there.'

Usther thought of finding the paladins buried in mushrooms and locked in a closet with Emberlon. She wasn't so sure.

A touch at her knee as Dichotomy asked for lap access. Usther uncrossed her legs and sat back in her chair and the chubby cat launched up and circled until, somehow, Usther was cradling her. Did the white-and-black cat purr more loudly, her rumble reminiscent of a rockslide? Usther scratched her ears and squished the skin between her shoulders and let herself imagine that her cat understood something of what was happening and wanted to help.

Even Misery seemed to have picked up on the mood. She sighed more often and moved restlessly from corner to corner, never quite finding the peaceful blank stare she so desired.

Emberlon brought them dinner from *The Bone & Brew,* both that first night and every night after. He stayed long enough to eat and then went home, doubtlessly to worry alone the way they worried in company. Igneus stopped by once on the pretence of bringing a book to Ree, and Ree shocked the room by standing up and giving her father a brief hug. After, both nodded to each other and Igneus left again.

Every second was a minute of experience. Every minute an hour of worry. None of them waiting here had any way to check on those out risking their lives. But Emberlon could scry on Andomerys, and Igneus was watching over Arthura, and both had promised to let them know if anything went wrong.

No news was good news.

So why did it feel so awful?

On the fifth day, when Emberlon arrived with dinner, he brought an update. 'They're on their way home,' he said.

'Are they safe?' asked Ree.

'Did they do it?' asked Usther.

Emberlon hesitated. 'They're safe,' he said, and left it at that.

When they returned, they gathered in the back room of *The Bone & Brew,* where the remaining council members, Igneus and Kylath, took their business. Tabris and Persephone leaned against the wall, neither in armour, both wearing thick bandages. It chilled Usther to see them. It felt wrong for healers to carry visible wounds.

'There was nothing we could do,' said Tabris. 'At first, it seemed like we were going to burn them to a crisp. We worked as a team, spreading our power as far as we could, and the mushrooms just shrivelled into dust. But then—'

'Then it reacted,' said Persephone. 'It all flashed and screamed. Started to flood out of the areas we hadn't gotten to yet, spreading and growing at an impossible pace. Even re-growing in places we'd cleared. If you miss even the tiniest bit...' She shook her head.

'It tried to cut us off from each other. Sent infested minions to surround us,' said Andomerys. 'It was almost an immune system response. It buried the paladins, focusing on the hands and mouths so they couldn't cast. And at the same time—'

'It cut at us,' said Arthura. Her face, feet, and arms were heavily marked with barely healed scratches and lurid red welts. 'With more precision than we expected without Mykol and Celia to guide them.'

'So Mykol and Celia are really gone?' Smythe pressed.

Tabris shrugged. 'We didn't see them. But...I dunno. I had a weird feeling. Did you have a weird feeling?'

'I had a weird feeling,' Persephone confirmed.

'We ran out of energy fast,' said Andomerys. Usther's eyebrows raised involuntarily. Andomerys had faced down the town council at the founding of the town and reportedly not broken a sweat, but she'd exhausted herself both times she fought the Many-That-Hungers.

'If not for Andomerys, we would not have made it out,' said Arthura.

'If you hadn't shot the infested minions pinning my hands, I wouldn't have been able to do anything,' said Andomerys.

'At least the Many are weakened from your attack,' said Kylath.

'I wouldn't count on it,' said Tabris. 'When we got out, there was more of it than when we arrived.'

'Perhaps we need to focus on preventing it from spreading further. Clearing it out from new areas before it gains a proper foothold,' said Igneus. He sat shoulder-to-shoulder with his wife, actually touching, which was the most affectionate Usther had ever seen them. She almost felt like she needed to avert her eyes.

Kylath said, 'Perhaps we could look at moving the existing resources of the crypt away from the Many's region...'

Discussion continued among the group but the words fell away from Usther and became muffled, distant.

Smythe met her eyes with calm certainty.

CHAPTER FIFTY

Ree

It didn't bear thinking about but Ree could think of nothing else. Smythe was going to die. It was right that he was willing. Maybe it was right that he would. But like clashing cymbals in her mind, all she could think was *wrong wrong wrong wrong*.

She bounded along a hallway on ratty feet, moving with the quick-footed pace of the small and swift. She ran past a lesser dead swaying on the spot and swinging its arms, and past a skeletal guardian on a plinth that watched her with glowing eye sockets tracking her passage. Then she unspooled from her skin in a swirl of shadow-edged light and pushed open the door to the library there.

It was small and unremarkable. Some of the hidden libraries had reading rooms and strange artefacts, or secret doors unlocked only by solving their puzzles, but this library was cramped shelves squeezed into a room narrower than it was long and with a dusty brown carpet picked with red and gold. She settled herself on the small stone steps leading to the bookcases and put her elbows on her knees and her chin in her hands.

'I didn't think I would care,' Ree said to the empty library. She tried on different words: 'I don't care', but they didn't fit.

She stayed there a long time. Eventually, she was aware of a quiet, rattling breath. She looked up and into the burning eyes of a spectre. 'Go away,' she told it.

The spectre glided back, fading from view. She hoped it had actually left; Usther had known the trick of making her spectres invisible for many years.

Later, footsteps approached. Without looking up, she said, 'I don't want to talk.'

'Oh. Terribly sorry. I'll just—'

Ree leapt to her feet, hands extended palm out. Smythe froze, already half-way through backing away. For a moment, she saw double. There was the man of now, ashen-skinned and tired, and the teenager of before, bright and arrogant and shocked.

She sat back down. After a moment's hesitation, Smythe sat beside her. For a while, he said nothing, neatly banishing her vision of the past. That Smythe had never been quiet.

Ree spoke first. 'Is she going to do it?'

'I think so. I hope so.'

They lapsed back into quiet. Then: 'You don't have to do it, you know,' she said.

'I know.'

'Do you want to die?'

'No.'

'Then why are you doing it?'

Smythe laughed, low and dark. 'I have to do something, don't I?'

He did. And he didn't. The bitter truths Ree had held so close to her heart all these years no longer seemed so sure. Smythe had done a terrible thing. He had been a teenager. He had been scared. She had been too, but she still never would have done it. He had hoped it would never work. He had done everything he could to make sure it would. He had followed Usther into danger to keep her safe. He had danced with Ree and smiled at her so sadly she had remembered she had a heart.

She didn't know what to say about any of that. She wasn't sure there was a point. Instead, she asked, 'Why didn't Lazarin's spirit scream?'

'Oh, that.' He wrung his hands in his lap. 'That's...that's been my big work, actually. For years now. I still believe that necromancy can reveal incredible secrets about the past, and I believe that soul summoning is the key to that. But hurting the souls to do it...it seemed wrong. So I decided to focus on changing that.'

'It doesn't hurt them at all?'

'No.' He reached into his pack and dug around a moment before pulling out a thick journal stuffed with notes and bound with twine. 'Actually, this is why I wanted to speak to you.' He handed her the journal. 'It's all in there. It's not very organised...there's quite a lot of history around the outside of it, truthfully...but everything about the spell I use to summon souls and the method through which I created the spell is in there. You could add it to the archive.'

Slowly, Ree unbound the twine and opened it. The pages were filled with Smythe's wild, flourishing script. She smoothed the paper beneath her fingers, then closed it.

'I was sort of in love with you, I think,' she said quietly. 'Back then. But I sort of hated you too.'

Smythe smiled sadly. 'I wasn't worthy of your love.'

'I know.' But even so.

They looked at each other a moment, then Smythe broke their gaze.

Ree cleared her throat and said, a little hoarsely, 'I don't hate you now.'

'We're both very different now,' he said, and the words hurt because they were a rejection.

'You're different,' Ree said. 'I never change.'

'I wouldn't say that.'

'How am I different, then?'

He considered. 'You're colder. And kinder. More watchful, but not as quiet. There is...a greatness in you, that was only a seed then, but I see it in you now, fully bloomed.'

'You mean my magic,' she said, and felt bereft. She never changed, but in that one solitary thing.

'I mean a greatness of spirit,' he said. 'I'm a soul summoner; I ought to know.'

'I was afraid that you would reject me then,' she said. 'Because I'm asexual. I didn't know the word, then.'

'I wouldn't have,' he replied.

Silence again. After a while, she leaned her head onto his shoulder, and he pressed his cheek against her hair. Steeling herself, she took his hand in hers; he returned her grip gently, and she found she didn't want to let go.

She didn't love him now. It had been too long, and they had changed too much. She thought, perhaps, she could love him a lot more than she had then, if she was given the chance. But he was going to die, and that was right, and that was wrong, and it wasn't her choice either way.

He asked nothing of her as they sat in silence, and something sparked in her. A cold fire that only grew colder as her determination crystallised.

She had stopped him from throwing himself into the Lich's magic once. She would do it again.

CHAPTER FIFTY-ONE

Usther

'You cannot really intend to kill that man for the sake of removing the Many-That-Hungers.'

Usther looked tiredly at Persephone. 'I don't have any other option.'

Persephone crossed her arms with a creak of metal. 'Of course you have other options. There is always a choice between killing and not killing. You've talked a lot about that yourself!'

Usther set aside her modified notes for the spell. She was only checking them now; if Smythe signed off on the spell, that would have to be good enough. 'I'm not going to kill him.' She hesitated. 'He's letting himself die.'

'You and I both know that's no distinction at all under the circumstances.'

She did know it; that was the problem. If Smythe didn't sacrifice himself for the crypt, he would live a long life. This wasn't something done in the spur of the moment, either. They were *planning* this. It felt wrong on every level.

'If you'd asked me a year ago if Smythe ought to kill himself to save the town, I wouldn't have thought twice about saying yes,' she said. 'He did some terrible things when we were younger. But that was a long time ago.'

'Usther.'

Usther sighed and closed her eyes. She thought about all of her neighbours and the family she had found for herself being forced back into the upworld—if the upworld would even be safe, at the rate the Many was spreading. They would lose everything if they didn't cast this spell.

She couldn't help but feel that *she* would lose everything if they did.

She looked at Persephone. 'Are you sure you can't kill the Many? You and Tabris?'

'With the Owl's help...I don't know.' She held her hands out palm-up, then let them drop. 'I don't know. You're right that it seems to spread too quickly. Even with your town healers, we barely escaped. Maybe with the right strategy? If we had more time to learn how it works. But all that time, it'll be spreading. And if we fail...' she trailed off.

'You'd be sacrificing yourself by fighting them,' said Usther. 'And with little chance of success.'

'It's different, for us,' said Persephone. 'Tab and I were trained since we were very young to sacrifice ourselves for the sake of others. Paladins are *meant* to risk their lives.'

Usther didn't think much of anyone who took children with nightmares and told them they needed to die so that other people could live, but she didn't want to get into that right now. 'Risking your lives for no purpose isn't really a sacrifice, though is it? It's suicide.'

Persephone stared at her, then after a moment, inclined her head sharply in acknowledgement.

'We should find out if Mykol and Celia are alive,' said Usther. She stood up, rubbing her eyes. 'I can't scry them. The Many seems to resist scrying.'

Persephone considered. 'Doesn't Ree have a piece of the Many in her heart?'

Usther raised her eyebrows. 'Yes.'

'Well...perhaps she has a unique connection to them. Has she attempted to scry?'

Usther frowned. 'Her magic doesn't work that way.'

'Why wouldn't it? Your magic and my magic are as different as life and death, and they both allow scrying. Her magic seems very similar to necromancy to me.'

Usther rubbed her eyes. 'We can ask her. I suppose there's no harm in trying.'

Though she couldn't shake the nagging feeling that there was something she was missing here. And that there could be a lot of harm in trying.

Her spectre informed her that Ree and Smythe were still in the library, so she gave it a pat on the cheek, causing it to give a shy chuckle, and dismissed it, collecting up the gravemould once more. She told Persephone she'd be fine alone, but the paladin refused to leave her. 'The council ruled that nobody travels alone,' she reminded Usther seriously, and Usther tried not to laugh at the thought of a paladin strictly adhering to necromancer law.

She left Misery and Dichotomy home to look after each other, with strict instructions for Tabris to feed the cat. It pained her to do it, but she could no longer tell herself that bringing them with her was safer than leaving them alone. Along the way, Larry started to trail them. Where he had come from, she couldn't guess. Persephone greeted him with a friendly pat, as if he were a wayward pet. He bit her hand, blunt teeth scratching ineffectually at the armour.

When they found Ree, she was sitting in silence with Smythe, hand-in-hand, head on shoulder. The sight was so shocking that Usther momentarily lost the ability to speak. Smythe looked embarrassed, but Ree only sat up straighter and reluctantly released Smythe's hand. 'Is it time?' she asked. 'Surely it can wait a few days?'

Smythe frowned at Ree, but Usther said, 'We have one last plan to try first. Ree, I know this sounds mad, but Persephone thinks you might be able to scry.'

Ree nodded. 'I can. That's how Smythe and I were able to follow you into the heart chamber.'

Usther's mouth popped open. She glanced sidelong at Persephone, who for the briefest moment looked uncharacteristically smug. It was a good look. Usther immediately lost track of what was happening.

'You can scry,' she said flatly.

'I can.'

'Then there is more to therianthropy than we thought. Maybe even than Witch-feather thought—'

'I'm aware,' Ree said steadily.

Morrin's teeth, but she was infuriating. She was about to tell her exactly that when Persephone said calmly, 'I believe there is a chance that you could scry on Mykol and Celia. To learn for sure whether or not they have returned.'

Smythe straightened his glasses. 'Do we need to know that to banish them? I think—Larry, mind those books! Come, sit here.' He pat the floor beside him.

'I believe we need to know that to *avoid* banishing them,' Persephone replied. 'If they are dead, then Tabris and I have some hope of exterminating the Many-That-Hungers from the crypt. If they don't—'

'Then they'll exterminate you,' Usther said sharply.

Persephone shrugged. 'Yes.'

Except Usther knew in her heart that they were still alive. The way they had built themselves from fungal fibres when transitioning into her cell...that was not a being that truly relied on its physical form. Could you even kill fungi in a way that mattered? Their spores would only be released for them to grow anew. For all Persephone's talk of sterilisation spells, Usther found it hard to believe that she could with certainly wipe out every last spore when the fungi seemed able to release vast glittering clouds of the stuff.

'It's my understanding that the Many resist scrying,' said Ree.

'They do,' Usther said, still irritated. She paused. 'But you just said you scried on me while in their domain!'

'I—' Ree stopped and frowned. 'I did, yes.'

'Then try now.' She reached into her pack and got out a scry-eye for her. It was a common focii for necromantic scrying, nothing more complicated than a treated chicken eye. It was hard and resinous, feeling like nothing so much as a marble. 'See if this helps.'

Ree accepted it. 'I'll need a—'

Persephone was already taking a small bowl from her pack and setting it on the ground, pouring in clear water from a small waterskin.

'Thank you.'

Usther watched her anxiously. Would the siblings be aware of being scried upon? It wasn't common, but it happened. And what would it mean, if the scry-eye did help Ree's scrying? Did it mean, as Persephone had suggested, that therianthropy and necromancy were related? Or would a scry-eye work just as well for a healer as it did for a necromancer?

Ree settled in front of the scry bowl, the scry-eye held firmly in one hand. She sang a few lines in Old Antherian, surprising Usther—her previous spells had been sung in a language she didn't recognise. The bowl took on a faint glow around the edge, which flickered and faded.

Ree frowned and tried again. Once again, the bowl lit up, as did the scry-eye in Ree's hand. But again, the light flickered out.

Ree's nostrils flared and her already thin lips thinned further. She gripped the edge of the bowl with one hand, thumb just barely avoiding disturbing the surface, and tossed Usther back her scry-eye. She placed her other hand over her heart and hummed the incantation again.

Usther held her breath. The bowl lit up, and remained lit. Ree's eyes took on a strange appearance that flickered between blue light and shadow. She stared intently into the bowl. 'I can see them,' she said. 'They're...they're in the heart chamber. Mushrooms are growing from their skin. They're as still as corpses. There's someone in the background moving around, I can't see who.'

'They must be alive,' said Persephone. 'Andomerys destroyed their bodies entirely. They must have reformed them.'

Usther knelt beside her friend. As Ree's brows knit together, she almost reached out to reassure her. Her early experiences of scrying had been disturbing; the sense of being pulled from your own body was deeply disorienting. But Ree's face shifted into an expression of shock. 'They're looking at me,' she said.

'It only seems that way,' Usther said gently. 'They—'

'They can see me!' She shunted the bowl aside. The water sloshed across the stone floor. Larry howled and lurched to his feet, rushing for her.

'Ree, it's—!'

'Get back,' Persephone said calmly. She'd unslung her spear from her shoulder and pointed it now at the door.

A single droplet of red fungi rested there. Usther took her friend and drew her back. She was clutching her chest and breathing hard. 'That wasn't there before,' said Usther.

'No,' said Smythe. 'It certainly wasn't.' He stood up and the air grew chill around him. Larry crouched over Ree and pawed at her shoulder, howling his concern.

'Larry, run!' said Smythe. When the minion didn't move, Smythe's eyes filled with ink. *'Run!'* he ordered, necromancy lacing his words, and Larry disappeared behind a bookcase.

The fungus gave a little twitch, the cap lighting up a brilliant red, and it released a glittering puff of spores. Within moments, there were more mushrooms sprouting up beside it, on the wall, on the ceiling above. Then more, then more, as cloud after cloud of spores were released.

Persephone tucked her spear under her arm and spread her hands, blasting it with holy light. Several fungi shrivelled, but more sprung up in their place. They reached up with their tendrils, weaving and twining together, growing a new shape of fungal sinew. Persephone blasted it again, but it only grew stronger.

'You need to get out,' Persephone said, blasting it again. 'Get Tab.'

Usther shook her friend. 'Ree?'

'There's no other way out,' she said tightly, then gasped and hunched over her own chest. 'Gods, it hurts!'

The figure was taking on a humanoid shape, but broad and misshapen. One leg resembled Mykol, the other Celia. It smiled with two mouths as the head split apart, leaving stringy, wet tendrils to stretch between. 'Our honoured guests,' they said. They took a step and the body split in half and each began to reform the other side, gory twins. Where once their gowns had been white, now they were red and dripping.

Persephone screamed, high and angry, and blasted them again. Silver fire licked up their bodies, burning the still-forming tendrils, but though they crumbled into dust more quickly took their place.

Both half-formed siblings locked their eyes on Persephone. 'We have no need of you,' they said at the same time. They waved a dismissive hand at her and fungi exploded toward her, leaping up her legs. She blasted it again and staggered back. She was dripping with sweat, her entire body heaving with the strength of her panting.

There wasn't any time left, Usther realised. All her hopes of second chances, all her faith in Persephone, it was all denial. They'd never had any options.

She looked at Smythe. 'Are you ready?'

He squeezed Ree's shoulder. 'I do have some regrets after all,' he said quietly, and stood up. 'What do you need me to do?'

Usther extended her hand. 'Throw all your will into expelling them from the crypt,' she said.

He nodded grimly and took her hand. Usther started to cast.

Ree screamed.

CHAPTER FIFTY-TWO

Ree

There was something gnawing at her heart, at her muscles, at the flesh of her chest. She could feel the teeth slide against each other, feel each rasping bite and the flash of fire that accompanied it. Beneath her hands, her chest bulged and crawled; the Many-That-Hungers was eating her alive.

Against that pain, she couldn't speak. Couldn't think. The room was full of silver light and angry fire, but it was nothing compared to the all-consuming agony of her chest where every breath of her lungs and beat of her heart was torture.

Distantly, she heard Usther chanting. Distantly, she felt the awful clash of ice and fire. But in a moment of sudden clarity, a voice rang out in her head. A voice unfamiliar and unspoken, with the echo of millions.

Give yourself to us...all this will stop...there will be no more pain...there will only be us...

Yes, she thought. I want the pain to stop. I'd do anything to make the pain stop.

There was a particularly violent bite in her chest, a horrible sinking and tearing that made her scream. Something...unfurled. Liquid and strange, but not painful. Something bloomed beneath her fingers, fleshy and alien, but not painful. She was sinking somewhere deep inside, drifting in her own mind in a cloud of glittering red.

Around her, vast structures formed in jagged lines of red. Beautiful spiderweb shapes that grew and changed and spun around her, ever more complex.

Dimly, she wondered, *Where am I?*

You are part of us, came the reply, and she found she wasn't afraid.

Points of light sparked among the spiderwebs. She realised each one was a mind, a consciousness. A unique being in constant communication with the others via these increasingly complex structures. She drifted further, deeper into the structures, brushing past these sparks and feeling a frisson of electricity at the touch. Each time, she felt a chime of acknowledgement: *I know you.* But she also felt a drain, as if each touch diminished her. Took something from her.

She started to panic as she brushed into light after light. Her thoughts became hazy, as did her sense of self. She clung to her image of herself; of the archivist, therianthrope, cartographer. Daughter of Arthura and Igneus. Reanima. Reanima!

You aren't Reanima. You are one of Many, came a billion whispers, each leeching away more of her essence.

I am, she thought. *I am.*

I am what?

You are one of Many.

Her panic ebbed.

The Many continued to leech at her. She found she no longer minded. She subsumed herself in their light.

USTHER

The siblings screamed as red light suffused them, ripping at their fungal flesh and sending it flaking off into some other place. They reached for Usther with twin expressions of hatred, but the force that pulled at them held them fast for now.

Usther was a conduit for terrible power. A vessel too small to hold the magic raging through her. At any moment, she would crack, but until then she gritted her teeth and directed the otherworldly energies like only a true necromancer could.

Smythe held her hand tightly, like a clamp. The power that ravaged her was crashing through him as well and where she bore it with a snarl, he bore it with a quiet stoicism. In her mind, she could see the modified diagram of the overlapping realms. Spheres overlapping spheres, belted with incantations, and she spoke them with confidence even as her voice choked from the strain.

Mykol inched forward, arm stretching, fingers lengthening into spidery claws as he attempted to reach her; she only raised her chin and continued to chant, refusing to so much as flinch. At the edges, his substance trailed away into the light and vanished; it was like he was disintegrating before her eyes.

But it wasn't happening fast enough. That they could make this progress was terrifying; it meant that she needed to give more. Necromancy had always favoured the arrogant and she had arrogance in plenty, but it wasn't enough. She glanced sidelong at Smythe and could see from his grim expression that he knew it, too. Lazerin had been right. Something more was required.

She couldn't make him do it, wouldn't even if she could. The sucking wind of the energy pulled at both of them, fierce and terrifying. Her dress whipped at her legs, her cloak streamed out in front of her. Frequent flashes of silver light hit the siblings and burst across their skin, a reminder that Persephone was still here and still fighting, but she had no thoughts to spare for her right now.

Smythe cried out; she couldn't help but follow his gaze. Ree lay prone on the floor, covered in a pulsing coat of red mushrooms, her eyes blank and unseeing. Usther screamed and lost her grip on the spell, the symbols and incantation falling from her mind. The spell shunted her out with a burst of energy, sending her crashing into a bookcase, pain cracking up her back.

Gasping, she crawled to her friend. She reached for her hand. The fungi lashed at her with tendrils, forcing her back as they struck her with a force to draw blood.

'Ree,' she whispered, unable to prevent the tears from streaming down her face. 'Oh Morrin, I beg you—'

Mykol and Celia laughed in unison, their voices echoed by myriad others. Usther glanced up; the red energy of the spell had not entirely faded, but they were forcing their way through it, now that the maelstrom had eased.

'Ree, please! Morrin, please, she can't be dead! Morrin...'

An armoured hand took Ree's, heedless of the attacking tendrils, and a silver glow suffused it. 'She's alive,' said Persephone. 'At least...her body is.'

What did that mean? Usther continued to pray and cry and reach for her friend even as the crimson fungi struck her and seized her blood.

A touch at her shoulder. 'Usther,' said Smythe. 'Cast the spell.'

The spell. She lifted her gaze to Smythe, but he was staring at Ree's limp form, eyes shining and mouth set into a firm line. She took his hand; power crackled at the touch, icy as a winter breeze.

She could see the spell in her mind's eye. The spheres, the incantations. The realms of gods and humans, laid out before her.

Ree, laid out before her. So still, so terribly still.

She turned, chanting the incantation. Mykol leapt at her, claws outstretched, teeth bared into terrible fangs, hair a mess of writhing tendrils. Smythe tried to pull her aside but it was too slow. Then, with a crack, Persephone took the blow, spear up and shunting Mykol back, only to dodge a blow from his sister.

She couldn't think about that. The spell. She tightened her focus, chanting louder. Her throat tore, the cold threatening to freeze her vocal chords, and still she chanted. The red light flared up stronger still. Mykol and Celia screamed with one voice and leapt for her again, but Persephone was a wall of armour and silver flame and would not let them pass.

The pull of the spell became a sucking wind; it took everything she had to keep her footing. Part of her wanted to throw herself into it but Smythe held her fast. And then it came, the point at which she was not enough. Her body was a wineskin filled to bursting; her mind screamed along with her voice, over Mykol and Celia, over the terrible vacuum of the realms outside.

She ran out of words, out of spell, and still the red light blared and pulled. She looked to Smythe.

'Is it time?' he asked.

She nodded, unable to find her voice.

He moved forward, still gripping her hand, still maintaining his connection to the spell. Persephone tried to block him but he moved around her and into Mykol and Celia's waiting claws.

'You chose us,' Celia said wonderingly. Mykol stroked his cheek with one clawed finger. Celia bared her fangs and tore at his throat.

The room exploded the moment his blood hit the air. The energy threw Usther back and sent books and bookshelves flying, but she clung stubbornly to Smythe, who pulled further in. Mykol and Celia disintegrated into a cloud of red. The crimson fungi became glittering particles that were sucked into the light of the spell. And Smythe tumbled into it.

REE

She was part of everything. She was the cycle of life and death itself. She could see it now, feel it; that life fed on death. A beautiful decay, a hunger that could never be satisfied. She was myriad and wondrous, a consciousness too broad and too complex for categorisation. Somewhere in this crystalline confluence of minds were the memories of the woman Reanima. It meant nothing more to her than any of the other memories archived here.

This was a world within a world. She could sense the other minds and think with them. She could feel what they felt: the familiar warmth of the white marble, the delicious flesh and consciousness of the undead, the sudden ecstasy of teeth in precious blood. And then, all at once, everything exploded. The entire world was screaming and flashing pain in blinding lights, she was in a kaleidoscope structure of spinning, flailing agony. The world started to pull away from her; the other minds were ripped from hers. She reached for them–

A new, specific pain, biting into her arm. The screaming of the Many abruptly cut out. She opened her eyes, startling forwards, to find Larry with his blunt teeth clamped so hard to her forearm that it bruised. 'Larry, stop!' she said. Larry growled unintelligibly, not loosening his bite. She felt disoriented, in too many places at once. This room was whipped by strange energies that were at once terrifying and relieving. The fungi coating her body crumbled away into glittering dust, sucked into a vast red void.

She was Ree. She was Ree, and this was the spell to send the Many back to their own realm. Conflict roiled within her; she felt like part of her was falling screaming into that void. Like part of her family was. But she also knew that the Many had been consuming her as surely as it did the undead it infested. As surely as it would consume everything, if given the chance.

Usther stood with feet planted in front of the portal, hanging on to something while the light whipped at her. Persephone held her too, with arms wrapped firmly around her waist. This was important, somehow. This mattered...these were her friends.

Ree eased her arm away from Larry, who watched her with dull, worried eyes. She stood up and swayed forward on legs that felt startlingly singular. The portal sucked at her with a terrible wind, but it wasn't enough to unbalance her. She needed to see what was happening. She needed to see what was in the portal.

She came up beside Usther and saw her hands clasped to Smythe's. He dangled there, nearly listless, blood streaming from his neck in shining rivulets while a glittering cloud of spores spiralled around him. Ree came back to herself with a feeling like a kick in the guts. She lunged forward for his hands as well, helping Usther to pull. A strong arm circled her waist; Persephone grabbed both her and Usther.

'Just let me go,' Smythe said. Though his voice was gasping and weak, it echoed around the portal, amplified. 'They're almost gone. It's almost done. I have to go to make this work.'

'Like fuck you do,' said Usther. 'Pull harder!'

'I'm trying!' said Persephone. 'Three people is a bit much, even for me!'

Smythe's eyes found Ree's. They were nearly blank with hopelessness. A look she had never seen on his face, never expected to see. 'It's right that I die here,' he said.

Maybe it was. It had a kind of symmetry.

'No,' she said. 'Usther is right. Dying is easy. And I'm not done with you yet.' She heaved with all her strength but it seemed to do nothing. But, there was a change in Smythe's eyes. A sudden gleam of life and will. He gripped Usther's hands back, and the pull of the portal suddenly lessened. They heaved him free and Usther cried out in Old Antherian, and the portal swirled shut, taking the Many-That-Hungers and the people it had built with it.

The four of them collapsed on the floor. Larry howled in glee and flung himself onto the pile, biting everything he could reach. Ree barely had the heart to fend him off.

On the floor, she stared at Smythe, who looked back at her with an expression of shock and fear.

She smiled. He smiled uncertainly back.

VEO CORVA

CHAPTER FIFTY-THREE

Usther

A hooded figure robed in flowing black lace knelt before a small shrine, rubbing a pouch of human teeth between her fingertips. The mosaic stone columns around her resembled broken fingers reaching up from the earth.

'I did what you wanted, didn't I?' Usther asked of the teeth. 'The Many-That-Hungers is gone.' She didn't voice the rest of that sentence: but so is Ree. Maybe you were supposed to be honest with your goddess. Usther wasn't sure she could bear to be honest with herself.

Her friend had retired to her room and rarely emerged even to eat or wash. She wasn't reading or writing, wasn't doing the archivist work so important to her—even though Emberlon was too unwell to do it himself. Physically, she was fine; Andomerys had healed her and both paladins had checked her as well. Everyone agreed that there was no sign that the Many-That-Hungers had ever touched her.

But still she withdrew, whether from depression or some phantom impression of the Many, Usther couldn't say. But they had done something to her. Something lasting. Something none of them knew how to heal.

But Morrin was happy, wasn't she? Her town was safe. What did it matter to the goddess if Ree, who wasn't even a necromancer, had been sacrificed for the cause?

'Something on your mind?'

Usther spun. Arthura stood barefoot, framed by an archway of broken stone. Instead of her brown cassock and fur mantle, she wore her ceremonial white, the hem thick with dust yet still stark in the shadowy crypt. The white of Morrin's high priestess wasn't pure; closer to the faded, yellowing white of old bone.

'Praying,' Usther said, not quite able to hide her bitter tone. She rubbed the pouch between her fingers, feeling the teeth through the rough fabric.

'May I join you?'

Usther inclined her head and the priestess swept over, lowering herself bonelessly into a kneeling position. Though her eyes were closed and her mouth moved soundlessly in prayer, Usther wondered whether this was Arthura the high priestess, or Arthura, her friend's mother. The woman had many sides, all overlapping, and Usther found it hard to tell which she was dealing with.

It wasn't long before the quiet dragged the words out of her: 'Did Morrin really choose me?'

Arthura turned slowly to regard her but said nothing.

Usther hurried on, 'You said you felt a connection between us. That you thought she had chosen me to help you protect the crypt. And then, with everything that happened...did she really? Or was it just that I was already tied up in everything.' Usther took a deep breath and added bitterly, 'Maybe she just wanted me to clean up my own mess.'

Arthura inclined her head, but it was a long moment before she said anything. Usther imagined what might be going through her mind: that she had made it all up, that Usther had misunderstood, that it had been a joke or a prank.

None of which was characteristic of Arthura, but it wasn't characteristic for Usther to be chosen by anyone, let alone a goddess.

'I don't know the mind of the goddess,' said Arthura. 'I merely interpret the signs she lays in my path. I saw around you a web of devotion and pain, fate and cleverness, and these are the things Morrin's chosen are made out of. I saw threads tying you to what happened before and seemingly to what was ahead, though I had no notion of just how entwined you would be. It is now fully clear that Morrin chose you for this; only you had the knowledge necessary to banish the Many.'

'The Many wouldn't have been here, if not for me,' said Usther.

'No?' said Arthura. 'There is much that you and my daughter have hidden from me, but I have ever been comfortable in the dark. Would

Reanima and Chandrian Smythe be here today if you had not saved them in your girlhood?'

'I...no,' said Usther.

'And what of the knowledge used to return them to this world? Many denizens would use that knowledge to gain power over their fellows. You have used it only to save them.'

'We caused the Many to come here!' Usther hissed the words, then looked around in sudden fear of being overheard. The Altar was empty; only the gods enshrined here could have heard them.

'So you seem to think,' said Arthura. She turned fully to face Usther now, shifting from her kneeling position to sitting cross-legged on the ground, her bone-white robes shifting with a rasp of rough fabric. 'The gods shape fate using what tools best fit the craft. And you, Usther, are a tool Morrin would find irresistible. Indeed, I don't believe she is done with you yet. I still see her shadow over you.'

'Great. Excellent. Happy to help.' Usther bit off the words. She didn't know why Arthura's god-talk so upset her right now. Why it didn't bring her the warmth and reassurance she was looking for. Maybe it was because her friend was suffering. Because she would never know for sure whether this was anything other than a huge accident.

Maybe she was broken, and even being chosen of a goddess could never be enough to fill the void of ambition and hurt inside her.

She stood up to leave but before she'd taken three steps she felt Arthura's hand on her shoulder. 'Usther.'

She turned. The priestess looked wild and harsh, her mane of ashen hair as thick as a beast's, her pale robes lending pallor to her skin and her cold eyes. For a moment, her otherworldly mask broke. 'I am proud of you,' she said, and her voice was unusually rough. 'Never doubt that.' Gently, she touched Usther's chin.

Something hot and knotted burned inside Usther. She nodded, not trusting herself to speak, and turned away before Arthura could see her tears.

She felt better and worse and needed time to think.

REE

'I'm meeting Smythe at Mortana's. Are you coming?' asked Usther.

Ree shook her head. As she stared at the wall, she thought she could see the faint impression of millions of red threads hanging in the air.

Usther sighed. 'Alright. Well...call Misery if you need anything.' She closed the bedroom door, leaving Ree lying on her stone-and-straw bed in her book-strewn room. Leaving her alone.

The Many-That-Hungers was gone, but she still felt an echo of it in the way her heart twinged painfully sometimes when she moved, and in the way her brain felt suddenly isolated, as if she had been abandoned in a once-crowded hall suddenly made empty.

In the days since they'd been banished, it had been hard for her to reconnect with her former life. Things that once had made her feel like a part of something—her family, her neighbours, her town—now felt hollow and distant, an intangible, frail tether as easily snapped as a cobweb.

She should be glad they were gone. She was glad they were gone. They had intended to consume everything she cared about. But she could not shake the sense that the fungus planted in her had hollowed out her heart. She didn't know how to fill it.

Time passed in a blur of coming and going. Of people appearing and disappearing. Separated from her by a distance she couldn't close. Everything shrouded in a fractal red haze. She heard people saying that she needed more time. She didn't know if time was enough to replace what had been lost. What had been damaged.

Then came someone she did not expect.

'Ree?' A green-haired paladin leaned in the door. For a moment, it seemed like they were made of crystalline red filaments, but then they faded and it was only Tabris, looking oddly soft without their armour. 'I hear you haven't left bed in days.'

'I've left,' said Ree. She'd eaten a little. Used the privy when necessary. Even washed once.

'Yeah...you know that's a figure of speech, right? It means you haven't left bed the expected amount.'

Ree cast around for something to say but found she didn't want to bother.

'Can I come in?'

She said nothing.

'I'll take that as a yes.' They settled on the floor, knocking a stack of books sliding. Ree struggled to care. Why be annoyed about books? Why be angry at someone so distant from her? The cavernous emptiness in her own mind was more concerning. She couldn't seem to stop herself from probing at it.

'You seem pretty lost in your thoughts,' said Tabris.

More apt than they could know. Ree's mind was, at times, vast and shadowed, at times, dense with overlapping pathways. Rarely familiar.

'And your friends seem to think the Many-That-Hungers has something to do with it. Sef said it nearly devoured you.'

Ree shrugged.

Tabris raised their eyebrows. 'I got special training in helping people deal with their trauma,' they said. 'Maybe talking to me will help.'

'Did you learn that at paladin school?' Ree asked bitterly.

'No, actually.' Tabris stretched and put their hands behind their head. 'Got it much later, when it became clear that killing the monsters preying on people is the smallest part of helping them.'

Something about that resonated with her, in the hole in her heart the Many had left when the ritual purged it. But did it matter if it did?

'You don't know what it's like,' said Ree. 'I'm alone now. I was part of something...huge. Part of the Many. And now it's just me, and I don't even feel like enough to fill up my own body, and I see shadows of it everywhere.'

Tabris nodded, their expression thoughtful. They didn't say anything for a while and Ree thought: that must be it. No amount of training could give them insight into what had happened to her.

Then they said: 'You're right, that we don't know what that's like. Maybe you could tell us about it? We know it's not the same, but we do know something about being part of a larger system.'

Ree sat up. She'd noticed that switch in pronouns before. 'You're plural?'

Tabris nodded. 'Tabris is our group name.'

'Why do you say "I" most of the time?'

Tabris shrugged. 'Well, sometimes it's because it's only one of us talking. But sometimes it's just easier that way. We got into the habit of it early because people can get uncomfortable about it, especially when they're already vulnerable enough to need a paladin.'

Ree thought on this. There were a few other plural systems in town that she knew of, and they were all very different.

'How many of you are there?' Ree ventured. 'If that's okay to ask?'

'Six headmates. There's a seventh that comes and goes.'

She wasn't entirely sure what that meant. 'And you're all paladins?'

Tabris laughed. 'Well...we're all in a paladin body. Three of us do the bulk of the paladin work. Nara does most of the therapy—hi, that's me you're mostly talking to right now—but we all pitch in. This is all of our life.'

Seven. Among the Many, she'd been part of uncountable millions. But that had been for a breath of time. Tabris—and Nara—had surely been plural for much longer.

'Nara,' said Ree. Tabris smiled and nodded. 'What would you do if...if the others were suddenly gone? If it was just you?'

Tabris considered. Their eyes seemed...shuttered. Their expression darkened. 'It would be lonely. Awful, maybe. I know some systems wish to be singular but that's never been the case for us. I'm not sure I would know who I am without the rest of us. What is it like for you?'

A void with the ghosts of a beautiful structure. A chamber where once there had been a harmonious chorus and now there was only a lonely, echoing voice. 'Before, I was me. And that wasn't easy but it wasn't...I knew who I was, even if I didn't always like it. Then with the Many...I wasn't me anymore. I was the Many. Ree's life was just one memory among millions. And then suddenly I was Ree again, but...now I know how small I am. I know being me isn't enough.' There were tears in her eyes. She didn't bother to dash them.

'Do you wish you were part of the Many again?'

Did she?

As the Many, she had been beautiful. She'd had companionship that didn't make her skin crawl. That didn't fill her with restlessness. She had known...so much.

Causing the life she had here to lose all meaning to her.

It still felt meaningless.

'I wish I could go back to who I was before,' she said. She was surprised by how many words Nara had dragged out of her. It did feel good to talk about. To let some of her hurt and frustration whistling out into the air, like releasing a steam from a kettle

'And what do you think it would take to do that?'

Ree shook her head. 'I don't know,' she said. 'I don't know.'

Tabris thought a long while. 'It sounds like what you're lacking is connection. Maybe the way back to yourself isn't trying to find you. It's trying to find the people who know you.'

The people who knew her?

'Think about it,' said Tabris. 'Take your time. You've been through a lot. But Ree?'

She raised her eyebrows, waiting.

'You are enough. I hope you can find your way to knowing that.'

USTHER

Usther banged on the door to Ree's bedroom, then opened it without waiting for a response. 'You coming?'

Ree glared at her from her bed. Her eyes were unusually shadowed, though Usther knew she must have been awake for hours. 'Go without me,' she said.

Usther crossed her arms. 'This is too important for you to miss,' she said. 'It's the trial.'

Ree put her arm over her eyes. 'I don't want to see it.'

'Well, get over it,' she snapped, then glanced at Smythe as he joined her.

'I'll wait with her, if you like,' he said quietly. 'I mean...if you don't mind, Ree?'

'I don't mind,' Ree said. Usther thought it might have been the quickest response she'd ever heard from her.

Usther pointed at her. 'You'd better be there when the trial starts,' she threatened vaguely, then turned on her heel and left. As she opened the front door, she thought she heard quiet voices.

Well. Good that she wouldn't be alone, at least. Ree'd been avoiding people for days—though thankfully she'd started taking visits from Tabris for 'talking healing' or some nonsense.

A little bell jingled at her feet and she felt two paws at her knee. She crouched down and ruffled her cat's ears. 'Of course you can come, darling,' she said. 'Misery? Do you want to come?'

Silence was her answer. Misery was in Usther's bedroom and, it seemed, would not be coming out.

It was nice to see people out on the streets again. She felt good this morning. The normally musty air of the central mausoleum had picked up a fresh damp scent from the distant river, and Dichotomy trotted proudly beside her, stopping every now and then to roll in dirt or smell the doors of other tombhomes.

Though things were hardly back to normal, the news of the Many's banishment a week prior had certainly lightened the mood in town. People were still not quite ready to travel alone, but they chatted on street corners or shopped in the town square. Mazerin the Bold hawked his bone-crafts loudly, and there was fresh bread for sale for the first time in months, as Lurga Nightcreeper had finally felt safe enough to return to her minion-run mill.

Usther took in the return to town life with a small smile. She wondered if she would ever see the streets full of denizens and not feel a slight bubble of relief. It was hard to take for granted now, especially when the memory of the barren streets was still so fresh.

She made her way to The Bone & Brew. Inside, there were already many denizens sitting and discussing their various works. That was still a strange new normal. She didn't have to search for Persephone, however. Even in casual clothes, she stood out; tall, round, and flushed with life. And today, she was again wearing her blue armour, no longer scuffed and pitted from their adventures but polished to a shine.

She lit up as Usther approached, her smile wide and her eyes bright. As always, Usther felt momentarily intimidated by her beauty, but she gestured to the seat across from her so Usther gratefully took it.

'Didn't manage to get Ree out the door?' she asked, taking a sip of her tea. 'I thought perhaps you'd have dragged her out by her ear, the way you were talking about it.'

Usther waved a dismissive hand. 'I'll let Smythe handle her. Why are you wearing armour?'

Persephone knocked on her own breastplate with a faint ring. 'Tab and I have been requested as official witnesses. Tradition dictates I wear armour for all official purposes so people don't forget I'm a paladin.'

Usther raised her eyebrows. 'I doubt anyone here is likely to forget.'

Persephone shrugged. 'It's tradition. Besides, I want to be prepared if anything happens.'

'The whole town is going to be at that trial. If any of them try anything, the town'll rip them apart.'

Persephone smiled ruefully and shook her head. 'See, that's exactly the kind of thing I'd like to avoid.'

'You can't convince me that upworlders don't have mobs,' Usther said. 'I've had to run from one myself.'

'I like to avoid upworlders forming mobs as well,' she said. 'It's hard for there to be justice when people are threatened. But,' she raised a hand before Usther could protest, 'I don't intend to interfere in your justice process. I must respect the rule of law here.'

Usther decided not to mention that the 'law' here was very informal. She'd see how Tombtown operated for herself soon enough. 'How are you finding your tea?' she asked instead.

Persephone took another sip and nodded. 'Oh, it's quite nice. Your Mortana has some interesting methods of mixing different leaves and brewing at different temperatures for flavour. I think this is citrus and winterflower mixed with a black tea. Very fragrant.'

'You didn't opt for the mushroom teas then?'

Persephone made a face. 'No, I think it'll be a little while before I order mushroom anything.'

They smiled at each other. Usther got herself a cup of tea as well—she asked for the same as Persephone, which pleased the normally surly Mortana—and they drank together with mild, companionable conversation for a little while, which took the edge off Usther's nerves.

She wanted Tarantur to face justice, of course. But Ellenil was so young, and as for Symphona...

Gods, she wished she never had to see Symphona again.

'Hey.' An armoured hand rested lightly over hers. She looked up in surprise into Persephone's sympathetic eyes. 'Do you want to talk about it?'

Usther felt her eyes sting and forced back tears. She did not want her kohl to run. 'About a child I used to look after going on trial for treason, or about the lover who tried to kill my cat going on trial for treason? Because it's all just...a lot.'

'Either. Both,' said Persephone. 'We have time.'

Usther drew a shuddering breath and nodded. 'Gods, yes. I'd like that very much.'

REE

'Are you ready to go?' Smythe asked gently.

Ree shook her head, so he took a book out of his pack and sat beside her, reading in silence. She hadn't expected that. She was still getting to know him; who he was now, rather than who he had been then. And if he was going to be quiet, she didn't have to care. She could instead turn inward, to the ghostly imprints the Many had left in her mind.

No. She wasn't supposed to do that. She was supposed to look outward. She decided to watch Smythe.

Time passed. Smythe didn't look up or speak to her. The only sound was his even breathing and the small, crisp noise of a turning page. Something about that was soothing; though she'd been struggling to read herself, she enjoyed witnessing another doing it. 'What are you reading?' she asked at length. She was surprised by her own interest.

Smythe blinked and looked up at her, his eyes refocusing on her. 'Burial Architecture of Ancient Iyada,' he said. 'I thought it might give me some insight into identifying which cultures created which parts of the crypt. I still find the existence of this place a terrible mystery.'

'There's definitely some iyadi influence in parts,' said Ree. 'You can see it in the stonework.'

Smythe smiled and shook his head. 'Of course you already know. Well, it's informative reading for me, at least.'

They lapsed back into silence. After a moment's hesitation, Smythe returned to his book. Something about the feeling of him drawing away tugged at Ree. 'Wait,' she said.

He looked up patiently, but Ree found she didn't know what to say, only that she wanted to keep talking. She cleared her throat and tried to summon moisture into her dry mouth. 'Thank you,' she said. 'For keeping me company.'

That was something Nara had encouraged her to do as well. To thank people, if she was grateful.

Smythe smiled. 'It's no trial for me.'

She liked this man. Much more than the boy he'd been. It was a surprise, this like. Something dragged out of the mist. She wished she liked the woman she'd become too, but she could hardly feel who that was anymore. She said, 'Um. About your advances in summoning?'

'Hmm?'

But she only looked at him helplessly as she tried to continue the conversation.

Smythe was plenty able to do so himself. 'I just wanted to...do something good, I suppose. At first, I was just frustrated that souls are so fragile and difficult to talk to but...I realised I felt guilt about summoning them, too. Worse than the guilt I feel when I issue Larry with a command. And I wondered why it had to be that way.' He smiled, a little bitterly. 'Though honestly, I wasn't sure where to send my research, once I'd found it. I didn't know whether anyone would really see and learn from the work I'd done. I couldn't take it to the Grand University. I couldn't take it to the town. So, I just sat on it uselessly.'

'You could have taken it to the town,' said Ree.

'Perhaps,' said Smythe. 'But they might have killed me for it. And coward that I am, I didn't want to die. Not even if I did good in the process.'

Ree started to say he wasn't a coward, but her thoughts caught on those last words. 'What changed, then?' she asked. 'Between then and now. You nearly died for the town.'

'Easier to give up your life when there are other lives you value more, I suppose. I didn't want anything to happen to Usther, or you, or that sweet little cat—'

Ree made a face at the description of Usther's monstrous feline as 'sweet'.

'I...I don't know, really. I only know that it felt necessary.'

And here was a connection she could feel. A warm tether to hold onto, a path out of the sudden loneliness she had been abandoned to. She took Smythe's hand in hers. He watched her uncertainly. 'Are you sure this is a good idea?' he asked.

'Not at all,' she said. 'But I hope it is.'

He nodded and she leaned in, pressing her nose against his neck and closing her eyes. He embraced her gently, and they stayed like that for a long time. She felt a little less alone; a pair in the vast emptiness of existence, instead of just one.

The first of many ways back to herself.

THE TRIAL WAS A DARK thing, and Ree wished she and Smythe could have stayed home to avoid it. She had expected the denizens to be loud and brash, but instead there was a kind of shocked misery about them. Perhaps the betrayal had struck them deeply. Tarantur was executed as a sacrifice to Namura's Ward, which guarded the town from feral undead and restless spirits, and also from scrying eyes from outside the bounds of the crypt. As a council member, he was deemed to have had a duty of care to the town, and his betrayal was therefore that much deeper. Ree did not shed any tears for him. He'd been a cruel and unpleasant man for as long as she could remember, always advocating for the harshest punishments and quick to denigrate other denizens, including children. But others did—though whether they were for him or for the harm he'd caused, she couldn't say.

Symphona met the same fate, though her trial was more drawn out, and the denizens were much more vocal during it. She'd been exiled once before, and instead of leaving the crypt, she had instead chosen to work against the town for vengeance. By all accounts, she was the closest with the siblings, and had encouraged them in their quest for dominance, rather than steering them down a different path.

Usther trembled the whole time Symphona was on trial. She offered no testimony and never added her voice, though she kept her eyes fixed on the dais where Symphona stood restrained. Ree held her hand tightly and sat with her shoulder pressed to her friend's. Usther only hid her eyes when Symphona was at last sacrificed to Namura's Ward, putting her head in her hands. Smythe squeezed her shoulder and gave Ree a pleading look. Ree hesitated, then wrapped her friend in a hug, letting her sob and shake within her embrace.

Others came and went for the trial; some were exonerated, some exiled. No others were sacrificed to the ward. The vengeance and justice the denizens so often craved seemed to have been drained from them after the first two. Persephone and Tabris flanked the dais like shining statues, not meting out any punishment themselves but implicitly lending their support to the will of the town. Ree wondered that such a thing was possible; that they had been betrayed by their own practitioners, and yet these paladins now stood with them. The world had never felt darker, nor stranger, but she clung to that strange new connection, the tether between the paladins and the town, using it to remind herself that none of them existed in isolation, no matter how cavernous both mind and crypt might be in the absence of the siblings.

Last to be held on trial was Ellenil. They strode up with their hair loose and unadorned, the small horns that curved from their skull fully visible for the first time, a long whip-like tail that they'd kept hidden their entire life trailing behind them. They looked shabbier than Ree could remember seeing them; their robes were ripped and dusty, their face smeared with dust. The kohl lining their eyes ran in ugly, smudgy trails down their cheeks, though they showed no sign of crying. They stood in silence while their crimes were listed, their head lowered and their hands clasped in front of them. Even from the seats below, Ree could tell they were shaking.

They were only eighteen. They'd been born in the town; one of only a handful that could claim it. They were obviously old enough to be responsible for their actions, but they were still grotesquely young to face the kind of consequences Symphona and Tarantur had. Their parents pleaded for them. Usther stood and spoke on their behalf. And it was decided that young Ellenil would be kept under watch, rather than exiled, and would not be permitted to leave the town without the permission of the council.

Perhaps they had learned, Ree thought. Perhaps the memory of sentencing a boy Ellenil's age to death still clung to them, and the memory of what that had led to. She could see so much of Smythe in Ellenil, none of it good. She looked sidelong at him; he looked grim but determined. Catching her eye, he inclined his head minutely. That decided her. It might not be fair that Ellenil should escape true punishment, but it was right, nonetheless.

At the end of the trials, the three of them were called up to the dais. 'Without the actions of these three, the Many-That-Hungers would still roam the crypt.' Said Arthura. 'Morrin smiles with bloody teeth and touches her head to these, the heroes of Tombtown. Reanima Crow-feather, Smythe Townslayer, and Usther of Morrin's Shadow!'

A great cry went up from the town, hoarse and fierce with desperation. Denizens stood up and shouted or stamped their feet; in the crowd, she saw Emberlon clapping his hands. Andomerys whooped and the paladins struck their weapons against their chests with a clang. The force of it hit her in the chest. This was connection. This was belonging.

She looked at Smythe, who had a small, shocked smile, and Usther, who had tears streaming down her cheeks.

They had, each of them, finally been accepted.

EPILOGUE

Usther

They sat atop the mountain on a large flat rock, overlooking the plains below. The sun was still rising on the horizon, so bright that Usther had to shade her eyes. The sky was full of soft summer colours, a painting come to life. 'I'd forgotten how beautiful the sky is,' she said.

Beside her, Persephone smiled and stretched. 'There are some benefits to the upworld,' she said. Her armour had been left behind, as it was on most of their trips. She trusted Usther to keep her safe. Instead, she wore the fawn and yellow dress she'd worn to the feast, her bare legs round and soft where they showed between the strips of the skirt. Usther had learned well just how soft those legs were, and now she casually rested a hand on Persephone's knee just to remind herself. Persephone brushed her lips against Usther's cheek, an almost absent-minded sweetness that Usther found maddeningly endearing.

'Do you really have to go?' Usther asked, though she knew the answer. She had always known that this thing between them, a paladin and a necromancer, couldn't last.

Persephone wrapped her arms around Usther's waist and pulled her closer. 'I really have to go. I can feel it in my gut. And Tabris will probably drag me out rather than let me stay another month. It wasn't easy to get them to leave without me the first time.'

'An understatement,' she said, snorting derisively, but her sombre mood returned almost immediately.

She wanted to say, 'You're the most incredible person I've ever met.'

She wanted to say, 'I never knew relationships could feel like this.'

She wanted to say, 'I love you.'

But Persephone was leaving soon and the words turned to ashes in her mouth each time.

Persephone suddenly tensed. 'Usther?'

Usther pulled back to look at her properly. She hadn't seen her look so worried in weeks. Perhaps ever. She was so calm, even in the face of danger, always there with a steady eye and a gentle smile. Now her gaze shifted, as if bracing for a blow. 'Well, spit it out,' Usther said, hoping her tone would hide her nerves.

Persephone took her hands. She looked her steadily in the eyes, warm brown meeting near-white. 'Come with me,' she said.

For a moment, the world spun on its axis. 'What?'

'Come with me,' she said again. 'I have to go, and that is right, but this is right too. More right than anything in my life has ever been. I know it's a huge ask—I know it's awful for you out there, even with my protection. I've been trying to think of a way to ask for weeks—'

She wanted Usther to travel the upworld with her, righting wrongs. Rescuing people from dark magic. Her grip on Usther's hands was tight, as if she feared Usther would tear away. But, in spite of her strength, it was still gentle enough that Usther could pull away if she wanted to.

Usther's thoughts spun wildly. She'd never dreamed of returning to the upworld. Never imagined it was safe to. She'd missed the sun, and the trees, and the wildlife. She'd missed the breeze against her skin. She'd buried and mourned those feelings, knowing them to be dead.

But she was a necromancer. She, of all people, ought to have known that nothing that died needed to remain dead.

Persephone gazed at her with a desperate, worried hope.

'I'm not done here yet,' she said. 'There...there are things I need to put in order. But if you come back in a few months—if you still want me—'

'I will always, always come back for you,' Persephone said.

A paladin's promise. Usther's stomach swooped, but not with fear. With a bright, sunlight warmth that mimicked the dawnscape before her. 'Yes,' she said. 'Yes, I'll go with you. I—'

Persephone kissed her fiercely, with a heat Usther willingly matched as they rolled back against the stone.

'I will always come back for you,' Persephone repeated, running her hand down the line of her neck. And as she kissed her again, Usther thought that perhaps it didn't matter that she couldn't say the words yet.

They had time.

LATER, WHEN SHE TOLD Ree, there were tears. There was a rather startling and clumsy hug. 'But you'll come back, won't you?' Ree said.

'I thought you'd be glad to be rid of me. You hate having a housemate.'

'It's not so bad,' Ree replied with a sad smile. 'What about Misery? What about Dichotomy?'

'There are...things that can be done,' Usther said. 'I'm not leaving for a few months yet. I have time to work out how to bring them with me.'

Ree nodded, and was quiet for several breaths. 'But you'll come back?'

Usther scoffed. 'Of course I'll come back. I'm not done with Tombtown yet.' She paused. 'And you and I will never be done with each other.'

Ree looked away, tears sparkling in her eyes. 'Gods, you were a terrible friend,' she said.

'You were worse.'

Ree shrugged and nodded, and they both laughed.

'It's so weird,' Usther said. 'I always thought it would be you who went to live in the upworld.'

Ree shook her head. 'I never thought about it. I sort of thought it would be like this forever. You and me.'

Usther tried to swallow around a lump in her throat. 'I could have been happy with that.'

'Me too.'

'But I guess...you have a bigger destiny than being my long-suffering housemate,' Ree said.

Usther raised her eyebrows. 'So dramatic.'

Ree shrugged. 'I've been thinking about it. About the paladins and their god-feelings. About the prophecy mother cast in the teeth for you at the Toothday festival all those years ago. And about you being Morrin's Shadow, now. You'll be a necromancer working with paladins, in plain sight. Maybe...maybe the world is changing.' She fixed her friend with a serious look. 'Maybe you're the one changing it.'

It all seemed too big and serious for Usther. She would return to those words many times over the course of her life, but for now, she only gave her friend an insufferable smile and said lightly, 'Well. I think I'm up to the challenge.'

And the gods would judge whether she was right.

SPECIAL THANKS

Without the support of these wonderful folk on *The Beautiful Decay*'s Kickstarter campaign, this book would not be published.

In no particular order, thank you to:

Tak!, Rob & Jenny Haines, Robin Hill, Paige Kimble, Vhalesa, tastytea, L. Rowyn, Aura V, Robin Swift, chimerical girls, Sergey Kochergan, RedGryphon, Neil Hart, Sean M, Hairy Larry, josh giesbrecht, Sally, Greyor, Benjamin Slade, Natasha Liff, katre, Lorelei Thee, Kiki, Jez, Sarah Jackson, R Beaumont, Lisa Padol, Neo, yuu gamon, and D. Moonfire.

And to The Selkie Delegation, Geekosupremo, Brian D Lambert, Kit, Jonathan Veguilla, Eko Punataival, Socheata Chan, Ranmilia, AingealWroth, Briony Woodman, Ryan C, David P., Sam, Ashton Green, Christina Bloszinsky, Alex Q, Yncke, Cheryl Trooskin-Zoller, Carl-Eric Menzel, David Gow, Kuba =)K, Shad, K. M. Gildemeister, Del, Jonathan Vernersson, Sario, Cefiar, Michael Warren Lucas, xenia dragon, B. Findley, Kai Mara, Ollivier Robert, Kay Rhodes, Tuula Turto, Waffelpokalypse, Sentinel Ark, Simon L. B. Nielsen, and Cyberfossil.

And to Gwenfar, Jonas 'Zatty' R. E., Ben Hamill, Bas van Haastregt, Alison Boulton, Sambience, Terri Oda, Ri Guijt, Marjo Hämäläinen, Marc Grondin, yewscion (cdr255), Gil ANDRE, Rin Seilhan, aletheridae, Lloyd Vickroy, Zeta Syanthis, Femke, Kelly M., Florence the Ghost, the Rat Goddess of Vengeance, Rachael Edmonson, Samantha Vente, Arturo Abruzzini, maloki, Rebecca Södergren, pawsies, James 'Jubal' Baillie, Fraud, Adam Nemo, Willard Goosey, Algot, Sasha Fox, Flo Songweaver, Azaliz, Aleana Cantu, Talon the Dragon, and others unnamed.

I couldn't have done it without you!

ACKNOWLEDGEMENTS

This book was harder to write than any other. Something something my first sequel, nobody wants it, I'm not good enough for this...you get the idea.

Well, as it turns out, people did want it. And I'm so incredibly pleased I got to tell more of Ree, Usther, Smythe, and Larry's story. And that I was finally in a place to make it as openly queer as it was always meant to be!

With as much resistance as I had with it, it will not surprise you that this book would not have happened without help. So thank you to my partner Joh, who loves Tombtown enough that it made me believe other people might, too, who was the critical first reader that whipped the book into shape, and who is always overflowing with ideas and enthusiasm for my little necromantic necropolis.

Thanks also to Dona Vajgand, the best cover artist anyone could ask for. You turned out a cover so gorgeous it somehow makes all my other books look better, too, and you were a delight to work with.

Thanks to Nicole Evans of Thoughts Stained With Ink, who proofread my error-riddled mess and found many other snags besides. It must've been very odd to jump into the second book of a series, but you were so kind and encouraging nonetheless.

Thanks to the enthusiastic readers who messaged me after reading *Books and Bone*, overflowing with excitement and asking when the next book would be. I certainly wouldn't have written it without you.

And of course, thank you to the supporters of *The Beautiful Decay*'s Kickstarter campaign. It never gets easier to go to your readers and ask for help, and yet so far you've always been there for me. This book couldn't have been published without you.

Well, that's enough out of me for now. On to the next one!

SIGN UP FOR PUBLISHING UPDATES!

If you'd like to receive an email every time a new Veo Corva book is announced or published, you can sign up to their newsletter here: https://tinyletter.com/witchkeyfiction

No spam, no extraneous updates; just letting you know when a new book is available.

About the Author

Veo Corva writes things and reads things and reads things out loud, and sometimes they get paid for that, which is nice because it means they can feed their cat.

They live in Wiltshire with their partner and their furry familiar and as many books as they could fit in their small flat.

They are anxious and autistic and doing just fine.

Read more at https://veocorva.xyz.

Milton Keynes UK
Ingram Content Group UK Ltd.
UKHW010703220923
429186UK00004B/351